THE ASCENDENT SKY

A LITRPG ADVENTURE

THE TRANSCENDENT GREEN
BOOK TWO

MATI OCHA

Robot Dinosaur Press
robotdinosaurpress.com

The author and editor have taken great effort in presenting a manuscript
free of errors.
However, editing errors are ultimately the responsibility of the author.
This book is written in Scottish English and includes relative diction as
well as instances of Scots spellings. We trust you'll keep up.

Lyrics of "Cumha na Cloinne" are in the public domain as a Gaelic
traditional song composed in the seventeenth century by Pàdraig Mòr
MacCrimmon. A recording of this song can be found here as performed in
this medley by the Alba Choir in Gothenburg, Sweden in 2019.

For my community. Please pardon my potty mouth.

Dham choimhearsnachd. Tha droch chainnt gu leòr ann—an dòchas gun gabh sibh mo leisgeul.

A Friendly Notice

This book may contain Scottish swearing, including but not limited to the following: damn, shit, shite, gobshite, fuck, bugger, bloody, arse, cunt (affectionate), cunt (pejorative), cunt (neutral), wanker, goddamn, gods damn (when one god isn't doing enough damning), bollocks, bawbag, balls, hell, fanny, piss, and pish.

Selected terms both vulgar and polite presented at intervals in context for your convenience and amusement.

This book has been rated as approximately three (3) blasphemies out of an unspecified number of blasphemies.

(We are capable of being reverent where it suits. But being precious about swearing is not something we're known for. If that's not for you, you have my sincerest well-wishes to find a wealth of literature that meets your every whim as well as the freedom to seek such things out. I've included this notice to save you time. Mo shoraidh leibh.)

PROLOGUE

G hilla could not recall how he got here.

He could not even begin to explain where *here* was. He remembered being flung upon the wave of spirit towards Earth. He remembered being severed from the bosom of his god. He remembered hovering in a formless state above the blue-green jewel that was the planet his mistake had annihilated.

Ghilla could not remember what had happened next.

He had flashes of memory; that was certain. An ancient tree in a strange meadow of green. A pull towards . . . something. An urge to respond, to rend himself from his torment.

But until that moment, Ghilla wasn't sure he had even had a name.

In a thousand cycles of service to the Ascended Alliance, he had presided over three ascensions. Every ascending world was different, but they had one thing in common: to qualify for ascension, they had to prove themselves worthy of the ascension directive.

Every world that joined the alliance had to show, for

lack of a better term, that they had learnt how to play well with others.

To minimise harm, greed, violence. To recognise the abundance of the breadth of the universe's bounty—to know that there was more than enough for everyone in it to thrive.

Earth, well.

To say Earth was an accident was like calling an active supervolcano's mass extinction power a bit of an inconvenience.

But Earth, yes. Earth. That was where Ghilla now found himself.

Beyond his own mistake, that infinitesimal miscalculation that had directed the ascension's wave of spirit not only to the wrong planet but, in the extent of that angle's ultimate trajectory, to the wrong *galaxy*, something else had gone terribly wrong.

His god had told him he would observe. Not just part of Earth's ascension, but *all* of it.

But he could not. He was not hovering above the Earth as he briefly had; he had landed upon the planet's surface somehow.

How, he could not say.

That wasn't supposed to happen.

Think, Ghilla.

First thing was that he needed to find out where he was in relation to . . . anything.

All he could see was green.

He tried to remember what he could of Earth, from the flash of a moment he'd had when frantically attempting to find out what sort of planet he'd targeted for ascension. Carbon-based life forms. Large oceanic coverage. Plants that photosynthesised by means of chlorophyll, hence the green. Ghilla had not visited a non-ascended planet in hundreds of cycles. And in truth, he hadn't still, for Earth's ascension had begun.

But why was it so green?

Ghilla could not make out whether he had a corporeal form. Everything felt hazy, as if he had lingered too close to the well when it was full. Perhaps he had at that.

One thing, however, maintained crystalline clarity.

Ghilla had not been an angry being. He experienced the full spectrum of emotions, to be sure, but he had never considered himself prone to pride or rage. What need had an immortal servant of the gods of such things?

But now, oh. *Oh.*

With no warning, with no chance at redemption or explanation, no *second* chance, his god had flung him into the abyss of this unworthy planet.

He had not truly realised that his fury had fed itself.

Energy existed at all times and none; time and space were obsolete when it came to ascension. They both were and were not. Earth's ascension had begun the moment Ghilla had made his error. And his travel to Earth, on the wave of energy—of spirit—that caused the ascension had happened as instantaneously as such things can.

Now, Ghilla realised that he could *feel*.

Again he heard the voice of his god.

"You do take responsibility," she had said. "You shall. For your foolishness, you shall bear witness to what you have caused. The planet affected was not ready to ascend; its people and its creatures were far from ready to ascend. Your folly has forced this upon them, and they will tear each other apart. And the world that has waited for its ascension will be forced to wait yet longer. This is the price of your failure that billions will bear in your stead. For that, I must act."

What right did even a god to condemn him for a single mistake? Ghilla's anger grew as his memories returned. To spend a thousand cycles watching this lowly planet fail in the face of a gift they could not even measure—how dare she decide this was justice?

So quickly, too. She had not hesitated; she had only flung him into nothingness without so much as a thought for the thousand cycles of faithful service he had rendered to the gods.

Now he was here. Now he had no choice remaining but to exist in this pitiful planet.

Contempt germinated in Ghilla's core, first a sprout, then a vine, then a creeper that wove its way through him until, against all his expectations and his god's, his essence clung to that creeper of contempt.

Around it, Ghilla was given form.

If he was to be an exile on this inconsequential rock, surely the universe itself had blessed him. It had freed him from the shackles of his unforgiving god; he took shape, and he took his first true look around.

The more he solidified, the more he *felt*. His fury burned away his guilt, replaced it with something hotter, more alive.

Ghilla was alive.

He was alive on a planet ascending . . . and he would take full advantage of his own accident.

The creatures here, they knew nothing of the ways of spirit. But Ghilla did.

Ghilla would remake this world.

If his god had shunned him, he would simply rise from

the depths of her disappointment. This planet had no gods. They had no magic.

Until now.

Ghilla already had magic; he felt it flowing into him through the veins of his fury.

He would be the first of this planet's gods.

When his thousand cycles had passed, he would face his previous deity not only as her equal, but as her better.

CHAPTER
ONE

I had to hand it to Eilidh.

How she'd been so certain I would come after her was a question I'd need to ask as soon as I caught up with her, but that was moot for now.

The intricate glyphs of spirit she'd laid out like breadcrumbs for us to follow, though? That was not moot. That was art.

I'd travelled with her for days on end, fought side by side with her in life-or-death battles gu leòr, and she knew for a fact that I used Connection almost constantly. More than that, she was familiar with the signature of my spirit. She knew I'd be the one looking for her.

She'd counted on it.

Every time I cast the spell, tendrils of spirit caught her golden glyphs. On tree trunks, on the winter-browned bracken just starting to give way to spring growth, on boulders—Eilidh had thoroughly and meticulously given us a path to follow, keyed specifically to me and me alone.

I wasn't ready to unpack that, so instead I just stayed glued to her trail like a goddamn magical bloodhound.

For three days we'd trekked away from Oban after working so hard to reach the town in the first place. We'd made it into the depths of a pine forest after skirting the northern edge of Loch Avich, and once we came out the other side, we'd once again be on the edge of Loch Awe, though this time on the western shore.

The forest would have felt oppressive, dense evergreens crowding in on us as we frantically searched. I had a vague memory of a deciduous forest on the western edge of Loch Awe, where at least the lack of leaves on the March trees would let more sunlight filter in, but for the present, that didn't matter. Instead, it just felt eerily quiet—all that mattered was that I knew there was a thread of magic connecting me to who we sought. I would have been tearing my hair out if Eilidh had actually been captured by Lord Edwin Thomas Sackington's arsehole thugs, but Eilidh was as canny as she was dangerous.

Which is to say very.

A fact that my best mates' banter behind me was trying to diminish as they cartoonishly argued over what her D and D class would be.

"Cleric," Iain was saying stubbornly.

"With that strength stat?" Rhona snorted, somehow right behind my ear, making both Iain and Meeksy jump— the teenage girl hadn't hit her second decade of life yet, but her own class was wraith, and none of us could ever really be sure where she was if she hadn't chosen to be visible.

Meeksy craned his neck to look for Rhona but gave up quickly, tossing his shiny black ponytail of hair over his shoulder. "The kid's right—"

"Not a kid!" came Rhona's voice, from farther away that time.

"—Eilidh's a paladin or I'm a block of tofu," Meeksy finished.

"She's neither," I said. Irritation threatened to overtake me. "She's a dìonadair. And Lord Bawbag's goons are going to drop the forest on our heads if *you* goons don't shut yer gobs."

"Well, chuck me in the steamer and call me edamame," Meeksy muttered. "How come she gets the Gaelic class?"

This was going to give me a migraine.

"If I ever encounter someone from the Ascended Alliance, I promise to ask them how they make their mercurial linguistic decisions," I said. "Now, if we could—"

I didn't get a chance to finish my sentence because Iain's arm cracked me across the sternum, stopping me in my tracks.

Ow.

Armour or no, my oldest mate had an arm like a bloody steel girder.

By now, we'd all learnt the rules of this ascended world.

Number one: if someone stops you in the wilds, shut up first, whinge later.

Number two: anything is possible.

As I followed Iain's gaze through the dense forest's tree cover, I immediately saw why he'd brought my talking and our movement to an abrupt halt.

Spunkies, as they'd be called in Scots. Sionnachain in Gaelic. And in English, glowing lights in the wilds were usually best known as Will o' the Wisps. And Jack o' the Lantern, before that got co-opted by the Americans as something you make with a pumpkin and a candle. My mum had still kept to the traditional turnips.

But the bluish light through the green of the dim forest

afternoon was neither pumpkin nor turnip related. No, this was just a glow, aloft where it shouldn't be, drifting like thistledown on a non-existent breeze.

Not just one, either.

A ragtag line of them led off into the woods, in the opposite direction to where we were tracking Eilidh's glyphs.

After a moment, Rhona appeared, looking exasperated. Her brown hair was plaited back from her face, but there was a bit of moss clinging to a spot just behind her ear. What on earth had she been doing?

"Why'd you stop?" she asked, then simply looked in the direction all of us were staring. "Oh. Never mind."

We all stood there, watching the wisps float through the darkened woods.

"Reckon we have two options," Iain said. "We can follow them and either wander pointlessly all night or run into some ascended monster out of nightmare itself, which could bite us in the arse . . . or we ignore them and go on our merry way and possibly leave something to flank us, which could more literally bite us in the arse."

Knowing it might be futile for decision-making purposes, I cast Connection, expecting only to see Eilidh's glyphs . . . except the one I'd found last was nowhere to be seen. I turned to seek out the previous one—she'd been diligent about keeping them in easy line of sight. But it was as if they'd never been there at all. Not even so much as a spark of spirit lit up gold.

"Shit," I said.

"Uh-oh." Meeksy shifted his broad shoulders and turned to eye me askance.

"I think the decision might have just been made for us,"

I said slowly. "Whatever this is, it seems to have somehow erased Eilidh's glyphs."

Rhona's eyebrows drew together in worry, and she opened her mouth, pausing before she seemed to think better of speaking altogether and shut it again with the click of teeth.

My entire midsection wanted to revolt at the very thought of losing Eilidh's trail, but if I let that take me over now, we might never make it out of these woods.

"Whatever those wisps are, it's too much of a coincidence to presume they're acting independently of the disappearance of the glyphs." Correlation wasn't causation, but it would be a muckle leap to think two bizarre occurrences out of the blue had happened at the exact same time without being related. When the others nodded, I went on. "Which means something wants us to follow the wisps. Whether they want to eat us or talk to us, though—that's the question."

"Calum," Rhona said, as if she were speaking to a thick-headed toddler, "have you met literally anything yet that just wanted to talk to us and not eat us?"

"Sailean," I said promptly, which also triggered a pang. I missed that wee furball. "And the starling that spied on Bawbag. And the stags, and the horses. The pigeon that flew our message back to Oban."

"You're stretching the definition of 'talk' to breaking point there, mate," Iain muttered. "But fair play. Not everything wants to eat us."

"If this whatever-it-is wanted to eat us, it could probably think of a more fun way to go about it than sending us on a wild goose chase through the woods," Meeksy agreed. "Though mythologically speaking, I guess plenty of monsters thought that was a cracking good time, so who knows?"

Feeling like it was probably as futile as the first attempt, I cast Connection again, this time focusing more on the wisps themselves. I tried to keep myself from panicking about losing Eilidh's trail.

The others' bickering faded into a hum as I quieted my mind, breathing with the flows of spirit around me. My new affinity was called Synthesis, and I could almost feel it as it worked in the background of my Nature affinity's passives. Gu h-Ìosal. Gu h-Àrd. All things below, all things above.

Taobh a-Muigh. Taobh a-Staigh.

Inside. Outside.

Spirit connected me to all of it.

And through that, a burning ember of pathos, almost too faint to see in the glowing wisps of . . . will.

Will.

I almost laughed when it clicked—Will o' the bloody Wisps indeed.

Gingerly, I felt for that thread of spirit that was my spell, prodded it until it came in contact with the nearest wisp.

The moment it did, I lost my breath.

Connection dropped away, leaving me dumbfounded as the patter of my pals' banter swam back into focus in my ears.

"Hey," Rhona was saying, looking at me even as she waved an impatient hand in Iain's face. "I said hey!"

At that, both Iain and Meeksy halted their back-and-forth bickering about the nature of ascended creatures' motivations, and they both turned to stare at me.

"Well," I said, clearing my throat when my voice cracked awkwardly on the word, "I guess every day's a school day."

"What the hell is that supposed to mean?" Iain asked, exasperated.

"It means we've just stumbled across the first ascended being who *does* just want to talk to us." I pointed towards the line of wisps, the certainty of that brief contact with the creature's will filling me with both eagerness and trepidation. "We'll find Eilidh's trail again afterwards."

"You're sure," Meeksy said. "Because if this thing tries to eat us and we end up dying and abandoning Eilidh to Lord Bawbag and the parade of sphincters he calls flunkies—"

"Believe me." I interrupted him before he could get farther than that. I did not want to think about Lord Bawbag or sphincters of any kind. "If I thought that was going to happen, I would be high-tailing it in the other direction."

"What exactly did it . . . say to you?" Rhona said, peering at me with an uncomfortable amount of trust in her brown eyes.

"It didn't say anything—I felt their intentions." I swallowed, shaking off the sense of just how daft that sounded and how hard everyone here would have laughed if I'd said such a thing a month ago. More to the point, everything in me screamed that I should trust this instinct. "All I know is that we don't want to ignore this invitation."

With that, I straightened my shoulders and started off towards the nearest blue glow, which gave a sudden surprised hiccough of movement, followed by a whirl that looked suspiciously joyous.

Brave new world, was it?

What on earth were we going to encounter now?

The forest came to life around us.

It took me a moment to pinpoint what was happening. One moment we were in the relative quiet, and the next thing I noticed, there was . . . life.

It had crept up on me like our wraith-like banshee of a teenager, but where Rhona was a harbinger of "you done fucked up, mate," this felt jubilant in a way I'd not experienced in the passage of time since the ascension.

Birdsong echoed through the trees, chirping out the dregs of winter into the lush promise of a newfound spring. When I triggered Connection, the flows of spirit around me were no longer barren currents but swirling movement that danced between living creatures. Voles and rabbits, the occasional hare or stoat, birds on the wing, placid deer just out of sight but aware of our presence.

And everything below the surface, too small to see with the naked eye unless it flew in front of our faces. Ants and clegs stirring to motion, a sleep-drunk adder dormant for winter, bees and beetles, ticks and spiders.

The new awareness washed over me with wonder.

I wasn't sure if the others could sense what I saw, but when I glanced over at Meeksy, he had tears in his eyes. He was always a bit of a soppy bloke despite his imposing appearance, and when he caught me looking at him, he gave me a wobbly smile.

"You see it, don't you?" he asked.

"Aye, I do," I said.

Iain gave us a questioning glance, straightening the belt at his hip where a dagger hung.

The Will o' the Wisps still danced before us, leading us deeper into the dimness. Their blue light bounced from tree trunks, lit moss with an eerie glow.

Whatever we were about to find, we were growing closer.

Even so, that didn't prepare me for my first sight of *her*.

All at once, the trees gave way to a clearing—or perhaps "bower" would be a better word for it.

Not only did the trees form a fairy ring around an open bowl of lush emerald moss, but their branches curved over the top of it protectively. Mushrooms grew in delicate towers from the moss, thin stalks giving way to thinner caps so translucent they glowed in the floating light of the Will o' the Wisps.

And at the centre of the clearing was a woman.

Cloaked in green to match the vibrance of the moss itself, at the sight of us, she pulled back her cowl to reveal her face.

She was as fair as the mushroom caps with skin as delicate, almost grey. Light from the wisps lit upon her and seemed to coax a glow from within to welcome them. Her eyes were dark as loam, and her hair fell in waves like yellow pollen past her shoulders. When she rose from where she sat, my mind clicked into place as her legs unfolded, back jointed and covered in deep brown fur and capped with lustrous cloven hooves. After a moment, her emerald-green cloak fell to cover them.

"Glaistig," I said, unbidden.

"Yes," said the glaistig.

Rhona had materialised by my side, and she gaped at the woman.

"Why did you bring us here?" I asked.

"Many reasons. Because you needed to see me," she replied. "Because I sense others in need of your aid. Because I have a message from the one you seek. She came to me in the night, and I was drawn to her as a beacon of truth and valour. It is she who told me that you follow."

"Eilidh," I breathed.

"Where is she?" Meeksy demanded, taking a step towards the glaistig.

"She has continued onward, on the heels of her quarry." The glaistig beckoned us closer and gestured around her at the soft moss. "Please, sit."

"We need to catch up with her," Rhona protested. "We don't have time to chat."

"You do not have time *not* to speak with me," the glaistig said cryptically. "Sit."

After a moment of hesitation, we sat. Rhona sat beside me, almost closer than I was comfortable with, but when I glanced over at her, I saw her worrying at a chunk of punky branch she must have picked up along the path, fingernails digging into the decomposing wood. Her fingers were grubby with it, but she didn't seem to notice. Around us, the trees seemed to lean in closer above our heads, the creak of branches melding with birdsong in the distance. Out of curiosity, I pulsed Connection, and I barely contained the gasp.

Spirit wove together with the branches above us,

protectively forming a net that blanketed this hidden bower and the glaistig within—and, of course, the four humans who had stumbled into her home.

It came on a wave of peace, like I had sensed the intent of the Will o' the Wisps, but my every instinct screamed that if someone were to violate the glaistig's hospitality, that net would catch them tight and serve them up to her for slaughter.

"Okay," I said to her, clearing my throat to disguise the momentary crack in my voice. "You say Eilidh sent a message. What is her message?"

To my surprise, the glaistig answered without dissembling or hesitation. "She was quite distressed. The man-thing beyond the loch has taken someone she loves, along with many others. He seeks the kind of control that nature will not allow someone to wield."

"Mòrag," I said at the same time Meeksy blurted out, "Shit, her gran."

Rhona fell still beside me, her fingers suddenly quiet on the branch. "First the simulacra, then the harts," she said, her voice empty and hollow. Then fury lit like a sparker catching gas in her eyes, and she turned her gaze on me. "I told you he would move on to people. I *told you*."

"I never disbelieved you," I said to her, and I reached out a hand to place on her shoulder. "We won't let him do this, Rhona. I promise."

"He already prepares," the glaistig said softly. "Your friend would have you ready yourselves to assist her. I would also require this of you—such an abomination cannot stand."

"As if we'd do anything else." Iain scoffed. "All of us had plenty reason to hate Lord Bawbag even before he went all Borg on Argyll, but if he thinks we're just going to—"

"You must know that however powerful you are, you can only be in one place at a time," the glaistig cautioned him. "That is my part of the message. You must prepare yourselves."

Dread pooled in my stomach, and I kind of wished I could steal Rhona's punky stick and shred it myself.

"You're saying it might come down to saving the captives or saving . . . something else," I said slowly.

"Just so." The glaistig met my gaze, her dark eyes almost black.

"Why are you helping us?" Rhona blurted out. "Everything else we've encountered has mostly tried to kill us. What's your game?"

"My game?" The glaistig's resonant voice drooped in confusion. "I do not understand your meaning. But I can answer your first question. This one"—she nodded at me— "has taken pains to help not only his own kind but others caught in the man-thing's web of suffering. All things are connected. All things speak to me. I hear their cries of relief, and I hear their lamentations. I help you because I believe through you, I can thus help *them*."

"The hart," I murmured.

"The horses." Rhona looked at me. "Sailean."

"Just so." The glaistig peered at me, and it felt as if I were on the receiving end of my own Keen Eye spell. I got the feeling this entity did not miss much. "I wakened not long ago. There is much I do not know about your people, but I do know mine."

"Who are your people?" Meeksy asked softly.

At that, the glaistig's face lit in a brilliant smile, and I caught my breath as the forest sprang to life around us.

The flutter of feathered wings burst forth above our heads, punctuated by the tick of beetles and the buzz of flying insects. In the distance, I heard a stag trumpet, followed by a fox's unmistakable scream. Closer came the squeaks of mice, the sleepy hoot of an owl woken from a midday nap.

"Who are not my people?" the glaistig asked fondly. Then she sobered, meeting each of our gazes one by one. "You see. All things are connected. Life and death and large and small." She paused, seeming to grapple with something beyond her ken. "The—the flow of spirit belongs to all. Together we live, or together we fall."

The ascension directive.

Without knowing why, I rose from where I sat and moved over to the glaistig. Throughout our mythology, a glaistig has been known as a ghost, a spectre, usually to be feared, but sometimes, just sometimes, she is the Maighdeann Uaine, the Green Lady, who watches the herds with an unflinching eye. A fierce ally and a fiercer foe.

"Ceud mìle taing," I said softly to her in my own language. *A hundred thousand thanks.* I took her hand in my own and kissed it.

If she had asked for what I thanked her, I didn't know that I would be able to tell her. All I knew was that for perhaps the first time since I'd learnt of the horrible advantage Lord Bawbag was using to gain power so swiftly, his thoughtless slaughter, it seemed we would not need to wait for aid from an indifferent Ascended Alliance.

The glaistig peered at me, bemusement written across her face. At first I thought it was my gesture of kissing her hand, but as her strange, velvety palm dropped from my fingertips, she spoke as if she had read my mind. Maybe she had.

"All things seek balance," she said. "All. Tides come and

tides go, but even storms serve their purpose, and they do not last forever."

We did not stay longer with the glaistig after that, and as we moved away from her, I caught sight of one of Eilidh's glyphs almost immediately.

When I said so, Iain let out an explosive breath. "Bloody hell, mate. Is sodding everything going to rear its head? If I go to Loch Ness, will Nessie be munching on the populace?"

Meeksy chuckled under his breath, reaching out to squeeze Iain's hand.

"I don't know," I said.

The farther away from the glaistig's bower, the more anxiety settled into me. I felt like I'd just faced down an ancient deity, but she wasn't one. She was a spirit, like the fuath and the beithir, given life and form with the ascension.

But even in a few short weeks, she had taken root in the earth, and her presence would ripple outward.

"What was that she said?" Rhona's voice cut through the drawn-out silence. "'All things are connected. Life and death and large and small. The flow of spirit belongs to all. Together we live, or together we fall.'"

"You remembered that verbatim?" Meeksy asked.

Rhona tapped her forehead with a knuckle. "Like a steel trap."

"It's the ascension directive," I said, to which Rhona nodded. "I ought to have considered sooner that it didn't only apply to humans."

Iain, though, frowned dubiously, stepping over a moss-covered deadfall and sinking up to his shin in a boggy dip with a squelch. He made an irritated noise and clambered back up to the rest of us.

"Was she saying none of us should kill anything ever again?" He asked the question with a raised eyebrow, gesturing at the forest. "Because honestly, mate, I reckon the beasties out there didn't get the memo."

"That's not what she meant," I said slowly. "Nature can be cruel, and plenty of things need to kill to survive. I think she was drawing a line between the natural order of things and destruction for the sake of itself."

Meeksy nodded along with me. "Everything we've seen about this ascension suggests it usually goes to planets that have reached some sort of . . . cosmic balance."

"And here we are, the cosmic whoopsie," Iain muttered, which made Rhona snort.

"They don't even expect us to survive," Rhona said, aiming a kick at a hummock of dead bracken. "They've just yeeted us into this with no real direction. Quests aren't normal—we're the only ones I've heard of getting them. And quests are the only way we've found to actually get information."

That sobered all of us, because she wasn't wrong.

"Then we'll just have to prove to the universe that we're better than that," I said. "We'll have to show them we can transcend their expectations."

I tried to smile, but it felt wobbly even to me. Rhona returned it as tremulously.

"If I, a pathetic hamster, can make it this far," I said, "there's hope for humanity after all."

My lofty sentiment only had a split second to hang in the forest's quiet air before Rhona blurred, and something buzzed past my head, precisely where she'd been standing, and an arrow thunked into a towering oak.

CHAPTER
THREE

S hit.

We'd been absolute numpties.

It was as if we'd forgotten what we were doing altogether and were acting like we'd been off on a wander in the woods.

But no sooner did the arrow stop quivering in the tree than all of us sprang into action. Rhona had already vanished; her stealth and speed were frankly frightening. I hadn't fought beside Iain and Meeksy against human foes yet, and if I'd been afraid they'd hesitate, I was immediately disabused of the notion.

Meeksy may have been a nurse, but he wielded his staff with a grace I could only hope I shared.

Iain was off with a bellow, following Rhona's cues as she lurked out of sight to close in on our attackers.

More arrows soared through the air, and I drew spirit to me to cast Connection, tracing their paths backwards to the bowstrings that had loosed them.

A blast of Spèird shattered the volley of arrows into splinters above our heads. Three archers, almost certainly some melee fighters to add to their ranks, and I'd put money on their having a mage or a stealth fighter in the mix.

The moment one of the melee fighters came into view, I cast Keen Eye.

Frances O' Callaghan
Level 11 Grappler
Affinities: Grappling, Arcane
This fighter is highly skilled in hand-to-hand combat and poses a threat even to warriors above his own level for his prowess.

Fuck.

"Iain, thoir ionnsaigh air na boghadairean!" I yelled in Gaelic, hoping he'd heed me and go for the archers.

He wasn't even level ten yet, and while he'd reached fourth dan in Tae Kwon Do, if this Frances O' Callaghan was a threat to higher-levelled opponents, I didn't want to gamble Iain's experience against a dangerous unknown.

On one hand, I was thankful as hell that Keen Eye's improvement had given me more information, but on the other, it highlighted just how goddamn lucky we'd been when we fought that reaver Steven Brown on the way into Oban. Maybe sometimes it was better to not know if we were biting off way more than we could chew.

The thought soured as I remembered Brown literally taking a bite out of Rhona, and I shook myself back to the battle.

I almost held my breath as Iain flashed towards O'

Callaghan, but I let it out in relief as his path veered away from the grappler.

A flash of light soared through the trees, veering uncannily around trunks and branches to explode in the grappler's face.

Meeksy's magic jolted me into action. Whatever he'd done didn't seem to damage the grappler, but from the way O' Callaghan stumbled, that flash of light had left him blinded.

I cast Tairm.

The forest roared to life.

Where in the glaistig's bower, that life had flowed with serenity, here in the heat of battle, the gnarled branches that soared overhead turned to grasping fingers.

The grappler may have been a match for a human opponent, but as his vision returned, he was *not* prepared to be set upon by the very trees.

Connection pulsed out from me—and not a moment too soon.

My agility was probably all that saved my life.

I'd been bang on about our enemies having a stealth fighter in the mix, and my reflexes were the only thing that kept me from getting skewered on a brutally hooked blade that flashed right through where my chest had been.

My new muscle memory reacted with alacrity, using the momentum of my dodge to pour my body weight into a devastating downward strike with my staff.

It slammed into the sneaky little arse right at the base of his neck. He'd been trying to fade back into stealth since I'd foiled his lethal attack, but the impact of solid oak connecting with his spine stunned him senseless, and he collapsed into a hummock of moss.

I channelled a flow of spirit into my staff, holding the humus-encrusted butt of it against his carotid artery.

"Who sent you after us?" I demanded.

"Lord Sackington will have all your heads," he choked out, and I added pressure to my hold.

"He sent you out here to look for us?"

The hesitation told me more than an outright answer. No—Bawbag hadn't sent them looking for *us*. He'd sent them looking for Eilidh.

Which implied that he had told them enough to make sure they didn't give away the fact that Eilidh was still on the loose. If this chap *actually* had Eilidh, he'd be bleating about it loudly and insistently enough to put every sheep in Scotland to shame.

I was wasting time.

If Lord Bawbag had managed to work out how to ensnare and puppet humans the way he had with the harts, I'd have had some compunction about dispatching this bloke. But he wasn't puppeted; he was just a person. A person who'd chosen to side with a monster.

I formed a blade of Purifire with the spirit I'd channelled into my staff, and I plunged it cleanly into the man's throat.

The rest of the battle ended quickly after that.

When I looked up from killing the sneak, Rhona had already dropped the grappler, as he'd been immobilised by the trees. They retreated to their previous branches as if they'd never moved in the first place.

Iain had made short work of the archers—with none of them trained for hand-to-hand, his lightning-quick attacks and ascension-boosted strength broke necks and crushed tracheas with terrifying efficiency.

Meeksy was going from corpse to corpse, and at first I thought he was just checking them for weapons, which was strange—harvesting them would have done that just as well—but then I heard a groan and a rattling last breath, and I realised our healer was making sure they were dead.

Jeezo.

And he'd said Eilidh was terrifying.

"Six total," Iain said, leaning against a tree and wrinkling his nose. "That seems daft if they were looking for us."

"They were after Eilidh," I said, "not us. Six of them against one of her is just . . . prudent."

"Overkill," Rhona chimed in. "But barely."

I cast Connection again, aware that the flash of insistent gold in the periphery of my vision meant that I'd notifications to dig through, but first I wanted to check for a glyph.

I had to walk in a slow spiral out from the site of the battle to find Eilidh's mark, but it was there, and this time I went all the way up to it, placing my hand against the tree trunk.

Part of me hoped touching it would give me something more, a whisper of her voice, a curse, her calling me an amadan, anything. But there was nothing. Just bark and moss and a dangling thread of a spider's gossamer, dotted with tiny dewdrops.

The attackers had clearly been in the right ballpark to find her, though it gave me a fierce amount of vindictive glee that she'd evaded them enough for them to overshoot her trail. They'd been moving in the wrong direction. Or maybe they were just that incompetent, but I didn't think it was smart to assume an enemy's stupidity.

I knew we should get moving, but I also knew that those lurking notifications were going to drive me up the wall if I didn't clear them.

Making my way back to the others, I caught Meeksy's attention first. "Screen time, then onward?"

"Aye," he said, straightening his shoulders. His dark eyes had a haunted cast to them, but the line of his spine only said resolve.

Rhona looked up at our voices and nodded, stooping near the grappler she'd nearly beheaded.

The now-familiar rush of spirit, pathos, and will flooded into me as she harvested the fallen. I still hated harvesting humans. It felt dirty to me, but I tried to rationalise it with the knowledge that they'd do the same to us without a single moment's hesitation. That and we needed all the help we could get—with Lord Bawbag's strategy of murdering anyone who got in his way and gaining power in leaps and bounds, it was a near certainty that he would be stronger than us, diminishing returns or no. But the same went for his people.

Resigned, I sat down on a damp, mossy stump, thankful for Eilidh's crafting skills that kept my arse dry.

I opened my notifications.

Through physical exertion, you have gained a permanent +3 to Agility and +3 to Stamina. Please note that such increases have diminishing returns as your base statistics grow.

Through arcane exertion, you have gained a permanent +3 to Spirit and +1 to Pathos. Please note that such increases have diminishing returns as your base statistics grow.

. . .

You have increased your affinities: Synthesis (Level 2), Staves (Level 2)

You have increased your specialised affinity: Wild (Level 4)

Thank the gods.

A flare of gratitude went through me at the increase to Pathos. I'd made the—possibly ill-advised—choice to go for the Pathos-based build when it was my weakest stat, but seeing it go up even a piddly one point made it feel less precarious.

I wish I could have pinpointed whether it was the encounter with the glaistig or my ongoing muddle of emotion soup from tracking Eilidh through Argyll. Until a few days ago, I'd been certain she hated my guts. Rhona was the one who'd turned that on its head. I still didn't think the cheeky wee teenager was *right* about Eilidh actually being in love with me, but I was prepared to admit that perhaps hatred wasn't the extent of our connection.

If I were really honest with myself, hatred was far from what I felt for Eilidh.

All the more reason to find her before more of Bawbag's goons could. I'd do the same even if she did hate me. I wouldn't have abandoned anyone in Oban to that fate.

Shoving those thoughts aside, I doggedly ploughed on with my notifications.

. . .

You have reached Level 10! You have six attribute points to distribute. You have three skill points to distribute.

Finally. I felt a surge of glee seeing my level tick into double digits, and I also remembered a previous notification I'd gotten when I hit level nine.

Adding skill points to existing passive skills or skills excluded from standard level increases will not boost their efficacy, but it can increase the likelihood of evolution.

As much as I was itching to find out what they meant by *evolution*, there were too many base-level spells in my existing skill trees that I needed to unlock, especially with my new class.

Only Tursa had been available when I'd hit level nine, and likely because the draoidh class only became available at level nine, there were nine total root-level spells in the class's skill tree. Of which I had exactly two. After Tursa, I'd gained access to Òran na Cloiche, a spell that meant "Song of the Stone" and lent my voice greater weight to those who heard me speak—or sing.

Even thinking about it made my skin heat with embarrassment. I didn't have time for that.

I opened up the Draoidh tree to look at the next available spell.

Mac-Talla
   Like Tursa allows you to connect with the turning of the

earth and the constancy of the stars above in the present, Mac-Talla opens you to echoes of the past.

When you use Mac-Talla, you gain insight into what has come before to better prepare you for what is ahead. Your Earth philosopher George Santayana once said that "those who cannot remember the past are condemned to repeat it"—the Draoidhean live by this understanding. It is also said that a smart person learns from their own mistakes, but a wise person learns from the mistakes of others. Listen to the echoes. Learn from them. Use them to chart a stronger future.

That was almost as esoteric as the others had been, but it was something that resonated with me deeply. I spent my first skill point to unlock Mac-Talla.

I wanted to venture over to the Wild tree, but I almost felt like I had to see what had unlocked on the Draoidh tree after Mac-Talla.

The sight of the next one would have stopped me in my tracks if I'd not already been sitting.

Darach (Passive)—Some believe that the word for druid, and thus all magic, originated from the word for oak. This word in the old language was dair, *and whether or not the etymology proves true, it is undeniable that the oak is a symbol of magic and protective power even now.*

As a Draoidh, you will slowly begin to demonstrate a Draoidh's connection to the power of trees. The first of these is always the oak, for it is within the stalwart oak your power finds its roots.

Darach allows the Draoidh to draw consciously from this

power, which grows stronger when using staves of oak or when in contact with living oak.

While Darach will not increase in levels as active spells will, your understanding of magic will, on occasion, trigger evolution.

Feeling as though I were almost in a trance, I unlocked that with my second skill point. In my mind was the image of the enormous oak that I had raised up from the wreckage of Kilninver's primary school. We'd been so busy on our journey—and the event had been so surreal—that I'd punted it into the recesses of my mind. Now it loomed before me once more.

The moment I confirmed the skill point, a paragraph materialised at the end of the description.

You have already demonstrated your connection to the oak, both in your creation of the living weapon Brac-Meanmna and with your spontaneous cultivation of an oak tree in Kilninver. Evolution of Darach: Imminent.

I didn't know what that meant. My heart gave a thump at the thought of a skill evolving, but I hadn't the foggiest idea what would happen when it did.

With only one more skill point remaining, I reluctantly left the Draoidh tree behind to look at Wild. I had so many other trees I wanted to explore, but I also knew where my strengths lay—more and more, I was feeling a fool for my first impulse to put those two early points into Strength, thinking that would change things. What had changed things was following my instincts, and right now, my instinct told me I needed whatever came next in the Wild tree.

My instincts had not steered me wrong.

Sgàthan—Like the mirror that gives this spell its name, Sgàthan draws wild magic into you to reflect back damage upon your foes and to twist their own spells and abilities from their intended paths.

Be wary at the chaos such things can cause. Once redirected with Sgàthan, enemy spells can and will strike wherever is in their new line of sight. What magic you turn away from yourself can harm your allies.

The warning was a good one, but if I were caught out alone, this spell could be the difference between life and death.

I confirmed my final skill point, leaving only my attribute points, and my internal alarm was beginning to tell me it was time for us to move.

Six points, and I already knew what I wanted to do with them. Three in Mind, two in Agility, and one in Dexterity. When I opened my stats, I was pleased to see the jumps I'd earnt organically, too.

I was ready for whatever awaited us on the road ahead.

Name: Calum Green
Age: 36
Level: 10
Class: Draoidh (Further class specialisation at: Level 27)

Affinities: Nature (Level 6), Healing (Level 4), Synthesis (Level 2), Staves (Level 2)

Specialised Affinities: Wild (Level 4)

Alteration:
>**Strength:** 13
>**Dexterity:** 20
>**Agility:** 25
>**Mind:** 46

Regeneration:
>**Constitution:** 18
>**Stamina:** 33

Manipulation:
>**Spirit:** 43 (+90 capacity for 24 hours)
>**Pathos:** 23 (+45 capacity for 24 hours)
>**Will:** 31 (+15 capacity for 24 hours)

CHAPTER

FOUR

Everyone in our party but Rhona had hit their next level, for which I was grateful. Rhona was still the highest, at eight on the cusp of nine, but Meeksy and Iain weren't far behind her now at level seven. That fight had pushed them all onwards, and I heard Meeksy murmuring to Iain about two spells on the Healing tree that I'd looked at myself—Pian-Sgiath and Dìon-Shlàinte, both of which would be of great use from here on out.

Meeksy also seemed mollified by getting the Gaelic-named skills. He'd grown up in Gaelic medium education in Glasgow with Eilidh, and though his family spoke Farsi and English at home, both his parents and his brothers had all learnt Gaelic, which was brilliant. The few times I'd been to his family's home in Finnieston, it had been a hodgepodge of Farsi and Gaelic that made me feel like I had holes in my hearing—I had approximately two words of Farsi—but nevertheless felt homely and comforting.

I wondered if Meeksy would gain any heritage class options like I had and what they would be. No one but assholes would have the audacity to say he wasn't Scottish enough to get any Scotland-specific classes or abilities, and I hoped his Iranian heritage would also be available to him. The system seemed to notice who we were and how we worked. I just wished I had some sort of guidebook.

Either way, it was a relief to me to not be the main healer in the group. My skills could still be useful in a pinch, but knowing Meeksy was there and could ease pain as well as heal and shield people? That took a burden from my shoulders that I had become used to carrying. My step was lighter as we moved through the pine forest.

Night fell as we walked, and though we were all exhausted, we continued to follow Eilidh's glyphs through the trees. We finally stopped when we emerged from the forest on what I think was an old logging track. It was almost unidentifiable in the dark, but beyond that, the trees seemed to already be reaching out to reclaim the marks of humanity upon the earth.

We stopped to rest in a clear patch of gravel road after deeming that the tree line would keep the flames of Purifire from being seen from a distance despite our elevation.

"We ought to set a watch," Rhona said. "And figure out how we're planning to get across the loch."

"We'll follow the path Eilidh took," I said automatically, and at Rhona's quizzically raised eyebrow, I went on hurriedly. "If we try to swim across and run into a fuath again, that's a problem. If we go south when she went north, that's another problem. We follow her trail until we find her or she leaves us another message."

I could hear the stubborn set of my words, but until I said them out loud, I hadn't quite realised how viscerally I was opposed to departing from Eilidh's trail. Part of me thought I could find her anywhere. Another part of me screamed that I would never forgive myself if we tried to find a shortcut and she ended up dead.

Rhona just dipped her chin in acceptance, yawning.

"We'll need to hunt tomorrow. Or fish," Meeksy said quietly. "We're burning a lot of calories and not replacing them well."

To punctuate his sentence, Iain's stomach gave a gurgle, breaking some of the tension of the day.

"I'll take first watch," I said.

"I'll join you," Iain piped up. He pointed to his partner. "That one could drop off in an active war zone, and I'm too keyed up to catch a wink yet."

"Fine by me," Rhona said, yawning again. "I think I could also pass out."

With that, she pulled her makeshift bedroll from her inventory and collapsed onto it with a vengeance. Before Meeksy could do the same, the teenage girl was out, snoring softly.

I felt my lips twitch in a fond smile. I'd gotten used to her little snores.

To give Iain and Meeksy a chance to say goodnight, I walked a short distance away to find an obliging bush for a wee. I felt dead on my feet myself, but I also knew myself too well. If I thought I'd be woken in a few short hours, I'd just lie there like an anxious log. Nobody would win in that situation, because an anxious log who hasn't slept tends to be rubbish at spotting imminent threats.

By the time I made it back to our bare-bones camp, Meeksy was sprawled on his own bedroll, which came closer to a proper camp setup than Rhona's. Hers consisted of her cloak and a bundle of old clothes for a pillow. I envied the pair of them their ability to fall asleep so easily. Meeksy didn't snore, but his head lolled, his mouth drooping open.

"You and me, then, mate," Iain said to me.

"Aye, it is," I agreed.

We were quiet for a time. I didn't know about Iain, but I hadn't yet gotten used to the new normal that was *feeling* the aches and pains and lactic acid of the day's exertion floating away with my body's new and improved healing. It was surreal.

"I'm really glad you're not dead," Iain said at last, breaking the silence.

"Likewise, mate," I told him. "Definitely had a close shave a few times on the way, but I made it."

"Fuckin' weird, isn't it?" He shook his head in seeming disbelief. "One second, we've popped up to visit Mum and I'm texting you to come visit, the next we're punted back into the Stone Age or something, but you know. With magic."

On the last word, he wiggled his fingers in a way that was likely meant to look magical but instead just looked like jazz hands. He ran one hand through his dirty blond hair, shaking his head again.

"What a time to be alive," he muttered.

"I know, right? Our Millennial arses have been through a wringer or three. Recession, more recession, Brexit—how many prime ministers?—pandemic, more pandemic, now literal apocalypse." I imitated his jazz hands. "But magic!"

"But magic." Iain chuckled mirthlessly. "How do you reckon folks are in Glasgow?"

"Fuck if I know, mate. I bolted. I want to hope people really *do* make Glasgow, but who even could say? Maybe a giant slime monster emerged from the Clyde and ate Govan. Maybe Nicola Sturgeon's become a level-fifteen mage and declared independence. Maybe the Old Firm teams have divided up the city like it's *West Side Story* and are having snappy dance battles in George Square." It was my turn to laugh at the absurdity of all of it. I wasn't sure which of those things were less likely, to be honest. "Maybe if we can deal with the monster on our own doorstep, we'll find out one day."

"I, for one, welcome our new Sturgeonesque mage overlord," Iain quipped, but like before, his smile didn't really reach his eyes. He glanced at his sleeping partner. "Worried about his family. He keeps a stiff upper lip about it, but—"

"No explanation needed, mate," I said softly. I ought to have thought to check on them before I left. The thought hit me with a twinge of guilt.

"If you'd told me a month ago I'd be hunting human beings because they were trying to enslave animals and people alike all because Lord Bawbag turned out to aspire to comic-book villainy for real, I'd have thought you'd gone round the bend." Iain took a deep breath. "But here we are. At least my obsession with martial arts has paid off with dividends."

"That's no small thing," I said to him. After a moment of hesitation and listening to Rhona's quiet snores, I went on. "I can't shake the feeling that I'm missing something important."

"Just one thing?" Iain asked wryly.

I rolled my eyes. "You know me. On top of everything, omniscient, moisturised, in my lane, thriving."

"Totes." This time, he grinned at me, the skin at the corners of his blue eyes crinkling. "So spit it out. Maybe between the two of us we can work the problem."

He wasn't wrong. Sometimes a new perspective could break something right open—or even just talking things through out loud. There was a reason in my industry of coding we had an entire term for it: rubber ducking. If you got stuck on a problem, you could talk to a rubber duck—literal or figurative duck—until you realised you knew the answer. I could only hope that'd be the case here.

I started by walking Iain through Bawbag's meteoric leap in levels. We'd gone over some of it with Rhona filling in gaps with her experiences in the days after the ascension, and from our encounters with Bawbag and his flunkies, it wasn't a leap to say he'd continued down that route. It also made it clear that his strategy—murder, harvest, rinse, repeat—necessitated an influx of people he deemed expendable.

While the thought made me queasy, if you looked at people like they were consumables, it did make sense. Horrible sense, but sense.

"What I don't get," I said at last, "is how the Ascended Alliance allows such an exploit to exist. It seems to go against everything they stand for. Not that we know much about them."

"If you squint real hard, you can even see Bawbag's shite as a twisted interpretation of the—what did you call it?—ascension directive." Iain sucked his lip against his teeth.

I shuddered at the thought; aye, he was right, but I didn't have to like it. The idea of literally burning through other people to survive definitely put a damper on the more Kumbaya-level "you all need each other if you're going to get through this" thing.

But I didn't think that was it. Capricious magical beings from across the universe? Sure, why not? After all, in Scotland, we were no strangers to capricious otherworldly beings toying with humanity. Even in the twenty-first century, folks trod lightly around fairy mounds and took care not to disparage the sìthichean themselves.

I must have been frowning, because Iain peered at me. "Whatchu thinking, mate?"

"I don't think Bawbag is in their design for ascension. I think he's the antithesis of it. The system's said as much, if we trust it, and while it's wildly unhelpful for the most part, it feels more aloof than capricious for the sake of caprice itself," I said, mind rummaging through thoughts and impressions, trying to get something cohesive to solidify into words. "It's like . . . okay, wait."

Iain raised one eyebrow at me, but he waited for me to go on.

"How have humans survived to become the most advanced species on our planet?" I asked.

"Large frontal lobes?" Iain said dryly.

"Beyond that. You can have whip-smart intelligence and still have the survival and common-sense abilities of a headless chicken trying to cross the M8 at rush hour."

Iain's gaze grew distant. I couldn't tell if he was looking at Meeksy or just staring into the darkness beyond the camp, but after a few beats, he turned back to me.

"We cooperate," he said finally.

"Got it in one. Well, two, since you said frontal lobes first, but—"

"You can get tae fuck," he muttered, but a smile quirked at his lips anyway.

"People love the idea of a lone ranger able to take on the world, but the reality is that humans really do need each other. We've only gotten this far because we communicate —we share information for the betterment of the group. We look after each other, learn from each other."

"And sometimes, we blow ourselves up."

"Also that," I said. "But you throw one person out in the wilderness alone and they might survive, if they're lucky. If they don't get an infected blister and die of MRSA or drink the wrong water and get Giardia and shit themselves to death. If you've got a village, though . . ."

"You've got penicillin." Iain gave me a sardonic smile as if to say *Yes, I know that's a logical leap, but you know what I mean.*

"You've got everyone's strengths instead of just one person's weaknesses. And that helps negate any weaknesses." The more I thought about it, the more I felt like whatever it was I was searching for lingered just out of arm's reach.

But something we'd landed on had to be the key—humans had always survived because we cooperated. Not because we killed each other for resources, and not just because, obviously, getting disembowelled by the guy in the next glen was the opposite of surviving.

We were close. I could *feel* it.

My notifications flashed gold just as a shriek pierced the quiet of the night, sending both Iain and me leaping to our feet.

CHAPTER

FIVE

E very hair on my body seemed to stand on end all at once.

We didn't have to wake Meeksy and Rhona with that violent assault on everyone's eardrums, and they rolled blearily into action even as Iain and I positioned ourselves to give them time to get up and gear up.

"What the ever-loving fuck was that?" Meeksy said muzzily, shaking his head to clear the sleep from his mind.

"As soon as I see it, I'll let you know," I said.

"Sounded like a bird," Rhona said, somehow alert and already armed.

"Raptor of some kind. Hawk or eagle?" Iain's face turned upwards, scanning the sky.

"A bloody horse-sized seagull was bad enough—you reckon we're about to have a slap fight with one of the sodding monster eagles of Middle Earth?" I hated that I'd just said that out loud.

"Aren't they usually asleep at night?" Meeksy asked.

"Not sure that matters in an apocalypse," Rhona said absently, her own sharp gaze turned upward.

"Maybe it wasn't hunting us," Iain said, though he sounded as dubious as his words made me feel.

"Announcing its presence is a bit daft," I agreed, but assuming our old world's logic would hold true in this ascended one was pure folly.

The only further warning we got was a sudden gust of wind.

Before I could even cast Connection to see where it was, the bird descended upon us. On sheer reflex, I flung Purifire at it like a spear, putting a hefty chunk of my spirit reserves behind the attack as I added the weight of Spèird to give it more force.

The bird was *fast*.

Granted, a blue-green glowing projectile in the middle of the night would be easy to see even without the eyesight of a bird of prey, but seeing something hurtling at you and evading it in midair are two very different things.

Two very different things this creature did without so much as flinching.

Magic attacks would swerve around obstacles, but if something outright dodged? Yeah, pretty useless.

We were not equipped to handle a flying foe.

Iain's hand-to-hand skills were an extreme sport against a bird the size of a horse with talons as sharp as foot-long shards of shattered glass. Meeksy and Rhona, with their daggers, were every ounce as buggered.

Which left me.

"Distract it however you can!" I yelled. "Without getting carried away!"

I left them to puzzle out if I mean literally or figuratively, mind desperately running through options. I cast Fuaran on the four of us. Despite the dip to my spirit, the buff to my regeneration could make or break this battle.

Rhona, apparently, has taken me at my word.

As the raptor screeched again, Rhona answered with her own—and she did it right into the massive bird's face.

I didn't think hawks or eagles had hearing as sensitive as an owl's, but I only caught the blunted edge of Rhona's banshee scream, and it sent me recoiling backwards.

It was a testament to the creature's fortitude that all it did was screech again, this time in apparent rage.

But it stumbled.

My spear had been easy to dodge, but as the enormous avian animal's wings shuddered, sending its weight to one large, taloned foot, I had an idea. We weren't going to be on *even* ground with a creature that could fly, but we could at least all be *on* the ground.

Its wings were still outstretched, and my staff glowed, illuminating the immense pinions that ran in a graceful arc down the length of the bird's wing. They were speckled brown and white—and I formed Purifire into a blade as long as both my arms outstretched.

I aimed it directly at the line of the bird's joint.

The monster raptor squawked, lurching sideways. It beat both wings hard . . . and from the one I hit came a barrage of suddenly free feathers.

"Keep distracting it!" I bellowed as I leapt counter clockwise around the bird's tail. It tried to whirl to face me, but my Agility served me well.

Thwarted from its attempt to seek out its attacker, the bird tried to take off. For one moment—a moment that stretched out precariously, teetering on the precipice of success or failure—I thought it might manage to fly with an entire wing disabled.

Its good wing beat down hard, propelling the right side

of the bird into the air much farther than the left, but it didn't get far.

Iain took the bird's momentum as an opportunity to seize. How he could gauge the trajectory of the fumbling raptor's head, I'd never know, but as the bird dipped towards the earth, trying desperately to stay upright, Iain launched a devastating jump kick directly into the animal's beak.

Somehow, somehow, the bird managed to retaliate, sweeping its wing out in a wide arc.

It could no longer fly—but for a second, it looked like Iain might.

The wing caught him right across the chest, slamming into him and throwing him into the air.

"Iain!" Meeksy bellowed.

I'd never in my gaming life expected to see a healer go berserk, but this was just real life, not a game, and Meeksy's bellow turned into a roar of rage.

My spirit had recovered enough for me to repeat what I'd done. I didn't know where Rhona was—I hoped she hadn't somehow been bludgeoned to death while in stealth—and I couldn't stop to look for her.

This time, I honed my Purifire blade and aimed it at the most accessible part of the bird: its tail.

When I put the extra force of Spèird into it, knocking my spirit all the way down to thirty percent, I thought I'd maybe pluck the overgrown pigeon's arse.

I didn't expect it to slice straight through the tail and hamstring the sodding thing in an explosion of feathers, down, and blood.

The bird screeched again, and this time its flapping seemed desperate. It knew it had overestimated its ability to take on this prey.

Part of me felt worse about killing this creature than I had about killing Bawbag's flunkies who'd attacked us in the forest.

This creature just wanted to eat; it held no malice towards us.

Like us, it was just trying to survive.

Meeksy had reached Iain; I could see the glow of his magic as he healed my childhood pal.

And Rhona, devilish, sneaky wee Rhona, had simply been biding her time.

She'd watched me with my magic, but she carried sharp blades.

Dodging the bird's flailing movements, she ran one dagger down its remaining good wing, slicing off feathers as she went.

Her head turned towards me once, and I knew what she wanted from me.

Rhona shrieked one more time, almost directly into the bird's ear canal.

The creature spasmed and stumbled, flopping over.

"Finish it quick," Rhona said, half a gasp.

I barely had enough spirit to do it—I wouldn't have if I'd not cast Fuaran at the outset of the battle.

This time, I only made enough of a blade to do what I needed. Nothing huge. Just precise.

My razor-sharp, fiery magic beheaded the bird like a guillotine.

You have killed a giant goshawk. Caught in a wave of spirit upon Earth's ascension, this bird of prey mutated far faster than can normally be expected for a creature of its complexity.

Such creatures frequently contain common crafting materials such as: bird meat, pinions, goshawk talons, down, bone.

Do you wish to harvest this giant goshawk?

Wearily, I thought *yes*.

My notifications pulsed with the influx of manipulation resources. A quick glance told me that, somewhat surprisingly, the goshawk had contained all three—Spirit, Pathos, and Will. With the additions from the human foes, my Spirit had ticked over the hundred mark, giving me both increased capacity and another permanent point. Pathos had too—or maybe not.

I did a double take. My capacity for Pathos had only gathered fifty-seven points with the humans and the goshawk, but *something* had given me a point.

Belatedly, I remembered the flash of gold right before the raptor had descended upon us. Digging through the rest of my notifications, I finally found it.

Through arcane engagement, you have gained a permanent +1 to Pathos. Please note that such increases have diminishing returns as your base statistics grow.

Arcane engagement? That was new. It usually said experimentation or something.

Then it hit me.

It must have responded to my conversation with Iain.

It was also striking just how difficult it was to increase Pathos and Will organically. I suppose that said something for me that my Will had started out at fifteen. I'd pretend my Pathos hadn't begun at an embarrassing eight.

If I were to reach the threshold of thirty for my class, it was going to take some doing. A *lot* of it.

Disappointment tried to take over as I perused the rest of my notifications. There weren't any of note beyond the Pathos increase. I'd been hoping my Synthesis affinity would have increased or something. My active combining of Purifire and Spèird had sparked improvements before. I was either missing an integral puzzle piece or simply hadn't practiced enough.

When I snapped out of screen time, the others were organising the bird bits.

Rhona in particular was having a ball, but then, she was the only one of us who breezed through the fight. She stood with a handful of enormous goshawk pinions in each hand and was miming flapping wings.

"Magic or no magic, I'm not sure you're going to achieve lift-off," I said to her.

"One can dream," she replied stoically, then gave me an impish grin.

Iain sat in front of a pile of—I had to assume—magically contained goshawk down, one hand pressing at his sternum as he winced. Meeksy hovered around him like an overly concerned bear.

"You're going to have to put the rest of this in your inventory," Iain said to me, grimacing halfway through his sentence. "Ours haven't expanded yet, and we already put the bird meat away."

"I call a drumstick!" Rhona said quickly.

"Mon the birdie bits," I said, rolling my eyes and holding my arms out.

The bloody bird was a mahoosive monster—I wasn't sure Rhona'd be able to hold one of its enormous legs, let alone eat the lot of it. Then again, apocalypse metabolism. Who knew?

Reluctantly, the girl handed over her makeshift wings, which I bundled into my inventory. I dug out a bag for the talons and bones, a little unnerved at the thought of what we could do with those two things. And finally, with the down, I settled on using Spèird like I had when fishing—I wove my still-recovering spirit into as fine a mesh as I could to scoop up the feathers, depositing them in an inventory slot.

"Nobody let me get them back out again until we are in a closed room and I have something I can dump them in," I said under my breath. "Last thing we need is to be covered in monster goo after a fight and end up tarred and feathered when I take them out to make space for a simulacrum or something."

Rhona had been gazing wistfully at the bundle of down as if yearning for a feather pillow—who could blame her? —but her entire face lit up when I said that.

"Oh, that would be hilarious," she said. "I am defo not going to warn you. I have to see you covered in slime and fluff."

"I hate you," I said.

"You love me."

All of the day's exertion seemed to catch up to me at once.

"I don't know about you lot, but I think Iain's and my watch is officially kaput," I said. "Meeksy, Rhona's all your responsibility. If I wake up covered in fluff *or* drawings of penises, I will blame you."

"Hey!" Rhona protested. "I would never. It's much funner if you're awake."

Meeksy must have been stressed, because he barely chuckled at Rhona's indignation.

I probably shouldn't have given her ideas.

CHAPTER
SIX

Despite the relatively light-hearted mood from our midnight fight, a sombre chill settled over us again as we made our way through a persistent Highland mist the next morning.

The light was diffuse, and the fog muted our voices and our footsteps alike. The only real brightness came from Eilidh's glyphs.

I could almost sense hesitation in them as we drew closer to the northwestern shore of Loch Awe, following the strands of her spirit through the oak forest just south of Inverinan and then to the lochside. It was as if she couldn't make up her mind whether she'd wanted to go north around the loch—back towards Kilchurn, where we'd been attacked by the second simulacrum—or south to loop around the way we'd fled.

The implications of that settled over me like the omnipresent mist.

Either she'd stopped tracking whoever she was tracking on purpose or something else had stopped her. Any number of things could have done it—a battle, an ascended badger, a boat. I could easily imagine Bawbag organising boats to ferry his people across the loch rather than sending everyone on haunted hart-back or on foot.

In the end, Eilidh veered south.

"South's safer," Meeksy said shortly when we'd definitively aimed in our new direction. "From everything we've heard out of the north end of the loch, Bawbag's got it in an iron grip."

"He could have the south side by now too," Iain argued. "How would we know if he's just killing everyone?"

"We wouldn't." Rhona stopped a short distance away, fully visible for once—if anything could be called fully visible in that soup. "But I don't think he's taken the southern bit of the loch."

"What makes you say that?" I couldn't imagine she'd seen anything that would point her to that conclusion. None of us could see more than twenty feet in front of our faces.

Rhona gave me a look as if I'd asked her to explain why she thought there was a bunch of floating water vapour all around us.

"Do you remember nothing from school?" She sounded exasperated.

"Social dancing," Iain said.

"I blocked that out of my memory," I confessed.

"Even the Strip the Willow?" Meeksy gave me a look of faux outrage.

"Have I taught you nothing?" Iain lamented. "Clearly, your example should have been the Gay Gordons."

Meeksy gave a solemn bow of apology.

Rhona, though, actually stomped her foot. "How am I the most mature person here? I'm talking about history, you absolute fuath-breathed arseholes. Fighting a war on two different fronts is just bad tactics."

"She's got a point," Meeksy said with a nod.

"More than you three put together," Rhona muttered. "I'm going to go make sure you don't blunder into a beithir."

With that, our teenage wraith vanished into the mist.

"Strip the Willow," Iain said, scoffing. "Missed the low-hanging fruit."

"You're a low-hanging fruit," Meeksy grumbled.

I suddenly wished I could also vanish into the mist.

The farther we walked, the more my apprehension grew. It felt as if Eilidh's glyphs had begun to impart more than just a trail of breadcrumbs; it was like her practice had given her the ability to infuse them with something of her emotion.

And if my instinct was correct, she was worried.

Very, very worried.

It wasn't that there was danger.

To the contrary, there was almost pure silence as we made the hike down the loch. We'd meant to hunt, but even though I pulsed Connection as often as I could justify, my tendrils of spirit returned nothing but the occasional plodding beetle and the gold glow of Eilidh's glyphs.

No ascension-mutated stoats, no murderous murmurations of starlings. Nary a badger nor vole.

When the diffuse sunlight began to fade, we all seemed not to need a verbal discussion—we simply exchanged a glance and kept on moving, Rhona ranging back and forth all the way.

By the time it was fully dark, the rain had begun in

earnest. I said a silent thank you to Eilidh for the water-proofing she'd done. Even walking through the mist for a day would have left us sodden to the bone, but the actual drizzle would have made it that much worse. Iain and Meeksy didn't have Eilidh's handiwork, but Oban had other crafters who'd managed similar feats.

Drowned rats or not, we were a surly bunch when we stopped. We'd two tents between us, but it was one thing sharing a tent with both Eilidh and Rhona and another thing with just Rhona. She was slightly over half my age, and neither of us would have made any kind of advances —but it felt an awful lot like a grown-arse man sharing a tent with a child. My solution? I gave her the tent all to herself.

"You're sure," she said, looking at me like I'd decided to substitute my cloak for toilet roll.

"Aye, I'm sure." I tried to look sure. "I'll take first watch. You three can get some sleep."

"Oka-ay," she singsonged.

Iain and Meeksy were already ensconced in their own tent, so I pulled up a patch of moss and sat down, full of weary hope that nothing would come swooping into camp upon our heads like last night.

I decided to try something new with my magic.

I'd succeeded several times in weaving a web with Spèird—what if I could do that with Connection as well and use it as a ward?

As the skill had levelled up, it had increased in range. Nothing massive, but unless something could practically teleport, it would give us enough warning to at least be on guard.

My first attempt fizzled out in front of my eyes.

I only wanted to try it in a small sphere at first, something I could literally poke with a stick to see what would happen.

But using Connection was a bit like reaching with my mind. Trying to move from a sensation of reaching to an actual framework clearly required a bit more of a bridge than I'd hoped.

Somewhat deflated, I tried again.

This time, I didn't try to make anything with it; I simply let the tendrils of my mind reach. Not far. I didn't try to use it to its full extent. I just wanted to get a feel for what I was actually doing with my spirit.

If it were something like a mystical appendage, that might mean my idea wouldn't work. It'd be like trying to cross your legs and then wear them as a hat. But if "reaching" were merely the easiest option my brain had used to conceptualise something foreign, maybe I'd have a shot.

The drizzle continued as I sat there pulsing Connection every so often. For every two times I used it on a small scale to study it, I'd cast it at full strength to make sure I was guarding our camp as well as possible. Nothing greeted those attempts except eerie silence.

The silence threatened to derail my efforts for the sheer surreality of its presence. I had grown used to Connection finding a wealth of life large and small—to have it encounter nothing at all, not even earthworms and mites, was enough to make me paranoid.

Regardless, I kept up my efforts.

It felt like an arcane version of Morse code: short, short, long. Short, short, long.

As my watch wore on, my mind calmed. Perhaps it was the nature of a spell called Connection; perhaps it was the repetitive action. Spirit flowed out with my casting, then back in as it regenerated, much like a breath out and a breath in. Moreover, the longer I let myself relax into the experience, the faster my spirit seemed to spring back.

I was so engrossed in the trance-like state that the moment Iain and Meeksy stirred to take over the watch, I *felt* them awaken. The sensation was like feeling someone's body heat vanish from your side. I realised, in shock, that my spirit had attuned to their own spirit wells' wavelengths of sleep, like the quiet presence of brown noise. It shifted in frequency when they roused.

Reluctantly, I shifted my own mindset away from my experiments. While I was a bit disappointed that it hadn't yielded what I'd wanted it to, I felt like I was grasping at the edges of something else.

"Madainn mhath," Meeksy said as he emerged from the tent, his voice gummy with sleep. He looked like a rumpled black bear emerging from hibernation.

"Madainn mhath," I replied automatically, charmed that he'd started his good mornings in Gaelic.

"Thalla a dh'Ifrinn," I heard Iain mutter from inside the tent, which made me crack a grin.

Him telling us to go to hell, well. Iain'd never been a morning person. Though to be fair, three hours past midnight was only morning in a literal sense.

I kept my thoughts to myself as I let them know it'd been eerily quiet, and like me, both of my pals immediately twigged the wrongness of the silence.

Settling into their tent should have been tough. For one thing, it was a bit weird to get into a still-warm sleeping bag. But I found as I lay down that though part of me felt strangely rejuvenated by my experience on watch, my body was bone tired.

Sleep took me.

"I'm not alone in thinking this is bloody bizarre, am I?" Rhona's voice, like the rest of her, appeared out of nowhere in the morning haze.

We'd reached the bottom of Loch Awe, and we'd still yet to see hide or hair of another living creature.

"Absolutely not alone," I told her.

We'd risen at dawn and started walking at a fast clip, making our way southwest as quickly as we could. Eilidh's glyphs held, as did the waves of apprehension that poured off of them. I had to admit that was creating a bit of a feedback loop with my own anxiety.

"Part of me wishes something would pop out of us to give me something to punch," Iain said.

"You could punch a tree if it'd make you feel better," Rhona said helpfully. Her heart didn't seem to be in the joke —her eyes kept darting back and forth, gaze scanning the wilderness.

"What'd the trees do to deserve that? With my Strength stat, I'd probably obliterate the poor thing." Iain glanced at the nearest tree as if he'd surprised himself.

He was probably right. Like that scene from one of the sparkle-vampire films where the vampire just started punching boulders into gravel—we'd pretty much become that.

Without the glitter.

Probably.

Hopefully.

"What d' ye reckon is causing it?" Meeksy asked.

"Bawbag," I said automatically.

"Definitely Bawbag." Rhona cocked her head sideways.

"I mean, obviously it's him, but *how*?" Meeksy tossed

his clubbed-back ponytail over his shoulder. "If he's doing something to repel all life forms, why isn't it affecting us?"

That ... was a good question.

"I don't think that's what he's doing." Rhona pronounced each word carefully.

"You sound like you've got a thought," I said.

"Let me think for a second."

We all paused in our walking to give her time.

The fog had partly burned off from the previous day, leaving behind it only a pale haze that the struggling March sunlight turned to gold. In other circumstances, it might have been beautiful—I'd always loved these moments in the Highlands when the sun came out over the haze and mist—but right then, it just made our journey feel otherworldly. It was like we'd fallen through some indescribable portal without knowing it, landing in a different plane of existence.

Rhona was quiet so long that I jumped when she spoke.

"I think it's incidental," she said finally. "I don't think he's *trying* to repel anything—or we'd feel it. Calum would, anyway."

"Then what is it?" Iain frowned the way he always did when thinking felt like too much work. His whole face crinkled up.

"The animals," Meeksy said without further explanation.

Oh, gods. I wanted to facepalm. "The *animals*."

"Will *someone* explain what you are talking about?" Iain said irritably.

"C'mon, mate," I said. "You should know this. What do animals do when a gale blows in from the Minch?"

Understanding dawned on his face just as the sun broke through the haze for the first time all morning, which lit him like a radiant finger from heaven. It would have been funny if my paranoia hadn't ticked upward like my damn heart rate with the realisation of what we were saying.

"They sense danger," Rhona said. "They're fleeing him. He is repelling them, but not on purpose."

"He needs them," I agreed. "Which means—"

"Which means he'll need to go farther afield to find animals," Meeksy said, and then he went on, his voice bleaker with every passing word. "Humans aren't as good at trusting our instincts."

"Shit," Iain said. "Rhona, you said he wanted to practise his puppet magic on people."

"I think we'd be absolutely barmy not to assume he's not got test subjects by now," Meeksy said just as Rhona muttered, "Aye, he was always hungry to control everyone. Now he can just do it much more literally. God."

"How is Eilidh outpacing us still?" Iain asked suddenly. "She didn't have that much of a head start. Like a couple hours tops, but she's clearly widening the gap."

I didn't know how any of us hadn't thought of that yet. "She must be running and barely sleeping."

"I don't know about the rest of you," Rhona said, staring at Iain, "but I think maybe we should make catching up with her priority one. Iain's right. We ought to have done already."

With barely more than a glance around at each other, we started to jog, then run.

Meeksy's huffing and puffing received no jibes. Not today.

CHAPTER
SEVEN

C atching up with Eilidh was easier said than done.

For one thing, even though she probably had to stop moving to leave her glyphs, she was still just one person—and one who had started the apocalypse at a fitness level that outpaced all of us, including Iain. He might have been a fourth-dan black belt, but he preferred to get his cardio from kickboxing, not pounding the pavements.

In my ascension-acquired Stamina and Agility, though, I was able to find a certain amount of my night-time meditative state with the rhythm of running. I continued with my experiments, pulsing Connection twice near to me and a third time at full range.

With each of Eilidh's glyphs, I started to notice new things as we rounded the butt of Loch Awe and started back northward along its southeastern shore.

Not only was I picking up on threads of emotion in the glyphs, but I started noticing strands of something else, something that felt almost like a time signature.

The sole reason I noticed it was because I was actively

trying to distinguish between the glyphs. It was subtle, like picking up on how faded ink on paper became after days in the sun. It came in impressions that felt like long car trips as a child, if you opened your eyes once and it was afternoon, a second time and it was dusk, and a third time and it was pitch black. Far less distinct than that—it felt like trying to tell time by one random glance at the quality of light around you when you were otherwise blindfolded.

And it was not reassuring.

We weren't gaining on her that I could tell. To the contrary, she seemed to be pulling ahead even more with each passing glyph. It may have been only a minute or two, but despite our increase in pace, Eilidh was going to be out of our reach.

The sun burned through the rest of the haze by midafternoon, leaving a brilliant blue sky and a clear view all the way up Loch Awe. Rhona and I'd just been here a few days before, but already, the landscape felt almost unrecognisable.

We finally stopped to eat when the sun began its downward slide at our backs, over the distant sea.

I used my Purifire to roast the goshawk meat from the previous night, which required magical assistance from Meeksy. He, thankfully, had also unlocked the Arcane spell tree and thus had Spèird, which he used to basically hold the meat in the air so I could flambé it.

The bird's drumstick was about the length of *my* leg, but Rhona still insisted on taking it for herself. She yelped when she tried to pick it up and burned her entire hand on the exposed bone.

"What did you expect to happen?" I asked her, bemused.

"Shut up."

Rhona eyeballed Meeksy. "Can you keep this up here so it doesn't fall on the floor?"

Meeksy laughed, waving one hand at her. "Aye, can do. Good practice for me, anyway."

"Reckon you get a spell upgrade for creating a magical plate?" Iain asked, elbowing Meeksy in the ribs.

It was easier for Meeksy to keep everything on a single "plate," so soon the four of us were standing awkwardly around an invisible table, pulling long strands of roasted poultry from the goshawk's thigh. We'd prudently kept it to just the drumstick and the thigh, but even as massive as the meat was, we were making it disappear at an alarming rate.

Once we'd finally been defeated and put the remains of our picked-at bounty back in Rhona's inventory, we gave ourselves a moment to tidy up, which also left us open to the unnatural stillness.

"How is it so different?" Rhona asked, sounding as unnerved as I felt as she broke the silence.

"Magic?" I shrugged at her, unsure of what else to say. "It seems like the ascension affects *everything* alive, not just animals."

Iain and Meeksy hadn't just been here, and both of them started looking around as if trying to see what was different.

I couldn't speak for them, but to my eyes, all of the trees seemed taller, the moss beneath them lusher. March was early for the real push of spring in the hills, but everywhere I looked there were shoots of wild garlic, other stalks I recognised as bulbs, even if I wasn't able to identify exact species.

"The plants aren't suffering," I said under my breath, which made everyone else turn to look at me. I glanced at

Rhona. "Animals are taking the hint to get tae fuck, but the plants seem to be thriving."

"Probably because Lord 'I'd Kill the Last Tiger on Earth' Bawbag doesn't even see a plant unless it's to fatten up his foie gras." Rhona scowled, then brightened. "Maybe you could convince the plants to impale him like you did with the sheep."

"You impaled *sheep*?" Iain gawped at me, a Highlander's horror scrawled across his face.

"In my defence, the sheep were mutated wee bastards with beaks and a bloodthirst to rival the beithir's," I muttered. "I wasn't out there poking holes in lambs for fun."

"Beaks?" Meeksy exclaimed, then shook his head. "Never mind. I . . . do not want to know."

"You really don't," Rhona said.

"We should get moving again." The farther the sun sank towards the horizon, the more urgency prickled at me. I didn't know what awaited us on this trail, but now that I'd recognised the mystical time stamps on Eilidh's glyphs, each moment we delayed felt like letting her slip farther and farther away.

Before the apocalypse, if you'd asked me what was scarier, no monsters or monsters, I'd have said monsters.

Hands down, no quibbling.

Now, I was reassessing that assumption.

By mutual agreement, we kept going through the night, the others sensing my increasing urgency.

We saw nothing alive that wasn't a plant. *Nothing*.

Not so much as a bat in the sky or a centipede. I'd have

shed a tear of relief if we'd stumbled across an ascension-mutated centipede like that one in Glasgow the night all this started, but there was nowt.

It set my teeth on edge.

For every mile we traversed and every glyph of Eilidh's I found scrawled on a tree or rock or on the path in front of our feet, foreboding crept over me like the build of atmospheric music, but the jump scare never came.

It was that more than the lack of sleep that started getting exhausting, and it ratcheted up when we finally turned away from the loch towards Lord Bawbag's manor. The sky was still dark, though I could almost feel morning approaching, and I remembered with a start that such awareness was part of my passive Draoidh skills—it came from Tursa.

"Shouldn't we have seen *someone* by now?" Iain burst out, his words quiet but explosive.

"Yes," Rhona said. "We should have."

"We really should have," I said, scanning around me. I turned to look back in the direction we'd come from, just to double check, and I was right. "I can't see another of Eilidh's glyphs."

"What?" Iain slowed to a stop, and the rest of us followed.

Rhona had been sticking with us the closer we got to Bawbag territory, and I couldn't blame her. She was terrified of the man, but here she was nonetheless, heading right back into the beithir's den.

Hopefully not the literal beithir.

"No glyphs," I repeated slowly. "I don't know why she'd suddenly stop—there's no signs of a fight."

"Maybe she didn't have time and had to run away? Or maybe she figured out Bawbag left the manor to start a base somewhere else and she's tracking him." Meeksy glanced northwards, gesturing at the vicinity of Kilchurn Suites.

"He wouldn't abandon the manor. Expand, sure, but that manor to him is his palace." Rhona grimaced. "At least, you know, until he can force all of Argyll to build him a bigger one."

"So where is everyone?" Meeksy argued. "He seems the paranoid type, and he's got those—what are they called? Simulacra. You'd know they were here if they were around, right?"

That last was directed at me. I gave a hesitant nod in acquiescence, though none of this sat well with me. Eilidh had been so diligent the whole way, leaving her little glyphs for me to follow despite moving at breakneck speed. For her to suddenly stop felt bizarre. And Lord Bawbag was gaining strength in leaps and bounds—who was to say what he was capable of now? He very well could have figured out stealth simulacra.

A truly horrifying thought.

Then I cursed.

"What?" Iain said, turning to me in alarm.

"I'm a numpty, that's what." I waved an irritated hand. "Gimme a sec."

I'd forgotten something vital. Thinking about Tursa had reminded me. It *was* a passive skill, but it also had an active mode. I pulled it up in my mind's eye.

Tursa—*The ancients moved twenty-tonne slabs of rock hundreds of miles to build their monoliths. From this we have gleaned not only their technological capabilities but also their astronomical understanding. Many of these ancient monoliths were built with an intimate knowledge of the stars in the sky and the movements of the sun's path.*

This skill is the bedrock upon which the Draoidh builds their power. In unlocking it, you will gain an instinctual knowledge of astronomy and its relationship to you. While this may not seem like much, it will root you in time, in the seasons, and upon the surface of the earth itself. For what is more constant than the stars for navigation? To get anywhere, you need to know where you are.

Both a passive and an active skill, Tursa will allow you to carry an instinct of time and the turning of the wheel, but upon casting, it will give you an innate understanding of your environment, a precious glimpse that can allow you to strategise in the heat of battle or work your way out of natural obstacles when you can see no escape.

That last bit was key.

We needed to understand our environment. Anything that could give us information about what we were walking into would be vital.

I took a deep breath and cast Tursa.

I'd never done it before, so I wasn't prepared for the way swirls of magic appeared around me. The others all took a step back in surprise.

Time seemed to freeze.

All of the work I'd been doing with Connection crystallised in my mind like the last twist of a tactile puzzle when all the metal pieces come together at once, showing you the secret for an instant of absolute clarity.

Ever since I'd first unlocked Tursa, it had been working quietly in the background of my spirit and my mind, gathering data. It knew what the land was supposed to be like as a baseline—which meant it knew what we were facing was terribly, horribly wrong.

It was as if I were staring at a piece of exquisite silk tapestry that had gotten infested with moths. Where there should have been intricate patterns of spirit and interaction between insects, mammals, amphibians, birds, arachnids— now there were rotting holes where gaps in the ecosystem were being slowly widened as Bawbag's influence devoured them.

Plants were thriving, but they were only *seeming* to thrive. They needed interplay between the bugs and the birds, just like they needed the delicate webs of mycelium, of fungus both beneficent and malicious. They needed the earthworms to eat through the dirt and leave rich fertiliser in their wake. They needed all of it. And they were left alone.

The plants were growing wild for now with no deer to prune their spring growth and no bugs to gnaw at their first leaves, but soon they would falter every bit as much as the animals who had fled.

Moreover, all those animals who had bled out of their usual habitats into the surrounding areas would need to eat —they would exercise a huge amount of destruction on a land thrown out of balance by their presence.

Bawbag's bullshit was, quite literally, earth-killing.

I didn't know how much time we had to correct this monstrosity, only that if it were to continue, his poison would spread out from here.

We couldn't leave it unchecked.

With a gasp, I almost staggered as time jolted into being once more.

CHAPTER

EIGHT

"**D**id it help?" Rhona eyeballed me like I was about to spontaneously combust.

"Define helped," I practically wheezed.

I reeled from the disorientation, though the part of me that had been held in tension since that bloody pictogram in Kilninver finally relaxed. One thing Tursa had made clear was that there hadn't been any sort of violence here—which meant Eilidh had stopped making the glyphs of her own free will. I could trust that she had her reasons.

A hand grasped my shoulder, and I turned to see Iain steadying me.

"Spill," he said.

"Erm, Bawbag's gonnae wreck the world if we don't stop him?" I took a deep, fortifying breath and, almost by reflex, restarted my pulses of Connection. Short. Short. Long.

"We knew that, ye bam," Meeksy said, but his words lacked bite.

I ran them through what I'd seen, watching their faces grow grimmer and grimmer.

"All I wanted to do was go visit my mum, watch some telly, sprawl out on the sofa, and eat too much of her rhubarb crumble with custard," Iain said at last. "But nooooo, the world had to end, and we had to get stuck cleaning up after the upper class's entitled fuckery because some arsehole across the universe made a boo-boo and gave the tossers magic to make feudalism a thing again. Have I mentioned this is pants? This is pants."

It was the most I'd heard him say in days, and in spite of the fact that he was using his words to whinge, I couldn't help the smile that cracked through the creeping over-whelm of despair.

"It is pants," I agreed. "But you're forgetting the impor-tant bit."

"Oh, aye?"

"Oh, aye—they gave a bunch of cheesed-off Gaels magic too. An leig thu leis an fhear ud an tìr a ghabhail bhuainn?"

Rhona blinked at my language switch mid-paragraph, and Meeksy whispered to her, "You gonnae let that man take the land from us?"

"Cha leig," Iain denied fiercely after a beat. He clasped my shoulder harder for a moment before letting it go and shaking his own as if to loosen them up.

"'S math sin," came a voice from behind us, making all four of us jump out of our skins. "About time you caught up."

The Eilidh who stood before us was not the Eilidh I'd last seen in Oban.

Sure, her auburn curls were the same, if twisted back from her face to keep them out of her eyes. Those blue eyes were still hard as agates, and her pale skin still held a smat-tering of light freckles. But the rest of her?

It'd only been a few days, but the gruelling pace she'd set for herself had changed her dramatically. She'd always been lean, but now she looked *honed*. It was the only word I could use to describe her. Eilidh stood in an easy stance I recognised from my own training, ready to spring in any direction if needed. Her shoulders back, spine straight, she had a confidence about her that, despite her hauteur, she'd always lacked. A clear delineation between fragile pride and hard-won strength of self.

Her armour, she'd clearly upgraded. Where she'd found the time was anybody's guess, but when I continued my reflexive Morse code of Connection, I felt the tendrils of spirit reach her—but only because she allowed it. I sensed more blackthorn, sharp and protective, as well as oak bark and something I couldn't quite identify. She'd managed to craft stealth into her very armour.

"Amazing," I said under my breath. "How did you—"

A Rhona-shaped comet flew past me, colliding with the taller woman with a startled grunt.

"You—you legendary jackass!" Rhona cried. "I've been worried sick about you for days!"

I wished I'd had a camera to capture the bemusement on Eilidh's face. "If you found me, Calum clearly managed to track my glyphs," she sputtered. "I wasn't exactly lost at sea."

To my surprise, Eilidh caught my gaze and gave me a tentative smile, and her pale skin flushed pink.

"The glyphs were phenomenal," I told her earnestly. "You may as well have been unspooling a magic ball of string behind you as you went."

"Had to be sure you'd catch on," she said, the smile turning lopsided.

For once, I didn't think she was calling me thick.

As soon as Rhona let her go, Meeksy wrapped her in a crushing hug, ruffling her curls, which made her wrinkle her nose and primly go to straighten the hopeless mop that had only barely been contained before the bear got a paw on them.

Iain followed, which left me as the only one who *hadn't* hugged Eilidh hello, and I awkwardly closed the distance between us with my arms out in what I hoped was a gesture of "you are not required to consent to embracing me" and not "I've got leeches in my armpits."

It seemed to be the former. After a moment of hesitation, Eilidh threw her arms around my shoulders, and suddenly she was right up against me. Maybe I'd had it backwards—maybe it'd been Eilidh crushing Meeksy. Dear gods, the woman's Strength stat was alarming. Then again, my own arms wouldn't seem to let go of her waist.

She still smelled of lilacs and leather, a ludicrous combo at any other time, but the scent of her hair somehow grounded me to the point that I managed to pull back right at the border of making the hug creepy.

Eilidh's face was full-on red now, and she took a couple steps backward, scuffing one foot on the tarmac.

"Your glyphs started to feel anxious as we got closer to this place," I said, not knowing why I voiced the quiet part out loud.

She obviously didn't know why either. Her mouth opened a smidge, moving as if she were about to say something, but thought better of it.

"There's not a living creature between here and the manor," she said after a long pause, darting a glance at me before turning her gaze on the others.

To their credit, they didn't acknowledge the awkwardness. Iain and Meeksy knew me well enough to know my limits with banter, and Rhona I thought was just so relieved to be back with Eilidh—or terrified to be within spitting distance of Bawbag's evil lair—that she didn't tease us at all.

That was almost scarier than Lord Bawbag himself.

Eilidh quickly caught us up on what she'd been doing whilst she waited for our arrival.

"They took my gran," she said to start, and I had a distinct feeling things would only get worse from there. "I also saw Diana from Kilchurn and Andy when they brought them in. The kid looked haunted—unstable. I can't blame him, but his decision-making skills weren't great before he got abducted by a monster. I'm worried he'll try something reckless—if he can."

My stomach roiled as she explained what Bawbag had been up to.

"He's literally got a couple hundred people corralled at his house. Like *in* the corral. It was the only part of the barn we didn't torch." Eilidh looked to me with a slight shake of her head. "They've been out there for days."

"How do you know?" Meeksy asked. His brow had furrowed, pushing his black eyebrows together into nearly a unibrow.

"From the smell," Eilidh said curtly.

Oh.

Bloody hell.

Rhona's hand plucked at the hem of her undershirt, her other hand running over the hilt of her dagger. Iain had gone dangerously still.

"Okay, what are we going to do?" I asked. "How many people of Bawbag's are guarding them? Any idea?"

"That's just the thing," Eilidh said. Her mouth turned downward, and she seemed to chew on the inside of her cheek for a beat. "I didn't see anyone after Bawbag's bruisers dumped the Kilchurn folks into the pen. They mounted a couple of those puppeted deer and rode off northward again."

"You didn't see *anyone*?" Rhona cut in. "No one. And the people are just sitting there like—like cattle waiting to be slaughtered?"

"His ward game seems to have improved, or someone's has." Eilidh looked as if she wanted to say something else, but she stopped and took a breath, closing her eyes as she exhaled. When she opened them again, she went on. "I didn't dare try to poke at the wards. I only got close enough to realise they were there. I'm not much of a mage."

"But you got close enough to smell them," Iain said shrewdly.

Eilidh's face turned bleak. "I didn't have to be close to smell them. Just downwind."

"Has he done anything to them yet?" Meeksy pressed. "Or are they just . . . sitting about in their own mess?"

"I couldn't tell. They are very placid, which doesn't seem right."

"*None* of this is right," I said softly. "Which brings us back to what we're going to do about it."

It took about half an hour of hashing out plans for us to make one, and while I wasn't about to crow over it, it seemed like our best bet.

Which was how I found myself at the northwestern edge of Bawbag's estate alone with my Connection practise. One thing we'd all agreed on was that reconnaissance was priority one—if we went barrelling in there throwing spells and fists and sword strikes and Bawbag's people came back in force? Aye, that'd be us d-e-i-d.

Not to mention the people he'd saved for . . . whatever he was saving them for.

Rhona was the obvious one to get close, and between Iain and Eilidh, she'd be well protected. Meeksy was going to use his healing magic from a distance to see if he could diagnose what was keeping them placid. I wasn't sure if that would be helpful if the cause was more curse than contagion, but he seemed determined, and it at least gave him something to do besides worry about the others.

With my magic as an early-warning alarm, I felt as safe as I could in my own role, but the sense of something evading me stuck hard in the back of my mind like an elusive word on the tip of my tongue.

There was what I'd learnt with Connection practise—I tried to apply that now. Like it had before, my steady usage as I sat unmoving slowly calmed me, bringing my heart rate down and my breathing in time with my pulses of spirit.

And like the last time, my efforts yielded similar fruit: as I settled into that rhythm, I felt my spirit regeneration tick upwards.

That came secondary to the other effect that took root.

Seconds blurred into minutes, minutes into an hour, then two. My spirit stayed nearly full now, and the golden glow that suffused my vision told me either something had happened within my notifications or I'd triggered another type of magic.

Just like everywhere else I'd been exploring over the

past day, the land here was unbalanced. Animals had fled Bawbag's sphere of influence like sensing a storm nipping at their heels, and the plants were opportunistically taking advantage of the shift.

I was connected to all of it. *All* of it.

My spirit threaded through the ground beneath me, the layer of spongey peat that kept Scotland's rains tucked away and filtered into the ground water, the heather, the bracken, the gorse. Tiny mosses and nascent flowers, fungi and lichens, all woven into a massive network that, as time slid softly by, included me.

And because of that, I sensed something else.

My first impression of Bawbag's rot—like destructive moths devouring a precious silken tapestry—held true. But the longer I sat in stasis, my spirit flowing through my own channels, out into the webs beyond, and back into my being, the more I could *feel* the effect he had upon things. He knew nothing but brute force, something that the natural world had little tolerance for. Plants grew all the time, not all at once, and everything under the sun under-stood that there was a season for growth and a season for rest. A time to germinate and a time to bloom. It was some of the oldest wisdom of Earth's philosophies for a reason— to everything there truly was a season.

Yet he discounted it, and he perverted it. He tried to force everything around him to give way to his will and his will alone.

In that moment, understanding bloomed around me like a flower opening to the sun.

Ascension was the antithesis of men like him. Of *people* like him.

For perhaps the space of three heartbeats, my mind seemed to expand out from me in a ripple of spirit as I comprehended what ascension could be like in a planet *prepared*.

I imagined the people waiting, hopeful and at peace. I imagined children eagerly preparing themselves like Scottish children would for their birthday parties, wishing for wonders and oh-so-certain to get them. I imagined what a world could do to ease the transitions of their animals, to welcome their myths into being, manifested by the power of their minds not in fear, but in honour. In reverence.

The ache that filled me at all of those fanciful thoughts tore through me as I imagined.

Ascension should not have been synonymous with annihilation.

But what were humans if not programmed to perform feats of extraordinary courage in the face of calamity?

Maybe, just maybe, it wasn't too late for us.

CHAPTER
NINE

I knew without checking my notifications that something had shifted in me. Something big.

But I didn't have the time to check or quantify it—because as the wave of sudden clarity ebbed back into the greater power of the seas of spirit, I learned something else.

I'd been approaching my thought of wards the wrong way, thinking of it like laying a tripwire or building something I would leave behind. That's why my analogy of reaching didn't work if I thought of it like my spirit was an appendage.

Spirit was *everywhere*. It was energy. I didn't need to make something from it; I just had to open myself to what it had to say.

The moment that sank into my mind, I was moving.

I felt my own passage in the knowledge of the plants, their reactions, so minute most humans didn't think they had such things at all.

Without so much as turning to look over my shoulder, I knew that if I wanted to be alerted when any of Bawbag's parade of arseholes arrived, all I had to do was stop, breathe, and listen.

The newfound awareness spread throughout me as I ran over the moor back towards the manor. As I drew closer, I could feel my friends by their own personal signatures of spirit: Eilidh's blazing gold like the sun, Iain's everready steel grey, Meeksy's fiery orange, Rhona's whip-quick silver. And my own, a vibrant, seething green.

Within the manor lurked only a bare handful of bodies, and what stopped me in my tracks wasn't their presence— it was that they were all the *same*.

Worse, what I felt from the manor matched the nebulous, amorphous blob of spirit I felt beyond the burnt-out barn in the corral.

I should have felt despair, horror, terror.

A few hundred people, rounded up like livestock. Human history had existing experience with such things, imprinted on our collective psyche to the point that few in such a dismal situation would miss the significance—or the danger.

Except there was none of that.

No fear, only a mild sense of disinterest.

That brought horror upon me almost more than an outright threat of violence.

I couldn't see my friends as I approached, which was for the best. If I couldn't, no one else would. Keeping my own presence out of sight of the manor was, to my shock, unnecessary. Whoever was in there didn't *care*.

It was as if Bawbag had zombified not only his potential victims but his own staff.

Part of my mind screamed at me that I should be asking where in this ascended atrocity were the rest of Bawbag's flunkies, but that thought sheared away just as quickly. We would cross that burning bridge when we came to it.

Until then, I was just going to thank every lucky star in the heavens that the most germane answer was "not fucking here."

Somewhat surprisingly, Rhona found me first.

"What are you doing?" she hissed at me. "You're supposed to be making sure they can't flank us."

"I already did. They can't," I told her. "We've got bigger problems."

"Aye, no shit, Sherlock."

"What shat in your tea?"

"Bawbag," Rhona retorted automatically, then immediately made a repulsed face. "Thank you for that. I'm never drinking tea again, because I just thought of Bawbag teabagging it, and it's all your fault."

"That's . . . fair. Sorry." I shook off the inappropriate conversation, turning back to the more pressing matters at hand.

Though I had regrets about instilling that particular imagery in both our minds. All the more reason to stop the man, preferably by killing him, burning the remains, and making a magical rocket or twelve to yeet the ashes into space.

"Where are the others?" I asked Rhona.

Instead of answering, she just grabbed the shoulder of my cloak and tugged.

I followed after her for about five minutes. We passed the hunting hut where we'd stolen Sailean's mother's pelt what felt like an age ago. Bawbag had felled a heap of trees around the hut itself, and disconcertingly, new ones had already grown to shoulder height in their absence. We'd been gone a matter of days.

Rhona caught me staring and glanced over her shoulder. "I know," she said shortly. "It's bloody weird."

When we found the others, it was just Iain and Meeksy.

"Where's Eilidh?" I asked without pause. She wasn't far away, which was puzzling.

Iain raised an eyebrow at me. "Having a wee, if you must know."

Oh. My cheeks grew warm. Right. People still had to piss in an apocalypse.

"Calum here says he left his post because he's developed a sixth sense," Rhona said.

"We've . . . all developed a sixth sense," Iain replied, bemused.

Rhona scrunched up her nose at that.

"What'd you lot find out?" I asked.

"Fuck all," Iain said at the same time Meeksy sighed and said, "I can't heal them."

They looked at each other, Meeksy with a disgruntled cast to his slouch and Iain with a helpless shrug that seemed to say *Like I said.*

Eilidh's presence drew closer in my mind. When she said "That's because they're being puppeted, which hasn't technically harmed them," I was the only one who didn't jump.

Rhona, of course, noticed. "Huh," she said, giving me a sidelong glance. "Guess your sixth sense is doing its job."

Eilidh looked momentarily confused, but she didn't ask. She met my gaze instead, motioning in the general direction of the corral.

"I take it no one else mentioned that?" she said to me. When I shook my head, she pressed her lips together and adjusted her shoulders. "He's figured out how to puppet humans. Surprise."

"That's not so much a surprise," I said slowly. "What's surprising is that he's managed to do it to so many of them. It's not just the ones in the corral—he also did it to the ones in the house."

"There's people in the manor?" Rhona squeaked.

It was my turn for incredulity. "You didn't know that?"

"I didn't exactly go peeking in windows. I couldn't hear anything, and I didn't want to get too close, but there's no movement in there. None."

"Aye, because they're basically zombies," I said. "I'm not sure they aren't sitting in puddles of their own piss. He's left them all the capability of an automaton."

"Why would he do that?" Iain asked. "I mean, he's an evil bastard, aye, but he seems the type to shoot a puppy for piddling on the floor, let alone a person."

"Control," Eilidh and I said at the same time. Our eyes met for the briefest of moment before we both hurriedly averted our gaze.

Meeksy, though, turned pensive. "He doesn't trust even his staff."

Eilidh's attention swivelled to Meeksy. "More than that," she breathed. "He actively distrusts them. Think— Iain asked a great question. Why *would* he basically turn out the lights in their brains on purpose if he had any smidgen of trust for them at all?"

My mind caught onto what she was saying. "Because it's the only way he'd leave them here with the others—he must have thought they'd somehow free them."

"Wouldn't you?" Rhona said. She aimed a kick at a tree root half-heartedly. "I mean, obviously, you would. Bawbag's people aren't you, but at least before the ascension, they weren't genocidal fiends."

"How has the bar dropped that low in three weeks?" Iain muttered.

Meeksy turned a bland gaze on his partner. "Bold of you to think the ascension kicked that ball down the hill."

Iain opened his mouth for a second and then just shook himself all over like a wet dog. "Aye, that was a stupid thing to say."

My brain was already moving through other things. "How paranoid is Bawbag?" I asked slowly. "On a scale of Pharma Bro to tin-foil hat?"

"Is that even a question?" Rhona scoffed.

"Touché, just checking," I said.

"What are you thinking?" Eilidh shifted her weight, her eyes as pensive as Meeksy's had been.

"Bawbag isn't paranoid," I said. "To the contrary, he's an arrogant arse who expects everyone to grovel at his toe jam."

"Yes," Iain said impatiently. "And?"

"So why would he zombify his own staff if there was little chance they'd succeed in freeing the people he's kidnapped?" I said, gesturing with one hand and bracing myself against my staff with the other. "He moved from quadrupedal mammals to humans faster than a footy bloke can down a bottle of Buckfast, aye, but for him to maintain control over that *many*?"

"Oh," Eilidh said, this time meeting my gaze and holding it, blue eyes wide. "*Oh*."

"Will one of you explain? Fuck's sake," Rhona muttered.

Meeksy stood up from his slouching posture, straightening his shoulders as he looked at the teen girl with a glint in his eye. "They're saying that whatever is keeping the people mindless has to be fragile—fragile enough that even an arrogant arse who expects people to grovel at his toe jam thought his *staff* could break through it."

The whites of Rhona's eyes became more visible with every word Meeksy said, and she let out an explosive sigh.

Eilidh, though, was still looking at me. "This means you're up," she said. "If he's dipped this shit in the River Styx, find me that Achilles heel, and we'll make this all come crumbling down."

Easier said than done.

Just knowing an answer was simple should have made it a given, but nothing really worked that way. It was like a difficult riddle; once I found said Achilles heel, I was sure I'd think it was the most obvious thing to ever slap me in the face. But until then? It felt instead like trying to slap the sun.

Getting closer to the corral was less fraught, at least. Eilidh and Meeksy had felt out the border of Bawbag's wards, which—much to my dismay—were far more sophisticated than the simple asinine trip line his flunky had used to hem us into the hunting hut.

There were two problems we had to solve, and the wards were the first one—and the most potentially dangerous.

My instincts told me I could dismantle them. Whether I could do that without triggering them was another story. This meant if I planned to actually free the people inside and not, for instance, watch them get immolated or pelted with Bawbag's terrifying glass-like magic before I could stop it, I had to first figure out how to rouse them from their collective stupor.

And once I did that, I'd have to also be ready to make sure they didn't panic outright.

Meeksy had the healing spells that both shielded someone from damage and from pain, but as close as we could count with them milling about aimlessly, there were over three hundred people in that corral. He couldn't protect all of them if the wards went wrong.

Because of that, I perched on the side of the corral where we'd escaped with the horses when Eilidh and I set fire to the barn.

More out of habit than anything, I worked on my Connection pulses. Short, short, long. Short, short, long. Short, short, long.

I could tell the others were getting impatient. They were behind me a moderate distance, within the tree cover that hadn't been logged away, but the ripples of spirit they caused with their antsy shifting told me they wanted me to just fucking *do* something already.

Short, short, long.

Tuning their agitation out as much as possible, I actively slowed my breathing, feeling an awareness of my heartbeat's relationship to breath take over along with the ebb and flow of spirit.

Short, short, long.

At first, the sense of Bawbag's destruction was nearly overwhelming. It was like trying to float in the sea when the waves were too big and muscles too tired—each swell threatened drowning.

It took me longer to ease myself because of it. It felt like purposely sitting in a hot tub everyone'd pissed and shit in and trying to convince myself it was relaxing over the tang of sewage and chlorine. And the urine and faecal odours were literal, because it was like whatever Bawbag had done to these people, losing control of their bowels and bladders was an immediate side effect. The stink was wretched. I only hoped Meeksy had started working out some substitute for antibiotics for all the UTIs he was going to have to treat.

Pushing all of that out of my mind? Yeah, that was not easy.

After almost an hour, I finally stumbled on *why*.

It wasn't just proximity and the stench of humans subjected to utter indignity that was causing my revulsion. Not directly. I'd thought it was Bawbag's influence causing the desiccation of life here, but I'd made a mistake. An understandable error. In coding, when I would get to know something I was working on, I'd start to get a feel for where the problems cropped up. Half of tech assistance was knowing where yourself and other devs had patched something and how—the equivalent of knowing where on the machine to plant a well-timed kick to get it running again.

I'd been looking at this like it was a corrupted file altogether, and it wasn't.

It was a single line of faulty code, and I was staring directly at it. Zeroes where there ought to have been ones.

Bawbag wasn't the source of the poison spreading out to envelop Argyll. Not the man himself—he wasn't moving about in a noxious cloud of his own stench.

He'd just created a stink bomb and left it to fester.

CHAPTER

TEN

As soon as I realised that, things fell into place like I'd flicked the first of a line of dominoes stretching out into infinity.

One. What he'd done here was vulnerable and currently impermanent. That didn't mean it wasn't dangerous; quite the opposite was true.

Two. He likely had no idea there was a ticking time bomb in his own back garden that he'd manufactured himself in his arrogance. He'd just buggered off somewhere.

Three. He had indeed buggered off somewhere, which was worrying. That he'd left with most of his force at once suggested he had a substantial target. They had gone north, towards Kilchurn. We would need to find out where exactly as soon as we solved our more immediate problem.

Four. Bawbag thought his work here was fragile enough to protect by doing the same to his own staff.

Short, short, long.

Spirit flowed out, spirit flowed in.

I tried to relax into the knowledge that spirit was energy, not an appendage. In my increasing desperation to solve this, it felt like a Sisyphean task. For days now I'd been trying to push this particular boulder up the hill, coming tantalisingly close to success only for it to roll right back down again.

But the stakes were higher now. It wasn't just me and my friends—I could see Diana and Andy in there, and far back, standing motionless at the most distant edge of the corral, Mòrag. Eilidh's seanmhair.

Gritting my teeth, I repeated my sequence.

Short, short, long.

I held the longer pulse, trying to shift my awareness from *reaching* to *listening*.

And when I did, I almost laughed in pure glee.

Spirit had a flow to it, a flow I had been observing for days upon end. That analogy of moths eating silk? It was almost painfully correct. Bawbag's magic had nullified the paths of spirit within the corral—and within his manor.

He'd disrupted the connections, broken the chain of code with an error.

This was against everything in the universe's natural order.

All I had to do was turn some of those zeroes back into ones.

All I had to do . . . was something wild.

"Are you sodding *serious*?" Iain said when I told him what I wanted to do.

The others all looked like they were one hundred percent on board with Iain's question.

"Yes," I said.

"Tha thu 'n da-rìreadh." Eilidh's echo in Gaelic of Iain's

sentiment was much quieter, an odd light glimmering in her agate-blue eyes.

And hers wasn't a question.

"Tha," I affirmed to her. "Tha mi cinnteach gur ann an-seo a tha an t-adhbhar agus an fhreagairt."

"He's sure this is the reason and the answer," Meeksy translated for Rhona, whose fear had seemed to slowly melt away over the past few hours.

The sun had reached its zenith as we skulked about, and the clear sky had given way to clouds rolling in from the islands, but light still dappled the hills in the distance where they broke. We were losing daylight.

We needed to move.

"Right, ma-tà," Eilidh murmured, then glanced at Rhona and reflexively switched to English. "What do you need from us?"

"Be ready to help the people." It sounded so simple, so sodding simple, but if I was right—and I was indeed sure I was—once I unravelled the wards and started bridging the gaps of spirit, the people *would* likely panic.

I didn't know how much they were aware in there or how much they would remember. But from what I knew of Bawbag and his henchmen, whatever they last remembered was almost certainly terror. For themselves, for their loved ones, for their homes.

Scared people could lash out. They could hurt someone without meaning to, including us and each other. Without me casting Keen Eye on every single person in there, I didn't know what their levels were or their classes. They could all be classless and below level three—or they could be level ten specialists who'd go nuclear.

We had to be careful.

Together, we made our way back to the paddock of people.

My eyes scanned the crowd of milling human beings. The wind shifted as I did, bringing with it another wave of stink. I tried not to breathe through my nose, but with my mouth open, it was almost worse. To be left alone in such ignominy was horrific—a human rights violation to a near-unbelievable extreme. Whether they were aware in there or not, these people were going to be traumatised.

"Be ready to move," I said to Eilidh, still looking out over the crowd of hapless humans. "I don't know how long it'll take me to safely bring the wards down, but depending on what they were designed to do, it could disrupt the people in there either wa—"

I broke off as my gaze fell upon a face I'd not recognised until that moment.

The last time I'd seen the man, he'd been wearing spectacles and a cardigan, and without the specs, I'd not really placed the face. The cardigan was gone, replaced with a fleece that itself wore a smear of red up one side of the torso, and the man's face was caked with dried blood. His trousers—well. What had once been waterproof hiking bottoms were now wretched, coated in waste both drying to a crust and still wet, seeping through the beige fabric with a colour that was obviously not just urine.

"Ronald," I said, raising my hand to point.

Eilidh's head snapped up, and she followed my finger.

The stick-thin Kilninver teacher shuffled aimlessly through the paddock, bumping into an old woman I didn't know whose own spectacles remained, implausibly, half perched on her nose with one arm of them dangling in front of her left earlobe.

I'd tried *very* hard not to look at the children in there. Now I did, seeking out the smaller forms.

"They got here fast," Eilidh said. "Really fast."

"Let's get them the fuck *out*," I said. "I think I'm evolving enough to feel at least three entire emotions, Eilidh, and if I don't use the rage right now, disgust and grief are going to make me a lot less helpful."

"Do whatever it takes," she said fiercely.

Rhona made a small cry from a short distance away as she figured out what had caught our attention, and Eilidh gave me a pointed look, going over to the younger woman.

Iain did the same, but to my surprise, Meeksy came over to me.

"One thing," he said. "I wasn't able to do anything to help them, but my diagnosis spell gained two levels from all my trying different things, and it won't help you with the people part, but it might help with the wards."

"Oh, thank the gods. Anything you got, mate," I said, slapping him on the back a little too hard.

Meeksy didn't even flinch. "I don't think they're alarm wards," he said after a brief pause as if considering his word choice carefully—that was the Meeksy way. "I think they're more of a . . . metaphysical corral to go with the physical one."

It *did* feel like finding out the answer to the riddle was as simple as "you don't bury survivors, of course."

It was the Occam's razor of solutions, and it made my job that much easier.

"Ceud mìle taing," I said to him earnestly, then, more hesitantly, "I don't suppose you have Purifire, do you?"

"I don't," he replied, bewildered. "But I do have a skill point in reserve."

"You do?"

"Aye, just in case."

I swallowed. "You know how I've used it to clean our armour?"

Comprehension dawned. Meeksy's brown skin was slightly flushed as he glanced at the people mired in their own mess.

"That is more than worth the skill point," he said softly. "B' fhiach e, gun teagamh."

"Math thu," I told him. I didn't think there were many people as good as Meeksy.

As he moved back towards the others, I found myself a place slightly upwind of the paddock, trying to minimise the distractions of the stench and familiar faces alike.

Whether I knew them or not, no person deserved this. Except maybe the person who'd done it to them, and him I just wanted to fire into space. Maybe without killing him first. If we could eject him from Earth with a high enough velocity, maybe he'd immolate in the atmosphere.

It was likely the practise I'd had—or possibly the resolve and growing confidence of knowing better what to do—but this time, summoning the flows of spirit with Connection felt easier. On instinct, I shifted my rhythm away from the short, short, long.

I changed it to something akin to a heartbeat.

Short-long. Short-long. I timed it with my breath.

Short-long, inhale, hold. Short-long, exhale, hold.

As I did so, I stopped reaching and listened.

"Listened" wasn't really any more accurate than "reaching," but it came closer in some small way to the sense of receptivity.

I could observe the flows of spirit, direct them, or I could be part of them.

My choice? The latter.

Short-long, inhale, hold. Short-long, exhale, hold.
Short-long, inhale, hold. Short-long, exhale, hold.
Short-long, inhale, hold. Short-long, exhale, hold.

The sense of wrongness in the corral ate away at me, but it couldn't touch me. Spirit shielded me. The plants beneath me whispered that they knew something wasn't right; though they rejoiced in their safety from gnawing jaws and teeth, they fretted for their future flowers that would go unpollinated. They were here, now.

And they were ready to help.

As it had before, I started to see threads of gold and green weaving together around me. At first I thought it was all my own, but something shifted in the spirit at my back, and I almost lost my concentration.

Eilidh.

I didn't know how she was doing it, and I didn't dare stop and question, but somehow, she had managed to meld her spirit with mine. She bolstered it effortlessly—it was only my own surprise that almost made me falter.

Distantly, I was aware of the sound of Rhona's gasp. Just as I was aware of the shuffling feet of the corralled people and the whisper of the breeze blowing my curls into my face. I heard the sibilant sound of wind in branches at my back, the gurgle of my own stomach and those of the unfortunate souls trapped in front of me.

Short-long, inhale, hold. Short-long, exhale, hold.

My spirit barely even dipped with each pulse of Connection now. It was as if I were simply cycling it through the veins and channels of my body rather than gathering it and expending it.

I was one bank of the river. It was the water. Eilidh was the other.

Short-long, inhale, hold. Short-long, exhale, hold.

My entire body burst into gooseflesh as the river we guided encountered the dam: the wards.

It was no match for us.

Spirit surrounded the circle of the wards like water rushing towards a drain, except that this water was far from stagnant—it was alive, and it was on the move.

The force of our combined magic crashed into the wards like a wave hitting a tidal wall, but instead of splashing back upon us, it kept going. It swarmed over the wards, filling in all those empty gaps, those zeroes, with energy that flowed, flowed, flowed.

Behind me, I heard sounds of alarm, but I couldn't stop.

I knew exactly what I had to do here, at the nexus of this wound in the countryside.

My Wild affinity leapt to me, fusing and synthesising with my magic—and Eilidh's.

What I needed was a summoning cry. What I needed was a gathering of the powers of the earth that lay in confusion, missing the vital presence of creatures great and small.

I had exactly the spell for that.

Power boomed from my core as I cast Tairm.

CHAPTER
ELEVEN

Before, I had only used Tairm offensively, against things that wanted me or my friends dead.

This spell calls upon the land around you, based on your affinities and your own intent.

Be clear in your need, and nature will respond to your call.

I didn't think I'd ever been clearer in my need.

At first, I felt the outrushing of spirit, heard Eilidh's sharp intake of breath as a counterpoint when the spell drew also from her power. For a moment, everything hung in stasis. It was as if every single cell on my body stopped its infinitesimal work, waiting for some ineffable sign that it could go on.

Then the ground shuddered.

And shook.

I heard Rhona yelp, punctuating Iain's bilingual cursing. Before me, several of the puppeted humans wobbled and tipped over, making me wince when they dropped like fruit from a tree. None made any move to protect themselves from the falls.

But just as suddenly as the earth had moved beneath

me, it settled, and wind burst forth, scouring through the corral with the scent of heather and peat.

I scrambled to my feet, knowing my active part in this was done for the present, but Tairm had only gotten started.

It was barely March in the Scottish Highlands—far from the idealistic showers-to-flowers transition beyond the early blooming trailblazers like Rhona's violets and the occasional patch of crocuses and snowdrops.

That suddenly ceased to matter.

Still tethered to the flows of spirit Eilidh and I had cultivated, the power washed over me, poured up through the ground at my feet. It rained down from the skies as the sun simultaneously burst through the clouds and a heavy-dropped spring shower glittered like millions of tiny topazes as it fell.

It was as if that downpour contained everything the land's flora needed to, well, flourish.

From one breath to the next, one *short-long* cycle of inhales and exhales, sprouts shot up from the earth around us.

I'd ignored, yet again, the memory of the oak tree that had risen up in Kilninver, but now there were three hundred witnesses as magic rippled through the sodden, soiled ground, leaving life in its wake. Where first horses and then humans had been kept contained, now meadow grasses sprang up from the well-fertilised earth.

They burst into bloom in a hundred species—I recognised some, like ryegrass and cocksfoot and Timothy grass and what looked like barley. Grazing grasses and wildflowers, a mix of whatever had gone through the horses and whatever Tairm had drawn up through the earth.

I stood in awe as the land responded to the need, filling

the moth holes left by Bawbag's horrid magic with alacrity. Pollen would soon float on the wind, drawing bees and butterflies back from wherever they had fled.

Part of me relaxed with the knowledge that this would right itself. The rest of me knew that this reprieve would be only temporary if we did not find the rot at the root.

Bawbag himself had to be stopped.

That was the only way this wouldn't happen again.

Almost before I could enjoy the success of freeing the captive humans, Tairm faded, and the sunshower slowed and stopped. While the eager spirit had devoured what filth lay on the corral floor, it had done nothing about the people's soiled clothing.

People who were, at last, moving and responding to the world around them.

Eilidh recognised it a split second faster than I did, and she was off like a fire arrow loosed from a bow, aimed directly at Mòrag.

Even as she moved, Meeksy was fast on her heels, his nurse training kicking in without hesitation. Iain followed —he had some first aid training from his long years working in martial arts, and he'd triaged broken bones and split lips plenty of times. Rhona trailed behind them, and I turned to her.

She was looking over the mess of people with apprehension. I couldn't blame her; I wasn't sure where to start, myself.

"Come on," I said to her, holding out an arm to give her shoulder a squeeze. "Meeksy might need us."

"I don't know what I'd be any use for," Rhona replied, uncertainty filling the crack in her voice.

Just beyond the fence—which now home to a plethora of climbing vines snaking through the poles—a wean stumbled two steps, looked around, and burst into tears. The child couldn't have been older than four.

I wasn't great with kids. Never really had been, even when I was one. But I didn't know who could look at a bairn and do nothing. I left my staff leaning against the fence and leapt over it, landing beside the child. On immediate reflection, this had been a mistake, because the poor lad startled and cried harder.

"Hey, there, pal," I said to him. "You're all right. I promise."

Without thinking over it too much, I drew on my spirit to conjure Purifire, keeping it to a small ball of sparks that danced in the palm of my hand. I felt Rhona clambering over the fence after her brief hesitation.

The blue-green sparkles did what I'd hoped they would —the wean hiccoughed, wiped the dripping snot and tears from his face with the tattered sleeve of his jumper, and stared, transfixed.

"Aye, there you are," I said to him. "You're all right. Want to see some more magic?"

The poor thing was likely traumatised, and the moment he realised his mum or da wasn't to hand, he'd probably be wailing again, but I was going to take the win. He nodded, still wobbly.

"Hold very, very still. This might tickle," I whispered conspiratorially, and then I directed my spirit into my version of the cleansing Purifire I'd perfected.

The kid made a wee squeak, but then he gave a startled giggle, squirming and scratching his bum.

Rhona giggled at that, which made the wean jump.

"All cleaned up now, pal," I said to him. "What's your name?"

Big brown eyes just stared at me.

"Fair play." I changed tactics. "I'm Calum, and this is Rhona. Why don't you stay with Rhona here, and I'll go find the other kids and send them to join you. You can tell them about the magic."

I was lucky Rhona's stabbing was confined to shrieking and daggers, because whew—the look she gave me when the wee mite determinedly grabbed her hand with his own chubby child's paw? Critical hit. I'd be down for the count.

Instead, I turned towards the sounds of crying and high-tailed it out of there.

It wasn't long until Meeksy twigged what I was doing. Though he'd occasionally flag me down to heal someone when his spirit was low, I think he appreciated me taking on the smaller victims of Bawbag's bullshit.

Some of the weans were with their parents—or, more frequently, parent, singular. I prioritised the ones who wandered on their own, the ones whose gulping sobs sounded shellshocked.

I recognised some of them from Kilninver.

Gods, what these bairns had been through. I wanted to kill Bawbag a wee bit deader with every kid I soothed. Some were untouched by the lure of magic sparkles, and those I settled as best I could. I managed to get them cleaned up surreptitiously for the most part, but one little girl started shrieking loudly enough to rival Rhona.

Daylight faded as we worked, and I kept up my pulses of Connection, occasionally interspersing it with Tursa for good measure. It wasn't until sunset when someone stumbled out of the manor, headed our way.

I was the first to see them, a mere shape in the distance,

but Rhona—now surrounded by about fifteen children and whatever adults were handy to help with them—took one look and stopped dead in the middle of telling them an implausible tale about Sailean vanquishing a fuath.

I'd face a fuath myself if it meant I could see that wee kitten right now. Her little milk-drunk face. Bless her.

"Excuse me," Rhona said to one of the adults. "Can you—"

The man she'd spoken to nodded immediately, though he had dark circles under his eyes, and his clothing was in worse shape than most, if thankfully clean of human waste.

"That's Nan," Rhona murmured to me. "Bawbag's personal chef."

By her name, I'd have expected her to be a granny, but she was a rail-thin woman in her mid-forties with black hair and a white streak at her left temple. Her olive skin looked stretched too tight, and it seemed to somehow grow tighter at the sight of Rhona. She wore a chef's loose-fitting trousers and shirt, unfortunately all white, which most definitely showed stains down the legs.

We pushed open the makeshift gate, leaving the newly cut rails—that explained some of the logging Bawbag had done—on the ground.

"You—what are you doing back here?" she said, with an authority that contrasted a bit with the stench of her soiled clothing.

I supposed no one in the manor had bothered to clean up.

"Cleaning up *Lord Sackington's* mess," Rhona said, steel in her voice. "As usual."

Nan's demeanour faltered as she looked over our shoulders at the people, and her face went slack altogether as she took in the new-grown meadow of wildflowers and grass that spread well beyond the formerly filthy corral.

All at once, the older woman seemed to smell herself, and her skin turned ruddy with humiliation.

"I can help, if you'll let me," I said to her gently. Servant of a walking ballsack or not, she didn't deserve what that sentient scrotum had done to her.

Nan managed a nod, looking from Rhona to me as if she were just now noticing me at all. When I kindled Purifire, though, she jumped, eyes widening.

"You're the one who burned the barn!"

"Well, yes," I admitted. "Though for the record, I'm not the only one with this spell."

"Spell?"

"Jeezo, Bawbag has pulled so much wool over their eyes, it's practically an entire *fleece*," Rhona cut in, exasperation making her fingers twitch. "Spell, Nan! Magic. You know, like what Bawbag used to keep you a zombie and pissing yourself for however long he's been gone?"

"You mean *Lord Sackington*," Nan said primly.

"No, I really don't," Rhona replied. "Look, just let Calum clean you up. You reek of arse, and for once it's not from having your nose so far up Bawbag's you cannae see the sun."

I hastily moved to cast Purifire on Nan to cleanse her, waiting only for her barest nod of acquiescence. The blue-green glow diluted some of her furious blushing.

The moment it was done, Nan heaved a sigh of relief— as did Rhona, who'd been downwind.

"How long ago did he leave and where did he go?" Rhona asked without wasting any time.

Nan swallowed, glancing over her shoulder as if she

expected the man himself to be looming there like some sort of omnipresent spectre of shittiness.

"I don't know," she said finally. "I don't—I don't know what day it is."

"The fourth of March," I told her, and her blushing face drained of colour, leaving it blotchy.

"Two days ago." To her credit, Nan pulled herself together enough to answer, but then she hesitated, eyes darting back and forth. "If—if I tell you where Lord Sackington went, will you help me?"

"Help you what?" I asked as gently as I could.

"I don't want to stay here," she said, all in a rush. "I didn't know where else to go, when it started."

She didn't have to explain what *it* was. From her accent, she wasn't local, though I couldn't tell if it was east coast of Scotland or farther north, like Orkney, toned down considerably with Received Pronunciation that made her sound like she'd lived in London for years and taken on the flavour.

"We need to get all of these people out of here and as far away from that man as possible. We'll be going to Oban. Far as we can tell, that's the safest place. Everyone there's working together to survive this mess." I glanced at Rhona, who had her unblinking gaze trained on the older woman warily. She saw me looking and gave me a hesitant nod. "But yes, we'll help you escape too."

Nan, though, grew more distressed with every word. Her head shaking back and forth caught my eye, and I turned away from Rhona to see what was wrong. I wasn't even certain Nan had heard the last thing I'd said, because clearly something had triggered a full-on anxiety attack. Through the spirit around us, I could *feel* it pouring off her, her heart racing, a tinny sheen of adrenaline-fuelled sweat blossoming across her upper lip. Her breathing bordered on hyperventilation.

"Nan," I said with as much authority as I could muster, and I'd forgotten about Òran na Cloiche, which made my words resonate in the air like I'd struck a tuning fork. "Breathe in with me—one, two, three, four, five, six. Hold it."

I nearly fumbled it in surprise at the unintentional use of my skill, but I talked her through her exhale, watching Nan's wild eyes calming ever so slightly. Rhona joined in, though I could see worry creeping across her face.

"Better?" I asked the chef.

She didn't answer except to dip her chin half an inch.

"Can you tell me what just happened?" I didn't want to bombard her, but clearly, something I'd said had set her off, and dread slithered its way into my own stomach.

"Your people are in Oban? You said it was safe there?" Nan asked, a slump to her shoulders suddenly pulling the entire weight of the moment yet further downward with its gravity.

"Yes, as safe as we can be," I said.

Both Rhona and I seemed to know what Nan was about to say. It hit me like a full-speed freight engine anyway.

"He went to Oban with everything he's got, including that—that horrid giant snake."

CHAPTER
TWELVE

Nan's words hovered in the air as if suspended on spirit itself. But I didn't have time to have my own panic attack. We'd all known this was coming—just not now. Not so soon. Not on the heels of the beithir.

With the enormous lightning-snake monster, this took the term "blitzkrieg" to an entirely new level of literalism.

I didn't even need to signal Rhona. One shared glance and she was off, back towards the corral with a purpose to her stride that most nineteen-year-old kids wouldn't have a prayer to match.

"Nan," I said, "is anyone else in the manor going to want to come with us?"

Nan looked back and forth between me and Rhona's retreating back. "I—I can't go where he is. I can't!"

She was going to break if I wasn't careful, but I didn't know if I could thread that particular needle.

"Listen to me very, very carefully," I said to her. "Have you chosen your boon yet?"

I gambled on the idea that saying something bizarre might snap her out of it if she didn't know what I was talking about, and if she did, that was a slight advantage. It'd been at least a couple weeks since the ascension, or close to it, so if she *hadn't*, that also told me a lot.

The gamble paid off—in a manner of speaking.

"My what?" Nan asked, some of the strength returning to her visage in the form of annoyance.

I let out a long breath through my nose.

As gently as I could, I walked her through the ascension, thanking whatever powers who created this system that the boons didn't expire. She surprised me by choosing the same boon I'd picked: Blessings. And Nan also asked me a heap of questions about where to put her attribute points, which I answered as quickly as possible. What wasn't a surprise was that she had above-average stats in Constitution, Stamina, Dexterity, and Strength—cooking was an endurance sport in the commercial world, and working for Bawbag probably mirrored a kitchen in hell itself.

As soon as I helped her sort all that, I deputised her to go back into the manor and find out who wanted to come with us.

I also told her to get them to sort their ascension stats and boons if they hadn't already. The fact that their fear of Bawbag really had kept them from investigating what must have been the equivalent of a weeks-long migraine aura only made that worse. That kind of fear hadn't germinated in the past fortnight. It was rooted deep.

By the time Nan headed house-ward, Eilidh and Mòrag were coming my way.

Mòrag gave me another wee jolt when she pulled me into a crushing embrace and kissed my cheek soundly. "A ghràidh, mo cheud mìle taing dhut."

"Chan e ach ceartas a th' ann," I said to her effusive thanks. Only the right thing to do.

"Ma dh'fhaoidte," she said dubiously, "ach cha dèanadh a' mhòr-chuid e."

Most wouldn't have done it.

"Chan eil sin fìor, a Sheanmhair," Eilidh disagreed softly. Rhona was coming down to join us, and Eilidh switched to English. "You'll see in Oban—most people are doing everything in their power to make sure we survive."

"Meeksy and Iain are organising folks," Rhona said, "but we might have a problem getting people to all leave at once."

"Everyone leaves at the same time," I said without missing a beat. "If we need to remind them what happened in Kilninver, we remind them what happened in Kilninver. Safety in numbers—we are stronger as a unit, not in easily picked-off groups of prey."

"I mean, *I* agree with you, but others are scared and might get spicy." Rhona gave me a tight-lipped smile.

"I'll talk to them," Eilidh said, her face going blank into what I was beginning to recognise as her resolve face. "Bawbag's arrogance did us a favour—he moved too soon and underestimated us. If he's moving on Oban, we'll come up behind him and hamstring him from his flanks."

"Something must have spurred him to move faster," Mòrag mused. Her blue eyes turned on me. "Rhona said the beithir is with him, and you've fought it before, that it seemed to have broken out of his control then."

"You sound like you have an idea," I said to the older woman with a genuine smile. Thank the gods for this reprieve and thank the gods that she was still alive. "Please. I'm all ears."

"If he's again taken control of it, a luaidh, perhaps he moved when he did because he doubts he can hold it for long." Mòrag said this very matter-of-factly.

"He went all in." I pronounced the words slowly, savouring them. "The bastard went all in this early, because he really thinks he can win against an entire town."

"With the beithir, it's not unthinkable that he could," Eilidh said, voice soft. "We need to go. As close to 'right now' as we can manage."

With that, resolve face was back, and she spun on her heel, striding back to the corral with Rhona at her side.

Mòrag peered at me as I watched them depart. "You have gotten more confident, m' eudail," she said.

I wasn't sure what I'd done to merit the affectionate pet names from Eilidh's gran, but I wasn't about to object—I'd lost all my grandparents early, two before I was even born, and there was just something about having an elder present that made me feel more at ease.

"It's definitely been a sink-or-swim sort of situation," I told her. "We're all just doing the best we can out here."

"Aye," she said. "Well, keep it up. My Robert would be proud to see it"—her voice cracked on her late husband's name—"and proud to see Eilidh with fire in her eyes again."

Robert.

I reeled for a moment, only holding her gaze because the old woman's blue eyes bore into me relentlessly. I hadn't *forgotten* how I'd met her, how I'd run into Eilidh— far from it. But it struck me in that moment that tragedy had become a daily occurrence to the point that my timely arrival with the monstrous seagull hadn't stuck in my head as something notable or worthy of pride.

"Sin thu fhèin," Mòrag said, as if she could sense my thoughts. She pulled me towards her in another crushing hug, this time kissing me on the forehead.

With that, she turned to follow her granddaughter,

leaving me standing alone with her words ringing in my ears and gold pulsing around the edges of my vision.

I was the one with the Òran na Cloiche skill, but when Eilidh's voice rang out across the grounds, *everyone* turned to stare for its pure magnetism.

"You have fifteen minutes before we move out—gather anything useful! I don't care if it's begged, borrowed, or stolen. Sackington stole days and dignity from you all. Don't let that turn into your life. If he catches you again, it won't be time and dignity—it'll be blood."

The timbre of pure truth resonated through her words. It was neither a long nor a particularly eloquent speech, but where someone else might have been met with argument, not a grumble came from the crowd.

It would have taken a braver soul than most of us present to argue with Eilidh MacIntosh at that moment. Her armour was clean, but the rest of her screamed hard travel and sweat. Power. Curls slipped out of place as flyaways, drying in the cooling air, and her pale skin had a flush to it that made her seem to glow.

The resonance of her spirit was all too easy for me to pinpoint, and what the others might not have registered consciously, I felt buzzing in my bones.

You know when you gawped at something as a wean and a parent would tell you to shut your gob before something flew in there? I had one of those moments right then and had to force my dangling jaw to click closed.

Fifteen minutes.

I moved off to the side, away from where everyone was organising. With the constant pulse of waiting notifications, I didn't dare ignore them. We'd need any tiny bit of advantage we could muster. It was as if Kilninver had been a mere trial run. We'd learnt from the experience—everyone stays together—and this time, the journey would come with an extra few hundred bodies.

To protect, yes.

But these people would also have strengths to add.

And the kids, at least, had Shield.

I'd forgotten about that in all of the hubbub. All children seemed to have the ability—an impenetrable shield of spirit and will that would protect them for one hour.

As I remembered, further horror dawned with the relief.

Bawbag and his goons wouldn't have been able to harm the kids for an hour after they first tried.

Which meant every child here had had to spend an hour in terror after seeing all the adults meant to protect them incapacitated.

Fuck that. Fuck Bawbag. If I could have, in that moment, I would have incinerated him remotely with the pure force of my fury.

It took me three of my precious fifteen minutes to simply calm myself enough to open my notifications.

Quest updated: The Hills Have Eyes: Part III

While defending Oban is personal to you, there is more at stake than simply the town itself. You have seen with your own eyes what is possible to do in an ascended world when the ascension directive does not yet hold weight with the people.

But it is clear you still hold the attention of Lord Sackington —every time you thwart him, his hatred of you grows. Now, you have unravelled yet another of his plans.

You have a choice: leave his grounds quietly or take repara-

tions from his holdings. By law of the Ascended Alliance, all possessions, lands, and domiciles belonging to perpetrators guilty of violating other sapient beings' right to free will are forfeit. Lord Sackington has previously been notified of the consequences of his actions and chooses to ignore them.

Continue on your path of ascension. Do not grow complacent. More than lives depends on your actions.

Objectives:

-Complete your personal quest (Calum Green) (Complete)

-Complete your personal quest (Eilidh MacIntosh) (Complete)

-Complete your personal quest (Rhona Smith) (Complete)

-Work together to craft infused armour (6 sets) (Calum Green, Eilidh MacIntosh)

-Create alchemical solutions to aid your party (6 sets) (Rhona Smith)

Optional: Take items of value from Lord Sackington's manor. Nothing within its walls belongs to him any longer.

Reward:

-1 skill point

-5 attribute points

-1 item (ascension dependent)

-All cooldowns reset

Despite the sudden shock at being given explicit permission to loot Bawbag's house tae fuck, I got just as much of a jolt from one of the more subtle updates: Eilidh had completed her personal quest. I didn't even know what the quest had been. Then again, Rhona and I had both completed our own without sharing too.

Maybe if I wanted to hear news, I ought to offer some.

What a novel concept.

I didn't have time to dwell on interpersonal relationships. The next notification gave me the fear.

Quest updated: Defend Oban

You have followed your instincts and tracked the lost Kilninver group to Lord Sackington's estate. There, you discovered the atrocity he has committed in order to exert control over those he deemed otherwise useless.

You have already observed that Lord Sackington employs ruthless measures—but even his brute strength can be neutralised by those working in the spirit of the ascension directive.

In combining your spirit with another's willingly, you have discovered one of the core powers of the ascension directive itself. Shared spirit is stronger than the sum of its individual parts.

Nan Reynolds has informed you that Lord Sackington marches on Oban. Not, as you presumed, by sea, but over land. Mòrag MacIntosh's hypothesis that Lord Sackington's timeline was adapted due to his need to maintain control over the beithir may prove vital to your success.

Objectives:

-Reach Oban (Previous Instance) (Complete)

-Seek out the following inhabitants who are most likely to believe your story:

-Catrìona and Iain Whyte and Farid "Meeksy" Meeks (Complete)

-Ross and Jo MacIntosh (Complete)

-Ruaraidh and Ciorstaidh Smith (Complete)

-Jack Miller (Complete)

-Tina Dunlop

-Convince at least twenty fighters of level five or above of the threat (31/20)

-Formulate a plan to aid Oban's defence

-Reach Oban with the survivors of Lord Sackington's magic and liaise with the town's defenders

-Survivor population: 312/312

-Optional: Reach Oban with all ultimate survivors having gained at least one level

Rewards:

-Experience (commensurate with current level progression)

-1 item (ascension dependent)

-1 skill point

-5 attribute points

-???

-???

Jeezo.

I decided to move on before I got mired in the metric shit tonne of responsibility that had landed on our shoulders.

Through physical exertion, you have gained a permanent +1 to Constitution and +2 to Stamina. Please note that such increases have diminishing returns as your base statistics grow.

Through arcane exertion, you have gained a permanent +5 to Spirit, +3 to Pathos, and +1 to Will. Please note that such increases have diminishing returns as your base statistics grow.

Through diligent use, you have increased the level of your skill:

Connection (Level 8), Purifire (Level 8), Slànaich (Level 3), Spèird (Level 2), Tairm (Level 2), Tursa (Level 2)

You have increased your affinity: Nature (Level 7)

You have increased your affinity: Synthesis (Level 3)

You have increased your specialised affinity: Wild (Level 6)

It was with some relief that I came to the end, reeling over the leaps in Pathos, Connection, and my Wild affinity.

As much as I wanted to dig deeper to find out what all of that could mean, there was no time.

I'd taken five minutes, leaving less than ten if I wanted to loot and run.

CHAPTER
THIRTEEN

"Eilidh!" I said her name with as much urgency as I dared, because I didn't think turning three hundred people loose on Bawbag's estate would help us leave in a timely fashion. I also didn't want anyone to panic.

She was about ten yards away from me, survivors eddying around her, and she homed in on my voice with almost bat-like precision.

Sometimes, Eilidh really *was* terrifying.

Making her way over to me, Eilidh paused briefly to reassure someone who seemed to be asking about whether they could steal a rake.

From the way the middle-aged man clutched the garden implement, I assumed she'd told him to go for it.

"What is it?" Eilidh asked me in a low voice when she reached me. She shifted her shoulders as if working out a kink.

"If you can run through your notifications, it'd be good, but the truncated version is that the quests have gotten more complicated, and we need to loot Bawbag's manor before we go."

"I'm sorry, *what?*"

"Apparently, the Ascended Alliance already hates this man as much as we do, because they said everything he owns is forfeit due to his crimes against humanity. Or the universe. Or something." I tried not to think of the group of people waiting for us to lead them to Oban like Loch Awe was the Red Sea. "We can choose to leave without bothering, but . . ."

"But if there's anything we can use, we should take it and use it against him," Eilidh finished.

"Aye. I've got Keen Eye, and Rhona knows the manor." I didn't need to continue.

"Go. Fast." Then she hesitated. "I've got some inventory slots open. Give me whatever's least . . . stackable."

I'd barely looked in my inventory in days, it felt, and while it had expanded to fifteen slots, they were all full. I offloaded some of the goshawk meat, mentally shuffling through everything else. I was about to hand her the down for one dangerously precarious second, but before I could make that fatal mistake and entertain three hundred onlookers with the two of us taking an explosion of bird fluff to the face, I remembered at the last second.

My face must have looked like I'd stuck my hand in roadkill, because Eilidh took an apprehensive step back.

"Something worse than twenty kilos of raw poultry?" she asked.

"Not worse, exactly, just dangerous. I'll explain later."

"Okay," she said.

I didn't know what was weirder, that she sounded sincere or that any trace of her previous animosity seemed to have vanished.

"Five minutes," she reminded me after a beat.

"Right." I jogged towards the manor, calling for Rhona over my shoulder.

Rhona caught up with me right as we got to the door, eyeing me warily. "What are we doing? I don't think there's anyone I want to see in there."

"Anything you want to nick?" I countered blandly. "Ascended Alliance says go on a thieving spree. I reckon you might have an idea of what could be useful for us. Think crafting, armour, weapons."

"You're serious," she said.

"Four and a half minutes. You find it, I Keen Eye it for merit. We've got as much space as we've got bags to chuck in inventory."

"Oh, bloody hell."

With that, she was off, and I hurried to keep up.

I'd expected her to make straight for Bawbag's quarters, but instead, Rhona veered off in a direction I hadn't explored. Not that we'd been on a grand tour last time.

We ended up in a room the size of my Hyndland Street flat's bedroom, and the walls were absolutely stocked full of a supermarket's bounty of food.

Rhona made a beeline for a lower shelf, where she grabbed a roll of bin bags, tore one off, and tossed me the rest. "I'll fill, you tear."

"I—okay." This hadn't been what I had in mind, but it was imminently practical with three hundred mouths to feed.

That goshawk would only go so far.

I had to marvel at Rhona's laser focus. Boxes of oats, dried fruits, nuts, protein powder in five different flavours —all of it disappeared first into the bin bag and then into her inventory. She snatched the next bag out of my hands and ran with it. Tinned tuna, tinned fruit, tinned veg. I didn't reckon Bawbag touched the stuff, but he had a whole staff living here. Tinned mackerel in oil. Two enormous jars of peanut butter. She had to set the bin bag on the floor so the weight of it didn't tear through the plastic.

Legumes, pastas, pumpkin and sunflower seeds. An entire flat of protein bars and three open boxes of mini pies.

I performed my duty handing her bags, occasionally pointing out something on a higher shelf and grabbing it for her, but Rhona knew precisely what was needed. Within a minute, she'd filled three entire bags with high-protein, high-calorie, and as high-nutrient food as she could.

"Upstairs," she said shortly as she shoved the final bag at me. "I'll meet you there."

"What are you—"

"I'll *meet you there.* Go!"

I ran, using my newfound comfort with Connection to navigate my way to the only bit of Bawbag's enormous manor I could claim with any familiarity.

As I found the servants' stairs that led there fastest, I heard voices at the other end of the house.

I couldn't stop to worry about it. Eilidh would know we could catch up, but I knew she wouldn't want to delay leaving at all. We'd gained their trust enough to get the survivors to leave with us all together—we had to keep our word from the first step of this journey.

Lord Bawbag's quarters were every inch as horrible as I remembered. The ivory statues in their niches stared at me. Animals and mosaics and people. Some were clearly ancient, which likely meant taken by force. Others were pristine and looked far too new to be anything but something Bawbag had acquired in the recent past.

I cast Keen Eye on the closest statue to me.

. . .

Antique Ivory Figure: Mwene Kongo, 1457 CE

This statue was looted from the Kingdom of Kongo in the southwestern part of the African continent. Ivory was a symbol of prestige where elephants are indigenous, due to the animal's revered status. Known for their intelligence, longevity, social cooperation, and wisdom, elephants have long symbolised power. This statue represents the ruler of the Kingdom of Kongo.

In an ascension, many things are possible. Perhaps one day, you may find a way to return this priceless relic to its rightful homeland.

Time was ticking away. I didn't have time to inspect everything and contemplate post-ascension shipping.

I ran into Bawbag's bedchamber and, without further thought, grabbed the massive super-king duvet.

Laying it out flat in the middle of the large anteroom off the stairs' landing, I grabbed as many statues as I could, placing them on the duvet with some space between them. Then I started to roll it up around them.

Thankfully, my next habitual pulse of Connection told me Rhona was coming.

The moment her head crested the top of the stairs, I pointed at the remaining statues.

"Grab them and be careful—they're literal treasure, and they're not ours. But they're *really* not his."

Rhona's quick mind grasped my meaning, and I left her to do that task. We were already at time—the flows of spirit told me the group was departing.

But there was one other thing I wanted to take.

The massive double doors to Lord Bawbag's bedchamber were works of art. Deep red-brown mahogany, polished to gleam, inlaid with more ivory carved in the shape of the Bawbag family crest.

Eilidh could have kicked the doors off their hinges; I'd no doubt. But I didn't want to damage them.

Working as quickly as I could, I gathered spirit to wield Purifire like a blowtorch.

It melted through the metal like butter. When the door started to teeter, I grabbed hold of it, lifting it just enough to get it into my inventory. Rhona started to sputter behind me.

"You're stealing his *doors*?"

"I'm stealing his goddamn doors."

The next one went even faster, and my helpful inventory deposited it into the same slot, stacking the two together.

"I got us enough food to get to Oban, and you steal a blanket full of relics from Ye Olde Sunset Empire and a door." Rhona finished rolling the duvet, depositing it into a bin bag and stashing it in her inventory. "A *door*."

She shook her head as we bolted back down the stairs. The kid was a hair faster than me, but she almost tripped when I called at her speeding back, "Technically, it's two doors!"

Three hundred people don't move very quickly, especially when there's a dozen weans in the mix whose little legs simply can't keep up.

By the time Rhona and I barrelled out of the manor, the group still on the move past the manor itself. We went the rear, where a pair of older men gave us a sidelong glance.

"Yous robbin' the place or something?" The man closest to me had a piece of new-grown spring grass between his teeth, and though he looked as tough as shoe leather and every inch as scuffed, there was a twinkle in his eye that belied the banter.

"Yes, actually," I said, making the second bloke startle. "We figured you lot might be hungry at some point today."

"You figured correctly," said the second man. "I'd say we ought to hunt along the way, but even if I had a rifle, the ascension took care of that option."

"If we see anything we can hunt, we will," I assured him. "But that's if we see anything at all. On our way in, the only animal we encountered at all was an enormous goshawk the size of a moose that tried to murder us at midnight."

The man blinked.

Before he could ask for clarification, Mòrag's face appeared, moving against the tide of survivors and clearly scanning their faces for us.

I raised a hand to get her attention, and she made her way to us.

"Your lovely friend Farid had a suggestion so we can move faster," the older woman said, smiling at the two men, who both gave her a respectful nod before increasing their pace.

We fell in behind them, and I resumed my monitoring of our surroundings. A short distance ahead, I could see the black hair and white streak that revealed Nan's presence. I was strangely relieved to see her.

"Farid?" Rhona was asking blankly.

"Meeksy," I said, snapping back to the others as I walked. "Farid Meeks. Meeksy. What's his thought?"

"Anyone who's boosted their Strength above twenty

will carry one of the bairns. When they tire, we'll all take a break for whatever food we can manage." Mòrag looked at us with some apprehension showing in the crease between her eyebrows. "Eilidh says you . . . relieved Lord Sackington of some items that may help?"

"Aye, we did," I said at the same time Rhona said, "Well, *I* did. Calum stole a door."

"It's not just a door," I started to say irritably, but then I closed my eyes and stopped. "We've got food. Enough to at least get some calories in people, though it won't be much."

"The protein powders won't be ideal now, but we've got heaps of other stuff, including beans and rice we can throw together in a pinch." Rhona looked immensely proud of herself.

Mòrag frowned. "Beans and rice need to be cooked, a ghràidh. And beans need to be soaked first."

Rhona's mouth had opened in indignant protest at the first bit, but at the second, she cocked her head to the side. "Soaked?"

"They cook much faster, and they're easier to digest when soaked overnight. Reduces . . . wind."

Now Rhona's bewilderment was even more pronounced. "Wait, what? How does soaking beans prevent it from getting windy?"

I couldn't help it. The guffaw escaped before I could rein it in, and when I looked up, the two older chaps' shoulders were shaking in what suspiciously resembled restrained laughter.

"What's funny?" Rhona demanded. "God, Calum, why are you laughing at me? You steal a door and I get laughed at. What the fu—heck do you mean wet beans reduce wind?"

The two men ahead of us lost their battles. Their

laughter rang out through the dismal countryside, and Mòrag covered her mouth with her hand—I think because she didn't trust herself to answer.

No, she left that to me.

"Farts," I told the hapless nineteen-year-old. "Soaking the beans keeps the people who eat them safe from excessive farting."

This time, the laughter erupted from everyone within hearing distance, and it spread like a symphony over a group of people who, a couple hours ago, were trapped within their own minds and within their own waste.

After a moment of helpless staring—with a significant reddening of the girl's pale cheeks—Rhona joined in the chorus.

If we ever made it back to Oban and survived whatever awaited us there, this story was going to spread; I just knew it.

But I'd take it—laughter was a melodic medicine, especially in times of trauma.

I guess today, in an unexpected way, beans really were the musical fruit.

CHAPTER

FOURTEEN

The mirth faded all too quickly as the reality set in.

All conversation leached away into the silence of the empty wilderness, and when Rhona resumed her scouting duties, ranging off into the distance and checking in only every hour or so, that left me alone.

Aside from the two blokes who we'd so charmed with our flatulent conversational topics, none of the other survivors seemed keen to speak with me. In fact, they acted like they found me intimidating.

That would have been hilarious if I couldn't see their point. Whether I liked it or not, Eilidh and I were the two most powerful people here, and it showed.

Some people dream of power over others, but that's never been me.

To quiet my mind, I concentrated on expanding my awareness of the spirit around us. Again, we faced that seemingly endless quiet. My own spirit encountered all flora, no fauna. I hoped it wouldn't be long before they came back, but I feared if we didn't finish off Bawbag once and for all, this part of Argyll would suffer even more than it already had.

On we trekked as the sun sank in the sky. Most of the children were too exhausted to fuss, but as popular as a cokie-back ride tended to be among the next generation, they *weren't* fun for hours on end. Carrying a squirming bundle that weighed four to five stone on one's back was not delightful—not for the adult and not for the weans.

We stopped at sundown, and to my surprise, Nan sprang into action. She targeted Rhona like a sniper, and at the centre of globulous circle of humans with the two of them as acting bullseye, I watched over the heads of strangers. Nan had Rhona empty her inventory of food-stuffs, which made gasps ripple through the circle. I blinked when I realised what Rhona must have darted off to get: there was a mahoosive stock pot amid the bin bags of staples, and when she pulled the lid off, there were heaps of others nested inside it.

Nan made an approving cluck. She set about unpacking the bin bags with the skill and efficiency of someone who had run entire cooking teams for an entire career.

I'd not asked if the rest of the manor staff had joined us. Watching her now with a small team of efficient people bustling around her, I thought I might have my answer. When Nan had everything categorised and organised—to the dulcet accompaniment of hundreds of grumbling bellies—she again demonstrated the precision of a heat-seeking missile.

Her eyes found what must have been a familiar face, and she barked, "Scott—fill this stock pot with water from the loch."

"From the loch?" Scott sputtered.

"Our friendly arsonist rescuer can make a soiled nappy

into spring-fresh cotton. You really think he can't make sure the water's drinkable?"

Far too many eyes turned to look at me, and I heard more than one person whisper, "Arsonist?"

Just the reputation I was hoping for. Swell.

"No pressure," I muttered to myself. If nothing else, I could boil it, I supposed.

Scott took the massive stock pot—an unhelpful thought pointed out it was large enough to fit a small child in with the lid on—and bumped his way through the crowd and over the single-track road. There was a deserted house at the loch side, and I wondered where its owners had gone. If they were still alive.

The loch wasn't far, and we'd stopped in a small carpark where a bulletin board sat with a few scraps of information for tourists. Off the top of my head, I wasn't sure what hamlet or village was nearest, but it was moot for now. On the landward side of the road, bracken grew all the way up to the tarmac, red-brown fronds not yet springing back to life. Beyond that was a field and some clumps of heather and grass, but what really drew my attention was the trees, at least until Bawbag's former personal chef started rattling off orders.

I watched in barely veiled awe as Nan delegated tasks. I guessed I already had mine.

Rhona had been sent round with bags of nuts and dried fruit for the kids. They'd get some fluid from whatever Nan planned to make for dinner, but water was going to become an issue—all this walking, and people needed to hydrate.

Whilst I was waiting to be a one-man water treatment facility, I had a spark of inspiration.

Standing in the middle of a crowd of traumatised strangers, I felt a bit uneasy asking for volunteers to play mad scientist, but if I didn't ask, I wouldn't know the answer to that question or the one that had popped into my head.

"I need about five adult volunteers who think they might want to focus on magic use," I said. "While we're waiting for Scott to trek to the loch and back, I want to try something that could also help us with dinner."

Blank looks all around were my only answer—at first.

First, there was an uncertain aversion of a gaze here, a twitching arm there, and a cleared throat or two.

Then, a tentative hand went up. The owner was a middle-aged man, one of the two who'd been near me when we set out. I waved him over, and it was like that flipped a switch. Hands shot up. *Way* more than five.

"Erm, I don't even know if this is going to work," I said. "But I'll take ten of you, and if it does work out, we'll go from there."

Ten was more than I had expected. No one seemed to want to fight for the privilege, so in a few moments, I had a slightly untidy queue of ten adults ranging from "probably preparing for their Highers" to "more wrinkles than a Shar Pei."

"Let's move on down the road a wee bit. If Scott comes back before we're settled, yous can wait there while I sort the water," I told them, gesturing at the crowd to let us through.

We emerged from the main group in front of a sign proclaiming the hamlet's name: Portsonachan.

"What do you want to try?" The speaker was the older bloke from my earlier conversation. He had replaced the blade of grass in his mouth with a fresh one at some point, but it was looking a bit battered.

"Have you all allotted your first stats and boons yet?" I asked. "That's the first order of business."

Only one of them nodded—to my surprise, it was the oldest person there: a woman who had to be about ninety, though her brown eyes were clear and canny, and her hair was a shock of white tinged with blue from silver-brightening shampoo. Around her neck, she had a pair of filthy spectacles with lenses as thick as the bottom of a pint glass. How she could see anything without them was beyond me.

"Where'd you put your points?" I asked her, wondering if she'd somehow used them to correct her vision.

"Oh, mostly in Agility, but the other two in Mind," she said. "By the time I did it, I'd already increased my Stamina and Constitution from walking to Falls of Cruachan from Taynuilt, so I figured they'd keep going up on their own."

I grinned at her. "Perfect instincts." When I glanced over my shoulder, I saw Scott was returning, so I turned back to the old woman. "Can you help the rest of them take care of that? At least two of the five to Mind, and the other three they can put wherever. Also for boons, everyone should take Blessings. I promise you, you can make up the difference for Brawn and Brains a lot easier with a bit of effort. I'll be back."

Behind me as I moved back towards Nan's impromptu kitchen, I heard the old woman getting straight to business. I'd need to ask her name, but first, I needed to fulfil my destiny as a glorified filtration jug.

In the few minutes I'd been gone, Nan and Rhona had transformed that cleared circle of space into, well, a magical kitchen.

Meeksy had joined them, and he'd circles of Purifire burning merrily under a handful of pots and pans, one of which already smelled suspiciously of sautéing garlic.

I had to shake myself to make sure I hadn't mysteriously dozed off. Scott had wrangled the stockpot of water into the circle, and he stood there gaping at the arcane practicality.

Slapping Meeksy on the back as I moved past him, I stopped by the stockpot.

Scott tore his eyes away from the magical hob to look at me dubiously, which was vaguely offensive. If he could see garlic sizzling on a magical fire two yards away, could he not stretch his suspension of disbelief far enough to believe me capable of a minor miracle?

Maybe not.

"Nan," I said, catching her just as she finished grumbling about not having more than a pair of wooden spoons to work with. "What temperature do you want this water?"

Unlike Scott, she had adapted to the idea of cooking with spirit eagerly—almost scarily so. She didn't miss a beat. "Boiling, eventually. If you can filter out the sediment, that'd be ideal, but if not, I suppose it will do."

Hey-ho.

That part I'd done before, when I was chasing the fuath into the depths of the loch to save Rhona from a watery grave.

Now, I figured I'd try to spice it up a bit. Figuratively speaking. I'd leave the literal spiciness to Nan and her sous chefs, who looked like they'd been dragged through the pits of hell and landed in a restaurant kitchen in the wilderness.

Basically, this evening was quickly growing to resemble something like surreality TV.

I pulsed Connection just to be sure we were still alone.

So far, so solitary, if you counted three hundred twelve human beings as one entity. No threats, no signs of other life that wasn't growing from the ground.

That sorted, I began to pull on spirit.

I wove strands of Spèird together in as fine a mesh as I could at the bottom of the stockpot, snug up against the metal. As soon as I felt satisfied that it was as tight as possible, I threaded Purifire through the weave. Not much of it, just a hair-thin tendril that moved in and out of the existing potential force.

Steam rose from the water almost immediately, and Scott did a double take.

While what I was doing wasn't overtly complex, it *was* a level of precision I'd not attempted before. With the fuath, I'd been acting out of desperation. I'd just flung my net out in front of me, but if I did that here, I could very well end up splashing Scott with scalding water.

I didn't think he'd find that sort of magical demonstration worthy of awe. Nobody liked a second-degree burn.

Slowly, I eased my interwoven spells upward from the bottom of the stockpot. Though I knew it was indeed filtering the water, condensing the sediment made it appear browner and browner as the weave moved towards the surface.

By the time I reached the top of the pot, it was steaming profusely, small bubbles already rising. Though I could sense the strands of my own magic, it was definitely bizarre to see what looked like a circular disk of slop hovering in midair.

I dropped it onto the tarmac with a splat.

Scott jumped.

"Water's ready," I said to Nan.

"I'll call you when we need more" was her only thanks.

Chefs.

When I got back to my group of magically inclined hopefuls, the elderly woman had them well in hand, and her sweet face burst into a grin.

"They're ready," she said. "Now what?"

"Now we try some practical experience," I said. "Full disclosure: I don't know if this'll work."

"If what'll work?" asked the bloke with the grass in his teeth.

"I'm going to do a couple things with magic. When I learned, it was all trial and error and fumbling into the occasional success. I want to see if it's smoother sailing with a navigator at the helm." I wasn't sure that was the best metaphor, but from the sudden eager look in the ten sets of eyes peering at me, I didn't think they were here for flowery turns of phrase. "Spirit is everywhere now. Think of it like electrons. It's not like that, not really, but for lack of a better explanation, electrons are in every atom of every molecule that makes up air, the earth, and everyone and everything here. You all have access to it now, but it *is* a new sense. It takes getting used to."

"What do you want us to do?" A man in his twenties leaned out around a middle-aged woman.

He was in what had once been a tracksuit and football strip, though the football strip in particular looked like it'd been scrubbed against a cheese grater.

"Nothing too strenuous. I want you to focus on what *I'm* doing and tell me what you feel." I shifted my shoulders, hoping this wasn't a completely futile undertaking.

"That's it?" The guy sounded disappointed.

"Wade before you try to swan dive off the board into the deep end, mate," I told him.

"What are you going to do?" the older woman asked.

"What's your name?" I asked her in return.

"Elizabeth Masson," she said immediately.

"Ms. Masson—" I began, but she cut me off.

"Oh, please, dear. I was Mrs. Masson for sixty years in the classroom, and I'm more than happy to have a given name again."

A chuckle rippled through the group, which I joined in.

"Well, Elizabeth, I thought we'd see about helping people have something to eat out of."

I hadn't expected a chorus of cheers, but anything less lukewarm than the responding squints would have been preferable.

CHAPTER
FIFTEEN

To be fair, if someone had asked me a month ago if I wanted to learn magic and the first thing they'd set me to do was "watch me make a plate," I'd probably have been a bit perplexed.

That said, people *did* need something to eat out of, and I had woodworking knowledge to make that happen—with the help of the nearby trees.

I'd grown so used to my habitual use of Connection that when the middle-aged, matronly woman who'd been standing in front of Mr. "That's It?" suddenly said, "What was that?" right after the longer pulse, I almost tripped into the ditch I was trying to straddle at the road's shoulder.

Only my Agility kept me from landing in soggy runoff, and my arms windmilled—very elegantly, I'm sure—until I got my bearings.

"You felt that?" I asked.

She nodded . . . along with two or three others.

Excitement bloomed in me. That boded extremely well for this wee experiment. The others looked somewhat crestfallen and confused.

"It's a spell I use to connect to the ambient spirit around us," I said to a handful of incredulous—or outright suspicious—looks as if I were taking the piss. "I'll explain more later, but it's good that a few of you noticed that already."

This time, I made it over the shallow ditch without incident. My target, a healthy, mature oak, seemed like the best place to start. While I didn't plan to cut three hundred plates out of a single tree, this one could give us a decent number.

I also reckoned bowls would be more useful. They could hold anything a plate could and plenty a plate couldn't, like drinking water.

Stepping up to the tree, I reached out a hand to touch its fissured bark. The moment my skin made contact with the tree, I nearly pulled it back in shock.

For the first time, despite all my use of Connection to reach out, something reached out to *me*.

I'd never expected to feel curiosity from a tree.

Perhaps that wasn't the best word, but it was the most appropriate I could come up with on short notice. I would likely never know if this was something new from the ascension or if the tree had always had some level of awareness, but right then, it didn't matter.

It had asked a gentle question, one I couldn't put into words, and I needed to answer.

Just in time, I remembered to say something to the observing humans. "Try to keep track of anything you can sense now."

My awareness of their crowding closer to the ditch receded as I cast Tursa, offering up a connection to the oak.

I was not prepared.

The oak seized the connection with an eagerness

bordering on grabby hands, which for a two-hundred-year-old tree felt jarring.

It found my awoken connection to its species and rejoiced, its branches above twitching. Had it been one branch moving at the normal speed of plants—slow—no one would have been the wiser. But this was all its branches. Anything slimmer than perhaps an inch in diameter moved, and even without leaves to rustle, it was unmistakable.

Well. If my protégés couldn't puzzle out what I was doing with their shiny new sixth sense, they'd definitely catch it with one of the old-fashioned five.

I hoped.

The oak tree felt parched for connection, like without the buzz of insects and the sensation of hundreds or thousands of tiny beasties making their home within its canopy, it had been set adrift at sea with no compass to navigate home. A hell of sensory deprivation.

I wanted to promise that they would return. It was as if the tree had reached inside me with its roots and squeezed, so hungry it was to work out why it had been so abandoned.

The problem was, I didn't know whether it would be the truth. If I assuaged the oak's fears, would Bawbag make a liar out of me?

Discomfort flooded me at the thought. I wasn't sure trees had a concept of deception, but it wasn't something I wanted to tinker with or explore.

Instead, I tried to communicate our need, our own bereavement. That the tree had experienced a similar trauma of alienation within its own being as the humans gathered a stone's throw away had suffered—that was a common ground. I could build a foundation there.

That's precisely what I did.

Through the flow of spirit between myself and the oak, information travelled both ways. It learned about me, and I learned about it.

I learned that trees can perceive light—they have no eyes, but they can see. They depend on light for energy, sustenance, survival. The idea that they could *see* felt preposterous . . . except that it didn't. When the revelation settled into me, my perspective flipped. Suddenly, it seemed preposterous to think they *couldn't* see. Their entire beings depended upon their tens of thousands—or hundreds of thousands—of leaves and needles catching enough light. It was why they grew upwards, why they spread out.

Trees communicated with one another through the mycelium beneath the earth, symbiotic relationships with fungus that networked between root systems, tying them all together as efficiently as humans used the bloody internet.

And they helped each other.

That, more than anything else, stunned me.

When one tree suffered, be it by aggressive insects, malicious fungus, or human destruction, the trees around it could *send it nutrients*. They could feed it, water it, protect it through the winter. Trees negotiated for the sky, giving each other space to fan out their branches.

This oak wanted to help us.

I realised as my mind spun through the intense influx of information that to the oak, I was part of its forest. A strange and unfortunate tree that had no leaves but could move, a tree that had value nonetheless. This tree didn't see my difference and decide I was without worth.

How could that acceptance rock me so deeply? Even as

something in me wanted to scream that I wasn't deserving of the honour, the tree whispered that I was, that every sapling deserved the sun.

Above my head, the branches swayed, and some began to fall to the earth.

Instinctively, I knew that they were the branches at highest risk of death. But they were oak, and oak was strong, and everything that fell would eagerly become whatever we needed of it.

I felt the oak's wonder as I removed my hand—it had marvelled at humanity even as I had marvelled at trees.

When I opened my eyes, I was surrounded by fallen boughs large and small.

And then something even more miraculous happened: stretching up the line of trees that spread up the gentle slope of the hill, a ripple passed through them, spreading outward from the oak.

I watched as tree after tree shuddered and shed branches it no longer needed.

As if that were not enough, I heard the same creaking shiver behind me.

The oak's communication had traversed the road, through the soil.

When it finally settled, every human was silent.

Had so much as another twig fallen from a barren branch above our heads, every ear would have heard it.

It took me a ten count to gather my wits. My spirit felt drained, but elated. Bloody hell—I was down to five percent. I didn't want to know what would have happened if I'd stayed connected longer.

I had only enough energy to turn round and slump, my back against the oak's trunk, which steadied me in more ways than one.

"Well," I said hoarsely. "I hope you got something from that. Time for a game of Pick-Up-Sticks."

Prudently, Scott chose to bring the next batch of loch water to me, proffering also a saucepan like some sort of offering.

"What's with the pan?" I asked, my voice still scratchy and dry. I slowly slid down until I was sitting in the crook of two roots. "I'm not putting it on my head, no matter how much the weans beg."

"Nan thought you might be thirsty after that," he said. "We don't have any cups."

Oh.

I'd have to do something about that, but . . . after I took care of the water.

The moment my spirit regenerated enough, I cast Fuaran, the relief of it an instant balm. Gods, that had taken a lot out of me.

"The water'll be a minute," I said.

I felt dizzy, like putting my head between my knees might not be the worst idea if I didn't want to vomit up some bile. Not like there was anything else in my stomach to speak of.

Scott said something that had the tone of assurance to it, but I couldn't make out the words.

All ten of my wannabe mages were scrabbling up the hill with armfuls of sticks already. Even Elizabeth—I wondered if she was one of those ninety-year-old gym rats I'd read about. I'm no ageist, but the woman was *spry*.

Minutes ticked by, and finally, I felt safe to try my human water filter trick again. I hoped it would be easier the second time—a hope that thankfully went fulfilled.

I scooped out a saucepanful of water with an apologetic glance at Scott for the dip in the remaining water level in the stockpot, but he just gingerly patted at the big pot's handles until he was satisfied he wouldn't end up leaving bits of his palms behind, and he sloshed away back over the little ditch.

Within moments of his leaving, people started depositing sticks at my feet.

"Stick" was perhaps not the best choice of word. Some of them were full-on branches that took two people to carry. Others would make any dog instantly covetous. In fact, I felt a bit like a canine deity with humans paying homage by bringing me stick after stick after stick.

This line of thought was not helpful. I slurped some Purifired water out of my saucepan and was grateful for it.

Wafting over the heads of the gathered survivors came the smell of food. Good food. Like home-cooked, honest-to-gods sustenance. When was the last time I ate something that wasn't spit roasted on a foraged stick and some magic fire?

Too long, that's how long.

I felt like I was suddenly in a three-way race between my recovering spirit, the people who were foraging non-spit sticks, and whatever Nan was cooking.

Thankfully, though, I had one way of making it go a bit faster.

Perhaps it was practise or exhaustion, but when I started my conscious pulses of Connection again and matched my breath to their rhythm, my jittery heart calmed.

Unlike the last times, I didn't stay in that meditative state long, just long enough to get my spirit to tick up over eighty percent.

I had an audience when I opened my eyes again. To tell the truth, I probably hadn't *not* had an audience since my wee communion with the tree, but they were much more noticeable now. Andy from Kilchurn skulked among them, his pale face peeking out between two larger blokes' shoulders. Hopefully, he'd take this chance to find a less dangerous way to act upon the world—for his own sake and everyone else's.

Might as well give them something to stare at.

Remembering what I'd done with my staff was one thing, but looking at a pile of gnarled wood, "bowl" was not the first word to pop into my head as a logical progression.

That was my pre-ascension brain talking; I knew it. My post-ascension brain had all of *A Guide to Woodcraft in an Ascended World* dumped into its synapses, so I was well aware this feat was possible.

Gathering the nearest sticks to me, the ones from the oak itself, I took a deep breath. Here went nothing.

I selected a medium-sized stick, about four feet long and an inch around. That would do, I hoped.

Spirit was blue, sometimes so pale it was almost silver, and it threaded through the red of pathos, though, like last time with my staff, it was the blazing gold of will that dominated.

This time, I wasn't crafting something from the entirety of the tree itself but from fallen branches. The process felt different. Where the first oak, days ago, had offered me something of its heart, this one today gave deadfall a chance to live on as something else. That distinction felt important.

Almost as if they were flexible reeds or spindly willow branches, the pile of sticks became malleable in my hands. I began to bend them, strengthening them with spirit and pathos and will, telling them it was okay to give way. They were used to needing rigidity, but as I fed into them the knowledge of the swaying willow and black birches whose branches fell like cascades of hair rather than reaching outward, the wood seemed to understand.

Slowly and carefully, I moulded the wood at its thickest part first, bending it until it formed a circle about six inches in diameter.

I kept on in the shape of a spiral. Spirals, I knew, were sacred shapes to the peoples who had inhabited Scotland long before the present day. Pictish stones wore them proudly—a difficult shape to carve into unforgiving rock.

The wood took to it, and as bark sloughed away from the flow of its grain beneath, spirit bolstered the shed skin of the tree. It filled in the gap at the centre of my circle. First in a thin layer, then growing thicker. I continued shaping the branch bowl until it was about nine inches across and deep enough to hold soup or porridge or tea.

Just before finishing, an impulse struck me, and I pulled the last bit of the branch away from the edge to form a small handle on each side of the vessel, bending it in an arc to reinforce the bottom and come up on the other side to meet the rim once more. It felt right to create such a shape —easy to hold for bairns and adults alike, and easy to string to a belt with a bit of rope or a clip for easy reaching if one didn't have the inventory space.

With a surge of satisfaction that came from the oak at my back as much as from myself, I released my hold on spirit, marvelling at the vessel I'd created.

It was . . . a quaich. A quintessentially Scottish vessel, often used ceremonially these days, but it had a long history in Scotland and in the Highlands as something much more pragmatic before they became popularly cast in silver and hawked on the high street to tourists.

Murmurs surrounded me, both from the hopeful mages and the people farther beyond.

I ignored them long enough to cast Keen Eye.

Spirit-Crafted Oaken Quaich

Formed from the willing sacrifice of an awakened oak tree, this vessel will imbue anything it holds with extra nutrients to nourish the body. It is a simple creation, but what it lacks in artistry, it makes up in intent.

Water drunk from this vessel will always be pure.

Goddamn.

People were waiting for an explanation I didn't think I could offer. I simply knew who I wanted to have this first creation.

"Eilidh," I said softly. "Where's Eilidh?"

CHAPTER
SIXTEEN

Eilidh accepted the gesture with bemusement, though a pinprick of pink bloomed on her cheeks as she took it, spreading into a proper blush I didn't dare attempt to interpret.

"Tapadh leat." She thanked me in Gaelic, and I gave her a nod with as much grace as I could muster.

"'S dòcha gum bi an ath-fhear nas fheàrr," I said. "Ach . . . 's ann leatsa a tha a' chiad chuach."

At the blank looks around me, I coughed, but Eilidh beat me to the translation.

"He said the next one might be better," she said with a slight quirk of her lip that wasn't quite a smirk.

Elizabeth, however, had pricked up her ears like a puppy who'd heard the word *walkies* at our use of Gaelic, and when Eilidh moved away, I saw a strange war play out on the elderly woman's face. Yearning and joy and despair all at once, like she had seen something precious but was afraid it had been a mirage.

"Ealasaid a charaid," I said to her, using the Gaelic form

of her name. "Tha Gàidhlig aig agus Mòrag, Iain, Farid, is eile. Cha bhi sibh nur n-aonar."

Perhaps it was fanciful of me, but communicating to her that she wasn't the only person among us who spoke her native tongue felt . . . vital. Languages only live as they are spoken.

To my surprise, her eyes welled up, and she only barely managed a nod.

"There are at least five of us here who speak fluent Gaelic," I said, figuring the others could probably understand the names I'd listed even if I'd lost them on the rest. "Once we're all safe, I reckon any of us would be happy to teach folks if you're interested. I know we'd love to have anyone at all."

With that, I gave myself a wee shake. Time was ticking, and I was . . . experiencing things that were suspiciously emotion-like.

I suddenly missed Sailean more than ever. Her wee face —she must be growing so fast, and part of me regretted not bringing her with us, even if it felt like the right choice at the time. Nothing I could do about it now.

"Ceart, ma-tà," I said brusquely. "Which means *right, then*. Raise a hand if you felt anything I was doing there."

To my enormous surprise, every single hand went up among my ten protégées—and moreover, another full dozen onlookers who had crept over from watching Nan cook.

"Holy . . . okay." The unexpected success tickled at my consciousness and left me flustered. I floundered onwards. "Erm. Out of all of you—including you lot who weren't with the first group; come closer if you want—does anyone feel comfortable giving it a go?"

This time was less of a surprise; people clearly felt a lot

less comfy with the idea of being guinea pigs. Fair play to them. I wisnae bothered. The one hand I had hoped to see was up. I grinned to see it.

"Do you mind if I call you Ealasaid?" I asked her in English, and she beamed in acquiescence. "Magic."

A nervous chuckle went through the assembled group, which had indeed gained the dozen or so who'd inched closer at my invitation.

"Guess our slang may need a bit of workshopping in this brave new world," I told them. "If you've any notes on the subject, we can chat after we make sure people have something to eat off of."

I pawed through the piles of sticks until I found one of similar size and shape to the last one, and I handed that one to Ealasaid. For myself, I decided to go with a bit of a challenge: a reedy bit of hazel that branched several times from the knob that had attached it to the tree.

Something struck me. When Eilidh had lent me her spirit back at Bawbag's manor, our intent had fused together. Right here, we likely had a good opportunity to try to replicate those results. All of us had the same goal here: make bowls.

"When we get started," I said to Ealasaid, "see if you can connect to what I'm doing in any way. Don't force it and don't worry about it if that doesn't make sense or you aren't able to intuit how once we're working. I'm just curious about something."

Ealasaid nodded eagerly.

In the short break, my spirit had mostly recovered. It was good to know that making quaiches wasn't as draining as making a staff, but we were one down and three hundred sixteen to go, and at this rate, we'd finish sometime next week.

Please let this work, I thought.

"Deiseil?" I asked Ealasaid.

"Deiseil is deònach," she replied. Ready and willing.

"Let's do this."

Once again, I opened myself to spirit. I couldn't feel Ealasaid's own magic at first, but I kept on rather than stopping. I may have had woodcraft downloaded into my brain, but we *had* to be able to share knowledge the old-fashioned way.

Working with the hazel was wildly different to working with oak from the start. Where oak was unyielding by nature, hazel bent with alacrity. Maybe a bit too easily for an instrument that was meant to be more solid. I gently nudged it the way I had with the oak, but in the opposite direction. Where I'd encouraged the oak to emulate birch and willow, I whispered to the hazel to keep the shape I gave it and to hold strong.

Halfway through my work, I felt a tentative touch upon my spirit, almost like someone poking me in the shoulder.

I kept my concentration, trying not to chuckle as the poke came again, stronger this time. Then softer, then less of a poke and more of a gentle hand laid upon mine.

With that, it was like a tributary flowing into a stream. Ealasaid was on the move.

If I wasn't careful, the flare of triumph would distract me. I refocused myself on the work of my hands.

My attention fully on the hazel again, this time I tried to let my intent filter through the wood—and for the first time, felt a gentle rebuff. Instead, the hazel seemed to guide *me* to best work with its inherent properties.

Hazel was flexible and wise, happy to be helped along and eager to shape itself to the greatest need. Its redirection of my intent was less the rebuff I'd interpreted in that moment and more of a nudge towards where its uses were best put to work. Hazel loved to heal, to protect, to nourish —the latter even more than the oak.

When I finished, I was almost energised rather than drained. Ealasaid was still working, and I didn't want to pull back in case it disrupted her flow state, so instead I just observed. The old woman's face was almost a scowl of concentration. Her eyebrows knitted together, eyes in a squint—the only thing that broke the intensity of her expression was the fact that, through her parted lips, the tip of her tongue stuck out.

I wasn't sure if she'd take to being told she was adorable, so I decided I'd keep that to myself.

When she was finished, she had her own quaich in her hands. She was breathing heavily and looked a bit woozy.

My spirit had still taken a hit, but not *quite* as much as it had with the first attempt, so I immediately cast Fuaran over us both, including everyone close by in the radius. A few people gave a sudden shiver, and Ealasaid jumped like I'd yanked on her tail.

She clutched her quaich, then relaxed as she felt the effects of Fuaran bolstering her spirit regeneration.

"I did it," she crowed.

"Sin sibh fhèin!" I congratulated her with a grin, defaulting to the polite usage out of respect. "You did indeed!"

"Oh," she said suddenly, eyes going distant. "Oh, my."

"What is it?" A small spike of alarm struck me with a pang.

"I hit level two!"

My mouth fell open.

People could—people could level by crafting.

People could level by crafting.

It seemed so bloody obvious the moment it hit me. Most ascended worlds weren't unstable messes—they were prepared. Peaceful. Making experience solely the purview of death and combat would be anathema to the ascension directive. It made sense that fighting *did* gain experience, and maybe that was a loophole in the grand scheme of goals for peace in that it would be difficult to differentiate between causes of violence, but my mind still took a minute to catch up.

A ripple went through the crowd, hushed awe following in its wake.

"Well, my friends," I said with a helpless laugh. "Guess we just got a major lucky break. Spread the word—crafting with spirit can help you ascend."

Around me, I saw hungry eyes—and I wasn't talking about the growling bellies.

When I asked, "Anyone else want to give it a go?" nearly every hand shot up.

Maybe we'd finish before next week after all.

It wasn't *all* as easy as with Ealasaid. There were a few misshapen fumbles and blobby balls of wood before we'd managed to distribute quaiches to everyone, but it was as if people thirsted to do something. I thought it was human nature, maybe—as a species, we didn't like to feel helpless.

But they'd been given a heady drug: hope.

They knew ascension meant a better chance of survival, for themselves and for the bairns. They knew Oban needed us. They knew Oban was our best hope for a peaceful settlement where folk looked out for each other.

Which meant they knew to carpe this particular diem.

Because of that, woodworking spread like a contagion through the crowd, newly initiated mages passing branches to others and pods of spirit-sharing focus sprang up, each with a more experienced person at the core.

Over the next half hour, the occasional "Yes!" burst through the murmur as people hit level two, and when I took a brief pause from my own crafting to take a wee turn around the now-bustling carpark, quaiches weren't the only thing I saw them making. A pair of industrious pods had decided to use the smallest twigs to make forks and spoons, and I saw a middle-aged Korean man triumphantly brandishing a pair of beechwood chopsticks that made me almost trip when I cast Keen Eye and saw that they would double the energy provided by any food they touched.

Beech, apparently, liked to make sure folk had enough calories.

Something had started to grow in my mind as more and more people—far more than the initial couple dozen—dove into magical crafting. I didn't think all of them wanted to go full-on mage, nor did I expect they would all fancy becoming a three-hundred-strong company of Calum's Calamitous Woodworking Brigade.

But what became abundantly clear as I made the rounds was that all of them *could*, if they wanted to, use magic to make miracles.

I stopped where I was and summoned the message from the day this had all begun, skimming it over again with a thudding pulse.

Our recommendation is to use your points not according to the life you have led thus far but according to the life you wish to lead. Upon ascension, your world is subject to vast changes, and your survival, however unlikely, will depend on your abilities, your mental acuity, and the emotional connection you share with your homeland and those who share it. . . .

We can offer little more guidance than this: no one, even the prepared, can survive alone. Every sentient species known to us has one thing in common, and one thing alone.

Strength is found in connection, not isolation. You will never have every skill needed to thrive.

The limits, such as they are, of your new world are far enough beyond your comprehension so as to be irrelevant. Should you survive long enough to discover them, you will have proven your own mettle and that of your planet.

Everyone could use spirit. Everyone.

Which meant something even more tantalising in the face of the beithir and Lord Bawbag.

We could, with our combined strength, *survive*.

CHAPTER
SEVENTEEN

I wouldn't dare say the mood at our long-awaited meal was *jolly*, but it was jubilant.

Nan had commandeered Eilidh's quaich the moment she heard it could purify water, and she'd set Scott to use that to fill her stockpot.

As more and more people took their first fumbling steps into the world of the ascension's wonder and away from its horrors, I watched in pure awe as people exclaimed over the boons of their new vessels and set about sharing them. The Korean man walked around with Nan, stirring every single dish with his chopsticks and a swirl of spirit to impart their blessing on the food.

Someone else followed with a pine ladle—very carefully!—that subtly increased the volume of Nan's stews.

As for Nan, she'd gone all out. With Rhona's stockpile of foraged herbs, Nan had created a full-on goshawk masterpiece. Someone had been cheeky enough to go into the nearby deserted houses and borrow their cooking pots, so there was a row of mismatched pots bubbling away with

Nan and her deputised sous chefs making sure nothing burned.

We prioritised the weans, giving them quaiches as soon as they were done so they could eat the second food was ready. By the time I got my own quaich-ful of goshawk stew, the kids were settled down on a pile of blankets— likely also raided from the neighbours, to whom I uttered a silent apology—looking sleepy.

Eilidh was not far away from them, and I was about to go over to her when a shy "Excuse me" got my attention.

I turned to see a gorgeous young woman and, I presumed, her just-as-attractive fiancé, from the ring that flashed on her finger and the way he had a steadying hand on the small of her back. She was tanned in the venerated Scottish sun-bed tradition, as was he, though in the bluish light from Purifire melding with the more traditional camp-fire made with the rest of the wood we hadn't used, every-one's skin looked greenish.

"I noticed you didn't have anything to eat with," she said, and she looped her own empty quaich through her the pinkie finger on her left hand to open a tattered handbag.

She dug around for a moment with her free hand, then made a noise of relief and fished out . . . a spork.

A very nice applewood spork, to be precise, but it was definitely a spork.

"You made sporks," I said, mystified.

"I thought they'd be practical." The woman grinned. "Also funny."

"Right on both counts," said her fiancé with a fond smile creeping across his face.

Gods, were these people models? Their teeth looked like adverts for bleach.

"Aye, sure thing," I said to cover for my being momentarily blinded. "Thanks very much!"

"You're welcome!" With that, they turned away, leaving me with my stew and my spork.

Not wanting to risk further interruption, I wolfed down half my stew before anyone else could talk to me. The spork *was* practical, I thought with some exasperation. She'd made it deep enough to be a functional spoon with tines long enough to actually spear goshawk meat rather than just poke it full of shallow holes like the average plastic spork.

What a time to be alive.

My eating speed, however, revealed that our eager helpers had, perhaps, overshot a bit. The brief use of Keen Eye proudly informed me that this maybe five hundred millilitres of hearty home cooking contained a whopping *fifteen hundred calories* and seventy grams of protein. I'd not exactly expected Keen Eye to double as a nutritional label, but it was simultaneously surreal and a relief to know that the bonuses did what they said on the tin.

With that much protein, I started feeling full fast.

Doggedly, I finished what was in my quaich anyway, giving it a careful scour with Purifire when I was done. My own, I'd made from the original oak, and I had—for whatever reason—not tried anything spectacular with it. It was a bit more refined than Eilidh's, but I'd hoped mostly it would come with the same boons, which it did.

I made my way down to the loch, as much to escape momentarily from the press of people as to get a drink. A soft footfall behind me as I picked my way through the brush alerted my ears—I must have been out of it to not sense Eilidh coming.

"Hey," I said, moving aside to give her access to the water as well.

I dipped my quaich into it, lifting it to eye level at first to peer into it and using Purifire to illuminate it. Not a hint of sediment. Jeezo. I emptied it in one go and immediately refilled it. I didn't think I'd ever tasted water so delicious, and that was saying something in Scotland. I'd spent my younger years accustomed to drinking right out of springs at their source or little waterfalls on hikes—sweet, clean water was something Scotland had in abundance.

"The weans are knackered," Eilidh said after she'd had a drink herself. "Ronald and the parents think they should be allowed a few hours of sleep now that we're at least a couple miles from Bawbag's, but I told them that might not be possible."

"What do you think?" I asked her.

"I think if we have to tote three hundred people all the way down to the southern end of the loch and then back up the coast to Oban, there won't *be* an Oban when we get there," Eilidh said. "So a few hours is moot."

Oof.

"Aye." I drew the word out, a more radical idea taking shape in my head. "That is indeed a problem."

I'd gotten so used to carrying my staff at my back that for a moment, I panicked, thinking I'd left it where I'd been making quaiches, but when I turned, I indeed felt its familiar weight. I looped my quaich around my pinkie like Spork Lass had done, reaching behind me for my staff, which I then used control Purifire enough to make blue-green light blossom.

It reached the trees on the far side of the loch. "About how far is that, d'you reckon? Five hundred metres?"

Eilidh turned to face me as I let the fire fade and replaced the staff in its sling-strap.

I habitually pulsed Connection, still finding only our group even with the longer reach.

"I know you're not thick enough to suggest we swim it," Eilidh said. "Whether there's another fuath in there or not, that's too far for the bairns and too far for most adults, assuming everyone even *can*."

In answer, I removed the quaich handle from my finger and set the quaich itself on the surface of the loch, where, naturally, it floated.

"We're not going to fit in there," she said dryly, but for maybe the first time since we'd gotten thrown together on this journey, she cracked a genuine smile, which I returned as impishly as I dared.

I made a mock gasp. "We won't? Maybe half of us?"

Eilidh snorted as I retrieved the quaich before it could float away. Her eyes lingered on it for a moment, like she was noticing how similar it was to her own.

I hastily moved it out of sight.

"It could take a while for us to figure out how to make a boat, let alone one big enough to transport people," she said after a moment. "It's a gamble."

The unspoken stakes hovered in the air—we linger too long, maybe Bawbag would return. Were we to take the known route south to skirt the loch, maybe we'd just arrive too late and find Oban occupied by a beithir and Bawbag himself.

If we tried and failed to make boats—or if it turned out there was another fuath or more lurking in the depths of the loch where I hadn't sensed them—everyone here could be at risk. A bunch of newly ascended level twos and a handful of threes and fours? No chance against a fuath. I suspected it would again take me, Eilidh, and Rhona at least, working in tandem. Even Iain and Meeksy would struggle without help, I thought.

Eilidh seemed to be doing the same maths I was, and I was just about to check whether we'd come to the same conclusion when Rhona came barrelling down the hill.

"Hurry," was all she said before gasping a breath. Then, "Calum, Connection."

Shit. *Shit.*

I wanted to protest that I just had, but instead I just cast the spell. At first, I didn't know what she was on about . . . but then I felt it.

My spirit shrivelled back from the contact with revulsion, and I physically recoiled where I stood. Whatever it was, it wasn't close, but it was getting closer with every passing heartbeat.

It was barely past the edge of my range, which was why I hadn't sensed it sooner.

Without another word, Rhona was off, Eilidh and I on her heels.

Even if someone else in the camp had Connection, there was no chance it was anywhere near my own level. I resumed my pattern with it as we closed the short distance back to the road to locate Meeksy and Iain, who were thankfully together with Eilidh's seanmhair. Mòrag looked up in alarm at our approach, and we slowed our pace so as not to frighten everyone.

"Keep everyone here," I said in a low voice, handing my quaich to Iain since I had no space in inventory. "There's a threat—if it gets past us, you're the next line of defence."

"Bawbag?" Iain asked automatically.

"No." I swallowed. "It's something . . . else."

"I'm coming with you," someone said from not far

away, and I turned to see Ronald, armed with—improbably —the shillelagh I'd left him with in Kilninver. The skinny man stared me down, defiant.

We didn't have time to argue with the man; he'd gone from primary-school teacher to captive to refugee at break-neck speed, and if he wanted to come, I wasn't going to deny him.

"Okay," I said shortly. "We go now. Rhona, I can track it with Connection. You get ready to flank it."

"I'm gone," she said, and a few people closest to us gasped, quickly muffled, as her words became reality.

"Keep up with us as best you can," I told Ronald. "If you fall behind, you stay behind—we don't have time."

Without waiting for him to acknowledge the ultimatum, I took off, veering around the edge of the camp and crossing the road and ditch in two leaps.

My boots sank into the far side, but I didn't care. Snatching my staff from my back, I used a targeted burst of Spèird to clear the bracken and brambles between us and the grass beyond.

I tried to match my use of Connection to the pounding of my feet, breathing in time as best I could whilst running uphill. Eilidh matched me pace for pace, and to my surprise, so did Ronald. When I glanced over at him, he gave me a tight smile.

"Ultrarunner," he said. Suddenly, his rangy physique made extra sense.

I wasn't sure how long he'd be able to keep up this speed, but if there were a contest in who could run fifty kilometres without stopping, he'd win hands down.

Almost as alarming as the sudden incoming threat hurtling towards our camp of vulnerable survivors like a meteor was the eerie fact that, aside from flora, Connection otherwise returned *nothing*. No beasties—biped, quadruped, or any other number of legs.

Just this one thing.

Worse, Connection coming in contact with it filled me with disgust, like biting into a cake and finding it full of rotten meat.

We ran for about five minutes, not covering as much ground as we would have on tarmac, but considering we were having to trailblaze through the underbrush, it was an impressive distance. Before the ascension, I would have preened for weeks if I could manage such a feat.

Now?

Now, the creature was here, and all I could think of was that if we'd been five minutes later, it would have hit the camp with no warning.

CHAPTER
EIGHTEEN

E ven in the dark, malice poured off of the creature as tangibly as the odour of rot.

Its shape in my vision was barely more than a blur, and I cast Purifire to light up the area, which made the thing *scream* the moment the light touched it as if I'd just slaughtered its entire brood of babies.

A fox.

I thought it was, anyway.

Its ginger fur was patchy, covered in ooze from hairless, gaping wounds where it seemed its flesh has rotted off.

The fox's outline was somehow incoherent, like something barely perceived out of the corner of your eye.

"What the fuck is that?" Eilidh said, her claymore in hand.

"Whatever it is, it doesn't like Purifire," I answered grimly. "Remember the first simulacrum?"

"Yes," said Eilidh.

"No," said Ronald.

"I'm going to try to immobilise it—when I do, get in there and hit it with all you've got," I told him.

But before I could, the thing darted out and around us.

"Fuck!" I spun, trying to track it, but it skirted the pool of light from my staff, and I gritted my teeth.

I could barely see the damn thing *with* the light, let alone without it.

The others turned uneasily, similarly trying to follow the rotting fox's movement. Was this thing a zombie? Were there zombies now? Gods, I hoped not. That was one major part of Earth's general mythos I did *not* want to deal with.

"I'm going to try something else," I muttered, letting Purifire go out momentarily. "When I turn the lights back on, that's your signal to move."

Casting out with Connection, I felt the stomach-turning presence of the creature hovering just beyond where I'd last spotted it. I couldn't tell if it was mindlessly reacting to Purifire or if it was calculating its best chance for victory. Rhona was making her way around it, moving slowly and silently through the brush like a shadow. The fox didn't seem to notice her.

It also wasn't moving.

Saying a prayer to any lucky stars willing to bend an ear to a hapless hamster, I lashed out with Spèird, not as a frontal assault but like a piston plunging straight downward.

At the fox's grating scream, I poured Purifire on top of the force spell, lighting up the patch of meadow in a flash of watery teal.

Eilidh and Ronald charged, blazing past me even as Rhona materialised on the other side of the fox.

I hadn't tried to crush the thing, only immobilise it, and its jaws snapped furiously where it lay pinned to the grass.

It didn't stand a chance.

Like before, the moment the others' weapons touched

the Purifire, the arcane plasma raced up the length of blade and bludgeon, and where those weapons came down upon the hapless monster fox, they set fire to flesh and fur alike.

The fire seemed to *tear* through the creature almost more than the blades did—within moments, it was dead and burning.

I ran towards them, again not quite fast enough with Keen Eye. Instead, I got the death notification, which made my goshawk stew turn to sludge in my stomach.

You have killed an anomalous fox.

While the ascension triggers mutations in indigenous beings and breathes life into deeply held mythologies, your instinct that there was something wrong with this fox was correct.

Such creatures frequently contain common crafting materials such as: fox pelt, fox tail, fox teeth, fox bones. These anomalous creatures, however, contain only a petrified heart. This is of unknown value.

As you did not strike the killing blow and there is only one petrified heart to be harvested, there is nothing for you to harvest. You have received experience.

"What the fucking fuck is this?" Rhona said, dropping what looked like a croquet ball-sized rock to the earth, where it landed next to the smouldering fox remains with a thud.

She had clearly struck the killing blow and thus harvested the fox—but it didn't disintegrate into motes like everything else we'd killed and harvested. My spine veritably buzzed with unease.

Better late than never, I supposed.

"Gimme a second," I said to her and cast Keen Eye on the petrified heart.

Petrified Fox Heart

Harvested from the corpse of an anomalous fox, the petrified heart contains the very essence of the corrupted being. Unlike harvesting Spirit, Pathos, or Will, which are nebulous manipulation resources that do not hint at their origins, a petrified heart is the soul's last defence against an overwhelming force seeking to consume it. They are a mark of defiance even as they are a mark of violation.

Without second-guessing myself, I pushed that information out to my friends, who reacted with audible starts and one yelp from Ronald.

My notifications thrummed like a heartbeat.

Dread gnawing at me along with the acrid stench of burning anomalous fox, I had the sudden urge to scour its remains from the earth.

"Stand back," I barked, and the others took stumbling steps back as I channelled a full quarter of my spirit into my staff, targeting the burning corpse.

I had perhaps been overzealous. Rhona yelled as the fireball blasted into the earth, leaving a furrow around its edges almost deep enough to be called a crater.

Eilidh reacted more stoically, but she did eye me askance, tugging Ronald's arm to encourage the gaping schoolteacher to move to a safer distance.

With that done, I opened my notifications with trepidation—trepidation that was rewarded by five little words I *really* had not wanted to see again.

You have discovered a quest.

None of us spoke as we made our way back to the camp, terror swirling around us like a cloud.

I grew even more intense with my use of Connection

and Tursa, using Connection more frequently with Tursa as a guidepost.

There was no sign of any other anomalous creatures nearby—no life at all. It had been the only thing.

And it wasn't Bawbag's doing.

That was the kicker.

Whatever this new anomaly was, Bawbag hadn't created it. I'd bet money—or in the ascension reality, whatever emerged as a valuable noun—that he had no idea it was out there.

Fuck.

When the camp came into view again, illuminated by the glow of fire both mundane and arcane, I wanted to plant my arse in the grass of the hillside and stay there. What were we supposed to tell them, that some *new* terrifying thing had turned up? That we were possibly going to get sandwiched between Bawbag, his beithir, and some unknown evil? That was a rock-and-hard-place scenario you couldn't pay me to get into, yet here I was. Freud would have a field day with the imagery of a bawbag, a phallic snake monster, and . . . whatever this other thing was. I couldn't be arsed to workshop my analogies in the face of evil.

Evil was a strong word, but it was the only one that seemed to fit what we'd encountered.

Thankfully, I wasn't the only one with reservations about barging back into the camp to all the questions that would certainly await us.

Eilidh stopped when we were still in the top third of the slope, holding up a hand. "I think we ought to . . . discuss this."

"You're right," I said automatically, unsurprised to see Rhona's vehement nod and Ronald's still-shocked echo.

On one hand, we'd dispatched the anomalous fox with about as much ease as one could hope.

On the other, what if there were more?

"This quest is unsettling," Eilidh said after a moment of silence.

"Yup," Rhona agreed.

"It's more than unsettling." I braced myself on my staff, stretching my upper back by curling my shoulders in. "This isn't 'Local Arsehole Does Arsehole Things, But Magically' level shite. This is—" I paused to scrub my hand through my hair, which would probably make the curls go pure frizz, but if I couldn't be arsed to care about metaphors, I *definitely* couldn't be arsed to give a flying fuck about my hairstyle. "Look, it's already an apocalypse, so the thought of making it even more apocalyptic is just exhausting."

"You get this quest and your first thought is that you're tired?" Ronald said, sounding mystified.

"Scunnert," I muttered. "There's a difference."

"Can you blame us?" Rhona piped up for the first time in a while, which was unlike her. "You've had a bad couple days, mate—nobody's denying that—but Calum's been fighting for his life for over a fortnight already, Eilidh too. And I spent the first week of the ascension watching Bawbag murder people until Eilidh and Calum rescued me. Second week was busting our arses to save yours, only to get to Oban and find out Bawbag'd gotten you, too. Forgive us if finding out there's a looming fucking tsunami on the other side of the warship bombarding us and thinking it's all a bit much."

Ronald shut his mouth with a click of teeth. "Right. Sorry."

"So what do we do?" I said finally. "Right before this

thing nearly landed in our laps, Eilidh and I were discussing our options, and none of them are good."

"Basically we take the tortoise route and Bawbag murders us, or we take the hare route and cross the loch and a fuath murders us." Eilidh's lips turned upward in a mirthless smile. "Six of one, half dozen of the other."

"Don't be glib," Ronald said sharply.

"I think I'm allowed a bit of gallows humour," Eilidh shot back. "Anyway, my very serious thought is this: we don't know if more of those anomalous foxes are coming. We've no way of knowing. But we *do* know Bawbag is making for Oban, if he's not there already. We have loved ones there. And if tonight taught us *anything* at all, it's that the ascension directive is right."

"Ascension directive?" Ronald asked.

"A group is stronger than the sum of its parts," I muttered. "I'm with Eilidh. I think we try for boats, cross the loch, and hoof it to Oban. Now that I know what these things feel like, I'll know them the moment they cross into the range of my spell. Buys us five to ten minutes' warning, which is more than we got with the goshawk."

"It's enough," Eilidh agreed.

"And what if you're out of commission?" Ronald countered. "Not to play devil's advocate, but I have to think of the safety of the children, and we can't depend on just one person's psychic sensing abilities to know danger's coming."

"Seanmhair always said the devil doesn't need an advocate—and if he did, he could afford a better one than you," Eilidh said. "The *children* need a community, not a ranging group of refugees fleeing for their lives from unsafe hamlet to unsafe hamlet with monsters nipping at their heels."

Ronald's face grew outraged in the soft glow from my staff, but before he could say anything, Rhona piped up.

"She's right," she said. "About both of those things. Oban is their best and safest bet, and with the time we have, we can prepare the adults as best we can to protect them. We need to make boats? Bitches, we made three hundred bowls out of a bunch of sticks in less than an hour *and* filled those bowls with nutritious goodness."

"Prepare the adults to do what, exactly?" Ronald asked, already sounding like he knew he was overruled. He wiped drying sweat from his forehead, a vein pulsing in his temple.

I gave him a cold smile, thinking of the possibilities we had before us. Three hundred adults, a bit less if we made sure each child had two guards.

Ronald just stared at me like my smile unnerved him. Probably did. "Prepare them to do *what*?"

Letting the smile die, I instead reached out and clasped the teacher's shoulder in what I hoped was a more reassuring gesture. "To be an army."

CHAPTER
NINETEEN

We gave the people in the camp a vague game plan when we returned: they were to take a few hours to rest, and then the most experienced crafters were to meet me at the side of the loch.

Part of me wanted to take Eilidh aside—things had shifted between us, and while I couldn't pretend I was upset to not feel like I had an ineffable archnemesis, there was too much weird history between us to go too far down this road without a frank discussion. But the moment we'd sent people around with instructions, she was off like a shot to Mòrag's side, and I was woefully exhausted.

I ended up going back up the slope of the hill, away from the crowded camp. A few people had given up propriety and just gone into the houses to sleep on beds and sofas—and I suspect to raid wardrobes—and I wasn't going to begrudge them that. Hopefully, they'd leave a note in case the owners ever returned. If they were even still alive.

Once I was alone, I sat down in the grass. It was damp with dew.

Looking at the quest again was the last thing I wanted to do, but I also knew it to be necessary.

You have discovered a quest!

Quest discovered: A Quick Brown Fox . . .

Upon ascension, many strange things happen as the balance of ambient spirit in a host planet tips from mundane to magic. But as you have already begun to suspect, something is wrong on Earth.

To the south, Will Grayson and Ezekiel Bosworth III have also encountered and identified this anomaly, which has since claimed the latter with its corruption. It seems this phenomenon is not localised to England's Peak District.

Something may have drawn the fox north to Scotland.

Be on your guard, and investigate the crafting properties of the petrified heart.

Stay vigilant and take any opportunity to seize further information. Perhaps it would be ideal if Calum were not the only person present with the ability to sense the anomalous creatures.

Objectives:

-Utilise the petrified heart in crafting or improving an item (Eilidh or Calum)

-Train others to use Connection and to improve their skill (Calum)

-Unlock the Nature affinity and learn Connection (Rhona, Ronald)

-Learn Connection (Eilidh)

Rewards:

-Experience (commensurate with current level progression)

-1 skill point

-Increase Nature affinity

-1 item (as ascension permits)

First of all, the system was starting to feel almost

insultingly familiar. Was there some beleaguered alien copywriter in a galaxy far, far away, frantically scribbling magical quest notifications? Did I even want to know the answer to that question? Probably no to both.

Second of all, it was really out there naming names now. Apparently, Lord Bawbag didn't merit a wanted poster, but these two unfortunate blokes got their names megaphoned out to us.

And thirdly, did it just tell us that a bloody Tory politician got corrupted by something other than the odour of their own farts? Ezekiel Bosworth III. What a name. I didn't spend heaps of time memorising the hundreds of Tories down south, but Bosworth was notorious up here for the fact that he owned an entire Scottish island and had effectively evicted all the locals to make room for his wanker pals to gun things down and then pat each other on the back for their immense bravery.

Such bravery. So manliness, wow.

Wait.

The third, it had said. Ezekiel Bosworth the *Third*. The member of parliament wasn't "the third" or he'd be utterly insufferable about it—this must have been his son.

Thrice named and twice cursed, it seemed, to have Zeke Bosworth for a father and fall victim to Extra Apocalypse in the regular apocalypse. Terrible luck. I hadn't a clue if he was anything like his old man, but I almost hoped he was, just so he'd deserve that fate.

Of all of those things, the third was the least pressing, but my mind was a bit done. And as I didn't have the petrified heart in my possession and also didn't have anyone handy to train in the mystical arts of the Nature affinity, I lay back on the grass and stared at the stars through a break in the clouds.

The eerie silence crept closer and closer the longer I lay there. It was a bit like living in the city where there was always a buzz of electronics, the boiler, the fridge. Computer fans and cars going past, neighbours banging doors or listening to music, council workers emptying wheely bins. All that stuff was background noise until it vanished. In a power cut, it was a lot easier to realise how *loud* everything was.

Out here, it was a different kind of sudden silence. There should have been the hoot of owls or the trilling coos of doves. Maybe a stag making a ruckus somewhere or bats squeaking their way through the night sky.

Without it, the earth felt barren. Bereft.

That was it.

As knackered as I was, I wasn't about to lie here all night in a funk.

No, I was going to see if I could convince a log to become a boat.

A few weeks ago, if you'd told me I'd be wandering about Argyll and asking nearby trees if they knew of any deadfalls, I'd have given you a look akin to that wee lass with the epic side eye and slowly backed away.

Now, naturally, that was exactly what I was about.

Never let it be said I am not capable of personal growth.

I also wanted to test a theory. In my experience with the oak earlier, I'd gotten a taste at how information could travel through the root system and mycelium. Now I wanted to find out how far that would stretch. Were there swathes of land that'd be out of range? There was really no telling.

Not wanting to venture too far afield—pun not intended—I did want to see if it were possible to gather enough wood for boats at all. Most people around these parts burned peat for fuel if they needed to burn something at all, and while peat was excellent for filtering carbon out of the atmosphere, keeping you warm in winter, and absorbing our plentiful rainfall, one thing it didn't do with finesse was float.

And hey, no one was really asking it to. But it did mean that I wasn't likely to luck into someone's woodpile.

The good news was—just to the northeast of us, there was a massive forest. We'd avoided it when we were hunting after the anomalous fox, since that had come at us from the south. But now I made a beeline for the trees, hoping for the best.

They were largely pine, which seemed promising, but whatever I found was likely to be wet. It didn't mean I couldn't leach the moisture out of the wood—another random bit of know-how I stumbled across in my mind thanks to that book—but depending on how much wood we needed, that could be quite the undertaking.

Even as I made for the tree line, my woodcraft mind started doing the maths. Not really *maths*, per se, in that I hadn't magically developed an advanced scientific calculator in my noggin, but it thought through the issue in instincts and experience.

The sensation was bizarre—all this knowledge I hadn't actively learnt was there, simmering in the background like a programme on a computer. I wasn't going to fuss about it, though. It'd already saved our arses myriad times.

While there were a lot of us, the last thing I needed was to build a fucking barge. We could row five hundred metres with relative ease; hell, with Spèird, I could probably turn a canoe into a motorboat, magically speaking. Regardless, I wasn't about to form the Loch Awe Shipyard's inaugural fleet.

I thought we could probably get away with something like a birlinn but smaller and without sails, a traditional galley used in our islands for centuries. That and some oars could get us to the other side of the loch without too much fuss. Plus, whoever did the rowing would maybe get a nice increase to Strength.

Traditional birlinns were made with overlapping planks, but with ascension woodcraft, we wouldn't need to worry about shaping things that way.

Humming the Gaelic song "Birlinn Cholla Chiotaich" under my breath, I entered the cover of pine trees.

Pine immediately felt different to the oak, the hazel, the apple, the beech. They were all deciduous trees, relieved to rest through winter on their stored energy, but the pines seemed much more steady. They would have their bursts of activity, make their pollen and their pinecones, but they felt somehow more nurturing.

I stepped up to the first one I came to, placing my hand upon its bark like I had with the oak.

It felt like being embraced by a brother, borne on a wave of sharp, aromatic sap and needles. Pine reached into the earth and pointed at the sky, regal and straight backed, but at its heart, it whispered secrets of abundance. *There is enough sunlight to go around,* it seemed to say. *Enough water, enough squirrels to spread our seeds. There is plenty for all.*

Gently, I reached towards it with our need. I hadn't tried to cast Connection whilst in contact with the oak, but I tried to do that now.

Nothing in my life could have prepared me for what happened.

Always before, when I had used Connection, I maintained my sense of self in time and space. I was a point on a map in four dimensions, and I learnt of my surroundings in relation to myself.

Now? As my spirit expanded with the spell, the pine eagerly drew me inward.

All at once, my consciousness rushed through golden veins of sap. Sap was blood, life—antiseptic and sacred, carrying nutrients from root to branch to needles and back again just like our veins carried the same in a human body.

Had I been aware of my breath, I would have lost it in that moment of understanding how strangely alike we were. Our bodies had structures that mirrored one another, and just as the trees depended upon the symbiosis with fungi, so *we* depended on our gut flora, the billions of tiny creatures that made their homes on our skin and in our bodies.

Connection felt like too simple a word to describe how all of this fit together.

And it didn't just open a conduit to this one pine.

Like dropping food colouring into water with a stalk of celery in it, I watched as awareness of me shot outward through the reaching, entwined veins and branches of flora.

Webs spiralled outward through the midnight forest, sleepy with the lack of sunlight but willing nonetheless. I could taste the earthy loam and peat beneath my feet, the shed leaves and dead fronds of the underbrush that had fallen to the floor to decompose into humus, that life-giving wealth of nutrients that would feed the coming spring.

As I reeled within this spreading movement, I felt something fed back into the network.

The voice, if I could call it that, was tired. It felt root rot creeping, battle after battle fought against beetles burrowing into its flesh. Its bark was scarred and scabbed over with sap from these many intrusions, and the absence of the culprits now could not make up for years of trying to heal and survive all at once.

My heart nearly burst as a sigh echoed through the networked mycelium and roots, rustled through the pine needles above my head.

Yes, it seemed to say. *Take me, that I may lend my life to something beyond myself.*

What swelled in the forest in its aftermath was a susurrus of movement, a whisper alone, but to my ears and in the silence of my spirit's web, it sounded like a song.

CHAPTER

TWENTY

The forest knew—so I knew—that the old pine would feed new life in its death no matter what. All fallen trees gave small creatures homes and shelter from the elements, food and sustenance in a million different ways. But, as the younger tree at the forest's edge had shown me, the world was a bountiful place. This tree sharing its trunk and branches and roots with us would not diminish the forest's wealth.

It was still some hours before daylight this early in the year, but I arrived back at the camp to find people stirring uneasily. Meeksy sat with Nan on a large rock in the carpark, the two of them clearly in deep conversation. Not far from them, Iain lay sleeping, one arm sprawled onto the gravel as if he didn't even notice the arm's rough resting place.

Eilidh and Mòrag were nowhere to be seen, but Ealasaid saw me coming from where she seemed to be doing yoga. My instinct about the elderly woman had been right. I chuckled when she straightened up from what I thought was one of the warrior poses and waved at me.

"Madainn mhath," she said to me, and then the old woman peered more closely at me. "An do chaidil thu?"

I was touched by her concern about whether or not I'd slept. Regret would be mine before long, but we'd too much to do.

Sheepishly, I scrubbed a hand over the side of my neck and answered her in the negative. "Cha do chaidil."

Ealasaid was about to show me the meaning of the Gaelic word "trod"—scold—but she didn't get the chance.

"Calum!" One of the kids from Kilninver came tearing across the camp, narrowly missing a sleeping person's tangle of legs and the puffy down coat they were using as a blanket.

I swallowed as I finally recognised the lass. She was the one who'd tried—and failed—to inventory a live spider.

"Morning, love," I said, wracking my brain for her name. Out of three hundred people, I could muster up maybe ten.

"You forgot my name," she accused me.

Ealasaid chuckled at that, but she made a show of sobering up immediately when the child scowled. That almost made me laugh—Ealasaid had *definitely* been a schoolteacher.

"I did," I admitted. "You all have me at a disadvantage. There are a *lot* more of all of you than there are of me."

"It's Rachel!"

"Rachel," I repeated. "Aye, I'll remember that. Find any good spiders around here?"

"No," Rachel said, sounding disappointed. She looked around conspiratorially and then whispered, "I heard they can get as big as a coo now."

"Och, I'd not fancy that!" Ealasaid said, shaking her head in a violent rejection of coo-sized spiders.

"I'm with Ealasaid," I said to Rachel. "But I did fight a centipede as big as a dug."

"What kind of dog?" Rachel asked. "There's all different sizes!"

"The size of a golden retriever." At my answer, the wee lass's eyes went wide with excitement.

Oh, gods, this kid was going to get some sort of entomology class and someday have a legion of giant arachnids at her beckon call, wasn't she?

Eager to change the subject, I looked down at the budding bug fiend. "You came running over here like it was important," I reminded her.

"Oh! I was supposed to tell you that Mr. MacTaggart and some other grown-ups want connections."

I blinked. "Mr. MacTaggart? Is he the tall, very skinny teacher with spectacles?"

"Yes!"

"Gotcha. Do you mean he and the others want the spell called Connection?"

Rachel's little face screwed up in concentration. "They said they want connections," she said doggedly.

"Brill, thanks." I thought I'd interpreted that well enough, but who knew? "Can you send him over with whoever he wants to bring?"

In answer, the wee girl barrelled off through the camp again, this time *not* missing the hapless sleeper's feet. Both Ealasaid and I twitched towards her as she tripped, expecting the kid would go sprawling onto the tarmac, but . . . instead, we saw the ascension in action.

Her scrawny legs compensated for the arrested momentum even as her arms counterbalanced her with a surreal display of near ballet-dancer grace, and Rachel didn't even seem to notice.

Perhaps more notably, whoever was under that down jacket didn't even stir.

"Maybe someone ought to go see if that person's alive," I muttered. "Or if they'll teach me how to sleep through a child kicking me in the shins."

I was about to turn back to Ealasaid, but Eilidh and Mòrag had awoken, and they approached us with Rhona not far behind them.

"You look terrible," Rhona said. "Magic or no, you need a nap."

"I'll nap later," I said, glancing at Mòrag and then at Ealasaid. "Mòrag, did Eilidh tell you our plan?"

"Aye, a ghràidh."

With a nod, I waved Ealasaid closer. "We're going to cross the loch instead of going around it," I told her as quietly as I could. I didn't want to spend the next hour fielding questions. "There's a very old pine tree in the forest up the hill—it's ready to die and is willing to sacrifice itself for us to build a birlinn."

I expected more of a reaction, but Ealasaid's eyes only lit up with excitement. For some reason, I got the impression that despite the harrowing experience in Bawbag's corral, Ealasaid was having the most fun she'd had in years.

"How are we going to do it?" she asked.

"That's a very good question I hope we'll all work out together." I let out a slow breath through my nostrils, feeling a nose hair tickle. Resisting the urge to sneeze, I went on. "What I want to do is gather a big group. Anyone who worked on woodcraft yesterday—the more experience, the better—anyone who feels drawn to the idea of a Nature affinity, and anyone who plans to prioritise their Strength stat."

"That casts a wide net," Eilidh said slowly.

"Exactly." My grin was probably lopsided, but it was there. "Hell, maybe we'll get lucky and Boaty McBoatface will come to life."

Eilidh cracked a smile. "I have to admit, that'd be a hell of a second world first."

Rhona guffawed, but Mòrag and Ealasaid looked perplexed.

Then Ealasaid's eyes widened. "You *are* the one who made the living weapon!"

Oh, no.

"Aye, he did!" Rhona boasted, pointing southward down the loch. "Not even that far from here!"

"You saw that notification?" I muttered, pitching my volume as low as I possibly could.

"Only yesterday—people were speculating about whether that was you or not," Ealasaid told me with a wink.

"We've got a boat to build," I said, suddenly feeling the need to be in the middle of the woods and far away from this forest of humans who could all start staring at me any second.

"Go," Eilidh said to me and Ealasaid. "I'll give you a head start before I sic them on you."

I could have kissed Eilidh for that, but I didn't have time to try, nor was I especially eager to get punched in the nose for making a pass at her. No, making a move on Eilidh—shift in dynamics or not—was something I felt would necessitate absolute clarity.

Obviously, I didn't want to kiss someone who didn't want to kiss *me*, because I'm not a fucking sex pest, but the longer we survived this apocalypse side by side, the clearer it became that any further shift in our relationship would need to be treated with care.

As Ealasaid and I wound our way up the trail I picked out, my ears started to burn as I realised that was, well. Cnag na cùise, as we said in Gaelic. The heart of the matter. Care. I cared for Eilidh.

Thankfully, I had a distraction. Also thankfully, it was still mercifully dark, so if my ears were bright red, Ealasaid wouldn't see them.

I hoped.

I tried to find the path of least resistance for the sake of my ninety-year-old comrade, but she kept pace without any help from me.

She caught me looking at her just as we ducked into the deeper dark of the forest. The sky to the east would be lightening now, but since the mile or so of trees and hill were in the way of that, it would make no difference.

"Ever since the ascension, my arthritis is gone," Ealasaid told me softly, stepping with careful feet over a fallen branch covered in moss.

I stared at her. "Really?"

The elderly woman gave me an almost bashful nod. She then clasped an age-wrinkled hand to the pair of spectacles that still dangled from a cord about her neck. "My eyesight is back, too. I keep these on me just in case it goes away again and I need them."

"That's—incredible," I said after a moment of floundering.

There was a much larger deadfall in our way, so I stepped over it, reaching back to offer her a hand to brace herself. Healed joints or no, I didn't reckon she wanted to slip and tumble arse over tit.

She took my hand with a small smile, clambering over the log. "How far is this self-sacrificing tree?"

"About another fifteen minutes that way," I said, giving Connection thread of spirit to check.

Spirit ebbed and flowed as we moved through the forest, and I hoped that if there were some other danger approaching, I'd have time to warn everyone. If absolutely nothing else, I could launch a bolt of Purifire into the air, boosted by Spèird like an arcane flare.

Nothing seemed evident, only the unending silence that felt like a smothering blanket.

For the rest of the walk, Ealasaid and I conversed in Gaelic, about nothings and our favourite songs—to my delight, Ealasaid had been part of the Taynuilt Gaelic Choir for most of her life, and she promised to sing a puirt-a-beul for us once we got back to Oban. I may have been sixty years younger than her, but at least when it came to quick-fire Gaelic "mouth music," her agility likely had me beat.

She was also, apparently, an avid Peat and Diesel fan. The cheeky Lewis lads' mixture of Gaelic and English rock and humour had won over a lot of people, including this delightful retired primary school teacher.

I felt a moment of gratitude right before we stepped into the clearing that housed the ancient pine.

While I couldn't be certain how Ealasaid would feel about being compared to a tree—I hardly thought she was about to lie down and die any time soon—there was something to be said about acknowledging and respecting the connections between ourselves and our elders.

"Nach i tha àrd," the old woman murmured, craning her neck to look up at the pine.

She was correct—this tree was massive, well over thirty meters tall and a relic of an age gone past. How it had

survived all this time, almost eight hundred years of defor-
estation and human meddling, was beyond me. Especially
with Loch Awe so close for transporting logs. Less than one
percent of Scotland's original tree cover remained, a
product of a landowning class who, for two hundred years,
had spent their time uprooting forests and human beings
alike to make a barren land full of more-profitable sheep.

Even more telling, the tree was a Scotch pine, not one of
the more common lodgepole pines or Sitka spruces, neither
of which were indigenous to Scotland.

And it *was* dying.

Patches of brown needles covered its branches, giving it
an odd, piebald appearance. Its trunk was crusted with sap,
the arboreal equivalent of suppurating sores.

"Ealasaid," I said, "nach fhaic sibh an dèan thu ceangal
ris a' chraoibh."

I wanted to see if she would—if she could connect to
the tree herself. If I had learnt spells just by experimenting,
maybe we didn't have to go through the exact process of
"unlock Nature affinity and skill tree, then spend skill point
on Connection."

Something in the quest made me think that might be
what it was hinting at—after all, Eilidh apparently had the
Nature affinity but hadn't spent a skill point on Connection
herself, and who knew when she'd hit her next level and
have a skill point to spare? Especially if she needed them for
other things that were more urgent.

Standing back as Ealasaid approached the ancient tree,
I watched and listened, keeping a tenuous hold on Connection but not otherwise interfering.

Nothing could have prepared me to see her throw her
arms around it and burst into tears.

CHAPTER
TWENTY-ONE

Flummoxed, for a moment I didn't move. I stood there gawping as the old woman embraced the tree like it was her long-lost love, not an ancient arboreal specimen.

Don't get me wrong, my Pathos stat was slowly ticking upwards, but this was still a bit alien.

Part of me rebelled, wanting to walk away and shut off whatever switch in my being that was suddenly jiggling dangerously like it might open a dam on my own water-works. I'd spent much of the past couple weeks joking—but not really—about having exactly one emotion.

Now, though, I seemed doomed to be mired in the full spectrum.

I'd known what I was doing, or thought I had, when I went for the Draoidh class. It had warned me explicitly that it was a Pathos-based class and that as it stood, I would not be able to use it effectively or hell, even unlock its founda-tional skills until I hit thirty in Pathos. Which meant I couldn't just shut off, retreat behind my walls. I had to let myself feel something that wasn't numbness and anger.

Anger *is* an emotion, of course. It just . . . probably

shouldn't ever be the only one a human being allows in. Pretty sure an ancient green alien with airplane ears once said something to that end, if more eloquently.

After shifting my weight awkwardly from one foot to the next, I took a couple tentative steps forwards and put a hand on her back. Soothingly, I hoped.

She didn't say anything in either of our shared languages, only held onto that tree for dear life.

With my light hold on my own spirit, I took a deep breath or two, finally relaxing enough to sense the tree myself.

And when I did, I understood all at once why Ealasaid's Highland stoicism had broken.

The pine had *recognised* itself in her.

Even only sensing the gist of it, the tree had felt her approach.

It had felt her grief.

The tree knew what it was like to outlive most of its generation, and indeed, its own species.

This tree had stood as forests fell, sensing their deaths through its root system and its fungus friends, yet it remained all this time. It had been curious about the Sitkas and the lodgepoles, made new acquaintances with them even as they grew as best they could, far away from the land that had made them. This elderly Scotch pine brought forth seeds every year, but every time they took root, they died.

Eight hundred years of mere survival. Never alone, but lonely.

Ealasaid, on the far side of Loch Awe under the shadow of Ben Cruachan, had done the same. At ninety-three, almost everyone she knew and loved was dead.

Her husband Seumas had passed two decades ago,

leaving her bereft and solitary in an empty home that echoed with the footsteps of the dead.

The people she had grown up with in the glen, picked blaeberries with and roamed in troupes who pestered tadpoles in the lochans—long gone. Her sunset years had been a litany of funerals, and with every burial, another piece of her language had gone under the earth.

I saw her as a child, Gaelic on her tongue and in her community, alive. I saw her at school, felt the sting of the switch as her English didn't come fast enough and her words came out Gaelic instead. I saw her aging, raging silently as she went through her life in a second language, her mother tongue always hidden away except when she got the chance to sing.

And I saw her growing older and more defiant, how she'd shed the shame that had been layered about her like being mummified alive, because bearing witness to death had forged her anew into living, breathing strength.

She'd taught children, adults, anyone who would listen. But much as I had for my own paltry reasons, Ealasaid had shut herself off to survive, grown a shell that had remained until I, unwittingly, had given it a sharp rap with a spoon, and now this ancient tree, this kindred spirit—it had cracked that shell and broken it wide open.

Not to hurt her.

It wanted to heal her.

Her sobbing turned into a keening sound, one that cut straight into me.

I recognised it.

Ealasaid's voice raised as she wept, and I heard sounds I knew.

Ho-rò, hi-ri hoireann ò
Hi-rì bròn ò hoireann ò

Hì ho-rò
Hì ho-rò
Rì, hi-rì, hili-ò bha hoireann
Ò bha hoireann
Hi-rì, hili-ò bha hì
Hi-rì, hili-ò bha hì

She wasn't just keening as a sound. She was keening the forest's collective grief, marrying it with her own. I felt the resonance of her voice through my palm upon her back. It seemed to emerge from deep within her chest as if she were pouring out feeling from a wellspring in her heart.

If I'd been a spoon rapping against her shell, that sound was a well-honed katana slicing through mine in one precise slash.

This time the pulse of spirit that surrounded me was not my doing.

It came like a drumbeat, a heartbeat. It thrummed through the air, through the earth.

And it did not come alone.

From behind us, before I even detected footsteps, came voices.

Ho-rò, hi-ri hoireann ò, a ghiuthais
Hi-rì liù ò hoireann ò, a ghiuthais
Hi-rì liù ho-rò
Liù ho-rò
Rì, hi-rì, hili-ò bha hoireann ò
Ò bha hoireann ò
Hi-rì, hili-ò bha hì a ghiuthais
Hi-rì, hili-ò bha hì a ghiuthais

For hundreds of years, my people had grieved like this —but never *quite* like this.

The church had stamped out the practise almost completely. I had never seen it. I didn't expect Ealasaid had ever seen it. And the people who came up behind us, their voices joined to the vocables that formed the flesh of her sorrow, there could not be even one among them who had seen what we called caoineadh.

Instead of a coffin beaten with hands, around us was the breath of living wood.

The creak of branches became its rhythm.

And then I saw Rhona.

The young woman moved as if in a trance, stepping over moss-covered fallen branches and stumps, making her way through the procession of people who had come to join us. Her face bore not a hint of immaturity as she slowly circled the pine's trunk to stand opposite Ealasaid, and her hands reached around its circumference as far as they could—but both of them were small. Their fingers didn't touch.

Rhona, with no Gaelic of her own, raised her voice.

It was fumbling at first, then gained confidence in leaps and bounds, higher-pitched, an octave up from Ealasaid.

Gooseflesh erupted along my arms.

Only then did I move from where I'd been standing, my hand still upon Ealasaid's back.

I shifted around the tree until I could see Ealasaid's right hand and Rhona's left, and I placed each of mine upon them.

A moment later, I felt another presence.

Eilidh.

She approached the tree from the other side, out of view, but I felt her rippling through the hum of spirit, and when she mirrored me to complete our circle, it was like touching lightning.

And then she, too, began to keen.

Dimly, I remembered that keeners used to position

themselves at the head and feet of the deceased. For this tree, we made a ring.

Until that moment, I hadn't joined my voice to theirs.

Eilidh's voice was a clear contralto. I didn't know what mine was; all I knew was that this was necessary.

My mouth opened, and my keening became one with theirs.

I'd forgotten Òran na Cloiche. Again.

The moment my voice melded with the others', it was as if we were singing at the heart of a vast cathedral, a choir but not a choir, paying homage to an aeon of life that would give itself to save our own. The morning had brightened around us, minutes slipping away into hours like water through our fingers.

It was as if the forest knew its own perfect timing, for just as our communal song rose to its zenith, so too did the sun.

Golden rays cut through the forest's canopy to bathe us in the buttery light of a nascent spring.

I instinctively cast Tursa, and for a moment, we all hung suspended in the cosmos, a point of shining will. Humans and forest alike—we laboured under a common cause.

A third of the camp had come to us to help. Ninety-nine of us, all told. Iain and Meeksy were among them, as was Ronald, though all of them were some distance from those of us at the tree's root ball.

When the pine creaked in the circle of our arms, the others moved.

None of us had to direct them—the connecting threads

of spirit did that on their own. The forest knew precisely where the pine should fall where it would not harm its neighbours on the way down.

We were simply there to catch it.

Nearly two hundred hands touched that trunk as branches gave way to make room for them. Those against the forest floor bent and cracked. The seven-hundred-year-old Scotch pine listed farther and farther until it rested on a moss-and-shamrock-covered bier.

And we were nowhere near done with our work.

Ninety-nine survivors of Earth's ascension. Ninety-nine minds connected to the trees and each other. Ninety-nine pairs of hands. Ninety-nine deep-rooted needs to have a safe place to land.

Most of us had crafted bowls, but I doubted there were any among us who could have accounted for so much as a washtub to float in before that day. But many of us knew the shape of a birlinn, and my woodcraft knowledge whispered words that meant little to me beyond the craft. Words like "clinker-built" for its construction of slats made their home in my mind. None of us spoke aloud; there was no need.

For all we were using magic, it demanded our sweat nonetheless. Every time I could, I cast Fuaran, moving down the length of the tree's trunk to make sure it caught everyone in a rotation. But even with the added regeneration, I felt my spirit draining with every passing minute.

Perspiration beaded in my scalp and ran down my face in rivulets. It dripped from my chin into the wood. I was aware of branches pulled inward, needles shedding in fragrant bursts. Had the forest not lent us spirit of its own, pouring into us more than our regeneration could keep up, I think we would have failed.

That truth reverberated through me and through the wood beneath my hands. Bark peeled away. It ground to dust and melded moss with resinous sap to fill in cracks and pock-marked knots where opportunistic beetles had woven warrens into the wood.

Patterns formed, spiralling through first a depression in the centre of the trunk and then a dip, then a deepening crevasse. Hands pulled at it to widen it at the middle; others moulded grains of wood like clay to form a prow and keel.

Where wood broke free, hands caught it and stretched it into oars. Every few people, I saw something strange—well, stranger than this miracle. There was a handful of helpers who held what looked like canteens made of the same pine. It was only when I happened to look up at the right moment, rubbing sweat out of my eyes with my shoulder, that I saw what they meant.

Living wood was full of sap—so full it wouldn't make for safe sailing.

Instead of the sap simply leaching out of the wood to spill into the earth, the tree formed fibrous membranes, into which the precious fluid drained. Once they were full, the tree's spirit closed them off, leaving small bladders of cellulose and sap, quickly moved to the side by human hands. It should have been grotesque.

The solution instead felt reverent.

Sap was blood and lymph in one for a tree—and for us it could be a precious boon.

Ninety-nine pairs of hands stayed in contact with the tree until instead of a pine's burls, we held a birlinn.

I was eventually going to make that pun if no one else did.

When we finally stepped back from what we created,

breaking away from the communal flows of spirit, we were exhausted.

Several people collapsed, almost flopping into the boat itself, which listed onto its side in its mossy berth.

I braced myself against the prow, hand grasping the rail along the side of the boat, which had formed for us to better be able to carry the birlinn.

A gasp startled me; now that my spirit was my own again, I felt strangely unmoored, sapped—pardon *that* pun —of strength but simultaneously ready to run up the nearest munro.

Heads turned along with my own, trying to see what had triggered the gasp.

When I saw it, I almost stumbled.

A tree the size of the Scots pine had a deep root system, one that had reached easily twenty meters into the earth straight down. When trees fell normally, many of those roots would break off when the weight of the tree and gravity took over.

That hadn't happened here.

Somehow, our combined magic had pulled the root system out from its long-occupied home beneath the soil, and while much of that wood had gone into the birlinn, what remained . . .

Those roots were vital things, connected to everything around them, and other trees' roots, fungi, and more were all intertwined beneath our feet.

This was an ascended forest now.

Instead of tearing those intricate, delicate connections apart, they had woven together into a web, going deep down into the hole left behind.

Up from the bottom of that hole, water was rising.

I wasn't sure I would ever be able to truly account for

that day, when all was said and done. Hell, in that moment, I couldn't account for not having noticed that everyone else from the camp, all two hundred thirteen of those who had remained by the shore of Loch Awe, had joined us as if called. The forest was full of incredulous faces. How long they'd been there, I could not say.

But to my dying day, I knew I would never forget the way ninety-nine weary people crowded around a magic-formed pool, gazing into its depths as roots and fungus siphoned out the silt, leaving it clear in the golden hour of the afternoon.

I would never forget how at that moment, we heard an altogether joyful sound, one that had been missing in the silence of the last days.

The unmistakable, quick-silver trill of a wren.

It flitted through the trees, fluttering into the branches of a lodgepole pine to the north, and more gasps echoed out around me as folk followed its path.

Because for a moment, just for a moment, we saw something else at the base of the tree.

A stag.

My beleaguered spirit was too drained for me to cast Connection, but I didn't need to.

The hart looked different to the last time I'd seen him, when I'd purified him of Lord Bawbag's puppetry and set him free.

Now, his snout had turned white, and cream-coloured fur spread outward from there, reaching all the way back to his shoulders and almost to his rump.

Then he turned and loped away into the trees, heading southwest.

CHAPTER
TWENTY-TWO

It was impossible for anyone to say we'd "lost" a day in the work we did in that forest. We stayed there to regain strength as the pool filled with pure, fresh spring water, and one wren became dozens, bursting through the canopy of the surrounding trees.

We had held a funeral for the pine, tying land to the work of our hands and the culture that had lived here for so long, and though most had no Gaelic and many were not even from Scotland, in my heart, I felt that even as one thing had died, something of Gaeldom had been reborn. Everyone here was a part of it.

It didn't matter where they came from or what blood ran in their veins. We had forged something in the tradition of the ancestors, with the magic of the ascension, and I was far from surprised to see a notification plastered over my vision.

World first!

In the Highlands of Argyll in the west of Scotland, there has been the first community ascension.

I had to stop right there, because *what?*

Glancing around, it was clear other people were seeing this too.

On the opposite side of the birlinn to where I was standing, Eilidh looked like she was literally holding her breath.

I figured I'd better read this thing fully.

World first!

In the Highlands of Western Scotland, there has been the first community ascension. One community has performed a mythic feat.

When a planet ascends, it is customary for community ascensions to occur the first night, but as Earth was not intended for ascension, it has taken eighteen days.

The people of Argyll have demonstrated their understanding of one of the ascension's most basic cornerstones: a community is stronger than the sum of its parts.

Together, in a time of desperation and great need, they connected not only to one another, but to the land itself, forging a bond that will ripple throughout your planet's future.

Communities who perform a mythic feat will receive:

-Experience equivalent to:

—2 levels if below Level 5

—1 level if below Level 20

—0.5 levels if above Level 20

-+10 Mind

-+5 Spirit

-+3 Pathos

-+3 Will

-1 skill point

You must accept these rewards in order for the Manipulation increase to take effect. Do so with caution in a safe place.

For being the first on Earth to accomplish a mythic feat, all community members receive, in accordance with and proportional to the feat accomplished:

- *Mark of Esteem: Mark of Connection*
- *Boon: Glòir a' Ghiuthais*
- *Unlock: Nature affinity or*
- *+1 to existing Nature affinity*
- *1 item (class and affinity dependent as ascension permits)*
- *1 community mythic item: Birlinn an t-Seann Ghiuthais*

Holy shit.

My still-recovering spirit flooded back into me with the sudden increase in level, expanded in capacity by the absolute leap in Mind. I shuddered to think how it would feel to accept the Manipulation stat rewards. We'd better warn people to not try to do that standing up unless they wanted concussions. The system warning was far too vague.

Something that had been gnawing at me for days finally crystallised. All at once, I understood why Bawbag rocketing to power on a wave of murder and blood only *seemed* effective.

I knew down to my marrow that what we had done was impossible to do by force.

It had to be in the spirit of helping *all* ascend. To protect not only one's self-interest but the interconnected web that made life possible at all.

People were buzzing all around me when I blinked out of that screen. I was itching to go through the rest of my notifications, but that would have to wait. Most of the people here hadn't even reached level three yet—which meant we were staring down the barrel of a couple hundred people who needed to choose a class before they could do anything else.

Even as I shook myself back to the glade, I heard

someone say, "It says I won't get my rewards until I choose a class—bollocks if I know what any of this means."

I met Eilidh's eyes briefly enough to see the lingering awe there before one corner of her mouth twitched upwards in a wry half smile.

The last thing I wanted to do was give a speech, but I needed to say something that would at least funnel everyone in *a* direction, preferably the right one.

"Today's been a lot, hey?" I called out, and the growing murmur around me faded as Òran na Cloiche kicked in. "First things first—there are a lot of you and only a few of us at the higher levels to go around. The good thing is we've got a fairly diverse spread of us, though I imagine there are a lot of classes we've never encountered yet. Wait until you've eaten and have a comfortable place to sit or lie down before you accept the Manipulation stat increase or it'll knock you on yer arse."

"Calum's right—listen to him. Everyone's tired," Eilidh chimed in. "And we're not going to try to ferry people across the loch in the dark. Let's move the birlinn to the shore and see what we can do about food."

I couldn't see Nan, but I highly doubted she'd stayed behind when everyone else came here, because everyone truly had come here—the children were held up on shoulders or standing on fallen logs. They stared around wide-eyed at everything.

My body felt refreshed, even if my brain was still weary.

Those who had joined us parted, streaming towards the pool. At first, I couldn't see why. When we picked up the birlinn, though, our combined strength enough to lift it, I understood.

We began walking, a slow procession through the forest.

Birdsong bloomed around us as more birds joined the wrens—starlings and even a cheeky wee robin that perched on one of the thwarts to regale us with a tune.

The others fell in behind us.

What had taken a quarter of an hour to traverse when it was just me and Ealasaid now took four times as long. Together, we found a pace of movement that adapted to the uneven ground. Where necessary, the bottom of the birlinn slid over mossy logs, but we were careful not to damage anything that couldn't easily heal.

The procession continued without stopping.

When we reached the edge of the forest, something bade me look back as the column turned to walk through the meadow, affording me a view of the path we'd trod. Without breaking the rhythmic stride, I craned my neck to glance over my shoulder.

Wherever we had walked, pine saplings grew in our wake.

Nan wasted no time in marshalling the troops.

Those of us who'd spent the day shipbuilding, after carefully lowering the birlinn onto the plush grass that spread out on the loch side of the carpark, were told to relax, but relaxation was the last thing on everyone's mind.

An excited buzz went through the group. For a moment, I leaned up against the tourist sign at the edge of the carpark, just watching. Yesterday, when we'd arrived, people were starving and exhausted.

Today, we were tired, but from sunrise to the sun setting to the west, we'd gone from being refugees to being a community.

It was palpable in the air, a hum punctuated by the occasional delighted laugh—not something I would have expected to hear when I'd reached that corral.

Before I could put my finger on it, Iain sidled up to me.

Without saying anything in greeting, he threw his arms around me and yanked me into a crushing hug, smacking me several times on the back to the point that I worried I might have somehow pissed him off.

"All right there, mate?" I asked him when he unshackled me. Phew. Someone's Strength stat had increased.

"Never better," he said, an odd light in his eyes. "I mean that. Never fuckin' better."

"I don't even have words," I replied honestly. "That was —unreal."

"You know how I always wanted to be a Power Ranger?"

To see a grown-arse man at age thirty-one, looking wistfully over the sunset-gold Highland hills and talking about Power Rangers felt slightly surreal.

"Erm, yes? Since we were kids." Of all the things that might make my mate tear up, this was not what I expected.

"I always just wanted to help," he said after a beat.

Oh. *Oh.*

"Mate, you helped even before you had magic on top of the martial arts—it's not like you've spent your adult life teaching kids to punch each other. You've taught them to be confident and kind, to only use violence to defend themselves and others." I shook my head, this time reaching out and giving him a side hug. "You're so good at that because you know what it's like to be bullied when you can't protect yourself, aye, but also because you know how to show them that their real strength is inside them all the time."

Iain coughed, then cleared his throat gruffly. "Wasn't fishing for compliments, man."

"I know, you pillock. I'm trying to tell you that you don't need a zord or whatever to help people. Just look around, for fuck's sake." Inspiring speeches: my new pastime. "We all just did something incredible."

"I hope Mum's okay," he muttered.

"Me too." I was about to say something else, but before I could, Iain looked over my shoulder and then punched me in the deltoid.

"Ow, what was that—"

"Think someone wants to talk to you," he said, just before Eilidh appeared from the direction he'd been looking.

Iain nodded to her, then headed off in the direction of Meeksy, who was helping Nan cook again.

"Hey," I said to Eilidh.

"Hey."

"People need help with class selection or something?"

She shook her head. "I think the general consensus has been to go with your instincts; anyone who's hesitating can ask literally anybody to weigh in. The stakes are high in general, but the system doesn't seem prone to allowing critical mistakes where it counts."

Fair point.

"Have you looked over everything yet?" I asked her.

"Not yet. I actually—I actually wanted to ask you if you'd be willing to come with me back to the pool."

After that slight hitch, the rest of Eilidh's words came out in a rush, like she'd had to work up to saying it out loud.

Maybe she had.

"Of course. But we were just there—did you forget something?"

"Just have a hunch."

On that cryptic note, she started walking, and I followed.

She was quiet as we made our way back along the path, which was frighteningly easy to pick out due to the infant trees peeking up above the soil.

"Wild," she murmured once.

We both gave the saplings a wide berth, taking care not to tread on them.

I didn't know if the birdlife returning was localised to this forest or what, but as we moved deeper into the trees, every cast of Connection returned more and more normalcy to my mind. It wasn't just the birds; wee beasties insectoid and mammalian scurried about, flooding back into the forest to resume . . . whatever it was they did all day.

On a whim, I cast Keen Eye on one of the saplings, and it almost made me stumble.

Mythic Scots Pine

Many things are possible in an ascension, and mythic feats make even more miracles come to fruition. Their effects, great and small, are felt for years—sometimes even longer—after their completion.

This mythic Scots pine sprang up with the death of this forest's most ancient tree, a tree that stood alone amid cousins who were brought to this soil from afar. With the pine's dying energy poured out into the building of a traditional Gaelic birlinn, this one also gave its final burst to propagating, as trees often do when they die.

The Caledonian Forest once covered most of Scotland.

Perhaps one day, it shall again.

This tree is sentient, if stationary. Those with strong Nature affinity may ask its aid once it is mature, if their need is great.

Eilidh saw me stumble, and without further prompting, I shared the information with her.

Her eyes widened. "Calum," she said, wonder in her voice as it dropped to a whisper, "can you imagine?"

"I really can't. But if we can rout Bawbag and save Oban, we'll get to watch this forest grow."

"We *will* save Oban," Eilidh said. The softness left her voice, leaving only steel. "We have to make sure he can't hurt people or the land ever again."

With that, she increased her pace.

I followed, the thought Iain had interrupted finally flourishing into something coherent that made me lengthen my own stride.

What Bawbag had done and was doing was monstrous. His contempt for anyone he considered beneath him was a virus, a pox upon anyone and everyone who joined him whether out of fear or a misplaced hope of one day becoming him.

Hatred was contagious.

Fewer things had ever been so obvious in recent years, but now, for the first time in forever, something else nudged that aside.

When I looked around that camp back there and saw people using new skills to help each other, using their magic to make the children giggle, and making sure everyone was okay?

It told me something vital.

Hatred was contagious, but so was hope.

Hope spread feverishly through our fledgling community, and we would bring it home to Oban.

CHAPTER
TWENTY-THREE

I wasn't sure why Eilidh had wanted to come back to the pool at first, other than the fact that it was a marvel of its own right. Mention of Oban had made me feel the press of time, and I had to tell myself that had we been walking, we'd make it twenty miles a day *maybe*, and that was if folks could carry the children. If we crossed the loch in the morning at first light, we'd cut our journey in half, if not more. Going around the loch instead of across it would take days.

We could afford to rest tonight.

As we approached the pool, I thought I understood why Eilidh had chosen to return, though not why she'd asked me to come too. In the brief time we'd been gone, moss had grown up around it, a raised lip in an uneven circle over-looking crystal-clear water.

Maybe she wanted to talk, but she wasn't talking.

When I cast Purifire to peek over the edge, light refracted all the way to the bottom. The effect was discon-certing.

"Can you cast Keen Eye on it?" Eilidh asked me.

Or maybe I *hadn't* understood why she wanted to come back here.

Feeling a prickle of disappointment, I did as she asked.

Mythic Pool of Plenty

Formed in the course of Earth's first mythic feat, this pool filled in with water from an artesian spring tapped by an ancient Scots pine's root system.

The spring has absorbed the properties of the pine, and as such, it is a well of abundance that will prove priceless to the people of Argyll as they ascend and for ages to come.

Its boons do not have diminishing returns, though they respond to need. Everyone's experience of the pool will be different, and it must be sought. Its boons cannot be bought; any attempts to commodify the pool will result in only the usual hydration properties of any other water.

Pine trees are traditionally known for healing, fertility, love, abundance in all forms, and safe births.

Without a word, I shared that with Eilidh as well.

Part of me wanted to drink from the pool; another part of me wanted to dive in and see if I could reach the bottom without getting so claustrophobic I wanted to drown.

Something held me back. It responded to need, it said, and there was simply nothing I needed to such an extent. We knew how to fight Bawbag and the beithir; we just had to get to them. First, though, I needed to look over everything this new world first had given us.

Sitting down was probably the safest option. I did so, leaving a healthy gap between me and the hundred-foot plunge into the pool.

"I'm going to do screen time," I said to Eilidh, and before she had a chance to respond, I let my vision fill with notifications.

There were a *lot* left over.

I decided to start with the most notable first.

You have been honoured with a Mark of Esteem.

For being the part of the first community on Earth to ascend by performing a mythic feat, you now bear the Mark of Connection.

This will be visible to all who have access to your information, whether by ability or your choice to share. A Mark of Esteem distinguishes you among your people as one who has taken vital steps on the path to ascension.

Should you survive, your name will be recorded in the Halls of the Ascended Alliance for all time.

The Mark of Connection also grants you the following bonuses, which you must accept to receive:

- A permanent +10 to Mind

- A permanent +5 to Spirit, Pathos, and Will

- An increase in an existing affinity of your choice

- 1 skill point

- +1 to all attributes

- 2 attribute points

Do you accept this Mark of Connection and its requisite rewards along with the ramifications of renown that accompany such esteem?

Bracing myself, I accepted, and the jump in attributes almost sent me to the floor even though I'd made the prudent choice to sit first.

It was like I'd been treading water in that pool only to suddenly realise the shore was gone and I was in the middle of Loch Awe instead.

That wasn't even all. I gritted my teeth as I went back to the world-first notification, which also needed my consent for the bigger shifts.

I'd thought a slightly smaller increase would have made it easier the second time, but I was wrong. Oh, I was wrong.

Maybe it was the combined total or just that I had not given my brain enough time to recover, but this influx made the mossy forest floor rise up to meet me.

"Calum. Wake up." Eilidh's hand lightly slapped my cheek, just over the line from what could be called a pat.

"I'm awake," I said grumpily. "Just made the rookie mistake of letting my Manifestation stats jump that whole chasm in two bounds. Really should have spaced that out."

When I pried one eye open to look at her, she was glowing gold and peering back at me.

Or maybe she wasn't what was glowing—oh. The ball of light in her hand was doing that.

"Duly noted," she said, moving back into a cross-legged position so I could sit up.

I groaned. "How long was I out?"

"Erm, like ten seconds? Not long."

"Why'd you slap me, then?"

Even in the gold-tinged light of her conjured sphere, I could see her cheeks redden. "Would you have preferred I just let you lie there? Or do you have a particular threshold where passing out spontaneously goes from fine to alarming?"

I snorted at that, pulling my knees up to lean my elbows onto them. Now that it had passed, I felt . . . phenomenal.

"Okay, maybe it wasn't the worst idea I've ever had," I said after a beat. "Jeezo, that feels good."

Eilidh eyed me sideways. "I think I'd like to avoid unconsciousness, myself."

"Ten seconds!"

She rolled her eyes, but I saw the hint of a smile.

Silence fell again.

I was about to go back into my notifications when she cleared her throat.

"I wanted to thank you," Eilidh said.

"For what?"

"For coming after me." She paused, passing her little sphere of light from hand to hand, which made shadows dance across her face. "I knew you would, but I didn't really know. You know?"

"Not really," I said slowly.

For a moment, her expression turned panicked, and I felt her anxiety through the ambient spirit, which in turn spiked my own.

"Wait," I said. "I just meant that there was no way I wouldn't come after you. Even though—"

When I broke off, she watched me over her ball of light, its rays shimmering on the surface of the pool beside her.

I'd thought we needed a frank discussion, hadn't I? Right. Frank it was.

"I would have come after you even if you hated me like I've always thought you did," I said finally. "I wouldn't have left John *Frost* to Bawbag, and he's a wankstain extraordinaire. You're the farthest thing from that—though if you want me to come up with an analogy, I'm going to have to start from scratch because I don't actually know what the antithesis of *wankstain* is."

The moment Susanna's arsehole boyfriend's name was out of my mouth, I regretted it, rambling on because I was bracing myself for a row.

But the row didn't come.

"You think I hate you?" When Eilidh said something at long last, it left me flummoxed.

"I mean, don't you?" I stared at her over my clasped

hands, leaning forwards. "You've always acted like you hated me. Or at least like you could barely put up with being around me."

"Calum—" she started, but then she put her head in her hands, and the light went out.

The glade was very dark without that light. Without the sun, the forest swallowed the remainder of the day whole.

Eilidh groaned, her voice muffled since she was speaking into her palms. "Ò, mo chreach."

"Erm, please explain," I said, thinking of what Rhona and Meeksy had said.

"I don't hate you, Calum," Eilidh said as she dropped her hands.

Her voice suddenly sounded too loud, but she didn't rekindle the orb of light. Maybe it was easier to talk about this when she didn't have to see my face.

"That's . . . a relief," I ventured. "I don't hate you, either."

"Very touching, thank you." Her chuckle took any possible bite out of the words.

I heard her suck in a deep breath and thought that sounded like an excellent idea, so I copied it. The air even *felt* healing in these woods. I didn't think it was just the oxygen.

"I came here to say this, so I should just say it, right?" She muttered this under her breath as if talking to herself, so I didn't think I was supposed to respond. When I didn't, she blew out the rest of the breath. "I always acted weird around you because it was painful for me to see you with her."

"Painful how?" I asked carefully. "Susanna is your best friend."

"Susanna doesn't have friends," Eilidh said, her voice turning cold. "She has sycophants."

Oof.

"Well, I'm certainly not going to defend her, all things considered," I said, feeling awkward, "but I have to admit it's kind of news to me that you feel that way."

"Is it?"

I heard her swallow in the darkness, her silhouette barely distinguishable from the shadows of the trees.

Somewhere nearby, an owl hooted, making us both jump.

With a nervous chuckle, I said, "I reckon we'll have to get used to animal sounds again."

"I know, right?" Eilidh echoed my laugh. Then, I could almost hear her shake her head. "Susanna. Right. Remember our *Dungeons and Dragons* game? The one that had gone on since uni?"

"Absolutely, since I still can't believe you managed to wrangle an entire group of people for a bloody decade," I said. "Susanna said the group fell apart because of 'group drama' or something, yeah?"

"It fell apart because of *Susanna*," Eilidh said. "Because of *Susanna* drama. There were ten of us, you know—the original six women and Rowan"—Rowan was a non-binary waif of a person I'd only met a couple times but had thought was excellent craic—"plus the lads. Susanna told Ainsley that Rowan had been trying to fuck her boyfriend and then told Rowan that Ainsley fancied *them*, knowing Rowan'd had a crush on Ainsley for like five years."

"Jesus fucking Christ," I said. "Did Susanna tell you that?"

"No, Ainsley and Rowan did, months later once they figured out what had happened. Their friendship took a massive hit, but thankfully, they're not fucking Machiavelli reincarnated. Remember the last night I went out to the club with you two?" Eilidh's voice had grown a little hoarse, and I heard her swallow again. "That's—that's right when I found out. I was supposed to go out with the two of you after I had coffee with the others, and they told me what she'd done."

I opened my mouth and shut it a couple times, unsure of what to say. This was enlightening—oh, it was very enlightening—but it was all water under the bridge. Or under the tree. Or under the birlinn. Take yer pick.

Before I could say that, Eilidh went on in a soft voice. "They also told me they'd seen her with John Frost."

I froze. "What?"

"I didn't believe them at first. I was actually low-key raging, because everyone was talking utter shite about everyone else, and I was fucking *scunnert*. Done with it. Literally, as I was grabbing my coat to walk out on them, Rowan shoved their phone in front of my face with a video of Susanna snogging Frost in the middle of Sauchiehall Street. From the night before."

My brain had, as the meme foretold, ceased to can.

"That's why she was on such a high that night," I said slowly. It felt like Eilidh had shone a spotlight on that night, illuminating every shadow all at once. "Night before, she'd said she was with you."

"I know," Eilidh said. "She made me lie about it. I'm so sorry, Calum. She'd been my best friend other than Meeksy since high school. Somewhere in that decade, something went wrong, and I don't think I'll ever be able to pinpoint it. It was like she sucked the life out of me, made it so all I cared about was her approval."

"I . . . know how that feels," I said numbly.

"It's not an excuse."

It was my turn to put my head in my hands. Or one hand, anyway. "It kind of is, though."

"What?"

"It's hard to want to blame you for being the enabler in a decade-long co-dependent friendship with someone like her," I said. "Any more than it's my fault she was unfaithful. Like, honestly, we're both well shot of her."

"There's more," Eilidh said miserably.

"Okay."

I wasn't sure how much worse it could get—and while aye, Susanna was an absolute gobshite, I hadn't even seen Eilidh after that night at the club 'til I ran into her, Mòrag, and the monster seagull. It wasn't like she'd covered for Susanna's rubbish except that once, and I wasn't angry about that. I braced myself anyway while again, I heard Eilidh taking deep breaths.

"Whatever it is, it's okay," I told her. "I'm not going to be angry with you or lash out at you. I promise."

The sound of a long, controlled exhale was my only answer.

"It's my fault you were ever even with her. It's my fault you got hurt like that, and it's my fault—"

"Eilidh, what are you talking about?" I asked, bewildered. "How could that *possibly* be your fault? Susanna is a grown-ass woman who makes her own terrible choices—"

"Exactly! And she chose to go after *you* because she knew I liked you!"

CHAPTER
TWENTY-FOUR

Okay, so maybe I'd been wrong about it not getting worse.

Sod's law or something—I ought to have touched wood. I'd jinxed it.

Still, my brain couldn't quite wrap itself around what Eilidh'd said. She was trying to take the blame for what Susanna had done because I was *collateral damage* in their radioactive relationship?

I wanted to say a million things at once, but unfortunately, tongues don't really work that way, so I was stuck with just one, and it naturally came out with complete coherence. "I'm sorry, what—I mean, no. Or I *do* mean what. *What?*"

"She went after you because I liked you."

"I heard that part, just can't process the causal relationship there. Give my brain a second to catch up."

Rhona was right. And Meeksy, I guess. But they were both so blasé about it that I hadn't really taken them seriously and had just shifted my Eilidh Feelings Meter from Definitely Hates Me to Maybe Doesn't Hate Me, Actually.

Plus, she'd said *liked*. Past tense. That didn't mean she still did.

I regained some sanity by triggering Connection a few times in my short-long, short-long rhythm.

The spirit around us buzzed with emotion, vibrating my skin—or something equivalent. I hadn't even really processed that Eilidh didn't hate my guts and want me dead. To hear that her weirdness, her prickly outbursts had all been *guilt*? Jeezo.

I couldn't change the past, but maybe I could at least punt us onto a better path for the future. Maybe I could do one thing to lessen that load for her; god knew we'd been through enough together. Eilidh deserved some reassurance.

Here went nothing.

"It's not your fault."

That was the most important thing here, the absolute heart of the matter. Cnag na cùise, sin e.

I was not going to sit in the dark to say this. I cast Purifire, wreathing us in a blue-green glow before I continued.

"I do not always make the right choices, and I am not the world's most awesomest anything, but one thing I know damn well, and you're going to listen to it: anything Susanna did, regardless of her cruel reasons for it, has *nothing* to do with you. It's about her. She is culpable. You made her do nothing. She did it all. It's not on you, Eilidh. I never want to hear you say it's your fault again. It's *her fault*. Doubly so if what you said of her reasoning is true— that's beyond cruelty. That's pure malice."

Back when we'd first escaped Bawbag what felt like a lifetime ago, Eilidh had almost died in my arms. I'd never wanted to see her look vulnerable again, and that sentiment ricocheted through me all over again. The context here was not life and death, but it was matters of the heart, and that could be just as damaging. Especially when someone like Susanna got their barbs in you.

Eilidh sat with her legs crossed and her back straight, hair in a messy bun atop her head, and white shone all around her irises. She was, if I remembered correctly, a year or so older than me, but in that moment, she looked lost.

Unsure of what else to do, I clambered to my feet, took one step towards her, and offered her my hand.

When she took it, I pulled her to her feet.

"Can I give you a hug?" I asked her.

Looking confused, she nodded.

I pulled her against my chest, and for one surreal moment, it felt as if I held the entirety of the universe in my arms.

Liked, past tense. *Get it together, ya bam.*

Eilidh drew a shuddering breath. Suddenly, it hit me that she might cry. I wasn't great with other people crying —never knew what to do or how to not make it worse, let alone make it better, which felt like some kind of ineffable eldritch magic.

I'd forgotten that Eilidh was Eilidh. She likely cried sometimes, but now was not going to be one of those times. The second breath I heard her take was steadier, and her arms squeezed me tighter for another few heartbeats. Then she pulled away, leaving me strangely bereft.

"Thank you," she said, not meeting my eyes.

"I meant it." I wanted her to look at me or at least to feel that I was in earnest. "You're not her. She's fuath toe jam. You're a fucking legend."

An indelicate guffaw burst from Eilidh's lips as if I'd caught her entirely by surprise. Maybe I had.

"She didn't deserve you," Eilidh said softly. "I'm going to finish sorting my notifications before we go back."

Before I could say anything to the contrary, she'd sat back down and gone glassy eyed.

She'd stolen my coping mechanism.

I had to chuckle as I joined her back on the ground.

．．（ ⸙ ）．．

You have received a boon!

Boon: Làmh na Glaistige

By fulfilling your word to the Glaistig of Earra-Ghàidheal, you have received a token of her favour. As she is guardian of the hind and hart, you receive a bonus to freeing the minds of those she protects. This can be used once between sunup and sundown and again between sundown and sunup.

New Skill: Saorsa

As a skill tied directly to a boon, Saorsa is part of no skill tree. It may be used twice per day and resets with the rising or setting of the sun. Saorsa affects all creatures within a hundred-metre radius of the caster and creates a web of Purifire and spirit that severs puppeted creatures from their bondage.

Be wary; whilst in the aftermath of Saorsa, all living beings may become violent or unpredictable, depending on the complexity of their minds, how sapient they are, and how long they have been in captivity.

For those who turn violent, they may attack anyone who threatens them, including their rescuers. In very rare cases, the trauma of their former puppet strings may cause irreparable damage.

Goddamn.

I'd forgotten we'd promised the glaistig that we would help where she could not, but it must have been the birlinn that somehow completed her task. Many questions swirled in my mind, but I was far from done.

You have received a boon!

Boon: Glòir a' Ghiuthais

With the creation of the birlinn and by virtue of its recognition as a mythic feat, you have been favoured by the forest.

When under tree cover, your spirit regeneration increases, the rate itself increasing the longer you linger.

Touching a pine tree will temporarily increase your total spirit capacity by 300 for one hour. This effect does not stack.

You have received an item! Book: The Power of Community in an Ascended World

You have reached Level 11! You have five attribute points and five skill points to distribute.

Through physical exertion, you have gained a permanent +2 to Strength and +5 to Stamina. Please note that such increases have diminishing returns as your base statistics grow.

Through arcane exertion, you have gained a permanent +1 to Spirit, +3 to Pathos, and +1 to Will. Please note that such increases have diminishing returns as your base statistics grow.

. . .

You have unlocked a specialised affinity: Coimhearsnachd. By acting on behalf of the greater good and not solely your own interests, you have discovered one of the greatest boons of ascension. Continue to explore the ascension directive to increase your affinity and your abilities. You have unlocked the skill tree: Coimhearsnachd.

You have increased your affinities: Nature (Level 8), Synthesis (Level 4)

You have increased your specialised affinity: Coimhearsnachd (Level 2)

That was a *lot* to process. I couldn't believe the enormous jumps this Ascended Alliance—if they were indeed the ones calling the shots—gave us for working together. Part of me couldn't understand how anyone could be enough of a daftie to go the Bawbag route if this were the case, but I'd seen enough of the world to know that common sense was thin on the ground and some people truly could not bear others' succeeding.

For some, it wasn't enough to achieve excellence if they couldn't smash other people down at the same time.

I already knew my stats had jumped, but I also had five stat points to allot. This time, I decided to give them a solid looking over before assigning them.

Name: Calum Green
   Age: 36

Level: 11

Class: Draoidh (Further class specialisation at: Level 27)

Affinities: Nature (Level 8), Healing (Level 4), Synthesis (Level 4), Staves (Level 2)

Specialised Affinities: Wild (Level 4), Coimhearsnachd (Level 2)

Alteration:

    Strength: 16

    Dexterity: 21

    Agility: 26

    Mind: 67

Regeneration:

    Constitution: 19

    Stamina: 39

Manipulation:

    Spirit: 54 (Glòir a' Ghiuthais: +300 capacity for 27 minutes)

    Pathos: 34

    Will: 38

Huh. I guessed that the plus one to all attributes didn't count the Manipulation stats, which I supposed made sense.

I also noticed that my Pathos had hit thirty. It was the bare minimum to be able to utilise my level-nine class, but I was thankful to have hit it. If I'd had to guess at where I'd gotten the organic growth in Pathos, it would have to be the caoineadh.

The keening.

When I thought about that moment, a sense of surreality came over me. I hadn't expressed grief in any sort of physical way in—well, in the eleven years since Mum died.

After having experienced the funerary rites we had given the ancient pine, though, an intrinsic understanding had germinated in me like one of those pine saplings that lined our path. Gaelic culture certainly wasn't the only one to have traditions of keening or loud expressions at grief; cultures all over the world knew the importance of catharsis.

Science had even confirmed it in myriad ways—yelling obscenities when we're in pain provides relief from that pain. Keening in grief is an action, one that allows the person grieving to feel like they can let something out instead of trapping it where it suffocates them.

Three points. I'd had to scrape for every increase in Pathos since I'd started down this road. To get three points all at once felt momentous, and I almost felt cheated by the fact that I'd gotten such massive increases from the mythic feat and its rewards.

I wondered what effect those would have spread across a populace.

We were going to find out.

While I vacillated a bit on where to put my five points, I decided to put it off a hair longer.

There were two other major notifications.

Quest updated: A Quick Brown Fox . . .

You have successfully participated in a community ascension feat at a sufficient level, causing this quest to evolve.

Stay vigilant and take any opportunity to seize further information about anomalous creatures.

Objectives:

-Utilise the petrified heart in crafting or improving an item (Eilidh or Calum)

-Train others to use Connection and to improve their skill (Calum)

-Unlock the Nature affinity and learn Connection (Rhona, Ronald) (Complete)

-Learn Connection (Eilidh) (Complete)

Rewards:

-Experience (commensurate with current level progression)

-1 skill point

-Increase Nature affinity

-1 item (as ascension permits)

Quest updated: Defend Oban

Nan Reynolds has informed you that Lord Sackington marches on Oban. Not, as you presumed, by sea, but over land.

By performing a mythic feat with your community, transforming an ancient, dying Scots pine into a birlinn, you have provided yourselves not only with the means to reach Oban faster, but with the personal connections necessary to be prepared to fight for the town.

Mòrag MacIntosh's hypothesis that Lord Sackington's timeline was adapted due to his need to maintain control over the beithir may prove vital to your success.

Objectives:

-Reach Oban (Previous Instance) (Complete)

-Seek out the following inhabitants who are most likely to believe your story:

-Catrìona and Iain Whyte and Farid "Meeksy" Meeks (Complete)

-Ross and Jo MacIntosh (Complete)

-Ruaraidh and Ciorstaidh Smith (Complete)

-Jack Miller (Complete)

-Tina Dunlop

-Convince at least twenty fighters of level five or above of the threat (472/20)

-Formulate a plan to aid Oban's defence

-Reach Oban with the survivors of Lord Sackington's magic and liaise with the town's defenders

-Survivor population: 312/312

-Optional: Reach Oban with all ultimate survivors having gained at least one level (Survivors having gained at least one level: 312/312)

Rewards:

-Experience (commensurate with current level progression)

-1 item (ascension dependent)

-1 skill point

-5 attribute points

-???

-???

My heart gave a thud as I fixated on perhaps the only thing I'd personally had nothing to do with—the number of people in Oban apparently convinced Lord Bawbag was a threat. It had skyrocketed upwards from thirty something last I looked to almost five hundred. That meant that there were almost five hundred fighters in Oban at least at level five, which was great, but with the beithir in play and

Bawbag's people probably around level fifteen, I honestly couldn't hazard a guess to how even a playing field we were looking at.

While I wanted to increase my Agility, I was likely to be the strongest mage we had, full stop. I decided to put three of my remaining points in Mind, one in Dexterity for handling my staff, and the final one to bring my Constitution up to a round twenty.

I shook myself out of my screens.

Eilidh was sitting by the pool, looking pensive. When I cleared my throat, she glanced at me, unblinking.

For whatever reason, that unnerved me. I looked away, reaching up to push a curl away from my ear as the wind made it tickle.

"Calum," Eilidh said, voice bewildered. "What happened to your *ears*?"

CHAPTER
TWENTY-FIVE

"My ears?" I moved my hand. Nothing *felt* amiss. No blood or anything I could feel, just a slight raised bit where it had been pierced once upon a time when I'd thought I wanted gauges.

"Higher up," Eilidh said faintly.

It was a surreal feeling to have my fingers seeking the curve of my ear's conch and . . . not finding it.

The ear kept going.

"What the—"

Scrambling to my feet, I conjured a ball of Purifire and leaned over the silver-smooth pool, which was about as reflective a surface as I was going to find between here and Oban unless I broke into someone's home.

My ear was longer. Not just longer, but the top of it now came to a slight point of cartilage I could feel with my fingers.

"What the fuck?" I said, breathing out through my mouth. "What is happening?"

"Your ear looks . . . elfy," Eilidh said, still looking at me sideways.

"I can *see* that!" My reflection was starting to look wild eyed, so I backed hastily away from the pool. "What I want to know is *why* my goddamn ear looks elfy!"

"Don't look at me," Eilidh said, hands in the air as if to show surrender, but she was still peering at me like I'd grown a tail.

Gods, I hoped I hadn't grown a tail. I twisted to look over my shoulder, but there was nothing I could see. Or feel. A tail would likely be noticeable, I'd think.

Don't look at me, Eilidh'd said.

She hadn't meant it literally, I didn't think, but regardless, I returned her stare.

She'd taken her hair down from the messy bun—must have beaten me at screen reading—and it fell in tousled waves over her own ears.

"Do me a favour," I said to her. "Check your own."

Eilidh's blue eyes widened, turned aquamarine in the light of the Purifire. Hesitantly, she flipped her hair back, pulling it all over to one side.

I didn't know if I was relieved or terrified.

Her ear had the point too.

She could clearly tell from my face what I'd seen, because her eyes got somehow even wider, and she patted at her ear until she felt it, then tripped and almost fell into the pool trying to look at it.

"Jesus," she said faintly. "What—what is this?"

"I haven't the foggiest idea," I replied. "I'd like to know too, but—oh, god. Wait."

Without losing another second, I cast Keen Eye on Eilidh.

Eilidh MacIntosh
Level 11 Dìonadair-Cheartais

Affinities: Broadsword, Daggers, Truth-Seeking, Justice, Nature, Unarmed Combat, Dualchas

A well-trained fighter even before the ascension, Eilidh MacIntosh has further honed her skills both on and off the battlefield. As one of the first sapient species members to participate in a mythic feat, Eilidh has begun her personal ascension into her true form.

"What the fuck," I muttered again. Wincing from anticipated impact, I sent her what it'd said.

Eilidh was spluttering by the time she got to the end of it.

"So that has to be you too, right?" she said, her voice taking on a tone that, improbably, managed to meld total confusion with detached numbness.

"Reckon it does." True form—what did that even *mean*? "But since it doesn't seem to have any effects that aren't . . . cosmetic . . . maybe we ought to just get back to camp."

"Right," she agreed. "Guess we should also go round and check everybody's bloody ears."

When we made it back to camp, though, there was no need. Enough people were either bald or had hairdos that didn't cover their ears that folk had noticed. Oh, folk had noticed.

Nan was in the middle of distributing food to people, and those who weren't actively spooning soup into their gobs were staring at each other's ears.

It was such a small thing, really. I'd never given my ears much thought except when, as a wean, I'd briefly been paranoid I'd sneeze and they'd balloon outward Dumbo's. But within a day, we'd gone from a camp full of three hundred humans to a camp of . . . people who were slightly *other*.

Eilidh gave me one last inscrutable look before haring off to find Mòrag, and I went looking for Iain and Meeksy.

There was a lot of discussion through the evening about what the cause could be, but exhaustion had bled through into my bones. When I'd finished eating, I stayed awake long enough to teach my very simple Connection meditation technique to a handful of eager folks—Ealasaid among them—and left them to station themselves around the camp.

Personally, I found a patch of grass at the edge of the bracken, lay down, and passed out into a dreamless sleep.

I woke several hours later to see the sky just beginning to lighten on the other side of the hill.

Today was the day. Over the loch and through the woods.

The camp was already stirring, either because of nerves or because none of us seemed to need as much sleep as we had done before the ascension. It seemed like Nan hadn't budged from where she'd been cooking the night before. I'd gone comatose when she was finishing serving up folks' tea, and she'd beaten me to waking up and was already sorting out breakfast.

When I wandered over to her, I stopped short.

People had been industrious, it seemed.

A basket of eggs sat beside her. Some were still in cartons, but others were piled in there along with bits of straw stuck to the eggs with chicken droppings. There were even a few that were a bizarre pastel green colour, like an Easter egg. Alongside it was a tea towel bundle of foraged herbs—heaps of fresh wild garlic and dandelion greens I could recognise. Other things evaded me.

Nan glanced up at me, stirring the giant stockpot with a large wooden ladle she'd not had when we arrived.

"Some folks might not be able to fight, but it doesn't mean they're not useful," she said softly. "They want to help. A few of the older generation have been taking the weans out to gather food, teaching them what's edible and what's not. Others are sharing knowledge like weaving these baskets. Not even with magic, just what's handy."

"No one is useless," I said. "No one. Every life here is important and valuable."

Nan relaxed a little at that. "Thank you. I'd not gotten a chance to say it sooner, but I don't think I realised until I was away from there how oppressive that manor was to work in. Lord Sackington, as you likely are aware, does not share your opinion that no one is useless and enjoys telling people just how useless he thinks they are at any opportunity."

"It's not an opinion," I said softly. "It's just the truth. Even if someone's doing something I don't like with their life, who am I to decide they don't get to live it? If someone's trying to kill me or mine, I'll fight them if I have to, but if they're not harming anyone, they can mind themselves."

The older woman's eyes softened, and she set the ladle down where its curved end hooked over the pot so it wouldn't fall in.

"So you're not looking to become the laird of Argyll?" Nan asked, and from her tone, I had to guess she was only half joking.

"Absolutely not," I said. "This land has been owned and passed about and torn out from under the people who live here long enough by people who don't give two shits about anyone but their own profits. I've not the slightest aspiration to join that long and storied tradition. Reckon we can start a new tradition instead, for the common weal."

Nan's expression was neutral, and while she nodded, I got the distinct impression that she was thinking she'd believe it when she saw it. Not that I'd blame her.

"Wouldn't that be something?" was all she said, and I knew I'd been dismissed.

I found Iain and Meeksy down by the loch, where mist turned the air a pale, blue-grey colour. The trees on the far side looked almost black in the pre-dawn light. The lads were sat upon a wide rock, comfortably side by side, and Meeksy looked up when I approached.

"All right, mates?" I asked them.

Iain turned to greet me with a small wave, which was somewhat dampened by the face-splitting yawn that accompanied it.

"Meeksy wanted to practise that Connection spell," Iain told me, blinking to clear the watering eyes in the wake of the yawn.

"Mostly want to know if we're going to get capsized by Niseag," Meeksy said under his breath.

"I reckon the commute from Loch Ness to Loch Awe might be a bit much even for a legend like Niseag," I said dryly. "But fair play. A fuath could wreak enough havoc to cause trouble. Anything in there you've noticed?"

"Nothing notable beyond a couple of terrifying large trout." Meeksy turned back to the loch, where, as if to punctuate his sentence, a fish jumped in the early morning stillness, leaving an abnormally big ripple spreading outwards from its point of impact.

"I don't suppose anyone's done any fishing," I said.

"Not yet," Iain answered. "Nan's trying to clear out some collective inventory space so people are as unburdened as possible in the boat. She's also worked with Eala-said to figure out the crossing order."

"Right." I frowned. "Do we know about how many people will fit in there?"

"One of the old bodaich worked in fishing for years. He reckons twenty on oars and another fifteen between them." At my wince, Iain gave me a tight-lipped smile. "Aye, not ideal, but with twenty crew on the oars, it'll be a lot of trips but won't take long. Could throw a rock from this side to the other."

"Pity we can't just yeet people," I agreed. "Or maybe we could, but they might not love it."

"I think I'll stick with Plan A," Meeksy said, then muttered something about tossing and dwarves.

"Mate, you're over six feet tall." I snorted.

"Size has nothing to do with not wanting to be tossed across a loch!"

I chuckled, clasping both their shoulders. "So we're set for tomorrow? Crossing order established?"

"Basic gist is two groups of higher-levelled adults first, then the kids all in one go, followed by everyone else. Best to have at least thirty or so adults with the kids at all times," Iain said. "Of course, the higher-levelled adults are level four at most, but that's safer than nothing."

I asked them a few more questions, sorting out the plan in my brain before making my way back up to the camp.

Even in the short time I'd been gone, things had sprung into action, and the maelstrom of movement sucked me into the thick of it. Before I knew it, we'd everyone up and running. Those who'd "borrowed" blankets from nearby houses brought them to me, and I gave them a quick scour with Purifire before sending them back where they'd come from.

There was no way of knowing for sure—short of following people around and watching their every move— that everything made it back to where it'd come from, but everyone here had a home somewhere. I got the feeling they were behaving as if doing the honourable thing would hopefully circle back to them, that they'd return home one day to find their own things unharmed.

This part of the loch had no easy mooring for a boat, even as small a boat as the birlinn. It meant that we had to be careful about how we planned to get people onboard, and despite my jokes about yeeting people, I didn't think throwing a person-sized weight at a boat on water would be particularly effective. Anyone who felt a burning desire to give that a go could wait 'til everyone was on the other side.

One thing, however, niggled at my mind. While Eala-said channelled her inner primary school teacher and wrangled weans and adults alike into groups, making sure they were as balanced as possible weight-wise, I sneaked down the road a wee bit, using Connection to seek out any wee advantage we could get.

The advantage I found was very wee indeed.

"Madainn mhath, a charaid," I said in greeting to a wren perched on the Portsonachan sign. "An cuidich thu sinn?"

Asking a bird to help in Gaelic was not—contrary to pop-cultural belief—an inherently mystical endeavour. What *was* mystical in nature was the thread of spirit I extended to the tiny bird, which it almost seemed to peck at before grabbing at the thread, giving an adorable ruffle of its feathers until it resembled a very round ball of fluff.

Just thinking that made me miss Sailean—speaking of very round balls of fluff. It hadn't felt safe to bring her with us, but I missed her. And now it wasn't safe for her to be in Oban, either. The last thing I wanted was for Lord Bawbag to get his hands on her again. Even thinking about him using his vile magic to puppet *any* of our endangered wildcats made me think steam was about to come out of my ears, and in an ascension, who knew? Maybe it actually would.

Thankfully, I had the more present round ball of fluff to distract me.

The wren trilled and launched himself into the air. My head spun as those tiny wings beat frantically, beady little eyes absorbing information and processing it faster than I could keep up with. Phew. Using Tàth on a bird this flighty—no pun intended—might have been a miscalculation.

As it climbed in altitude over the loch, I watched as Argyll fell away beneath it. The effect of simultaneously seeing the tarmac of the B840 beneath my feet and the trees surrounding the Taychreggan Hotel flash past under the wee birdie made me dizzy.

I tried to breathe into it. The wren fed me information it thought I would find useful, and I had to smile wryly at its definition.

That bramble in the field was apparently a great place to gorge—if one was a bird and liked to eat bugs alongside the berries. And the wild barley that grew scattershot around the hotel also made for good eating. The wren knew where to fly to avoid raptors, where the sheep lived, and consequently, where I could find stray pieces of wool—or if I were cheeky, bits of wool still in use by sheep who made them—to line the inside of my nest.

He was, however, concerned that my nest would be large enough to necessitate perhaps an entire sheep, and that sentiment came on a wave of spirit through the bond with an undercurrent of worry.

Very thoughtful of him.

I attempted to assure him that I had no nesting plans for the immediate future, and with that, had to momentarily consider how that was *not* likely to be the strangest part of my day.

Tàth had levelled up, and I could feel the differences, particularly because I had a bonus with avian and equine animals.

But the wren also saw something else.

Smoke.

CHAPTER
TWENTY-SIX

I quickly found the limits of Tàth the moment the wren took notice of the smoke. The wee bird was skittish about flying any closer, but from the quick glances I got through his eyes, I could see two things.

One: it wasn't natural fire.

Two: it wasn't Purifire.

That alone was enough to make dread coil in my gut like an adder waiting to strike.

The wren was content to continue flying around the general vicinity of our crossing, at least. I was satisfied moving everyone over to the hotel, though it was maddening knowing that there were proper beds an ascended stone's throw away from where we'd spent two nights sleeping on tarmac and grass. Regardless, a dark crossing would have been too much risk. If it had just been me and my companions, I'd have taken the danger. With weans in the mix, though, no way in hell.

Making my way back to the camp, I kept the thread with the wren, if tenuously. Its pull on my spirit was negligible at this point. Such a small creature with a comparably thin bond apparently took far less upkeep than my bond with the horse.

That felt like it had been ages ago.

The time had come for us to cross the loch.

Ealasaid was a powerhouse even at ninety. She and Meeksy were passing out consolidated packs to each group, spreading the community inventory out as efficiently as possible.

The bundles themselves were impressive. Parcels of oat flapjack wrapped in foraged birchbark paper like we were on a trek to drop a ring in a volcano. Tightly woven grass packets of protein powder that could be mixed with water in a quaich in a pinch. Handmade baggies of nuts sat beside tins of fruit and veg, all nestled together into a larger basket that would fit neatly into a single inventory spot. The crafters had been busy.

It wasn't just so we could fit all the supplies we needed; it was a contingency plan. Just like when we'd left Kilninver, we wanted to make sure everyone had something to keep them going in case the group got turned into slivers.

The retired schoolteacher had everyone ready to go by the time I caught up with her. She waved Meeksy away, sending him to me, and Mòrag and Eilidh came over to speak with us too, along with Rhona and Ronald.

The rowers—a mixed group of people of a wide range in ages—had already manoeuvred the birlinn down to the loch, and I was surprised to see a glow of magic as they worked together to construct a small gangway. Perhaps I shouldn't have been surprised, but a glow of pride answered their glow of magic.

"Eilidh and I are waiting here until the last journey," I said, giving everyone a moment to nod. "Iain and Meeksy go over with the first group—"

"And Rhona and Ronald are on the boat to make sure nothing goes boom in half a kilometre of loch water," Rhona interrupted blandly.

"Meeksy and I'll cover the loch as soon as he's on the other side." I cracked my neck, making Ronald wince. "That's not what I wanted to tell you. I've got eyes in the sky, and there could be trouble towards Oban."

"What sort of trouble?" Ronald asked warily.

"Smoke. Fire. Neither Purifire nor of mundane origin, which means something else. I'm not well-versed enough in spells to know"—I almost did a literal facepalm as I realised I'd not spent my skill points, but that might have to wait—"what could have caused it, but I'll keep an eye on it."

"Eyes in the sky?" Mòrag peered at me. "Dè tha sin, a ghràidh?"

"I've a skill that allows me to bond with animals—they can be a bit twitchy, but I see what they see. Right now, it's a wren, and he doesn't want to go anywhere near the fire." At the bemused looks I got from those who *hadn't* heard or seen me do my little party trick, I shrugged. "He's happy to help, so long as I don't try to force him to do something he doesn't want to do."

Ronald shuddered at that, and I gave him a tight smile that I hoped was somewhat reassuring.

"He'll warn us if anything dangerous is coming?" Eilidh asked me, ignoring the look Ronald gave her.

"He will. Also might tell us where to find some good bugs to eat, wee lamb."

I didn't think that helped Ronald's confidence.

"We'll keep all our senses on high alert," Meeksy told me grimly. "We can do this."

"Then let's do it." Rhona swallowed, her anxious eyes

233

glued to the loch despite the bravado in her tone and in the straight line of her spine.

"Buidheann a h-aon," I called to Ealasaid to get her to move the first group towards the birlinn. Turning back to Rhona, I pulled her in for a hug, which she returned tightly. "Anything happens, Eilidh and I are right here. We'll be able to see you the whole time."

I felt the young woman swallow as she hugged me all the tighter for a moment before trading me out for Eilidh.

The first group was all adults—as we'd planned. We didn't have much in the way of weapons, but those who had picked up woodcraft in the past two nights had set to it with a single-minded fervour, and everyone in the birlinn at least had a club in hand. The oars would also double as bludgeons in a pinch. I just hoped they wouldn't need to.

While I was definitely recognising some familiar faces by now, I couldn't really name any of the adults in the boat yet, beyond the obvious ones who were my mates. I hoped someone knew who the others all were.

It was clear those with any maritime experience had taken over the responsibilities of mooring and launching our craft. We had no proper lines to cast off, but someone *had* found some rope, and as they snaked through the rail on the edge of the birlinn, I heard a few muted cheers.

I stood with Eilidh not far away. The sun had not yet crested the hill, but it would soon. The morning was misty, but the opposite side of the loch was still visible, if veiled.

"We'll see yous all on the other side," I said to the folks in the boat as they got settled, nervous expressions and sweat marring more than a few faces. "Just a couple hours, and we'll be on our way to Oban for real."

All I got in response was an anxious bob of heads that rippled through the birlinn.

Water splashed as oars moved, first nudging the birlinn away from the makeshift dock as the former fishers pulled their spirit-formed gangplank back from the boat and up onto the shore.

"Couple of them know how to make another," one of them said to me, a woman in her mid-fifties who looked like she'd spent a lifetime out in the sun and had bullied it into tanning her instead of burning. "Though they're going to have wet feet no matter what. First crossing'll be the slowest, since they'll need to figure out where they can safely disembark."

"It takes however long it takes," I murmured.

We all watched as time stretched out, oars kissing the water and moving in tandem. I wondered how they were keeping the rhythm—until one of my habitual pulses of spirit revealed their secret.

The rowers were using *Connection* to keep time.

My mouth fell open as I felt the echoes of it ripple through the surrounding spirit. They didn't need to listen to a drum when they could literally listen to each other's magic.

Even so, that first journey—its mere five hundred metres—drew itself out excruciatingly. They landed after what felt like hours but was in reality only a few minutes. A collective sigh cascaded through the folks on our shore when they made out that the passengers on the birlinn had made it successfully onto the western edge of the loch.

If I'd thought that was bad, the return journey was worse. Though I knew Iain and Meeksy could not only take care of themselves but could also take care of the folks who were with them, from this distance, they were barely the size of peppercorns. I didn't like how small they looked.

But then the birlinn came within reach of the makeshift

mooring lines, and though Rhona's face was so white she could go guisin' at Halloween as a ghost without makeup, she carried herself as if daring someone to tell her to let someone take her place.

I'd known Rhona was a brave girl since the moment I met her and she'd defied Lord Bawbag—she'd been so afraid of him that she'd demanded to come with me, a strange man over a decade older. She'd trusted me. I'd trust her now to know what she could and couldn't handle.

Naturally, that's when everything went to shit.

As the second group started boarding the birlinn, I did my usual short-long, short-long of Connection, and just when I did, at the very edge of my range, I felt something familiar.

Something familiar and *wrong*.

"Fuck," I said softly.

Rhona's head swivelled as if I'd shouted, as did Eilidh's.

"What is it?" Eilidh asked.

"Anomalies."

Her eyebrow went up, and I was already moving, looking for Ealasaid.

"Ealasaid!" I called.

She emerged from behind a pair of burly men who practically made a wall.

"What is it, m' eudail?" She squinted at me, clearly realising something was wrong.

"The bairns need to go in this crossing," I told her, my tone leaving no doubt as to my seriousness.

"There's not enough people on the other side to protect them," someone else objected, and I turned to look at them.

I didn't dare say it too loudly, because I didn't want to terrify the weans. Instead, I just looked the man very pointedly in the eyes, then gave a nod to the southeast and said, "The children. Go. Now."

His already-pale face went whiter than Rhona's, and he swallowed.

Ealasaid, bless her, was already moving. Her face gave no sign of her being afraid—she smiled and doted on the weans as she gathered them and told them they'd been so good that they were getting to cut the queue and go first.

I wasn't sure if they'd buy it—kids aren't daft—but they went without fussing.

Keeping Connection active, I slowly made my way around the crowd with Eilidh until we got to the group of adults who'd been meant to go after the kids. They also had simple clubs, not like the shillelaghs I'd made in Kilninver, but plenty serviceable.

"We might need you here," I said quietly. "Eilidh and I need to go head something off, but if it's too much for us or gets past us, be ready."

"If you can make any more weapons in the meantime, do that," Eilidh added.

"And anyone who's unlocked an Arcane affinity and has Purifire, be ready to use it." Purifire had seemed to have a startling effect on the fox; I hoped that'd hold true with the rabbits.

"What's out there?" The woman who had asked the question tightened her grip on the cricket-bat-sized club she wielded.

I reached out with Connection again, recoiling from the sense of the thing—things. When I winced, though, it wasn't because of disgust.

"Rabbits," I said reluctantly.

"That's all?" A man guffawed. "You got us worked up over some bunnies?"

"If it helps, they're the size of Rottweilers, and there's an entire warren's worth," I told him. "Also, there's something wrong with them, and it's *not* their size."

"I'd listen to Calum," Eilidh said. "He and I are the scariest things here, and if we're nervous? Get nervous."

I managed to keep my jaw from dislocating itself in shock, but only barely. I mouthed a "thank you" at her as we moved away.

"Think of the one in Monty Python, and you won't be far off," I said over my shoulder. "Hopefully, you lot'll avoid seeing them face to face—or any closer than that."

With that, we were off, Eilidh kissing her gran's cheek before we started to run.

CHAPTER

TWENTY-SEVEN

"How far are they?" Eilidh asked as we took off southward.

"Not very, and closing fast," I said. "Guess the saying 'quick like a bunny' really applies here."

I'd the sudden, intrusive image of an entire field full of murderous and rotting cotton balls flying at our heads.

"Plan? I've got Tuaineal, so with enough warning, I could probably catch at least some of them in it." Eilidh ran beside me, giving no sign that loping up a hill and speaking were incompatible.

Tuaineal—that must have been the name of her stun, since it meant a stupor or dizziness.

"That could work," I said. "Then I hit them from above with Spèird and Purifire and we go from there?"

"Aye, suits me fine." Eilidh glanced at me briefly before returning her gaze to the path ahead. "We've just got to make sure they don't get past us."

"We'll do everything we can to make sure of that," I said between breaths.

Despite my sky-high Stamina, I was feeling my low

Strength, because running up hills most definitely took some muscles. Especially running up hills in squishy ground. The magical boots Eilidh had crafted were the only thing keeping me from being soaked up to the knees every few steps where the spongy foliage of the terrain was more bog than solid ground. The muscle control to not pitch face first into a clump of heather was not negligible.

I really needed to start doing press-ups. And squats. Probably also some godawful interval training that would make me want to die. Ugh.

At least maybe the Stamina'd make it easier than the time Iain convinced me to go to one of those Grit Fit classes he loved where they did burpees 'til they boaked just for fun. Maybe it wouldn't be as bad now. Maybe they didn't actually get sick all over their own feet. A man could dream.

We were skirting the edge of a burn that ran on our right side, likely flowing down into the loch. The occasional rivulet caused tripping hazards under our frantic-paced feet, but my enhanced Agility helped mitigate that ignominy.

It meant I could concentrate on Connection—and on the burgeoning dread every time I cast.

I didn't want to say it out loud, but something made me very uneasy about these anomalies. The way they felt when I touched them with Connection made me want to scour my skin raw with pumice.

This was the second encounter that had approached from the same direction. With my next use of Connection, I felt them far closer than expected. These things were fucking speed demons.

"Shit, incoming," I said to Eilidh.

"Already?"

"Aye!"

We'd had more warning than with the fox, but these things had reached us far, far faster.

My first thought when they bounded over the hill was that we were being attacked by giant popcorn.

Our one lucky break was that the bouncing bastard bunnies were *not* as proportionally massive as that first centipede or rat I'd met. Unlike the goshawk or any number of other creatures we'd encountered in the time since the ascension, the rabbits didn't seem to have gotten the gargantuan gene. Be that as it may, a horde of rabbits the size of Rottweilers bounding over the hill like kernels popping? Still bloody terrifying.

Not all of the rabbits were white—most were more typical earth tones, plus the rotting flesh—but the way they spilled over the event horizon of the hill immediately put to mind the way cinema popcorn makers overflowed. Two hundred metres away, they rocketed towards us, shifting like a flock of birds as they realised they now had targets.

And they were spread out.

"Fuck!" Eilidh had her sword unsheathed, but I could almost see her calculating the trigonometry of her stun and finding it wanting. "Do you have any way of grouping them together?"

"No, I don—wait."

There was no *time* to wait.

"Fuck it," I muttered, grabbing my staff and drawing deeply on my spirit to cast Ring of Fire. I fed Spèird into it in a last-ditch effort to make a giant arcane lasso.

My spirit reserves plummeted to below fifty percent, which staggered me for a moment, long enough for me to register that it had worked.

Sort of.

The rabbits had been spaced out enough that I had only

caught about half of them, but the ones I'd caught were flung into the centre of the circle of Purifire, where they'd collided with an unholy screech.

Outwith the circle, I didn't think my magic had repelled the abhorrent creatures, but it might as well have. They went squealing away from the fire, scattering even more.

"Eilidh," I called out, but she already had her sword point down and golden magic swirling around her.

Now that I recognised that as nearly *pure will*, the spell was even more impressive.

Tuairneal erupted out from her in a wave even I could feel. It swept over the ground, making every hair on my arms stand on end.

The rabbits outside the Ring of Fire still careened away, but I didn't think that would last.

Wincing at the toll it was about to take on my remaining spirit, I made a disc of Spèird as wide as I could and slammed it downward within the ring.

"Go!" I yelled.

Eilidh was off like a shot, sprinting forwards with her claymore in hand.

I had three seconds to panic that the ring wouldn't let her through before she hit the waist-high wall of Purifire, claymore slashing in wide arcs with sprays of blood and putrid viscera.

My spirit was at thirty percent, and I cast Fuaran to help it recover even as a pulse of Connection made it dip slightly.

Fuck—some of the rabbits I'd scattered had barrelled on to the north. At least ten of the wee buggers hurtled down the hill along the burn.

"They're escaping!" I yelled, willing my spirit to climb faster.

Our plan had worked, but not well enough. Not with this many moving pieces.

Something told me we didn't want to find out what would happen if one of these things sank their teeth into us.

They weren't zombies, I didn't think, but even my mediocre Healing affinity practically *screamed* contagion.

Except they weren't escaping after all.

A split second before I felt a shockwave of spirit crack through the air behind me, I felt the rabbits turn with my use of Connection.

They didn't skid or scrabble; it was like after the initial panic that had sent them scattering, they'd simply loped onward and looped around in a wide arc.

But when Eilidh used her taunt?

Every single remaining rabbit let loose an ear-grating shriek and pelted towards her like they'd been fired from a fucking cannon.

Whirling my staff, I caught three of them as they sailed by me, one after another. Each movement of the living weapon seemed to solidify my intent, as for the first time, I consciously noted it acting in battle.

The oak of my staff was as repulsed by these things as I was; the book I'd used once I'd unlocked the Staves affinity taught that movement and spirit are one and the same.

Each form, each strike, each parry—they all brought spirit to bear with the intent of their action.

I just wasn't fast enough.

Whether there were ten left or a hundred, I couldn't tell. I spun to find that Eilidh had the anomalies a heartbeat away from swarming her.

My heart caught in my chest.

I did the only thing I could think of doing: Tairm.

The ground around Eilidh's feet exploded outward.

As did about half of the rabbits.

If Eilidh was shocked, she didn't show it; she swung that massive broadsword as if she'd been planning on the earth rupturing a foot away from her toes all along.

My spirit depleted, all I could do at first was watch as she fought through the anomalous creatures.

She was still going to get overwhelmed.

I sprang into action. It had only been a heartbeat since I'd cast Tairm, but it felt like an age as I leapt forwards.

Striking out with my staff, I caught the rump of one of the rabbits. The hit sent it flying tail over toes—and also broke Eilidh's taunt.

Just like the fox, the rabbits were hard to look at directly. They seemed blurred round the edges, like if someone poured turpentine on an oil painting and it launched itself at you to eat your face.

That was precisely what this one did.

My reaction was pure instinct, an extra *thwack* of Spèird along with my next strike. It was also a remarkably terrible idea.

It didn't hit Eilidh; the way spells worked in an ascension apparently made friendly fire very difficult and rare. It did, however, hit another five of the rabid little thumpers.

I didn't have much spirit left at all. All I had to keep me alive was my staff—a living weapon—the knowledge the system had downloaded in my brain about how to wield it, and the hope that Eilidh's many years of HEMA would help her keep us both this side of dead.

That—and Connection.

Something sparked in my mind, a combination of the book on staves and long hours of practise I'd had with Connection, breath, and heartbeat.

I felt my staff exult as if it had been waiting for just this moment, and even as I recognised it, it tugged me towards a form I'd barely used.

Barely used, but still knew like muscle memory passed down through my DNA.

Breathe in, spirit in, staff retracted.

Breathe out, spirit out, strike.

It wasn't just me.

I felt more than saw Eilidh mirror me. Together, we moved until we were back to back.

The anomalous rabbits attacked chaotically, as if there was some sort of random strike generator spurring them on with no discernible pattern. Even in their chaos, though, our response could be . . . calm.

Like when we had shared spirit to free the people in Lord Bawbag's corral, like when we had joined with the entire community to build the birlinn, a sense of *flow* superseded any fear, any panic.

I remained aware these things were dangerous; it was simply that in that moment, both I and Eilidh chose to effect the change within our power.

And because of that, our power grew.

More of the rabbits must have come over the hill at some point. We'd long since worked through the ones who'd arrived first. Even so, there seemed to be an endless tide.

The thought of that tide rolling down the hill and descending upon the low-levelled people of our fledgling community made me want to smash every single anomalous rabbit into a fucking crater.

As I fought, sometimes killing the rabbits with a well-placed strike to the head and sometimes only maiming, I became aware of my spirit regenerating even faster than it normally did with Fuaran.

I almost missed a hit as the realisation struck: even in the middle of a battle, the flow state increased my spirit.

Elated, I attacked with renewed vigour. Each time the rabbits lunged for us, we would counter, and they would retreat a short ways before running at us again. They were already blurred even when moving slowly, but that effect made them nearly disappear at speed.

Their screeches became more frantic and their own attacks more erratic. Even with the influx of spirit and Puri-fire now crackling down the length of my weapon and Eilidh's, my entire body felt like it had been doused in sweat.

Muscles burned with the continued motion of the fight, lactic acid building to near-cramp levels of danger.

But slowly, the rabbits' numbers slowed.

When the last one slid off Eilidh's sword—she'd skewered it when it leapt at her face—both of us were panting, hair dripping with perspiration. My eyes burned where it had dripped into them, and I almost boaked as the putrescence of the carnage around us rolled over me all at once.

You have killed an anomalous rabbit (113).

Both mutated by the wave of spirit in Earth's ascension and corrupted by an unknown anomaly, this rabbit was a tougher-than-usual foe—and more dangerous than one would expect.

Such creatures frequently contain common crafting materials such as: rabbit pelt, rabbit's foot, rabbit teeth, rabbit bones, rabbit meat. These anomalous creatures, however, contain only a petrified heart. This is of unknown value.

I didn't care how many of those I'd killed myself, but a peek into my inventory showed fifty-seven petrified hearts, which meant somehow Eilidh and I had killed almost the same number each.

"Dhìa," Eilidh said, stepping over a pile of rabbit corpses to come round and face me, and I couldn't tell if she was invoking god as a prayer or a curse.

On reflex, I ran through my Connection pattern. And froze.

I'd thought they could no longer shake me.

I was wrong.

Eilidh saw my face a moment later when I met her eyes, and I could practically *feel* the air suck right back out of her lungs.

"There's more," I said, leaning on my sweat-and-gore-slicked staff and pointing up the hill.

Eilidh's use of Connection didn't have to be as strong as mine then—because like a glass of water rippling with the vibrating thump of a T-rex's gait, spirit rippled outwards from a point of impact just over the crest of the rise.

Just as a pair of enormous fucking bunny ears protruded above the ridge.

CHAPTER

TWENTY-EIGHT

"You've got to be fucking *kidding me*." Eilidh stabbed her claymore into the blood-wet ground and put one hand on each knee like she was re-enacting the meme of the fed-up woman that had gone viral a few years back.

The ears grew longer, followed by the crown of the enormous rabbit's head.

Normally, had I thought about a rabbit the size of a moose coming towards me, I suspect my immediate impulse would be to pat it, not murder it.

I did not want to pat this rabbit.

It was the tawny colour one associates with the average wild rabbit, but between that and the ears, that was the only thing this one shared with its pre-ascension brethren.

Great chunks of rotting flesh hung off its body, exposing fat and muscle beneath curling flaps of blood-and-lymph-matted fur. The blur that characterised the anomalous creatures was even more pronounced at such a scale—as was the smell.

Dear gods, the *smell*.

I gagged even at this distance and saw Eilidh doing the same. Bile burned at my throat.

My spirit well and truly recovered, I cast Keen Eye.

Anomalous Giant Rabbit

Caught in a wave of spirit upon Earth's ascension, this rabbit mutated far faster than can normally be expected for a creature of its complexity. This rabbit had mutated thusly before coming in contact with the anomaly, which changed the creature from a placid—if abnormally large—specimen to one of truly threatening proportions and danger.

Remember that a rabbit's teeth are not its only weapon.

As you have already established, anomalous creatures are vulnerable to Purifire, but this creature is unlikely to be susceptible to control measures that would more easily affect smaller anomalies.

"Fuck a duck," I muttered.

"I'm sorry, what?" With a sharp tug, Eilidh retrieved her claymore, eyeing its gore-crusted blade distastefully. Clumps of fur clung to the steel.

"Purifire will hurt that thing, but I don't think our previous method will work here."

Eilidh made an irritated noise. "Fuck a duck indeed."

The rest of the rabbit emerged over the hill, and while it didn't seem to have seen us yet—I doubted it shared the T-rex's mythical inability to see us if we stood still—I harboured no illusions that it would.

"I don't feature us fighting this thing and slipping on dead bunny slime, do you?" I asked the question, but I didn't wait for Eilidh to answer, gingerly leaping to a relatively clean patch of tufty moor grass.

Eilidh followed, her gaze scanning the terrain. "You don't think your Purifire circle will contain it?"

"Keen Eye practically told me it wouldn't, and even if it

did, we'd still have to kill it somehow." I ran through my repertoire of spells in my head. Cumhachd had some potential if Ring of Fire actually *worked*, but Ring of Fire was a spirit burner.

"What exactly did it tell you?" Eilidh asked, motioning me to follow her.

I simply sent her the information, watching her lips tighten even just looking at her side on.

The rabbit monster had paused, ears swivelling and nose twitching. I'd always thought bunny nose twitches were one of the most adorable things on this daft planet, but now? No, thank you. Half the monster's cheek was hanging off, baring a mouthful of teeth that were decidedly *not* the grinding molars they were meant to have as a herbivore.

Some of the original molars had rotted away, but the ones that were left had either broken or otherwise transformed into sharp, jagged points. Rabbit teeth could already cause serious damage to human flesh when the rabbit was the size of a football, no need for serrated edges.

I hated this. Wasn't Bawbag enough to deal with without this cottontail cunt hippity-hopping through the Highlands?

The bit that implied even this Ascended Alliance in their aeons of arcane glory apparently didn't know what the hell this thing was? I'd worry about that later, if Rotting Fluff-Butt over there didn't bite me in half.

"I don't think you should taunt it," I muttered to Eilidh. "I'm going to—try something."

"Why hasn't it attacked us yet?" she asked as if I hadn't spoken.

"No idea. It's not like we're hiding."

"And we're not being particularly quiet." Eilidh stared at the thing.

Its ears still rotated like oblong satellites stuck to the top of its head.

We exchanged a glance.

Even if this thing wasn't attacking us right this second, we absolutely could not leave it on the loose in Argyll. Understanding passed between us, leaving a bleak, resolute silence in its wake.

"You'd mentioned you wanted to try something," Eilidh said slowly after a moment. "Why don't you find out if it can see first?"

That wasn't a bad thought.

With a sharp nod, I twined together Cumhachd and Purifire—not much of either—and loosed it from my staff.

Not at the creature itself. I aimed just past its face.

For a moment, both Eilidh and I held our breath. Just for a moment, it seemed like maybe the monster couldn't see at all. Only for one single, tiny moment.

The spell I'd shot towards it earned no reaction as it arced over the moor closer and closer and closer until it brushed so close to the creature's face I thought it might singe a whisker.

Then the mahoosive rabbit exploded into motion.

Its back legs were the size of canoes, but unlike a canoe, neither of those enormous feet were hollow, and when they pounded the ground with wet squelches from the spongy peat, they sent tremors through the earth even as water and disturbed flora flew outward from the impact.

"Got that?" I asked Eilidh.

"Aye, stay behind it at all costs," she said, and then she was off at a run straight up the hill.

I only had a fraction of a second to react.

We'd felt the concussive force of the rabbit's feet hitting the ground, but we'd forgotten this was still an ascended rabbit.

Both Eilidh and I had forgotten that there were senses beyond the usual five, and losing one of them?

Didn't mean others weren't terrifyingly strong.

With laser precision, the monster whirled, launching itself towards Eilidh like it had had a week to chart out the movement and another week to practise.

For the second time in the short span of time we'd been out here, my heart gave an unwelcome crunch.

Remember that a rabbit's teeth are not its only weapon.

The rabbit used those mahoosive feet to spring off of the boggy earth like a bloody trampoline.

I knew without a single doubt that if one of those feet hit Eilidh full force, it would break every bone in its path.

Eilidh was not one to be underestimated.

That was one thing I'd learnt to enormous effect since meeting her, even before the ascension made her more terrifying by an order of magnitude. She leapt sideways at the last possible second, using her dive to slash across the monster rabbit's foot.

Weaving together Spèird and Purifire as I'd done before, I aimed and loosed at fast as I possibly could at the clearest target I had: the motherfluffer's cottony tail.

Never in my life did I think I'd be firing off magic to goose a rabbit the size of a moose.

Here I was anyway.

As quick as she'd been, Eilidh wasn't out of danger. Her roll caused a thud to the earth that the rabbit homed in on like it was a hungry shark and she'd just dropped an entire side of beef into the sea.

A couple things happened at exactly the same moment.

The rabbit tried to twist in midair, and . . .

Its movement shifted the ultimate impact location of my spell.

No longer was it aimed at the disgusting creature's tail, which was, until that point, one of the few points on the monster that had not been made repulsive with rotting flesh.

The rabbit's attempt to twist had been partially successful, and my combined fire-and-force spell bypassed lighting a fire *under* the creature's arse and instead hit it directly in the arse*hole*.

Or near enough, anyway.

My own arse veritably puckered at the sight, but the effect it had on the unfortunate business end of the spell was, not unexpectedly, incendiary.

The rabbit's furry breeches went up in flames.

Oh, god, I'm sorry, I'm sorry, I'm sorry.

I didn't know if I was mentally apologising to any gods who would listen or if I were apologising to the rabbit itself. It certainly hadn't asked for any of this when it was hopping about, minding its own business.

It didn't help that my absolute dick of a brain helpfully yelled, *Fire in the hole!*

I was definitely, indisputably going to hell.

"Did you just set its *arse on fire*?" Eilidh yelled as the rabbit dragged its rump across the moor grass and heather, which accomplished exactly nothing except leaving a trail of gruesome putrid flesh smouldering in the heather.

"Yes," I replied miserably. "I was aiming for the tail."

The auburn-haired woman prudently removed herself from the line of literal fire. I could almost see the gears in her head turning as she reoriented on her target, shooting me a half-exasperated, half-bewildered look as if to say *Then what on god's green earth did you hit?*

She was already off, and I couldn't let my guilt distract me from putting this poor thing out of its misery.

With the rabbit well and truly diverted from attacking by a much more immediate problem, Eilidh and I circled it from the back, where Purifire eagerly climbed from its inception point up the monster's hips where rotted flesh sizzled and gave off a horrid, acrid smoke.

The moor was free of any brambles where we were, so I didn't think Tairm would be of much use. Cumhachd it was.

Gathering as much spirit as I dared, I said yet another mental apology as I threaded more Purifire through the other spell. Purifire most certainly damaged it, but this fight could not go on much longer. We needed to end it so we could go scour our brains.

I loosed the spell—and a solid half of my spirit—at the back of the rabbit's head.

This time, my aim was dead on. Mostly because the monster had planted its flaming arse in the burn, which despite the Scottish terminology, was water and not fire.

It wouldn't put the Purifire out, but the rabbit didn't know that. My spell hit it smack between the enormous ears just as Eilidh crouched and leaped directly onto the rabbit's back.

How she managed to keep her balance, I'd never know. She slammed her claymore down between the rabbit's shoulder blades even as it tried to buck her off, and I circled around to fire off another Purifire-Cumhachd combo, this time at the side of the monstrous rabbit's face.

It hit with a sickening crunch as it punched through the

skull that was met with a staccato crack as something in the rabbit's spine broke.

The creature spasmed once more and collapsed.

For all her grace in monster murder, Eilidh was less smooth on the dismount—though that could have been the fact that she slipped in a chunk of rotten rabbit meat.

She went sprawling into the burn, but she didn't even look angry about it. Eilidh had landed, after all, upstream.

"Uill, a Chaluim," she said dryly from her very wet seat, "Is tusa a mharbh e."

My death blow, then. I took her words to mean that she planned to stay right where she was until she was cleaner.

Purifire cleansing could only go so far.

CHAPTER
TWENTY-NINE

You have killed an anomalous giant rabbit.

Both mutated by the wave of spirit in Earth's ascension and corrupted by an unknown anomaly, this rabbit was a tougher-than-usual foe—and more dangerous than one would expect.

Such creatures frequently contain common crafting materials such as: rabbit pelt, rabbit's foot, rabbit teeth, rabbit bones, rabbit meat. These anomalous creatures, however, contain only a petrified heart. This is of unknown value.

My notifications flashing told me there was more to it, and sure enough, I saw the anomaly quest had updated.

It had gained no further objectives but it had gained an unnerving paragraph that simply said:

The anomalies, despite moving with alarming speed in the direction of your community, turned around after getting past you. Had they continued on, they could have reached the more vulnerable among you.

It would be wise to burn the corpses.

The implication there was clear.

They hadn't been aiming for the rest of the people. The anomalies had been headed straight for *us*.

It made it all the better that Eilidh and I had come here alone. Maybe if the giant rabbit had killed us, it would have, I don't know, gone about its terrifying and monstrous zombie bunny life.

A vain hope, and one not worth entertaining.

As soon as I finished reading that paragraph, I closed out of the notifications and set about burning the corpses —all of them. Eilidh emerged, shivering, when I was about halfway through and blue-black smoke rose in a column into the sky.

That smoke will be visible from miles away, I noted glumly. Without me somehow commanding the entirety of the elements, it couldn't be helped.

"Can you dry me off?" she asked tentatively.

My spirit was mostly recovered, even though I was using Purifire constantly with the rabbit sludge, and without a thought, I cast a web of it over Eilidh to warm and dry her.

Some bits of her armour sizzled alarmingly as the Purifire found chunks of gore even the current of the burn hadn't washed away, and she bore it stoically.

My main regret—aside from the horrible comedy of errors with the tail end of the rabbit—was that its corpse remained in the burn. I burned it until it was no more, but that stream was contaminated, and I didn't know how to fix it or even if I could. Worth a shot either way.

In the end, once I felt certain Purifire had burned away any contaminants from the corpses themselves, I asked Eilidh to go for a run with me before we returned to the group.

Together, we ran downstream, and I stopped every

hundred meters or so to weave a web of Purifire in the water itself. From the way it hissed, a grim feeling settled upon me, knowing I'd made the right choice.

The hissing reduced the farther downstream we got, but just to be safe, we followed the burn all the way down to the loch. There was no further sign of contamination by then, but I wouldn't have rested easy at the thought of leaving Loch Awe as an unwitting breeding ground of anomalous fish. I didn't even know how I was certain there was danger, except that the notifications had told me to burn the corpses with Purifire.

By the time we made it back to Portsonachan, everyone had been ferried across, and the birlinn awaited the two of us, with Rhona pacing back and forth on the shore.

"What the hell took you so long?" she blurted out the moment she saw us. "It's been ages!"

"Aye, well, it was more than a fox," I said.

"Lots of foxes?"

"Muckle fuckin' bunny," Eilidh muttered. "And a hundred of its pals."

"A *hundred?*" Rhona said, and the rowers' mouths fell open. "Damn, I wish I'd been there."

The rowers' mouths fell open a bit farther at that, one of them closing his jaw with an audible click of teeth.

"No, you really don't," I said, shuddering. "It was vile."

"Calum shot a magical bottle rocket up the giant rabbit's arse," Eilidh said, too loudly.

Rhona burst out laughing, but she was the only one. Everyone else just stared, including Ronald, whose string-bean frame was hunched over on one of the thwarts.

"I didn't *mean* to," I said, too defensively.

"Of course you didn't mean to," Rhona said through her

giggles. "You're the only person on Earth who could—and would—manage such a thing by *accident*."

Before I could work up the wherewithal to decide whether or not I wanted to be offended by that and if so, in which way, a tug on my mind made my gaze snap up to the sky.

The wren.

I'd forgotten about the bloody wren in all the . . . rabbit tornado.

Thinking of it strengthened the hair-thin bond of spirit, and I swayed on my feet as my viewpoint split once more.

Whilst we'd been fighting, the wren had been surveying the smoke in the distance.

The good news was that the smoke, whatever its source, was not getting closer to us. The bad news was that it *was* moving towards Oban.

We wasted no time rowing across the loch. The group we'd already sent over remained visible and clearly busy, though doing what was anybody's guess from our vantage point in the birlinn. It was getting on past noon, and

I hated the idea of leaving the birlinn behind. Crafting it had been a singularly powerful experience, one that I wasn't sure was repeatable. The birlinn we'd made was unique.

In the end, though, it was a boat. It wasn't alive like the three hundred people we were trying to keep breathing. Not to mention the thousands in Oban who could die.

I'd planned to take one of the oars to give a rower a break, but I must have looked haggard. When I'd gone to offer, the bloke with the oar had taken one look at me and said, "Naw, mate."

Sitting on a thwart next to Eilidh, I fervently wished for something to distract me from the radiating warmth on my left. Rowing would at least give me something to do that wasn't thinking about that heat or second guessing all the decisions we'd made in the past few days.

We could have taken the strongest of us and returned to Oban, leaving the other three hundred to take the slower route around the loch. Sure, that was a possibility. But if we'd done that, we'd have left them vulnerable, including the children. That wasn't acceptable to me or to anyone else. Oban had the advantage of numbers and at least some preparation at this point; the people with us did not.

There were any number of things we could be questioning, but if we sat here picking apart the instincts we'd followed, all we'd do was pick up an ulcer.

We were still alive. That was all that mattered.

I tuned back in to the birlinn to hear a couple of the rowers talking, both of them darting glances at me and Eilidh in the process.

". . . wrecked all of Sackington's guns and stole his grenades," one of them said, not really trying to be quiet.

Eilidh zeroed in on him like a bloodhound catching a whiff of the quarry. "Yes. We did."

"Erm, he wasn't saying it was a bad thing!" one of the rowers blurted out.

"Yes, I was! We could have used those instead of hitting things with sticks, for fuck's sake," the other one said. "No offense."

"Mate, they don't even work anymore," I said, and when I could almost *see* his thoughts pivot to *but there's magic now,*

I sighed. "We happened to be present when someone figured out how to use their magic to fire a rifle at one of Bawbag's simulacra. Not only did the bullet *literally* bounce right back, but it killed his daughter when it ricocheted, and his next shot was dead on. Can you guess what happened then?"

"He died," said the guy who had tried to reassure me they weren't questioning that decision. He had sandy brown hair that was a mess of waves half stuck to his head with sweat from the exertion, and his muscles were bulging out of his shirt—guess he was getting those Strength increases.

"Did he die?" the other bloke asked.

"Aye, he might as well have just shot himself in the heart. Even swords bounced right off that damn thing— piercing it with the point seems to be the only thing even marginally successful, and that might be imbuing it with Purifire more than the actual poke."

"I know how to shoot a gun," Eilidh said bluntly. "And amateurs with firearms tend to hurt much more than they help, let alone in a state of active combat. This isn't the fucking Wild West."

She sounded Done with a capital D, and I didn't blame her. To his credit, the bloke seemed to mull that over for a bit before nodding as if ceding the point.

Whatever the Ascended Alliance knew about friendly fire of an arcane nature, that did not extend to human-made explosives. If we got to the point where we were dealing with something like that again, we'd figure it out.

I was just as tired by the idea that random people could pick up a gun with limited ammunition, become sharp-shooter enough to hit the broad side of a burning barn without running out of said ammunition, and then survive longer than ten seconds against something like the beithir. Or that giant bunny, for fuck's sake.

Plus, most Scots had never held a gun, let alone shot one. Even in the Highlands, you might find a rifle like the one that had spelled doom for poor Donald in Kilchurn, but it wasn't like people had handguns or ammo lying around. A useful tool in certain situations—downright deadly so far in this one, and not for the thing it was aimed at.

No, thank you.

It seemed easy in the films, but if we were going to be in all-out industrialised warfare, we would have bigger fish to fry. Probably literally, because whilst we were all trying to blow each other's heads off, a kraken would likely emerge from the sea and eat one of the armies.

Yay.

The rest of the short trip across the loch was punctuated only by the splash of oars and the creak of wood. Being the highest-levelled person here meant I held the reins to a lot of horse races I'd never otherwise touch in my existence. I'd have to get used to people who thought they knew more than me questioning my decisions. Or, you know, we could maybe make some sort of governing structure that didn't revolve around a single leader.

Scotland wasn't too keen on monarchy or lords, but maybe this was our chance to figure out a better way.

Imagine that.

Imagining a better world was all well and good, but seeing it happen in front of my face in microcosm was something else entirely.

In the time we'd been gone, people hadn't been resting on their laurels. Or their haunches. Or resting at all.

To the contrary, Iain had a full-blown martial arts course going on the lawn at the edge of the hotel, with pupils wildly ranging in age. There was a *very* determined three-year-old with her tongue poking out in concentration as she kicked and threw herself off balance. And there was Ealasaid and an old man who looked like he had a decade on *her*—both of them were doing what looked like a simple kata.

Nan had a veritable pantry in front of her, and she was cooking up a storm with a troupe of assistants who all moved with purpose and laser focus.

If we ever needed a drill sergeant, I suspected we'd have our best bet in Nan.

And beyond them, *everyone* was busy. Again, one of the older folks had the kids and was teaching them about plants. The hotel had a herb garden off the back, and it had veritably exploded in the ascension, so there was enough mint for me to practically smell from the edge of the loch. Mint needed little encouragement before it got an influx of magic. Now, it seemed it had plans for world domination.

People were organising supplies, entertaining kids— hell, it looked like we even had a massage therapist who was working out the kinks in a sixty-year-old's neck.

"Glad everyone seems to be getting on fine without us," I murmured to Eilidh, who seemed as bemused as I felt.

"They didn't know when you'd be back," Rhona said, making me jump when she materialised by my right shoulder.

I ought to have sensed her coming—either I'd neglected my use of Connection or her stealth had improved. Maybe both.

"We're going to need to leave soon," I said. "We can't eat up the time we gained crossing the loch by sitting here for the next day."

"We need a plan first." That came, somewhat unsurprisingly, from Ronald. The man had the build of a skeleton and the sneaky feet of a fucking tiger. "If Bawbag's attacking Oban, we can't just bring the kids there."

In my slight irritation at being snuck up on, I perhaps poured a bit too much spirit into my next cast of Connection, because several people in my immediate vicinity jumped.

I barely noticed their sharp movement.

There was no time for me to be relieved that it *wasn't* an anomaly my spirit encountered. I couldn't be relieved, because my spirit encountered the one thing that was arguably worse.

Simulacra.

Not just one of them.

"Simulacra," I said. "Eilidh, Rhona—we need to find them and hit them *fast*. If Bawbag sees everything they see—"

"He'll know we're coming," Eilidh finished, already moving.

"What?" Ronald started to protest, but the three of us ignored him completely.

"Ealasaid!" I called the elderly woman's name. "Get everyone who can use Connection and Purifire and form a circle around the kids.

My stomach sank like someone'd dropped a boulder into it. I could already feel it was too late.

Bawbag's magic had improved, I realised, feeling sicker by the second. I hadn't tipped them off with my use of Connection; they'd already been making a beeline for us.

My mind raced through different possibilities. None of them altered what we had to do—and do quick.

"Piercing damage only—Nan, sharpen some knives as fast as you can. If a simulacra gets close, hit them with Purifire and stab them. Better yet if someone can sever Bawbag's connection to them."

New rule: everyone would need to know this shit as soon as humanly possible.

Rhona gave me a look that said *If you're done chatting, can we take care of the problem?*

At least I thought that was what it said, since she pretty much pulled an exasperated face and then vanished into stealth.

"Never in my life thought I'd spend so much time running," I muttered as we took off through the crowd, which was now on high alert.

Iain and Meeksy, to my surprise, both fell in with us, Meeksy huffing and puffing.

"We'll make a runner of you yet," Iain said to him fondly.

I wanted to laugh, but with our feet pounding against the tarmac of the single-track road leading away from the hotel, I was too busy sorting through the implications of the simulacra.

Trees flashed by as we ran, Connection telling me that as fast as these buggers were, they had nothing on the anomalies.

Small mercies.

From the direction the simulacra were coming from, I suspected Bawbag was scouting to the rear to make sure nothing was coming up to flank him. I doubted he was outright looking for the people we'd rescued, but that didn't mean finding them wouldn't be a world of trouble for each and every one of the survivors.

We were about half a mile from the hotel when I came to an abrupt halt. The simulacra weren't far now. They were moving straight at us, to be sure, but they weren't hasty about it.

The others slowed and stopped after another moment.

"What are you doing?" Iain asked me.

"What if we use them?" I replied. "We can't let them see everyone back there, but what if we let them see *us* without engaging them?"

"That . . . could actually work," Eilidh said slowly. "If he's just using them to spy, we could give them something to report. You said they're not intelligent."

"They're a fungus shaped like a jellyfish."

"Right. They just feed back whatever they see to Bawbag." Eilidh glanced in the direction we'd been running. "And we could make sure what they feed him is us."

"Let him think we're coming to flank him," Meeksy said.

"We *are* coming to flank him," Iain said. "Letting him know that's a terrible plan."

I felt a wicked grin forming on my face. "Not if we veer from it after we seed it."

If I stopped to think, I would have started to panic.

Anomalous beasties coming up from the south, Bawbag to the north, his simulacra on the move, three hundred people to keep safe—it was best not to dwell.

We picked our way through the trees, keeping tabs on the simulacra as we went.

The plan was to circle around them and get their attention. I didn't know for sure if Bawbag was looking for us specifically or keeping an eye out for more general threats, but I could guarantee that he'd prick up his ears if he caught wind of us.

Around us, the land wasn't full forest, which made it harder. I wasn't sure exactly what the simulacra were capable of sensing or how. Now that I'd a better spell for finding out, I planned to use it as soon as I got a chance.

Connection pulsed through the spirit around us, more accurate than a radar for gauging the simulacra's position. I kept track as we moved, paying specific attention to their behaviour patterns.

They acted like drones. The three of them stayed within twenty metres of each other, but each ranged out a short distance before returning. After a few cycles of this, I realised they were on a rotation. One would venture out in a slightly different direction, then it would circle around and rejoin the remaining duo.

It gave me a bizarre impression of an Orcadian strip-the-willow. While my initial assumption had been correct —they were indeed making a beeline for the group—they seemed to be scouting on the way as if to be thorough about it.

That unnerved me.

Eilidh came up beside me, a frown creasing the skin of her forehead. The others had moved a bit away, letting us take point, and Rhona was doing her wraith thing somewhere out of sight, but Eilidh seemed as unsettled as I felt.

"They know *something* is out here, but I don't think they know what," I said to her, barely above a whisper.

Her frown grew deeper, but she dipped her chin in assent. "I have a new passive spell called Gairm that alerts me when something is actively tracking me or those I protect"—I started at that, but Eilidh didn't seem to notice —"but it hasn't gone off yet."

"What do you think they're sensing?" I murmured.

"I wish I knew. Body heat maybe? Or use of spirit?"

"It could be either of those things." Then I joined her in frowning. "If it was the latter, though, why hasn't my use of Connection sent them after us?"

We were getting closer to them, bit by bit encroaching on the land that would put us in striking distance.

"No idea," Eilidh answered. "Nothing feels right here. I keep thinking we should run to Oban, leave the others to catch up, but then I see the kids and can't. It's too dangerous to leave them with these things out here."

The rage in her voice was barely contained—I've seldom found real-world examples for the phrase "right-eous fury," but hearing her then, it was the only possible description of what lurked within her words.

There was no way either of us would let Bawbag repeat what he had done to those people. Oban stood a much stronger chance than they did—and if we were lucky, we'd be able to keep the survivors safe *and* defend my hometown.

I tried not to think of the odds.

Another pulse of Connection told me that this was it.

"Game face on," I whispered to Eilidh.

She held up a hand for the others as I crept forwards. I couldn't yet see the simulacra, but I could sense them as I kept my spirit expanded, listening.

We were near the small hamlet of Annat, and I both hoped and feared there were still people there. I didn't think there were—Bawbag seemed to have led his own personal reboot of the Highland Clearances. Yet another reason he needed to be stopped. The man had treated the apocalypse like a fucking free pass to punt Scotland back into the Dark Ages, like he'd just been waiting his entire life for something to happen that would give him a chance to commit even more blatant atrocities.

I'd say "with impunity," but his pre-ascension activities proved he'd already managed that. This was just the logical progression of his gobshite ways.

Most people—the overwhelming majority—see a catastrophe and their impulse is to help; others exploit.

I'd be damned if I was going to let one of the latter get away with it when I could do something about it.

Eilidh and I kept off the single-track road that led into Annat. "Into" was being generous; the hamlet was a handful of buildings, and that was it.

The simulacra were just on the other side of a row of houses.

We moved laterally to come at them from the side. As Eilidh unsheathed her blade, I touched a finger to the flat of it, watching Purifire spiral around the steel.

If we wanted this to work, we needed Bawbag's attention, and we needed to act like the simulacra had stumbled upon us and not the other way around.

"You're sure about this," Eilidh said, barely above a breath.

I nodded in response.

Pretending I had no clue the simulacra were there, I turned and called to Iain and Meeksy.

"It's clear!" They'd know that meant to come out.

I didn't think either of them were about to win a BAFTA for their acting performances as they sauntered out from a copse of trees, but Rhona, on the other hand—she emerged from the north with a full-on rakish grin that made her look like the cat picking canary feathers out of her teeth.

"Bawbag's moving north," she announced. "I climbed a tree and saw the smoke—he's definitely going to Oban!"

"We cannot let that happen!" Iain cried passionately.

Eilidh's lip twitched as she tried to repress the laughter I thought was playing tug-of-war with her mouth. Her cheek started to quiver slightly.

"We *won't* let him hurt Oban," Meeksy declared.

I wanted to facepalm hard enough to risk serious damage to my nose.

To avoid that particular pandemonium, I triggered Connection—and not a moment too soon.

The first of the simulacra appeared from the side of a house and gave a sudden jump as if something had poked it in the bum. It would have been cute if they weren't basically Lord Bawbag's eyeballs roving over the land.

"Simulacrum!" Eilidh burst out.

The others were coming—I felt the threads of spirit as they moved. Unlike the others, which had rushed us head-on when we'd encountered them, these ones did nothing of the sort.

They moved to encircle us.

"Behind you!" I yelled at Iain, who spun to see the second simulacrum speeding his way.

"We have to stop them before they can tell Bawbag we're coming after him!" Meeksy started to cast Purifire, lighting his brown skin with the blue-green glow.

Oh, gods, the melodrama.

Bawbag was never going to believe this, was he?

It was too late now—the third simulacrum appeared,

having circled around us to the south, and now all three of them leapt at us.

Keeping my hold on the thread of spirit coating Eilidh's blade in Purifire, I extended it to Rhona's daggers as she came tearing into the fray like a vengeful ghost.

With a "here goes nothing" look at Eilidh, I slammed Spèird down on the simulacrum closest to her, following it up with Connection to trace the line to Bawbag.

"Your one o'clock!" I yelled to her, and without missing a beat, her claymore came down, severing the simulacrum's connection to Bawbag.

Iain had wanted to try out his hand-to-hand on one of them, and he did that with aplomb. His acting sucked, but his martial arts skills did not. Even so, it was a bit like watching someone try to beat up a rubber ball; his punches and kicks landed and bounced right off.

That was all we needed.

The other simulacrum was close to Rhona, and as she whirled, I hit it with my one-two of Spèird and Connection. I didn't even have time to tell her where to slice with those Purifire-wreathed daggers. She moved so quickly with a flurry of strikes that she'd already sliced through Bawbag's connection line. Like the first one, this simulacrum deflated like a jellyfish out of water.

"One more to go." Iain kicked the sole remaining simulacrum hard. "We can't let it get away!"

It took everything in my power not to roll my eyes at him—but terrible acting or not, it did the trick.

The simulacrum he was facing gave another one of those strange little hops and exploded into retreat. It headed northwest, just as I had hoped it would.

"I'll go after it!" Rhona vanished from sight almost as quickly as the simulacrum had.

We all held our breath as silence fell over the abandoned village. We were in someone's back garden, the two jelly-like puddles of simulacra lying pitifully on the grass.

Whatever urge any of us had had to laugh seemed to have passed. I wasn't sure if our plan had fully succeeded; we wouldn't know until we got to Oban and to Lord Bawbag himself.

But all I could do was hope.

If he was going to attack, we'd made sure he'd do it knowing that he had someone coming for his sorry arse. If absolutely nothing else, the knowledge that Lord Bawbag was going to have to look over his shoulder the rest of the way to Oban was worth whatever we'd done here.

We all stood there for about ten minutes until Rhona came back, her eyes bright but rolling in the most teenage expression of disgust I thought I'd ever seen.

"You lot are the *worst* actors I've ever seen in my life," she said, picking a piece of moss out of her hair.

"Which direction did it go?" I asked quickly, before Iain or Meeksy could start a war.

Rhona pointed.

Eilidh, however, was staring at the two globs of simulacrum jelly in their little grass craters. "Calum?"

"Yeah?"

"Reckon you could"—she waved her hand in what was likely supposed to be a magical gesture but instead looked like a cross between a wave and a wanking motion, and I was certain she'd not intended the latter—"you know, track Bawbag the way you did with the first one?"

My nose wrinkled. "Aye. I could do that."

"Why do you look like someone shoved a jobby up under your nose?" Iain asked, tactful as always.

"Go over and pick one of those things up and hold it for a few miles, and you'll get your own answer," I told him.

"Ew," said Meeksy.

"Exactly." I blew out a breath.

Eilidh was right—we ought to have thought of this option sooner. But before we did anything else, I wanted to minimise surprises.

Walking over to one of the simulacra, I cast Keen Eye.

Modified Simulacrum

This simulacrum has been upgraded by its user, which has enabled it to, among other things, work as a unit with other simulacra, scan the ambient spirit for signs of spirit vectors, and provide more efficient feedback to the user.

This simulacrum has been severed from its connection with its creator.

Well, that was mostly useless, except for confirming what we already expected. Though the idea of these things scanning for "signs of spirit vectors," which I presumed meant people. Or maybe just any being that could actively use spirit? Or who had the means to use and then draw in spirit? What I wouldn't give for a guidebook to this apocalypse—preferably one that wasn't parcelled out to only those fortunate enough to stumble into life-threatening quests.

I gingerly reached out and picked up the simulacrum I'd just examined.

Yep. Still felt like holding barely contained goo.

Bawbag was to the northwest, according to the goo compass.

I wanted to put it in my inventory, but that was packed full with random stuff that had been shuffled around in the past couple days. There was one slot that just had what looked like a white pillow—

"Bugger!" I only barely managed to *re*inventory the goshawk down before turning my jellyfish compass into a feathered tribble.

A few fluffy bits of down floated to the floor.

"One of these days, he's going to forget," Iain said to Meeksy as if I wasn't even there. "I think I'll follow him around until he does, just so I can see him absolutely covered in feathers."

It was hard to believe it had only been two nights since we had rescued the survivors at Bawbag's manor. It felt like it had been weeks. Bawbag's movements felt erratic but at the same time as if he were marching on Oban in slow motion. When he'd been sending his goons to skulk around Craobh Haven, we'd been certain he was aiming for sea access and the control of the marina there. I still didn't think that was wrong—but something had made him forsake that entire plot and do a more literal march.

He could have reached Oban by now, but the wren kept confirming to me that he hadn't, and the simulacra told me that he was watching his arse.

"I don't like this," I said to Eilidh as we made our way back into the camp. "Part of me really wants to just race ahead and see what we can do to harry him, but if we can't manage to *stop him*, stop him—"

"That'll put everyone here in his line of retreat one way or another," she finished for me. "They're safer with us. And Calum?"

"What?"

"We're safer with them."

For a moment, I thought about that. She was right, of course.

On impulse, I slowed our approach when people came into sight, casting Keen Eye on a few folks at random.

Mairead MacKenzie
  Level 6 Duellist
  Affinities: Nature, Small Blades, Husbandry

Wu Liqin
  Level 5 Nourisher
  Affinities: Nature, Small Blades, Enchanting

After the first two, I had to pick my jaw up off the floor. These people had been level *one* two days ago, and they'd not fought a single person.

I hadn't so much as a ghost of a clue as to what a "nourisher" was, but that sounded like a community-oriented class if I'd ever seen one.

And an Enchanting affinity?

Eilidh clearly noticed me gawping, because she stopped. "What are you staring at?"

"There's folk who have hit levels five and six," I said. "Without fighting."

"What?" Eilidh's eyes bulged. "I know we found out people get experience from crafting, but that's huge!"

I looked at a few other people, wincing as my spirit dipped with the repeated use of Keen Eye.

The highest person I saw was level seven, a man who'd clearly taken to woodcraft with a vengeance, because when my eyes fell on him, he was veritably surrounded by wooden implements, everything from what looked like garden stakes to a hooked wooden knife so wicked, I'd likely jump in front of a moving train to avoid running into the business end of that monster.

For a moment, my brain seemed to expand yet again, almost zooming out to see the scene from above with intense clarity.

Not only did the ascension reward peaceable actions, but it also made the people who didn't fight invaluable. They were never lacking in value anyway, though plenty of people would think "apocalypse" and assume it went full-on survival-of-the-most-murderous, when reality was that humans only functioned in a society.

"I've got an idea to pass the time while we nip at Bawbag's heels," I murmured to Eilidh, snapping out of my galaxy-brained moment.

"I'm all ears."

"Reckon you can steal a notebook or something from the hotel?"

"Aye," Eilidh answered warily. "But why?"

"Ascension census. Let's find out what we're really working with now," I said, flashing her a genuine grin.

For a moment, I thought I'd somehow said word soup instead of a sentence from the way her eyes grew large, and her pupils dilated visibly—then she swallowed, her throat bobbing ever so slightly, and a flush crept up her neck.

"I'm on it," she said.

Then Eilidh turned and fled towards the hotel, leaving me wondering what the fuck had just happened and why the skin on my arms suddenly felt unusually warm.

We'd made it about six miles when I saw the white hart again.

This time, the animal stood directly in our path. Or, more correctly, my path, because I was at the head of our column for once. Eilidh and Rhona were on rear guard duty, and Iain and Meeksy had our flanks. Ronald was with me, the string-bean man not my favourite company, since he badgered me with questions so constantly that I couldn't even get into my Connection rhythm.

He stopped mid-sentence when he saw the hart, as did I.

The hart wasn't entirely white. Like I'd seen when we made the birlinn—which we had covered in a tarpaulin at the back of the hotel and splashed with muddy water in hopes it would be there when we could retrieve it—the white fur seemed to have spread out from the stag's snout.

It was the same one; I was certain of it.

He gazed at me with limpid brown eyes.

I could still feel the wren flitting about somewhere, the thread of spirit tenuous between us. Now, I reached out to the hart with Tàth as well.

The stag didn't take it. I'd not yet had the spell rejected by an animal, and I tried to pound the dent in my pride back out again almost as soon as it went crunch. But the hart's rebuff didn't feel reproachful. To the contrary, it felt almost as if he was gently trying to tell me he had other things to do.

Or he wanted something from me first?

I only had bonuses with birds and horses. Until that moment, I hadn't quite realised the difference they made. The wren could communicate with me. In a very birdlike way, of course, but communication I could understand, nonetheless. With the hart, while I felt kinship with the creature leftover from healing him with my magic, it was a bit like trying to understand someone underwater with no body language.

Awareness crept into my brain, of the three hundred people behind me slowing and murmuring, but I couldn't heed it.

The sensation was confusing. Impressions swirled through my mind, thoughts that I couldn't account for. I didn't think I could have created such a bond with him before now, not like I had with Sailean.

Sailean.

The moment I thought of her, awareness of the kitten poured back into my mind. She felt altogether closer than she should, but I didn't have time to puzzle out why.

Watching me without blinking, the white hart then pawed at the ground. With that, he turned and walked away, in the direction we'd been travelling.

"What—what was that about?" Ronald asked.

"No idea, mate," I said.

Unnerved, I reached out for the wren. He wasn't far at the moment; he'd paused to eat, it seemed, which meant he couldn't be that distressed by anything he'd seen.

The smoke still rose in the distance, and though it was still a few miles away from us, we were somehow gaining on it.

On Lord Bawbag.

I hated to ask it of the wren, but I gently prodded him to see if he would be willing to look closer.

To my surprise, he gave a trill of assent that I heard both in my mind and faintly from a tree a couple hundred metres away before I saw a small blur in the distance that vanished just as quickly.

"Let's keep moving," I said shortly to Ronald. "I don't think anything's wrong, just—keep your eyes open."

I heard a nervous chuckle ripple through the folks behind me.

Aye, nothing was wrong. Just the apocalypse, same as any other Tuesday.

Assuming it was actually Tuesday. I didnae ken.

We were travelling at a brisker pace to what we'd started with. Even the kids seemed hardier; when we paused at mile ten and asked if they needed a break, they said no. It had only taken us an hour to go four miles—that was walking at a clip for the average pre-ascension adult, let alone a person with half the stride length, if that.

Not long after the hart left, the smell of smoke reached my nose.

It wasn't fresh smoke billowing through the air but stale, damp. Like if you sat round a campfire all night with the wind blowing in your direction and then it rained on the clothes overnight when you tried to air them out.

This smoke, however, was not campfire smoke.

It had a strangely metallic scent to it, like the time I left an old tin kettle on the fire in a bothy with Mum as a kid— that acrid odour. And while for most of my life, I'd not come close enough to lightning striking to memorise the scent of ozone, fighting alongside mages who could conjure it had imprinted the smell onto my memory.

The combination of metal and lightning screamed *beithir* to me.

Ronald had thankfully gone silent with the hart's departure, and now I held up a hand to halt the column of people behind me.

"I need to look around," I said to Ronald. "Stay here. If you see a flare of Purifire, alert the other fighters."

I didn't give him time to argue. Instead, I set off with Connection in rhythm. We'd decided to risk staying on the roads, since going overland would slow us down, but whatever I was tracking lay beyond the beaten path, into the trees.

Immediately, I felt the effects of my new bonuses. It was as if every breath I drew into my lungs invigorated me.

Unfortunately, every breath I drew into my lungs also filled them with that burnt, tinny odour.

The source of the smell wasn't far. I hadn't expected it to be, but it still came as something of a surprise when I almost tripped over a tree root something had wrenched from the ground.

We weren't far from Angus's Garden. Just past it, in fact. It had been one of Mum's favourite spots, a lovely wee lochan near a large pine forest. It was somewhere in this forest that the smell was the strongest.

It didn't take long to find.

The road was still in view behind me when I found the broken trees. Their trunks were singed and crushed in places, blackened in others. When I cast Connection, my spirit brushed up against exactly what it expected: a memory of the beithir. Here. No longer ago than a few hours.

Looking around me, I tried to categorise what I saw.

Aside from the damage to the trees, the ground was torn up in several places. Torn roots bled sap onto the floor, and that wasn't the only blood.

Red stained the green carpet of moss and early spring shamrocks. There was no body to be found, but there was certainly enough blood to merit a corpse.

Of course, Bawbag would harvest anyone who had the double misfortune of dying in his vicinity.

That thought turned my stomach.

A tickle started in the back of my mind. It wriggled there, not invasive but increasingly unignorable.

When Connection turned up nothing farther than the patch of forest I stood in, I tried to shake the feeling off. I wanted to get a sense of how many people had been here. Bawbag himself had been here, as had the beithir. Scanning the forest floor, in a few bare patches of dirt, I found hoof prints.

Mac-Talla.

I had a skill that could help—one better suited than Connection.

Without hesitating, I cast the spell.

"Unsure what to expect" was an understatement.

My hair seemed to stand on end all over my body, and I jumped as ghostly silhouettes of stags appeared in the glade. They were faint, barely there at all, but present. And they had the unmistakeable feel of Bawbag's mind magic.

So he did have the puppeted harts with him. My stomach continued turning like I'd skewered it on a spit. They weren't alone—as I swivelled in a circle, I saw the thrashing beithir, shapes of people barely visible, back what they might call a safe distance. I didn't think there was such a thing as a safe distance where it concerned that monster.

I ranged out in a small spiral from where the beithir had occupied. Beyond the intruding tickle I couldn't shake, something else niggled at me.

If the beithir were under control, why would it have been thrashing so much?

That felt like the obvious question to ask, and perhaps the question alone was an answer to something else: if

Bawbag had the beithir fully under control, he would have already been in Oban.

Instead, we were gaining on him.

Either he truly thought he could take over an entire town with his small group of murder-powered bastards and abused creatures or . . . he was simply too stubborn to divert from the course he'd set.

I didn't have time to work out more than that, because even as I resisted the urge to reach back behind my head and scratch my skull as if it would relieve the itch in my brain, something small and brown pelted into the clearing, skidding to a halt at my feet.

Staring down at it, I almost couldn't make a single word form. Finally, I managed exactly one.

"*Sailean?*"

The tiny fur-based missile that had come flying out of nowhere pell-mell and landed in front of me was Sailean, also known as the Scottish wildcat kitten I'd left in Oban for supposed safekeeping.

She didn't seem to need the recovery time I did, apparently. The tiny kitten launched herself at my leg, climbing me like a cat tree until she reached my shoulder, purring wildly.

I thanked every possible god—mostly Eilidh, to be honest, since she'd made it—for my armour.

Kitten needle feet were not to be trifled with.

"Sailean, dè fon ghrèin—"

Before I could finish asking the cat what in the world she was doing here, another one arrived, this one in the form of a human who only shared the first three letters of her name with "cat."

"Catrìona?" I asked incredulously.

Catrìona Whyte, Iain's mum and one of my own mum's best friends, half collapsed against a tree, scowling at the kitten on my shoulder.

Sailean, of course, was entirely unmoved by the display of disapprobation. The strange thing was that I couldn't actually feel her—other than the usual way. The bond I normally had with her still felt tickly and muted, as if something were blocking it.

"That wee bugger has just made me run a half marathon to get to you," Catrìona said between gasps, pointing at Sailean. "Gave me a fright, too. She bolted out of Angus's arms a couple hours ago, and I was the only one they thought could both track her and not be spotted myself."

My mind shuffled through all the information in that sentence, belatedly dredging up the fact that Angus was the man who had taken me, Eilidh, and Rhona in the night we'd staggered into Oban. As for the rest . . .

"I couldn't sense either of you with Connection," I said warily.

"I'd be surprised if you could," Catrìona answered wryly, seemingly recovered after only a few seconds to breathe. "I've got a shield spell that's meant to make me and my immediate party virtually undetectable, along with anything I target. Works for three hours and then takes two days to reset."

That was a hell of a defensive spell. And it made me feel ever so slightly better knowing the trade-off was so huge. The momentary panic of Connection failing me when I needed the most lessened accordingly, but I would need to remember that it didn't make me omniscient.

"Thank you for protecting this little monster," I said, a swell of something altogether too warm and fuzzy growing in my chest as I reached up to give the kitten's cheek a scritch. "We ought to go up to the road. Unless you fancy trotting back to Oban the way you came, you're welcome to join us as we attempt to skewer Lord Bawbag in the back."

Catrìona's eyes narrowed at the mention of his name. "I'd prefer to join you. Everyone in Oban is on tenterhooks waiting for him to arrive and kick off—frustrating to buggery."

"I think I know why he's keeping you all in such suspense."

I plucked Sailean off my shoulder and held her to my chest instead. She squirmed a bit, nuzzling against my collarbone. Her tiny purr vibrated my skin. I winced when those little needle feet found a piece of exposed throat.

"I don't suppose you happened to bring her carrier?" I asked hopefully as we turned towards the road.

Catrìona was demonstrably *not* my mother and the only animal here was a cat, but from the withering look she directed at me, I definitely thought I'd just earnt a bed in the doghouse.

The appearance of Catrìona was, much to my own internal sheepishness, overshadowed by the sudden arrival of a kitten.

I kept her close to my chest—literally—as I hurried about, giving a quick rundown of what I'd found and what I suspected to those who had become the de facto leaders of our motley crew's smaller cells.

A few times, I had to repeat myself, because most Scots will never see a Scottish wildcat face to face, but even if Sailean had just been the average moggy, I reckon folk would have still gone full pleading face at the sight of her. Once my words sank in, though, the mood sank right along with them.

The air shifted with the thought of the beithir. It wasn't just that most of the people there couldn't so much as imagine it—though that was part of it—but that it raised the already-high stakes.

Lord Bawbag and his brand of bampotery were one thing; actual, literal monsters were something else altogether. Something with more teeth and venom.

We kept hashing things out as we moved, getting Catrìona up to date on our progress even as she updated us on Oban.

Like us, Oban had discovered that crafting's experience gain was higher than combat's—and in a town that liked to work with its hands, that meant people were jumping to take advantage, with everything from throwing stars to macrame.

But we each had other salient discoveries to share. The news of community bonuses made Catrìona's eyes widen so far I thought they might actually pop out of her head.

She repaid that favour by telling us that Oban's people had found out that artisans who knew how to make things could fabricate blueprints—blueprints that could teach others how to craft them using the ascension's spirit methods rather than the old-fashioned way. Anyone with hands-on experience had set about with a feverish furore to create a library of blueprints, making one copy of each to store and others to share.

Everyone in hearing distance veritably swooned at that. The possibilities were staggering. Throughout history, humans have survived only by sharing knowledge. It was always war that got the attention, but the true notable aspect of humanity was our resilience and our teamwork— and the ascension was making it increasingly clear that it had upped the ante on our potential.

While sure, it was impressive to see what one individual could pull off alone, the truest feats of human existence were always what we could make happen *together*. It was how we'd put human feet on the moon and at the bottom of the sea alike.

With the knowledge now that we were absolutely and without a doubt *not* the only intelligent life in the universe? I'd put money on scientists somewhere already working on how to talk to them.

As it was, though, it took one pathetic hamster—me— to realise something obvious as we walked.

I still carried Sailean, now in a sling someone had gifted me, and she snoozed as if the rocking motion of my walking soothed her.

Rhona happened to be on one of her return appearances, and she had been walking beside me for a few minutes already. When the realisation struck, she didn't miss a beat.

"What is it?" she asked.

"I need Eilidh," I said, turning to scan over my shoulder where I thought she was.

"Finally, he admits it."

"What?" I said.

"What?" Rhona gave me a look as if she'd not said anything.

I decided to ignore the comment. "Both of us have a crafting quest. It could get us some more experience and also help us prepare. But we'd have to bugger off for a bit."

"We've got this. Go do whatever," Rhona told me with a bravado I wasn't sure was strictly real. Then she held out her arms and made grabby hands at the kitten. "Gimme."

Reluctantly, I handed Sailean over to Rhona, fighting the urge to look over my shoulder at the kitten as I made my way against the flow of survivors.

Ronald had chosen a post somewhere in the middle of the column where I couldn't see him immediately, but I did see Ealasaid. The older woman had a determined look on her face as she walked along the right flank of the group, and I felt a *thub-thub* of spirit when I got close to her that told me she was practicing Connection.

She looked up before I got *that* close, though, which would have confirmed it if I'd not already sensed her activity.

"Calum, what is it, a ghràidh?" Her dark eyes lit up at the sight of me, and she puffed up her chest. "I've increased Connection to level three!"

"That's fantastic!" I said. "'S math a rinn sibh! I'm looking for Eilidh—I don't suppose you've seen her?"

Ealasaid pointed backwards. "Air ar cùlaibh."

I murmured a quick thanks, confident that she and the others would keep the group well covered in case of emergency. Through the wren's eyes, I could tell Bawbag was still on the move north, but that didn't eliminate the possibility of more simulacra.

Eilidh was with her grandmother when I reached her,

though they walked in silence, arm in arm. The older woman looked tired, but she moved with the same fluidity I had seen in Ealasaid. The ascension's effects on ageing were something that would merit discourse one of these days—just not now.

"Can I borrow you?" I asked Eilidh, to a surprised look from both herself and Mòrag.

"Of course," she said slowly.

"If there's any trouble," I began, and Mòrag waved a hand at me.

"Siuthadaibh," Mòrag said, telling us to bugger off.

I guess part of being in a community was trusting said community to do what was necessary. I had to tell myself as I walked that I didn't *want* to be the one everyone turned to for answers or protection; that was a weight I neither needed nor wanted on my shoulders.

As soon as we were a short distance from the column, with Eilidh gazing after them wearing an unreadable expression, I pulled the petrified hearts from my inventory.

That got her attention.

"What do you want to do with those?" she asked warily.

"We're meant to craft some things for a quest, yeah?" I said.

"You want us to stop and craft things?" Eilidh now turned that unreadable expression on me, and I was starting to get an inkling of disapprobation from it.

"Yes. For the quest. Since we already raided Bawbag's manor, our bit and Rhona's alchemy bit are all that remains. If we finish the damn quest—"

"We get rewards before we have to face the sentient scrotum himself," Eilidh finished, her voice sour. "Aye, I understand."

"We can catch up to them in no time," I said.

"I'm not worried about that."

Planting my staff in front of me on the road, I was starting to feel exasperated. "Then what *are* you worried about?"

"We don't have time to craft enough armour for everyone," Eilidh said softly. "If we did, that would make me feel better."

Oh.

"As soon as we're close enough to Bawbag for it to matter, we'll think of something," I told her. "We're not the only crafters here anymore, and the bairns won't be following us into battle."

"I know. It's not just them I'm worried about."

"I know."

We stood there for a moment, time slipping away like grains of sand through the bottleneck of an hourglass.

Then, without a word, each of us started digging things out of inventory. I got the petrified hearts, the goshawk talons, the goshawk pinions. Eilidh had the giant rabbit pelt, along with a plethora of other items I couldn't identify at a glance, but a sniff said she still had trout oil left.

Eilidh's face changed again, smoothing out. "Let's get started. If there's anything you want to add to this experiment, now's the time."

She was the armour crafter; I was a woodcrafter. For a moment, I wasn't sure what I could even contribute to this quest item.

I pulled up the quest to look at what it said once more.

Work together to craft infused armour (6 sets) (Calum Green, Eilidh MacIntosh)

That was pretty damn clear—the system expected me to do *something* here.

"Are we making entirely new armour?" I asked Eilidh.

"I think that's what it wants." She didn't sound certain.

Looking around, I pulled on Tursa to get a better lay of the land. The trees nearby were mostly oak, which suited. I could also see a rowan, and just beyond that was a beech.

Eilidh made a frustrated noise when I started to walk towards the trees. "What are you doing?"

"Getting supplies so I can be a more useful contributor."

She fell silent at that, and I stepped into the small copse. We weren't in a forest here, not really, but even getting close to the trees made me feel more at ease.

I went to the oak first, and while this one was not as insistent as the first I'd communed with, it still reached out to me with curiosity. Communicating my needs came more fluidly this time. The trees here weren't like the ones on the other side of Loch Awe; they hadn't experienced the loss of their ecosystem's more mobile members. But they were not isolated from the others, either. These trees shuddered with uneasiness when they tapped into my memories.

With spirit forming Connection that flowed into the trees' own intertwined world, I felt the ripple through their network that told me they were conferring in their own arboreal way.

It both was and wasn't like it had been before. Again, I heard the branches moving overhead and the thumps of donated branches touching down, but this time, there was more of a sense of purpose.

When I pulled back, I had to brace myself against the ground with my staff. I went about wordlessly picking up the branches the trees had offered, piling them into my free arm until I could carry no more.

The trees had impressed upon me what we needed to do, but it was up to me and Eilidh to see it through.

· · ⟨⟨ ⟩⟩ · ·

If Eilidh felt at all dubious about seeing me come back with an armful of kindling, she didn't show it. Instead, she had been busy arranging all of her own crafting items. And rearranging, it seemed.

Was she . . . nervous?

I separated the wood out by type of tree. If we could pull this off? We'd have some seriously badass armour. If not, we might be going into battle looking like we were in terrible Ent cosplay.

There was a possibility that the latter was still on the table either way. We could end up with seriously badass armour that looked like terrible Ent cosplay. Though if that happened, maybe the element of surprise would work in our favour, especially if I could convince the others to bellow something in Entish.

We could keep that particular plan of attack in a back pocket.

Maybe it wasn't just Eilidh who was nervous.

Performance anxiety about crafting—who knew?

"We need six entire sets," Eilidh muttered, "but they shouldn't be all the same, should they?"

I wasn't sure she was talking to me, though that didn't sound like a truly rhetorical question.

"Who do we start with?" I asked, and Eilidh looked up so sharply that I thought she must not have been talking to me at all—or realised she was speaking aloud.

"Rhona," she said. "She's growing in leaps and bounds, but I worry if she has to face down Bawbag in the flesh— ugh, forget I combined those words—she might not manage to keep it together."

"Not entirely sure I'll manage to keep it together." I gave her a wry, lopsided smile. "Every day that goes by makes me want to feed that man to a passing shark more and more."

"You'll have to queue for that, I think," Eilidh said under her breath. Then she let out a long sigh. "But I also think there will be no shortage of people aiming for creative ways to see his end. Letting him get stabbed by his own beithir would be poetic."

"Aye, it would."

When we both stood in silence for a moment, I echoed Eilidh's sigh, nodding towards the materials.

It was strangely intimate, both of us kneeling to collaborate on something magical without being in a life-or-death situation or in the company of hundreds of other people. Just the two of us felt far more personal.

Perhaps it wasn't that strange at all. Spirit radiated off of Eilidh like body heat, melding with mine effortlessly.

Since I wasn't the armourer here, I let Eilidh take the lead.

I watched, transfixed, as she traced the tip of her dagger on the giant rabbit pelt, a perfect freehand outline of each part of a pattern only she could see.

To my eyes, it was only a series of shapes at first, but when she reached for blackthorn and pine sap, the elements began to rise into the air, buoyed on flows of spirit. When I opened myself to her spirit, lending her my own, the design seemed to come to life in front of my face.

Blackthorn was a powerful guard against malignant spirit, and on impulse, I reached for one of the petrified rabbit hearts. I instinctively held it up to the centre of the chest piece. As I watched, it absorbed into the leather. Not like a liquid, but almost the way the roots and fungus in the ancient pine's empty hole had woven through one another. The effect was, at first, grotesque, but when the vein-like tendrils of the petrified heart touched the long, sharp spikes of blackthorn, they fanned out almost all at once, symmetrical and foreboding.

This was for Rhona, and she needed stealth, swift strikes. Rowan was in my hand almost without my guidance, and its greyish bark lent a silvery sheen to the armour. Almost as if we were draping it in mist.

Eilidh hadn't been with us for the goshawk, nor had she seen Rhona's gallivanting about with the pinions, so when she reached for the enormous feathers, I nearly faltered.

I didn't know what she could possibly do with feathers that long. But even as the chest piece completed, Eilidh pulled the pauldrons to the fore.

There were a number of smaller pinions, I saw. Eilidh dug through them without looking, finding some that we had shorn off with my Purifire and Rhona's daggers. These, we began to layer at the shoulders.

Threads of spirit wove them together with plied strands of spun rabbit fur that had sloughed off the pelt.

The goshawk had also left us with its eight razor-sharp talons. Four of them made their home in Rhona's armour: two on each elbow where she would now be able to turn basic bludgeoning elbow strike into a devastating slash.

Piece by piece, we built armour for the youngest of our circle's core members. Working in tandem with Eilidh made it impossible for me to ignore the exacting care that radiated off of her—and I presumed the same was true of me. I'd already watched Rhona almost die more than once. If I never saw such a sight again, it would be too soon.

When we were finished, we both sat back, panting.

In front of us was, if not a masterpiece, at least something that didn't look like we'd cobbled it together out of Mum and Da's pots and pans.

A slight sheen of sweat coated Eilidh's forehead, and with the sun trying to nudge its way through the clouds above, she glowed in the brightening light.

To distract myself from the fact that we were both perspiring and breathing hard—and in a heightened emotional and sensory state—I hastily cast Keen Eye on the new armour.

Purifying Stalker Armour—This six-piece armour set has been carefully infused with druidic and arcane elements to create a cohesive whole that is not only highly resistant to the corrupted elements of the anomalies noted in Argyll but also is geared to combat them outright.

The armour has been fed with will and pathos to encourage its resistance to arcane corruption and as such, attacks versus anomalous creatures receive a bonus: +15% chance to inflict bleeding damage over five seconds, +3% critical chance. Additionally, the use of the purifying properties of pine sap, rowan, and the protective influence of blackthorn help the wearer resist any ill effects of coming into contact with the corruption with a bonus: +17% corruption resistance. Wearing multiple items from this set provides the following:

2 pieces: Wearer's stealth abilities activate 20% faster

4 pieces: Wearer's stealth abilities activate 30% faster

6 pieces: Wearer's stealth abilities activate 50% faster, and if the wearer is within three levels of a higher-levelled opponent, the opponent will be unable to detect the armour's wearer without: 50 Mind, 50 Spirit, or a detection ability at Level 5 or higher.

Holy shit.

I met Eilidh's gaze over the armour. My notifications had lit up, and I couldn't be arsed to care.

In her eyes, I saw the same eager hunger reflected as I felt.

One down, five sets to go.

With Connection, I could sense how far away the group was getting from us—with their increasing Agility and Stamina from the activity, the answer was creeping higher with every moment, but after that first set of armour, both Eilidh and I knew we'd made the right decision.

We set to the rest with similar determination, creating armour first for Iain—bonuses to speed and evasion as well as strength—and then for Meeksy. Meeksy's was tougher; as he was a healer, we piled on the rowan and beech for the protective and nurturing elements, but we also needed his armour to protect him from harm as best we could. For that, we used oak and hazel, layering them together to form something paradoxically stolid and flexible alike.

Ronald, we still didn't know well. The most we had to go on was "teacher, bit touchy, can outrun anyone we know." Because of that, we plied him up with smaller goshawk feathers for speed and beech to boost his energy levels and endurance.

When we came to Eilidh's, I could tell she was eager to fix things she perceived as flaws in what she had previously made for herself. *I* couldnae see a flaw when I looked at her current armour, but I knew that was my own bias talking. What I didn't know was whether that bias was my lack of expertise in armour crafting or simply the growing pull of admiration.

In game-world terms, Eilidh was our tank. A peek at her Constitution nearly staggered me when she showed me. Mine was nineteen, which wasn't great but wasn't horrible. Eilidh's? Hers was *fifty*. Her Constitution stat rivalled my

Mind stat, which was sat at sixty-seven, but had less direct effect on whether or not something could make me dead.

Her Strength was a whopping fifty-three.

Eilidh's armour, we made of oak.

The rabbit hide provided a template; the wood gave it form. With our combined practise, we had grown more efficient, but this time, I reached out with my personal affinity with the tree. I whispered through my spirit, which responded with a rustle of leaves as the wood moulded itself into just that: leaves. Each no larger than a thumbnail, they fanned out across the design in an intricate scale-mail pattern.

Hazel lent its pliability, rowan its otherworldly protection, and the petrified heart again provided an extra bulwark as it lent its essence to our task. When we finished, she had a suit of armour that wouldn't have looked out of place in a fantasy blockbuster—and this armour was beyond fully functional.

Purifying Oaken Leaf-Mail—This six-piece armour set has been carefully infused with druidic and arcane elements to create a cohesive whole that is not only highly resistant to the corrupted elements of the anomalies noted in Argyll but also is geared to combat them outright.

The armour has been fed with will and pathos to encourage its resistance to arcane corruption and as such, attacks versus anomalous creatures receive a bonus: +18% chance to stagger an opponent over five seconds upon hit and upon being hit, +12% damage resistance. Additionally, the use of the purifying properties of hazel, rowan, and the protective influence of blackthorn help the wearer resist any ill effects of coming into contact with the corruption with a bonus: +15% corruption resistance. Wearing multiple items from this set provides the following:

2 pieces: Wearer's vanguard abilities do 10% more damage

4 pieces: Wearer's vanguard abilities do 15% more damage

6 pieces: Wearer's vanguard abilities do 20% more damage, and if the wearer's Strength is more than ten points above their opponent's, they will gain a 10% chance to stun on their next basic attack, with a 50% duration increase on active stunning skills and spells

I could practically feel Eilidh itching to get that armour on the moment we finished it. A small twitch appeared above her left eyebrow as if her valiant effort to not simply snatch it, strip, and change on the spot needed an immediate outlet—no matter how small.

She managed to restrain herself, showing probably far more patience than I ever would.

"That leaves you," she said, tearing her eyes reluctantly away from her new armour. "Are we starting fresh or—"

"I want to keep what I have," I told her. "I want to see if we can improve it."

"Okay." Eilidh bit her lip uncertainly. "If you're sure."

"I'm sure." When she didn't move, I looked at her sideways. "What? You think I should start from scratch?"

"Erm. No? You just—you have to take off what you're wearing for us to improve it."

Oh.

It should have been a non-issue—I was pretty sure we'd all gone skinny dipping at one point during a heat wave when we'd fled Glasgow for Loch Long. But I suddenly felt like a gangly virgin all over again, seventeen and shy but trying to act like I got naked in front of folk I fancied *all* the time.

Bloody hell.

I turned slightly away from Eilidh as I removed the armour. Fuck. That's why this was doing my head in—I'd just admitted that I fancied her. I could feel the tips of my ears burning, a strange feeling considering they had changed shape. The heated sensation of blood-rushed skin and cartilage was in a slightly different place to where it had been before.

Hurriedly, I stripped off the rest of my armour pieces, which didn't even leave me naked since of course I had the undergarments she'd made beneath the armour itself.

Even so, I felt like I was on stage full Monty under a sea of floodlights.

Get it together, hamster man.

After making five other sets of armour that were brand new and far more badass, mine looked almost painfully prosaic.

The constant wear had scuffed it, and though I'd kept it clean with Purifire, the leather could have used a good oiling anyway. If nothing else, hopefully this would get it up to snuff again.

In what had become our routine, I used Connection to open myself up to spirit. It was the arcane equivalent of holding out a hand to someone where they could reach out and take it. Eilidh seemed to do that without thinking, her spirit settling against mine like interlacing fingers.

One thing was for certain: the sensation hadn't grown any *less* intimate.

For mine, I knew I wanted the petrified heart, knew I wanted the oak and rowan. But beyond that, I really wasn't certain. When Eilidh reached for one of the cellulose bladders of pine sap, which had been used for other armours already, I thought she was right to. I still didn't quite know what I felt was missing.

It wasn't until I glanced over at my staff that I felt it.

The living weapon.

My staff, Brac-Meanmna, was alive.

For the most part, it was content to go with the flow, unfazed by my choices. Now, for the first time in a while, I felt its desire.

Eilidh started when I reached for the staff, which lay next to my knee on the tarmac. I felt her confusion and apprehension ripple through our combined spirit, followed by a tentative brush of her mind against the staff—and its consciousness.

While I wasn't looking at her directly, I still saw her eyes widen out of the corner of mine. Without so much as looking, her hand moved with perfect precision for an element we had not used except for with Rhona's armour at the very beginning: the remaining goshawk talons.

At first, I wasn't sure what the staff wanted. A goshawk's foot had three forward-facing toes and one rear-facing one to grip with.

Then it showed me.

The bloody thing wanted *claws*.

I didn't dare refuse; instead, I took the talons from Eilidh's hand, feeling as our spirit melded with the staff's.

And that wasn't all.

Not only did I feel the stirring of spirit within the living weapon for the first time on a conscious level, but it reached for its *own* material. Both Eilidh and I stared as a low-lying juniper on the road's shoulder shuddered and dropped a handful of spiky branches.

They rose up on a wave of spirit until they touched the butt of the staff, and the juniper seemed to elongate, snaking up and around the wooden shaft like vines of ivy.

It left a pattern of stem and sharp needles ingrained into the whorls of oak, and at the centre of the haft, those vines pulled away from the wood to form a claw, waiting for the talons in my hand.

Dumbstruck, I held them out, and the staff took hold of them, growing around the bases of the talons like flesh until a goshawk claw protruded from the shaft of the weapon.

Eilidh and I both watched as that taloned wooden claw flexed and then retracted, slipping back to meld into the shaft and leaving a raised grip that hadn't been there before. Just before the smug satisfaction of the living weapon faded into dormancy once more, I got an image of that claw reaching out to hold onto a groove at the centre of my back. Until now, I'd been carrying it in its leather sling, which worked fine, if a bit cumbersomely. Sometimes the staff slipped down as I walked to bump into the backs of my knees.

This whole time, Eilidh had been working with my armour even as she kept one eye on the staff to see what it was doing. Now, it was nearly done.

In appearance, it didn't look too different to how it had started. It was in the details where I could see the shifts. The leather seemed to have grown veins, for lack of a better word. Or branches. Roots? This strange embossing covered every surface with near symmetry.

When our combined spirit faded, I was simultaneously underwhelmed and bewildered by the staff's own intervention.

But I didn't have time to fuss about it. We'd only been working for about a half an hour, yet that was plenty long enough for our people to get a few miles down the road from us. I quickly donned my armour once more and, absent the leather sling for the staff, I jumped when I felt the staff's clawed hand grip between my shoulder blades.

Squirming, I tried to minimise the obviousness of my

discomfort, turning to help Eilidh quickly store the crafting items once more.

She looked stunning in her new armour, the leaf—literally leaves—mail moving with her as she bent to pick up the now-empty vessel of pine sap. Had I caught a glimpse of her like this a couple months ago, it would have sent my head spinning even then. Gone was the straight-laced, studious woman I'd known. Even on nights out, she'd seemed to never let down her guard. Now, in some ways, the edges had softened, but that was only the effect of whatever had made her choose to trust me.

In the place of her previous coldness was a compassionate warrior, fit and fierce and competent.

I must have been staring, because she turned to look at me, a question in her eyes, as if she'd felt my gaze upon her.

Caught out, I fumbled for words. "I was just thinking how much has changed. For the better, in spite of— apocalypse."

The expression that greeted those words was a flash of her old self, the wary prickles I'd taken for so long to mean her dislike. Now I knew them for what they were: her attempt to guard against getting herself hurt.

Her wariness held on for a long, heavy moment that hung in the air between us even as I held my breath. But after that moment, it faded, leaving a curious softness to her face.

"Yes."

That was all she said, and then the last pile of gathered wood vanished into her inventory, and she took off at a sprint, leaving me no choice but to follow.

THIRTY

The golden glow of notifications hovered in my vision, but I still didn't trust myself to run and read at the same time.

That said, I did use the time to inspect my improved armour.

Purifying Hardened Leather Chestplate (Set Item 1/6)

Fashioned from oak-dyed ascended sheep leather, this chestplate is cured and treated with brown trout oil and beeswax for water resistance and reinforced with giant centipede chitin and blackthorn to add greater protection against ranged and melee attacks.

This item has been upgraded with the use of petrified hearts, rowan wood, oak wood, and pine sap and is not only highly resistant to the corrupted elements of the anomalies noted in Argyll but also is geared to combat them outright.

The armour has been fed with will and pathos to encourage its resistance to arcane corruption and as such, attacks versus anomalous creatures receive a bonus: +10% chance to create a bolt of Purifire on hit and upon being hit, +15% damage resistance. Additionally, the use of the purifying properties of rowan and the protective influence of this armour's initial crafting with blackthorn help the wearer resist any ill effects of coming into contact with the corruption with a bonus: +15% corruption resistance. Wearing multiple items from this set provides the following:

2 pieces: Strike your enemy with 10% of whatever damage they inflict upon you; wearer's Wild affinity skills do 10% more damage

3 pieces: Generate 50% spirit for every point of damage you take

4 pieces: Armour will actively channel spirit from your surroundings to keep you dry; wearer's Wild affinity skills do 15% more damage

6 pieces: Wearer's Wild affinity skills do 20% more damage; immunity to backstab damage when staff affixed to chestplate

I did a double take at the last one, feeling a surge of smugness from the living weapon attached to my back. It wasn't total immunity to being backstabbed, but if something managed to evade Connection and my perception skills and got close enough to stab me when I was unarmed?

Yeah, I'd say that would make itself worthwhile even if it only ever happened once.

Catching up to the others took longer than I expected. Not by *much*, because Eilidh and I were faster than even Olympic qualifiers by now, but they'd still made impressive progress, especially with a dozen weans in the mix.

Just as the group came into sight as we rounded a curve in the road, my vision flashed, and I stumbled.

World second!

In Apsáalooke Nation within the north-central United States, there has been a second community ascension. A community has performed a mythic feat.

The people of Crow Agency have demonstrated their under-standing of one of the ascension's most basic cornerstones: a community is stronger than the sum of its parts.

Together, in a time of desperation and great need, the Apsáalooke people's combined spirit, pathos, and will soothed the ire of a legendary thunderbird brought forth by the ascension. Thought by many to be the mythical creature that gave the Apsàalooke—known in English as Crow Nation—their name, the thunderbird is known for the eponymous thunder it creates by flapping its wings. By approaching this legend with respect and trust, the people of Crow Agency have forged a bond that will ripple throughout your planet's future.

The entirety of my skin burst into gooseflesh.

I had no connection to the Apsáalooke people—I couldn't remember ever hearing that name before—but in that moment, I felt a sudden, deep kinship with them along with a flare of triumph.

We may have been the first here, in Scotland, to achieve a community ascension, but across the world, the Apsáalooke had been the second. All would know—not just what they had done, but that what they had done was *possible*.

We would not be the last.

This would spread across our planet. Hand by hand and bit by bit, humans could and *would* adapt.

Heady and potent hope flooding me, I found my footing again, and not a moment too soon.

Even as the group ahead slowed and reacted to the projected message, my habitual pulse of Connection caught wind of a familiar presence on the far side of the column.

Already, I felt ripples of alarm.

"Wait!" I called out, projecting my voice with Òran na Cloiche. "Weapons down! She's not a threat!"

Eilidh turned to me, worried brow creasing at the sound of my words, and when I put on a burst of speed to close the remaining distance, she matched my pace.

There were cries of fear from the group, and while those closest to us turned to see me and Eilidh running, it wasn't fast enough.

A flash of lightning split the air, bringing with it the shriek of children a moment later.

"STOP!" My voice boomed across the stretch of road, and I vaulted the remaining few yards, drawing my staff from my back and spinning to face my fledgling community.

At my side, Eilidh began to glow gold with spirit and will, and before I could react, a concussive wave of energy burst from her gathered magic.

Ronald was closest, his shillelagh raised in his hand, but there were others I recognised as rowers from the birlinn and some I'd seen training with Iain and Meeksy. Everyone in fighting stance rocked back on their feet, stunned by Eilidh's spell.

I couldn't see Iain or Meeksy themselves—or Rhona.

Cursing to myself, I spun to face the reason for this altercation, already forming as contrite an apology as I could manage. In all of . . . everything . . . I'd not even imagined we'd see her again, not outwith her bower.

But here she was.

The glaistig had found us.

She stood in front of me with fire in her eyes, wiping a smear of blood from her nose.

To the side, I saw Diana restraining Andy, whose knuckles bore a splash of red and whose face contained a potent mixture of horror and rage.

"I am truly sorry," I said to the glaistig after healing her nose.

"You did not harm me."

"It doesn't matter—it still happened." I scratched the back of my head, skin buzzing and jangled. "Humans can be tetchy around newness."

"Humans," the glaistig said as if trying out the word. "You are not solely human."

It didn't matter that we'd moved a short distance away from the bulk of the crowd; people heard that. Out of the corner of my eye, I saw more than one surreptitious hand go up to feel an ear.

"Maybe not," I said dryly, "but we still have human habits, and a lot of the ascended creatures we encounter want us dead."

My hopes that maybe Andy would find some solace in magic seemed to have petered out with his ill-considered punch. I sighed.

"I do not think it is supposed to be that way." The glaistig's voice held an ache of sadness and bewilderment, as if she felt the grip of the emotion without being able to identify how she felt it at all. "That is not why I came. I came because you have done what I hoped, and you have restored balance to the blighted lands."

That sounded somewhat encouraging, though we already knew what we'd done, and I wasn't sure we could afford any more delays. Her next words, though, disabused me of any suspected futility of her visit.

"I think something else is rising to take its place," the glaistig said softly, and her peat-dark eyes held a glimmer of something I truly never wanted to see in a preternatural creature's expression: fear.

"The anomalies," I said, mirroring her volume.

Her gaze snapped to mine from where she'd been staring into the middle distance. She took half a step back with a crunch of gravel under her hooves. "You have encountered them?"

"Yes."

With as much economy of words as I could manage, I told her about what we'd seen, the foxes and the surreal giant rabbit.

Behind me, the crowd grew somewhat restless. Now that they were not fearing danger from this front, I thought their minds had returned to the known evil.

"I'm not sure what we can do about it," I told the glaistig. "At least not now, not with Bawbag headed towards Oban with the beithir."

The glaistig's eyes grew distant. "A piteous beast," she murmured.

"I'm not entirely sure 'piteous' is a word I'd use to describe the beithir, but that said, I wouldn't wish such a fate on Auld Clootie himself." I paused, torn between going on and apologising for being glib. After a moment, I settled for the former, with a twist. "Why do you say it is piteous?"

"A beithir is formed of death, and all it knows is revenge. People fear snakes and kill them; a beithir is what happens when one is killed without proper care." The glaistig returned her gaze to my own. "Some would say the beithir gives its victims more of a chance than it was given itself."

That was . . . a take I had not expected to consider.

Those we had saved from the beithir were indeed safe and

unharmed, if traumatised. I didn't think the plunge into fresh water to heal the venom from the beithir's scorpion-like sting eradicated the memory of that tail running someone through. Even if it did, *I* remembered what that looked like. Also, some weren't so "lucky," and the first strike ended up fatal.

Couldn't heal a crushed skull.

Feeling the antsy mood behind me increasing with each use of Connection, I tried to snap back to some semblance of direction.

"Did you come simply to warn us about the anomaly?" I asked.

"Simply?" The glaistig's eyes narrowed. "There is nothing simple about it. If it comes here in force, your people will perish at each other's hands. What brutishness is worst in them will be amplified. What impulses their decency restrains will run wild. What fears they have will grow until they are consumed."

I hadn't realised I'd started holding my breath with her first few sentences, but now I let it out. "Is this the choice you mentioned?"

Before, I had assumed the choice would be saving the survivors or saving Oban. Maybe that had been naïve of me.

"Both are threats," the glaistig said slowly. "Perhaps your people will defeat their attacker without your help; perhaps they will not. Perhaps if you leave now, you can track and eradicate the anomaly; perhaps it will instead make you its pawn."

That was enough to send a chill through me, and from the way murmured conversations around me cut off sharply, I wasn't the only one.

A voice I hadn't heard in some time burst through the air.

"So you're saying our choices are to become Bawbag's meat-suit zombies or this anomaly's?" The shrill voice held a thread of terror too strong to be called an undercurrent.

I turned to face Andy. The kid looked gaunt, haunted. Beside him, Diana wore an unreadable expression, her lips pressed tightly together and her brows knitted to form a crease in her forehead. She raised one hand to place it upon her grandson's back, but after a moment seemed to think better of it, and the hand fell listlessly to her side.

The lad still had a series of spots breaking out across his face, and his blue eyes darted back and forth, back and forth as he seemed to look everywhere but at the glaistig.

For all she *was* a preternatural creature and her dominion that of the animals, as she looked at Andy's wild-eyed anxiety that poured off of him in waves, the glaistig's head cocked to the side. She took two steps towards him, her hooves clopping on the tarmac. At first, he lurched backwards, but after a moment, he stared into her eyes, and his face went slack.

"What are you doing to him?" Diana asked pleadingly, her own fear bubbling over whatever wall she'd been keeping it behind. "He's young—he didn't know better. He's just frightened, and—"

"I am helping him," the glaistig said. "As I have helped others touched by the evil that did this to him."

With that, she reached out a pale, greyish hand, touching it to the side of the lad's face.

I couldn't see what she did, and at first, I hovered anxiously myself. Her dominion was animals. But after a beat, I realised I was being a numpty.

Humans—or whatever we were becoming—*were* animals.

Watching with spirit as much as with my eyes, I felt the peace that emanated from the glaistig, her soft insistence on his attention and her gently offered forgiveness.

THIRTY-ONE

No one spoke for a while after the glaistig left.

We had decided to pause for food, since the increased stamina had kept everyone going long enough that we all needed to eat, and our bodies weren't yet used to sussing out their new rhythms.

Despite not feeling hungry, I made myself spoon the stew Nan gave me into my mouth with my magically crafted spork. I didn't really taste it; everyone else seemed as on edge as I felt.

Eilidh and I had distributed the new armours, and then she had gone around to the other higher-levelled people who wanted to fight, adjusting the old armours we were no longer using to fit new people. Now, she sat cross-legged on the tarmac across from me and Meeksy. Iain paced beside us, taking a bite every few steps without even looking at his aim. Ronald sat in lotus position, looking far more sanguine than anyone else, but that might have just been that he seemed to be meditating successfully. I had to hand it to the man; if mindfulness was about existing in the present moment, I thought it would take a whole hell of a lot of willpower to want to exist in this one. Personally, I'd prefer a moment where I felt a bit less like I was about to be the meat filling in a rapidly forming evil sandwich.

Rhona fiddled with the feathers on her own new armour, and though I knew she was ecstatic about it—she had practically crowed when she saw it—her young face was pensive, her brown hair pulled back in a severe ponytail.

"I can't keep just *reacting* to things that come our way," I finally said, breaking the silence. "It was understandable at first, but if we have any hope of defeating Bawbag and whatever it is that is coming up from the south, we need an actual plan."

The wren had paused for a nap a couple miles away, and I was partially tempted to release him from our tenuous bond. That seemed like the wrong idea, however.

"There haven't been any other simulacra," Eilidh said, drawing out each word as if she wasn't sure she thought it was relevant.

"Reckon that means he bought our ploy?" Iain somehow managed to get that question out of his mouth without losing any of the stew he'd shoved in first.

"Our *ploy* was a bit like painting a smiley face on a tree trunk and expecting him to believe it was Harry Styles," Rhona said, her hand dropping from the feathers at her shoulders. "We should probably assume he did not, in fact, see Harry Styles."

Meeksy, who had been sitting quietly with his arms wrapped around his knees, added his head to the pile with a groan.

"There's risks whatever we choose," Ronald said without opening his eyes, surprising everyone. "I, for one, don't think we're worth much without some sort of home base to return to. Oban is the more immediate danger. Whatever is causing the anomalies must be affecting other communities—we can't be the only ones fighting it. But unless we do something to stop Lord Sackington and that beithir, we really will be caught between the rock and proverbial hard place."

"Between Bawbag and the beast," Iain muttered. "This is not the sexy fairy tale of my dreams."

"Thanks for that nightmare." Rhona's voice came out in complete deadpan.

"You're welcome, pal."

"Sackington is more of a Gaston anyway," Ronald added, surprising me yet again.

"No . . . one—"

"Don't you dare." Eilidh interrupted before Iain could burst into a terrible parody song. "Even in an apocalypse, I feel like you'd have corporate lawyers landing on your head if you so much as got through the first verse."

A chuckle went through the group, though it was mirthless.

"Anycunt got an idea?" Iain said after a moment. "Naecunt?"

I heard a snort from farther away at his choice of language, and a surge of affection went through me for my lifelong pal. If there was anything he was good at beyond generally pulverising bi lad stereotypes and martial arts tournaments with equal facility, it was a fearless dedication to the Scottish breadth and depth of usage of the word *cunt*.

"Hard to make a plan when we don't know for sure what we're up against," Eilidh said, though a smirk danced across her face that I returned with a half smile of my own. "All we've got to go on is Bawbag, beithir, and his menagerie of puppeted beasties. No way he's going up against a town of eight thousand with only that."

"Aye, she's right," I said. "From what the wren's seen, that's the extent of his party. He may be a bit desperate to keep a handle on the beithir, but I don't think he's a total daftie."

"You think he's got an ace in the hole." Meeksy looked up. "Something worse than the beithir."

I nodded. Until I'd voiced it, I'd not really grasped it. We could still be wrong—maybe he was a total daftie—but something was off here. Everything from his slowness to the intensity with which he'd pursued the beithir itself. After we'd almost managed to kill it in Connel, he must have sought it out all over again.

None of us wanted to consider "worse than the beithir," but we had to. The only thing I felt fairly certain about was that Bawbag didn't know about the anomalies yet. I did not want to find out what might happen if the two fronts of this conflict collided.

After another hour of hashing out ideas, we—reluctantly—decided that Rhona was best positioned to do reconnaissance. I hated the idea of her going out there alone, but I wasn't her big brother, just an overprotective friend. And even if I had been her brother, she was her own person. She was, by whatever law remained, an adult, if a very young one.

With a promise to cast a lightning bolt if she encountered any trouble, Rhona handed me Sailean back before vanishing into the afternoon's golden hour.

The sun had come out while we were eating, casting the

green-brown of the winter-dormant hills with its warm and near-sparkling gold. While I couldn't catch a glimpse of the sea from where we stood, Loch Nell lay off to the left, just south of us, and the sun seemed to trail its fingers through the dark waters, dancing patterns upon its still surface.

At least any lightning Rhona created would stand out.

I made the rounds of the group before we started out again, wanting to get a pulse on how people were feeling and if anyone else, like Andy, was looking volatile.

Plenty of nervous faces greeted me, which wasn't surprising. For most of them, the glaistig was the first sapient non-human they had encountered. I hoped in the long run that would be for the best; if their first meeting other sapients was with someone neutral at worst, maybe they would greet others with less bias.

Of course, there were plenty of examples where caution was wise.

Even so, I was surprised when Mòrag pressed a notebook into my hand. The older woman had a pensive look about her, and her silvery hair swept back from her face in careful plaits.

"What's this?" I asked her, glancing over my shoulder as the group began to move sluggishly onward.

"I think Eilidh called it the 'ascension census' you asked for?"

Oh. *Oh.*

"Mòran taing," I thanked her, quickly opening the notebook as if it were a precious treasure chest.

Mòrag gave me a wan smile, moving away again. Part of me wanted to ask her to stay; it was strange to yearn for the kinship of a family that wasn't my own. An image intruded in my mind of a cosy living room, a peat fire burning, fairy lights all around and a spread of cheeses and wine and half-eaten stacks of oat cakes sprawled out over a coffee table. Mòrag sat in a rocking chair across from me, and Eilidh's blue eyes danced in the glow cast from the fairy lights as she reached out and squeezed my hand.

I shook off the sudden daydream, swallowing. Bloody hell, increasing my Pathos had made me a ball of mush. Fighting the urge to gruffly clear my throat, I instead tried to employ one of Iain and Meeksy's meditation techniques. Acknowledge the desire, feel where it exists in the body—this one felt like it was lodged behind my sternum, pressing upon my heart—and let it exist without judgement.

One or two deep breaths.

Maybe three to be safe.

Clearer in my mind, I flipped through the notebook. Eilidh's scrawl alternated with Mòrag's careful block lettering for the first five or six pages whilst they just listed everyone on their own line with level, class, and any affinities.

Just scanning what was there revealed that we had just over fifty people who'd managed to reach levels four and five, another hundred and ten or so at level three, and the rest at levels one or two. The children were also listed, and it gave me a wee jolt to see that the bairns had somehow already unlocked affinities too. Most of their levels were two or three—which made me wonder how any adults were still level one, for fuck's sake—and I really wanted to see how their stats allocation went.

Flipping to the next page, which was the end of the initial list, a genuine smile spread across my face.

Notes.

Eilidh'd also included notes.

The weans are able to level through crafting, and though

their starting statistics seem to operate from a mean of one to five up to age ten and they have very limited ability choices, they are notably improving and unlocking affinities. The most common affinity is still Nature, which is unsurprising, but one six-year-old girl, Rachel, has unlocked a specialised affinity.

I had to chuckle at that—that was oor wee beastie aficionado, or I was a simulacrum. The next line confirmed it.

She's unlocked the Small World affinity, which gives her access to the eponymous skill/spell tree and pertains to arthropods in general. Though none of the offensive abilities are open to her, there is a path of progression even at her young age.

The other notable specialised affinity that someone has unlocked is simply—and somewhat enigmatically—called Spirit. It seems the man who unlocked it (Donnie MacLean) has discovered how to increase his Mind and Spirit attributes through meditation.

That also gave me a bit of jolt. I felt like I'd been on the cusp of that myself, and hearing that it was indeed possible set my mind aflame.

The rest of Eilidh's notes, while helpful, weren't particularly newsworthy.

Some of the classes were interesting, to be sure. Most were in English, but a few were in other languages—the Korean man's class was in Korean—and I was surprised to see more than a few rare classes within the level threes. Most were not combat specialists, but that almost excited me more. Knowing that ascension pertained to peaceable pursuits far more than violence was one thing; seeing evidence of it was something else altogether.

There was a middle-aged woman whose class was ascension architect, and not much farther down the list was a young bloke with a class called "spiritweaver," and I was itching to find out what *that* meant.

My mind spun through all of the different possibilities of this new system of existence. With each line I read, my resolve grew. Accident or not, we'd been given a chance to become something more than we had ever been.

I was not going to let someone like Lord Bawbag destroy humanity's hope.

A flash of jagged light in the distance snapped me out of my navel gazing.

Rhona's signal.

She was in trouble.

CHAPTER
THIRTY-TWO

I berated myself as I ran, ignoring the flashing notifications and everything else except for the need to close the distance with all possible haste.

The lightning had not forked through the sky a second time, leaving the sunset-hued Highlands blanketed in a silence somehow eerier than the one we'd experienced when Bawbag's magic had driven away all creatures great and small.

Yet again, I regretted that I'd have to leave tiny Sailean behind, this time with Meeksy. It was irrational, it was silly, and it was true all the same.

Connection spurred me forwards, Eilidh and I the only ones who had followed in case there was some sort of trap waiting behind. Of course, that meant we could blunder into any trap lying in wait ahead of us, but unless Bawbag's ace in the hole included the sneakiest of sneaks, we'd see an ambush coming.

Adrenaline rushed through me as we ran. After all the delays, the careful stick-together philosophy, here we were again. Just the two of us, sprinting headlong into the unknown.

I tugged on the thread of spirit that connected me to the wren, thankful for Tàth, thankful that I hadn't heeded my impulse to release the bond.

The wren startled, giving off a fleeting impression of puffed-up feathers, but he immediately let out a trill I heard only in my mind. He wasn't particularly close to us. Regardless, I watched the bough of a massive maple fall away beneath him as he winged into the sky.

Rhona hadn't been gone a very long time, and I didn't want to think of the implications of that. It meant whatever had happened wasn't far from the bulk of the group. Just beyond my sensing abilities, it seemed.

Mid-stride, I cast Connection again, stretching those abilities as far as possible.

I almost stumbled.

It wasn't that I couldn't sense Rhona; I could. It wasn't even that what I found sparked terror; it didn't.

What got me was that Rhona *wasn't* in apparent danger. She wasn't alone—at least five people were with her—but she was unbound, conscious, and giving off anxiety, not outright fear.

Eilidh noticed me missing a step, and she brought herself to a halt. I related what I could see, hoping she'd be able to make heads or tails out of it.

"How close can we get?" she asked.

"Without them noticing?"

"Aye."

"I honestly don't know. Depends on too many variables." I searched through the middle distance as if I'd suddenly develop X-ray vision. "We've got our eyes in the sky, so hopefully we'll at least get some advance warning."

"Get as close as we can, assess, go from there?" Eilidh glanced at me, her posture poised and ready to move.

"Aye, sounds like the best option."

We took off again, this time on hyper alert. Through the wren's eyes, I saw where we were aiming, and I wasn't sure whether to thank our lucky stars or curse.

Rhona stood surrounded by eight people, people I presumed had to be Bawbag's flunkies. She looked irritated but not overly worried, and they weren't actually attacking. Her daggers still rested in their sheaths, even. What the fuck was going on?

Despite my bonuses with birds, I still had to filter what I saw through a wee birdie brain. The wren couldn't understand what they were saying, so neither could I. It was a bit like trying to understand the parents in a *Peanuts* special.

Shaking off the double vision, I caught Eilidh's shoulder to slow her as we approached, flashing eight fingers at her.

The wren sang a bright tune from its perch above their heads, and even trying not to get pulled into its view of the tableau, I saw Rhona look up and notice him.

"She should know we're coming," I murmured to Eilidh.

Her only response was to nod. Eilidh pointed at me, then at my eye, then in the direction of the people.

Bugger. If I were to use Keen Eye on the lot of them, that would help, without a doubt. It would also leave me with only the dregs of spirit necessary to keep us alive.

I settled for a compromise, gritting my teeth as I left Eilidh behind to move through the foliage as quietly as possible. Thankful for the literal bird's-eye view of where I was going, I managed to avoid the bracken that lined the hillside just above the copse of trees where Bawbag's people had Rhona, and in keeping with our long and storied experience with his flunkies, they were not paying any attention to anything outwith their immediate vicinity.

If all his goons were like this, Oban would be fine.

With a pulse of Connection, I listened to the flows of spirit in the glade. I wanted to use Keen Eye as efficiently as possible, which meant trying to identify the biggest risks before triggering the ability.

Spirit was weak and sluggish around three of the men and one of the women; it grew stronger around a another man and woman who stood side by side, their proximity and body language suggesting they were together-together rather than just in each other's company.

That left two men, both of whom stood in the centre of spirit vortexes. They were burly bastards, each well over six feet. They wore no real armour, only what looked like Kevlar vests, leaving their well-muscled arms bare. Wincing in anticipation of the hit to my spirit reserves, I cast Keen Eye on the one who was facing Rhona even as he muttered something to the man next to him.

Gregor MacGregor

Level 15 Siphon

Affinities: Spirit, Arcane, Hand to Hand

Specialised Affinities: Stalker

This man has concentrated on his existing affinities to become an expert in tracking, magic, and close unarmed combat. The siphon class soaks up ambient spirit to create an ongoing personal ward that alerts them to immediate danger. This ward only triggers when the siphon themself is threatened.

Shit.

No wonder he'd found Rhona—he had a magic-based class and wraith-like affinities as well as five levels on her. I didn't know what a siphon was in the class sense, but I'd a feeling it had to do with the way spirit swirled around him like he was the eye of a supernatural storm.

My spirit took another hit as I used Keen Eye on the other one, and I immediately fought the urge to swear.

Benjamin MacGregor
Level 16 Siphon
Affinities: Spirit, Arcane, Nature
Specialised Affinities: Butcher
This man has honed his focus on the arcane, but he has a history in hunting and butchering his own meat, which he now applies to combat.

I'd had a feeling the Butcher affinity was meant to apply to non-human prey, but in the hands of someone like this bloke, that mattered about as much as a hunting rifle in the hands of a serial killer.

I really hoped my analogy would prove erroneous.

With both of them multiple levels above me, Keen Eye had taken almost half of my spirit. I used Fuaran before trying again and let my pulses of Connection ground me where I crouched in the underbrush. We were lucky it was late afternoon—the shadows stretched out from the pine trees and hedges of hazel, hiding me as well as I could hope. Even so, with the level-sixteen siphon brother there, every spell I used was a risk. With his Nature affinity, he would almost certainly have Connection unless he'd avoided that tree entirely.

Magic was all well and good if you could catch someone by surprise, but if they could see you coming?

My spirit replenishing at a faster rate, I cast Keen Eye again, this time on the woman half of the presumed couple. She and her bloke stood with their backs to me, but I could see a pair of daggers at her belt, so I wasn't surprised when her class came up.

Mary MacKenzie
Level 11 Nature's Blade
Affinities: Nature, Dual Daggers, Shadow, Healing
This woman has dedicated the early weeks of the ascension to mastering the Dual Daggers and Shadow affinities at the expense of her other affinities.

I let out a slow, controlled breath. She was my level, no specialised affinities, and it seemed we might have gotten a lucky break. The use of Keen Eye hadn't come as steep with the lack of level differential—only about ten percent of my remaining spirit—and I used it again on the chap next to her.

Robert Priest
Level 10 Hedge Witch
Affinities: Nature, Arcane, Shadow, Staves
This man has focused his energies on blending into the shadows, which has allowed him proximity to power. Underestimate him at your peril.

None of that sounded ideal.

He clearly wasn't in stealth just now, but that didn't mean he wouldn't be the moment we entered into combat.

The other four I couldn't call negligible, though I didn't want to waste spirit on Keen Eye four more times even with the faster recovery offered by Fuaran.

Time was ticking.

Eilidh and I needed to make a plan.

When I got back to where Eilidh was waiting, I quickly ran over what I'd seen. She stood there for a moment, looking pensive, but just before I was about to say something, she spoke instead.

"The siphons sound dangerous." Eilidh winced as if she knew she were stating the obvious. "But I think we've had a stroke of luck in that the one's self ward or whatever only gets triggered when he is in immediate danger himself."

"Aye, I agree. But there's still eight of them. If I had to guess, the four who struck me as the least threatening are likely around level eight. Maybe slightly below that, but I doubt they're much higher since the two in the middle felt stronger by an order of magnitude." I frowned. "Which means there's two of us at level eleven, two of them right where we are, four slightly below, and two significantly above. Plus Rhona at level nine."

"Bad odds," Eilidh murmured. "I don't think we can hope to fight them all, not without help."

"No way. That'd be how we get Rhona killed."

"We need to distract, disable, and—"

"Do a runner?" I said dryly.

At Eilidh's exasperated look, I noticed that the corner of her mouth was ticking upwards even as she tried to disguise it. Before she could say anything, though, a flash of inspiration hit me like one of Rhona's lightning bolts.

Eilidh homed in on my sudden shift in expression immediately. "What?"

"I think I know how we can get the siphons out of the way—and maybe shore up our ploy at the same time to make Bawbag think it's just us coming for him. It's a gamble. A dangerous one. But it could work."

"I'm all ears," Eilidh said fiercely, shifting her shoulders to adjust the weight of the claymore on her back.

Keeping an eye on the stalemate in the glade was easy with my wren friend, who trilled whenever they moved, and from the occasional irritated glance up at him, they thought he was simply an obnoxious wee beastie.

I ran through the plan with Eilidh as we moved into position. With a lot of luck and barring any massive disasters, we would hopefully get Rhona out of that pickle and eliminate two of Bawbag's stronger men.

That was the dangerous part. Their class was a wild card—I suspected it was a rare level-nine class, and that they'd both gotten it probably said something the Ascended Alliance would be able to explain. Here on Earth, though, all I knew was they were trouble.

And possibly murderers even before the ascension.

Likely, I'd never know the answer to that. All I had to account for it was a nagging sense of unease. Intuition, my mum would have called it. Trusting my gut seemed like the safest bet here—and there were no safe bets.

Once Eilidh seemed solid on the goals, she gave me an enigmatic look. I couldn't tell what was behind it; it seemed like part worry, part resolve, and part something else, something ineffable. To my surprise, she reached out tentatively and took my hand, giving it a squeeze.

"Thoir an aire ort fhèin," she said, and then she was gone.

Look after yourself.

Why did that make me more nervous than I already was?

It was up to her to get in position first, since with Connection I'd be able to tell where she was at all times. I waited a safe distance away from the group, using the spell to keep tabs on Bawbag's flunkies.

The four lower-levelled folks seemed to have gotten

bored. They were sat on the floor or leaning against a tree, while the couple—I dubbed them Bonnie and Clyde—stood in hushed conversation.

As I inched closer, I started to be able to hear snippets of talking, but it wasn't until I got close enough to see the woman's mouth moving along with a deep bass voice that I realised it was the siphon I was hearing.

". . . think we're stupid or something? You keep repeating . . . and think . . . true."

I pulsed Connection, willing it to help me hear.

Just a few more feet.

I missed the first part of Rhona's response, but she apparently had a lot to say.

". . . I'm telling you the same thing over and over because it *is* the truth. I only went with them to protect the wildcat!"

My heart skipped a beat.

"Soon as Benny's skill resets, we'll know for sure." The siphon—Gregor, it seemed, since I couldn't see who was speaking beyond Bonnie and Clyde—sounded very certain of that.

I could almost hear Rhona's answering eye roll. Had she actually betrayed us?

"The wildcat what's conveniently dead?" Benny piped up then, but his words brought a balm of relief. "That wildcat?"

If Rhona had told them Sailean was dead, she had to be protecting the kitten. Like she'd wanted to do all along. I had to admit she was a much, much better actor than any of the rest of us—she was threading enough truth into her lies to be able to repeat them with conviction.

"The fuath almost killed *me*," Rhona said with genuine pain. "You think it would have a problem with a literal kitten? I'm trying to tell you that the others are hunting Lord Sackington. I came to find someone as soon as I could get away, but if you *don't* want information that could help him win in Oban, fine. Kill me or whatever."

There was a moment of hesitation. Then Gregor turned to Benny and murmured something I couldn't hear, leaving Rhona in a small circle by herself with the two of them a few feet away. Perfect.

I moved forwards with a rolling gait, staying out of sight even as I kept my bearings with Connection. My spirit was nearly full again, and I renewed Fuaran to do my best to top it off and help me respond to what was coming next.

Coming to a stop beside a lodgepole pine that was thankfully just large enough to shield me from view, I took a beat to breathe.

Even if my hare-brained plan went off without a hitch, there were variables I couldn't reasonably account for. Namely, Bonnie and Clyde and the other four flunkies. It was suicide to think our luck could hold and they'd have none of their own. All it would take would be one of them looking over at the wrong time. Or, as I caught the flash of steel from a small blade in the hand of one of the sitting goons, a well-thrown knife.

One more cast of Connection, and I was ready to move. Eilidh couldn't miss my signal if she tried. I fought back the rising tide of reasons this could go very wrong.

Just as I was about to throw my arcane grenade, though, Rhona stepped forwards until she was out of my line of sight. The nineteen-year-old girl had gotten directly into Gregor's face, and I could hear her restrained anger in every word.

"Whatever you're going to do to me, just do it. Take me

to Sackington or don't, but stop pretending you think I'm lying, because you *know* I'm not."

Bold, Rhona.

But she was in my way. *Move, move, move.*

I tried to will her to move, but she stood there, barely over five feet tall and staring down a guy easily twice her body weight without flinching.

She needed to move. If she didn't back up again, everything Eilidh and I had planned would go down the shitter.

Rhona didn't budge.

With desperation creeping up my throat and ready to strangle me, I did something I didn't think I would have even thought of a day ago.

I put my staff on my back and latched onto the pine with Connection, whispering my urgency through its roots, through the tangled web of fungus and plant matter below the earth.

The moment the awareness touched Rhona, she sprang backwards.

Spinning fully two-thirds of my spirit into the spell, I made Ring of Fire into a blazing wall to surround the two siphons.

And everything descended into chaos.

THIRTY-THREE

I would be hard pressed to put anything that happened in that glade into chronological order.

Everything seemed to happen at once, quick as a pat of butter sliding across hot cast iron and somehow simultaneously as slow as a glacier etching out a new canyon.

One: Eilidh.

She blazed into being across the glade like an avenging angel, glowing gold with righteous rage and magic crackling along her blade.

That claymore caught the Clyde half of Bonnie and Clyde just as he was about to fade into stealth. He had jumped away from my Ring of Fire and directly into Eilidh's path—one lucky stroke for us.

Two: the siphons.

They clearly had not expected to be contained with arcane fire. Quite to the contrary. One of them—I couldn't tell which through the blue-green inferno that licked furiously a full two metres into the air—immediately tried to push *through* the Purifire barricade and just as immediately learned the error.

A smaller blaze flared up from his face and hair that came in contact with the fire, and I winced as his brother threw him to the floor and started kicking dirt over him to put the fire out.

Water had little effect on Purifire, but earth did, it seemed.

That was our second stroke of luck.

In the panic, MacGregor Number Two didn't think to try kicking soil over the Ring of Fire.

Three: Rhona flew at Bonnie. Her daggers moved like a whirlwind, her body a blur of motion.

For a moment, I thought we might actually win this in our initial strike.

I was wrong.

Four: the lounging goons.

They may have been sitting on the ground under a tree minutes before, but the moment things kicked off, they started moving. One vanished into stealth straight away; the other three made a beeline for Eilidh, drawing weapons.

I cast Fuaran on myself to give my spirit a boost, but that was nearly all I could do beyond my Connection pulses. Every second that passed by, my spirit recovered, but the Ring of Fire came another second closer to failing. We did not have time for this to be a protracted battle.

Tursa.

That was what I needed to use—*upon casting, it will give you an innate understanding of your environment, a precious glimpse that can allow you to strategise in the heat of battle or work your way out of natural obstacles when you can see no escape*—but it would drain me.

If I didn't use it, though, the MacGregors could escape their fiery prison, and this would be over for everyone.

I cast Tursa.

Time seemed to slow as it had before, threads of spirit elongating in flow patterns across the tiny field of battle.

Eilidh's sword was mid-strike, cleaving Clyde's trapezius muscle in two. Three of the flunkies were converging on her, and from the alert resolve on her face, she was well-aware of their proximity.

The other one-on-one battle teetered on the edge of one of their honed blades—Rhona was small, fast, stealthy, and vicious when she wanted to be, but Bonnie had two levels on her and had not split her focus. Rhona would not win this fight.

Ring of Fire held and held strong. With as much as my Mind had leapt over the past few days thanks to the community mythic feat, my capacity was much larger. That meant two-thirds of what I had went farther than it would have a few days ago—and thankfully, it was enough to hold a pair of high-level brutes.

Whatever I was going to do, I needed to do it fast. The next stage of the plan Eilidh and I had hashed out required us to be emphatically not here. It required lead time. And it required being free of any of Bawbag's barnacles.

Think, Calum.

I needed power, and I was almost out of spirit.

Bonnie and Rhona were most accessible to me. Eilidh and her satellite flunkies were on the far side of the two dagger-wielding women. Rhona had her back to me as she whirled, suspended in motion by the time dilation of Tursa.

Over her shoulder, I saw pale skin, flushed with exertion.

Bonnie's throat.

I needed power.

The word in my language for that was Cumhachd—and I had that spell in my arsenal.

Like dominoes, the next moves lined up in front of my mind. All I had to do was hit the first one.

Tursa vanished as quickly as it had come, and I took one more big gamble.

I poured a full ten percent of my spirit into Cumhachd.

It left me gasping as the arcane missile soared through the air, but the spell did not miss.

A flash of white lit the side of Rhona's neck at the crook, but it punched directly into Bonnie's exposed throat.

She dropped like an anvil had fallen on her head.

Rhona leaped to the side, spinning to look at where the missile had come from, her eyes widening when she saw me staggering from the expended energy.

No way would it be a killing blow. But it better be enough.

That was the last thought I had before something slammed hard into my back.

My vision went white and flashed gold, a gold so bright and burning it made me wonder if I was dead.

Dimly, I was aware of yelling, the rush of Purifire still reaching to skyward.

Putting my staff on my back had just saved my life.

The combination of low spirit and the blow at my back had dropped me to the floor. Someone scrabbled beside me, the only real sound a guttural gurgle that slowly faded.

Then Rhona was there, swimming into focus above me.

"Get up!" Her hand grasped mine, and she yanked me to

my feet so fast my head spun all over again. "That cunt tried to backstab you—he's dead now."

Bonnie was still down, unconscious and mottled with red at her neck but grey-blue lips.

I couldn't see Eilidh . . . because she was coming at me from the side.

"Come on," she said urgently. "They won't be stunned long."

That flash of gold—Eilidh's stun.

"Calum," she said when I didn't move.

Then her hand planted itself in the centre of my chest, and it felt like pure life flooded into me. Or like an adrenaline injection to the heart.

"What was—" Rhona started to say, but I cut her off.

"Talk later! Run!"

Seconds before, I wouldn't have been able to lurch through the trees back to the road, but whatever Eilidh had done was like the ascension version of amphetamines. I beat both her and Rhona to the tarmac, and we took off back towards the group.

For all we'd escaped that mess by the newly grown points on our ears, what came next was the riskiest part of our plan.

"Thank god you showed up," Rhona said beside me. "I was starting to be afraid you wouldn't."

"Rhona, you need to run back to the group as fast as you possibly can." I pointed back behind us. "Tell them to get ready to fight."

"*Fight?*"

"Those two siphons I put in a cage?" I said. "They're trackers. They are going to come after us the second they get free, and we absolutely have zero chance of beating them alone."

"But we wanted Bawbag to think—"

"Just *go*," Eilidh barked. "If we do this right, he still will."

Rhona gave us one last look of confusion, but something about the certainty on our faces must have hammered home her own resolve, because she nodded once more and was gone, threads of silvery magic trailing in her wake.

"You really think this'll work?" I muttered, concentrating on keeping my feet moving.

"Is beag m' fhios," Eilidh admitted in Gaelic, the equivalent of a *hell if I know*.

"Did you manage to say it?" Whatever magic she'd done on me was wearing off. Shit. It really had been like an arcane injection of adrenaline.

"I said it. Put the force of Mòr-Bharail behind it, and at least one or two of them ought to run straight to Bawbag."

Eilidh didn't sound certain.

"Any who don't? They die," I said bluntly. "If they're even marginally smarter than block of clay, they will go while the siphons are still trapped. If they're not . . ."

"We can't let them escape."

I heard the same grimness in Eilidh's voice that I felt in myself. The thought of luring anyone into a trap was not pleasant to me, but those siphons were bad news. Maybe that class had a good side; maybe the Ascended Alliance had need of people who could track the occasional antisocial cunts who felt the need to ruin things for everyone else. But these blokes?

If we didn't kill them, they'd kill us—and the people we'd spent days trying to keep alive.

When we reached the group, we encountered a solid line of fifty people, all armed, Rhona at the centre.

Sweat beaded across her forehead, gluing her straight brown hair to her head, but she had made it back in record time.

"I hope you know what you're doing," she said to me when I got close enough.

"Would you prefer if we'd left you with them?" Eilidh said pointedly.

At that, Rhona shook her head. "No. Not even a little bit. But there're kids here."

"I know," I said. "Believe me, I know."

"I'll get everyone else back and organised as best I can," Eilidh said to me. "You need to sit down and do your meditations or whatever will get you back in the game—also, you're our best shot at advanced warning."

"Just got to hope they can't stalk themselves around my magic," I said under my breath, wincing.

"Aye, we'll hope that. Beò an dòchas," Eilidh murmured, irony tinging the words. *Alive in hope.*

Doing my best to ignore the unsettled murmurs behind me, I sat down on the hard tarmac, crossing my legs.

The wren was our other contingency. Even now, he still flitted from branch to branch in the glade we'd left, and we'd know—I'd know—the moment Ring of Fire fell.

I took breath after breath, falling into the now-familiar rhythm of Connection. Short-long, short-long, short-long. My spirit crept upwards, though the blue bar at the edge of my vision throbbed like a wound. I'd pushed it way too close. My spirit had hit two percent with the cast of Tursa.

Thinking of that made my heartbeat skip, turning irregular. I drew another deep inhale. Trying to steady it might have been futile before the ascension. Now, I'd had practise.

Calm slowly seeped into me despite the discomfort of both of my arse bones against hard tarmac.

Spirit began to flow in and around me, moving with my breath and my blood.

Inch by inch, I found my way back to tranquillity. I couldn't change what we'd chosen, and our plan so far *had* worked. Not without hiccoughs, but we'd accomplished the most important thing: we'd gotten Rhona away from them. We could sort out how she got into that mess in the first place later.

My exercises had helped tremendously. With every cycle of Connection, breath, and heartbeat, my spirit returned. I helped it along with Fuaran, sensing as it poured back into me through a million infinitesimal tributaries.

It never became a flood, but maybe someday it would. Even as I thought it, I remembered one of my passive skills, Freumhan. Roots.

I was a draoidh; I had chosen this path.

Not in the sense it was used in pop culture so frequently. In an older and wilder reality that rooted me to the land. My land. My home.

Freumhan had formed the basis of what I did all along this path, and it would continue to do just that. Now, as I relaxed consciously into its embrace, I felt those tributaries light up.

Spirit, pathos, and will blended together like a tree's roots with the symbiotic mycelium. It didn't matter where one stopped and the other began; the secret was that all was connected.

I didn't need to put my hand on the trunk of a tree to feel the forests near and far. Even with my arse planted on the tarmac, I was connected to it and everything that touched it from beneath.

The wren trilled in my mind as Ring of Fire finally fell, and through his eyes, I saw the MacGregor brothers stumble out of it with a lurching, angry gait. Benjamin's face was badly burned, healing more slowly than I would have expected.

Only one of the lower-levelled flunkies remained, and Bonnie was only just now coming to. A groan reached the wren's ears, followed by her cry of pain as Gregor MacGregor yanked her unceremoniously to her feet. His brother grabbed the remaining flunky—a young man barely over twenty—and growled something, pointing at the forest floor.

"They're coming," I said aloud. "Five to eight minutes until they reach us. Two siphons, levels fifteen and sixteen, one dual-wielding stealth-based melee fighter at level eleven, and one lower-levelled kid who's bitten off way more than he can chew."

From the murmur behind me, that news spread through the small army at my back.

My spirit restored and my head clearer, I got to my feet. "Does anyone have water or food handy?"

Instantly, woodcraft canteens appeared out of inventories in at least a dozen hands, which sent a ripple of nervous laughter through the gathered fighters. The people with me spanned multiple generations, genders, skin colours, body types—the one thing that did not vary from person to person was the courage it took to stand there in the face of potential death.

I took the nearest canteen and drank half of it, handing it back. Though I'd little time to marvel over the way it tasted like I'd stuck my face in a burn and slurped up water right from the source, I had to appreciate the immediate refreshment. Someone else held out a chunk of grilled goshawk, which I downed just as quickly.

"Thank you." Even as I swallowed the cold meat, I felt my body making use of the energy. It steadied me.

Connection opened me to my surroundings; Freumhan rooted me in the earth. At my back, I sensed something else: the combined will of a community under threat.

The wren's song reached my ears, flying ahead of the siphons who I saw through the wee bird's eyes far below. The MacGregors moved like bloodhounds. Every line of their easy gait scrawled a tale of single-minded purpose. Behind them trailed the low-level flunky. There was no sign of Bonnie, but with her affinities, I had to assume she was near.

I didn't need magic to know the moment the siphons spotted us.

One of them let out a roar, making the people massed at my back jump, followed by sounds of rage and recognition.

Survivors *knew* these blokes.

The two men turned to one another, clasped arms, and as they loosed an ability I could only guess at, the ambient spirit in a hundred-metre radius flew to them like it had been magnetised.

"Get down!" I bellowed, throwing myself to the tarmac as the energy they'd sucked into themselves exploded into a maelstrom.

THIRTY-FOUR

E ilidh had been nowhere in my immediate line of sight when I hit the floor, but suddenly she had launched herself in front of all of us, claymore planted point down in the road.

With Connection active, I saw the taut lines of spirit solidify into a crystalline shield as wide as her arm span. The siphons' chaos struck that shield like a gale howling in from the Minch.

Fissures appeared like cracks in the Earth's crust across the surface of Eilidh's shield, but it didn't break.

The unmistakable crack of bone, however, threatened to break me.

Screams erupted.

The shield was shaped like an obtuse triangle, funnelling the siphons' magic back and to the sides, which gave it a much wider angle of protection—it just wasn't wide enough.

"Injured to me!" I heard Meeksy's voice cut through the air even as his spirit signature glowed in my mind as he began to heal people.

"Get ready!" Eilidh forced the words out through gritted teeth. "That was their offensive nuke, but if we don't finish this fast, they'll be able to use it again."

I *felt* everyone's sudden comprehension of what she left unsaid: they would be able to use that again, but she had spent her shield to make sure their first volley didn't spell our annihilation.

We wouldn't last through a second without her protection.

My blood seemed to turn to a glacial river at the stark demonstration of those interim levels. But there was no time to second guess ourselves. Our job now was to survive —and to make sure these siphons did not live to see the sunset.

That attack had taken a lot out of them, and its dubious success left them swaying on their feet. The other flunky still hung back, a war of emotions playing out on his face.

Another scream of pain cut through the air behind me, and I drew my staff, casting Cumhachd with every ounce of my intent focused on a blur of motion at our left-most flank where a flash of crimson became a splash of blood.

Bonnie.

My spell struck her in the shoulder, sending her spinning.

Cumhachd had put her down once, but this time, my goal was to get her off guard until—

Iain.

He sprang through the crowd of frightened fighters, delivering a devastating series of strikes to Bonnie's unprotected sides. Rhona joined him an instant later, a blur herself as she darted in and out, feinting and slipping away like water through an open hand.

Emboldened, a handful of our people surged forwards

to join in the mayhem, staves aimed at Bonnie's feet as she reeled under the combined onslaught of Iain's fists and feet and Rhona's snake-quick strikes. Rivulets of blood dripped down Bonnie's forehead and into her eyes from tiny cuts Rhona opened in her scalp.

"Calum," Eilidh said urgently. "The siphons are regrouping."

It was clear the MacGregors had gambled on that devastating first attack completely breaking us. Without Eilidh, it likely would have. They staggered, shifting their weight from foot to foot like boxers readying to take on a lightweight challenger who'd gotten in a lucky shot on the defending heavyweight champion.

Despite their surprise, they recovered quickly. They'd hit us from almost a hundred metres away—if they'd been closer, their volley might have done more damage.

"Can you hit them with your stun?" I asked Eilidh.

"If I do, it'll leave me without spirit. I don't think—"

"Then don't. You're the highest-levelled person here who can take a blow." I cast Fuaran on the both of us, watching Eilidh shiver as it rippled over her. "Once you can safely use it, do."

"What's the plan?"

I spoke only loud enough so the people nearest me—their chambered energy full of tinny adrenaline and nerves—could hear.

"Everyone on my left, aim for the one with the burnt face. On my right, the other. Our best bet is to keep them from being able to use that attack again—they seemed to need each other's help."

"Divide and conquer," Ronald said at my shoulder, his face grim in my peripheral vision.

"Go on my signal," I said, and Eilidh nodded. "I'll make it obvious."

With only a slight hesitation, Eilidh swallowed, raising her claymore.

The two of us broke into a run, Ronald beside us, though I'd not asked him to. Suspicion I didn't have time to entertain crept across my skin.

Benjamin MacGregor was the one with the burned face, and it seemed our group of survivors was not the only source of recognition—he took one look at Ronald and roared, spittle flying from the corners of his mouth.

Pulling my spirit to me, I infused it with will and pathos. Not only anger, though I'd plenty of that to spare, but something else.

A fierce, inescapable drive to protect this fledgeling community.

I didn't dare use two-thirds of my spirit again. This time I used only a quarter of it, and instead of a circle of fire, I threw down a line between the two brothers.

When I'd said I'd make the signal obvious, even I hadn't quite reckoned on the effect.

Purifire leapt into being, cutting the single-track road in two more clearly than any mere reflective paint could ever dream. It stretched nearly fifty metres, which would make the siphons need to either go through the fire—which they'd both learnt was dangerous, especially Benny—or lose precious time to go round the inferno.

The MacGregors stood so close to one other that when the blue-green flames went up with a *whumph*, the arcane blaze caused a flash of sparkles to ripple up the blokes' Purifire-adjacent arms as their arm hair caught fire.

Behind me, the survivors' footsteps joined the crackling of the flames.

The siphons merely brushed off the singed hairs and moved to meet us. I noticed that Benny in particular swerved away from the Purifire's heat. He was the higher levelled of the two brothers, but it was Gregor who's bellow of rage split the air as he drew a pair of wicked-looking hunting knives and charged Eilidh.

As much as I hoped their combined nuke had dealt them as big a blow to their spirit as my previous use of Ring of Fire had to mine, I didn't dare count on it.

I was a draoidh; meeting the siphons head on would be suicide.

That didn't mean I couldn't come at them from below.

The fighters streamed past me as Eilidh and Gregor collided with a clash of steel. The bigger man had no real advantage in an ascended world beyond level, and when his daggers caught her claymore's strike, surprise flashed on his face as he encountered her strength. Muscles bulged in his neck.

I struck before he could recover, pouring my intent of protection into the earth as I triggered Tairm.

Along the line of my Purifire wall, the tarmac cracked as the underground root system formed into deadly vines. Like had happened previously with Eilidh's sword and Rhona's dagger, Purifire raced along the vines, coating them in cleansing flame. They plunged outwards from the rift in the road, and a scream pierced the air as one of them found purchase in the unfortunate flunky who had been hanging at the back.

That unfortunate soul had no Kevlar to protect his innards.

My gut twisted in empathy; like the sheep in Kilninver, these roots dived straight through the bloke's midsection, spilling viscera onto the road where it caught fire and sizzled.

Play stupid games, win stupid prizes, I thought bleakly, wishing it helped.

The vines of plied roots were not as successful with the siphons.

With Bonnie clearly dead, Iain had joined the left-most attack, and with twenty low-levelled survivors at his back, he had Burnt-Faced Benny nearly pinned against my wall of Puri-fire, whose furious cursing was coupled by his whip-quick slashes of short daggers to cut himself free of the vines that could not penetrate the Kevlar he wore to protect his torso.

Desperation was dangerous.

Whether or not the MacGregors had spent the bulk of their spirit on their initial attack, Benny was far from helpless.

"Sackington will have your heads!" he screamed, wet lips drying almost instantly in the heat from the fire.

Benny grabbed hold of the nearest fighter, who tried to yank himself free from the siphon's grasp that held him like iron manacles. Before I could do anything, the fighter's skin began to pale, draining of colour—and that wasn't the only thing. The middle-aged bloke's beer belly seemed to droop, his thinning hair losing melanin visibly as it faded from grey-streaked brown to the colour of ash.

The man collapsed, and Benny kicked his corpse into the line of fire.

He'd stolen *spirit*.

Something deep in my core rebelled at the sight.

I knew beyond any shadow of a doubt that, like Bawbag with the simulacra, the siphon's abilities were not meant for this.

Ronald had rushed ahead towards Benny, but he skidded to a halt just before his toes encountered the victim's body. But Iain didn't hesitate.

He launched a devastating side kick into Benny's solar plexus, putting the full force of his considerable Strength stat and a lifelong study of the body's leverage behind it. In my mind, I heard Iain lecturing me on how to kick with the side of the foot, how to use the glutes and hamstrings and the weight of the body behind it, and now I got to see in the flickering light of Purifire exactly what that looked like turned to real violence.

Benny took the kick with a startled gust of an exhale— and then he grabbed hold of Iain's foot and twisted.

My heart crunched along with the sound of dislocating bones, and I heard rumbling roar from behind me that could only be Meeksy.

Even as I moulded together Cumhachd and Slànaich to target my oldest friend, I saw Eilidh miss a step.

"Miss a step" was not the best word when it was caused by a brute of a man aiming what would have, in any other circumstances, been a death-wish of a strike at her well-guarded face. It was a feint.

And it worked.

Gregor's dagger came up in the sliver of an opening her flinch had created, so fast that all I could see was a flash of blade going in and bloodied metal coming out.

I reacted on pure instinct, feeling my spirit rush out of me as I sent a wave of pure Spèird at the MacGregors.

It hit them across the chest like a clothesline made of steel. The crack of breaking ribs resounded through the startled gasps, but I was already moving, my gaze frantically moving back and forth between Iain and Eilidh.

"Go!" Meeksy shouted from my left, magic already flying from his outstretched arm.

The glow rushed across the distance to Eilidh even as Meeksy shot me an anguished look that told me all too well that he knew the terror of watching the one he loved hurt at the same time as his oldest friend.

Kinship bloomed in me at the strange comfort.

The others with us were not trained fighters, but they were firing spells at the MacGregors as best they could, and a trio advanced on Benny MacGregor. Benny had been thrown back a solid fifteen metres by my wave of force, and he lay gasping, trying to recover his breath.

Gregor was already up, and he had Eilidh in his sights.

My spirit was under half with the force of those spells. I wracked my brain for something I could do that would further delay them without draining myself completely.

Then it hit me.

The fucking bunny had shown us what to do.

"Eilidh!" I yelled her name, and even with the stab wound, healing or not, she looked to me immediately. "Danns a' choinein!"

True to form, understanding washed over her face at my words.

Dance of the rabbit.

I gambled on throwing another twenty percent of my spirit into Spèird to delay Gregor a few precious seconds. A guttural scream rose and died off just as quickly from my left as Benny's hunting knife caught one of his attackers across the throat.

The spirit around me shuddered with shock and grief.

Eilidh gritted her teeth and sprinted for me, yelling at the others to follow. "For Oban and Argyll!"

THIRTY-FIVE

If I were the MacGregor brothers, I think I'd have shit myself, higher levels or not. That or turned and run, retreated. Or run far enough back to get around my wall of fire, which I kept feeding a cord of spirit to keep it in place. Benny and Gregor were grossly outnumbered.

The fact that they did none of the list of pragmatic options told me plenty. As it was, Benny was flushed and snarling, and Gregor had paused to regroup, staring through the fire at his brother and then at us, Eilidh's blood still dripping from the blade of his knife.

They could look at a line of almost fifty people and still think they could win.

When Gregor triggered his next ability, though, I saw why. An arcane bolt flew from his hands, not aimed at me or Eilidh, but aimed at the lower-levelled people on my right-hand side. The magic crackled, the purple-red hue of a bruise shot with lightning. It sped through the air, distorting the flows of spirit around it in my Connection-enhanced sight.

The spell slammed into a woman I thought was a bare level three. She didn't even have time to scream.

I recognised the magic immediately as my own spell.

Cumhachd.

Mine was only at level three unless I'd increased it in the past couple fights; it was clear some of his skill points had gone into levelling it up.

Fighters were nearly hyperventilating around me, biting back sounds of panic.

"Open yourselves to spirit," I commanded, moving ahead of them with Eilidh as the MacGregors telegraphed some unknown plan to each other through my wall of Purifire. "And to each other."

Òran na Cloiche amplified my voice, and even the siphons twitched at the sound of it. I could only hope they wouldn't know what I was talking about.

It almost didn't matter.

Even as I nodded to Eilidh and she moved to position herself next to me, the siphons charged.

Everything in me wanted to react to it, but I'd committed. My feet stayed planted where they were, muscle memory taking over.

Only a fraction of a second had passed when Eilidh and I spun into motion. I felt the flow of her spirit reaching for mine and reached back, my staff spinning in time with my heartbeat and breath and the rhythm of Connection. Without needing to say it out loud, both of us opened ourselves to the other frightened fighters behind us.

Meeksy was the first to join us, then Rhona, who had been strangely absent through the fight until that point. I felt their surprise and then wonder as the web of spirit grew to encompass them. The wee wraith that was Rhona danced in and out of view in the edge of my vision.

There was no more time to wait on what the others would do. Benny MacGregor leaped ahead of his brother. Literal froth clung to the corners of his mouth, his burned face contorted in a pink-and-white rictus of rage.

Jesus Rachmaninoff Christ, the man was a fucking *berserker*.

His knives flew at Eilidh, and felt her surge of fear even as she parried his wild strike.

Gregor, it seemed, was mine.

Spirit surged in our web, a rejuvenating sense of well-being flowing through me. Meeksy. It had to be. My healing was nothing compared to this.

My staff completed a wide arc, and I channelled spirit into it, whispering mentally to Brac-Meanmna that we could not let this fight turn to a loss. The living weapon responded with a series of images that flashed through my mind even as Gregor got within striking distance.

It was as if the past few seconds had happened in slow motion and now time sped up.

Brac-Meanmna caught Gregor's arm at the wrist just as he attempted a thrust through my guard, and though the impact jolted up my arm, there was no crack of bone.

The siphon reacted seamlessly, retreating half a pace and shaking out the arm as if he'd simply gotten dripped on by a leaky pipe.

I knew my Strength stat sucked, but that was just insulting.

My staff began to emanate a strange sensation, almost like smug satisfaction.

Without any time to question it, my body already moved into the next stage of the staff form. Grunts and the clash of steel arose from my left as Benny tried to react to not only Eilidh but also Rhona, who had materialised behind him, her dagger catching him just under the arse cheek to slash open his hamstring. At the same moment, she let loose a gut-curdling banshee scream directly into Benny's ear. Most of our fighters hadn't previously heard Rhona's sonic ability, and even though the damage was directed entirely at the siphon, a collective flinch jerked through the entirety of the battlefield.

The siphon somehow managed to resist.

Benny's answering elbow flashed out quicker than even Rhona could dodge, catching her in the ribs with a startled *oomph* that sent her stumbling backwards.

I had to trust she would be okay.

Gregor hadn't moved, which was almost worse than if he'd gone berserk like his brother. Instead, he stood there, simply assessing me as I hovered in a grounded stance, my weight centred.

The spirit between us moved only fractionally, the barest hint of disturbance. It was the sole warning I had as he struck like a snake.

Brac-Meanmna was ready to meet him. Shifting my weight, I spun the staff around to bring the head up in a sharp upward arc. This time it almost felt as if the weapon lunged at him, anticipating the trajectory of his attack.

The spirit-enhanced oak caught him in nearly the same location on his right arm, and this time, there *was* the distinctive crack of bone.

How Gregor managed to hold onto his dagger, I'd never know. Without missing a beat, his left hand lashed out, catching hold of the staff just below the globe of wood at its end.

I did the only thing I could think of doing. Instead of trying to yank it back from someone who clearly could best me in a game of tug-of-war, I threw my entire weight behind it, pushing the staff as hard as I could into his grip.

Gregor had not expected that.

Again, Brac-Meanmna flared with approval and satisfaction, and the flash of spirit from the staff then did not come from me. The globe of the staff's head slammed into Gregor's unguarded face before I could grasp my own triumph.

His nose crunched with the impact upon the fragile cartilage, and blood burst from the wound.

Even then, though, he did not release the staff.

Adapting quickly, he flexed his broken wrist and grabbed hold of the pole of wood, ignoring both pain and danger as he tried to yank me off balance.

So I let go of the staff.

Gregor stumbled backwards, and I lashed out with Cumhachd as I felt his spirit gathering to retaliate, his reflexes and response times clearly superior to my own even if I'd gotten lucky twice in a row and surprised him. My arcane missile struck him in the chest, sending him to the floor.

I could feel Eilidh still dancing warily with Benny. She was growing tired, and while my spirit was recovering from the careful movements melded with hers, beyond Meeksy and Rhona, no one else seemed to have joined us.

Whether frozen in fear or simply afraid to clutter the field, I didn't know.

"A little help here!" I yelled the words.

I did not expect the help that arrived. A familiar pulse of spirit poked into mine, finding its place a moment later as Ealasaid appeared by my side.

Mòrag and Ealasaid both had come.

Gregor MacGregor burst out laughing.

Without missing a beat, he leapt to his feet, taking hold of my staff with both hands. He completely ignored the two old women, instead making eye contact with me. Blood had coated his upper lip, the nose fracture already healing. He paid it no heed, only licked a drip away, coating the tip of his tongue with a swath of crimson.

"Watch me as I demonstrate what I'm going to do to them," he said, ignoring everything else.

My body tensed as I realised what he was about to do. Gregor raised up the staff horizontally and brought it down viciously over his knee.

I braced myself for the splintering of breaking wood—but it didn't come.

Instead, Gregor howled as Brac-Meanmna went super-nova, first with the blue-green glow of Purifire and then paler, paler, paler until it was bright white. The flesh on Gregor's palms began to sizzle.

And the women struck.

Mòrag moved faster than I thought possible, the only weapon in her hand a shillelagh someone must have made her. She brought it down hard on Gregor's knee, and he roared in pain. Too late, I saw that the staff had not limited its burns to his hands—it had seared straight through the denim of his jeans and into the angry red flesh beneath.

The staff went clattering to the floor, and I darted forwards to retrieve it. Ealasaid had gone for the siphon's fallen blade, and she held it in a reversed grip, stabbing downward at Gregor's other knee.

Perhaps not wanting to be shown up in bravery by a couple of elders, more fighters joined the fray. I felt the swirling spirit behind me even as I hefted Brac-Meanmna once more, letting the Purifire wall die at last as I called to the earth with Tairm.

Above my head, the sky exploded into the screeching of what seemed like every possible bird in Scotland.

At first, I thought it was the effect of my spell somehow, creating a hurricane of feathers and beaks and claws.

But it wasn't.

The wren had taken his own initiative.

Ravens and magpies swooped down from the air, their corvid cries shredding the other sounds of fighting. Songbirds punctuated it as they dive-bombed the MacGregor brothers, their shrill tweets making the hair on the back of my neck stand up straighter than wire bristles.

The true effect of Tairm came on an altogether different set of wings.

If my magic couldn't teleport a thousand birds to a battlefield, it *could* kick a literal hornets' nest.

A loathsome buzz resonated through the fight, a low drone that got my hackles even further up as hornets the size of golf balls poured in from the southern side of the road in a writhing black river of rage.

Benny, in his berserk state, tried to swat at them.

Eilidh leapt backwards from the murderous insects despite certainly sensing that they were my doing—I wanted to do the same. Instead, I threw myself back into the fight with Gregor, Brac-Meanmna practically pulling me towards the siphon even as he fended off attacks from Mòrag's shillelagh and his own blade in Ealasaid's hand.

I conjured Purifire once more as I'd done back at Bawbag's manor the first time I'd been there, melding it with Spèird to send it hurtling at Gregor's eyes in a blinding flash of fiery light.

He dodged, but only barely, and I saw his eyelashes go up with tiny plumes of smoke.

Melding together flows of pathos and will, I tried something else I'd done once before, with the rabbits. I circled to get around to Gregor's back, and though he was under attack from the front, he still discounted Ealasaid and Mòrag to try to face me as if I were the greater threat.

Maybe I was, but he could underestimate old women to his own peril.

Gregor lashed out with his remaining dagger, spinning to strike at me with still-expert precision. I dodged, but not fast enough. His blade caught me across the deltoid, and I reacted instinctively again, delivering a counterstrike aimed at his throat. The siphon danced backwards—right into a full-on swing of Mòrag's shillelagh.

He barely grunted in pain, but an enraged shout drew both our attention.

The hornets coated Benny's burned face, and he furiously attempted to bat them away . . . until they started to sting.

His screams cut through the air as berserker fury gave way to desperate panic. "Get them off me! Get them off me!"

Gregor bellowed, and like it had before with his siphon abilities, I felt the spirit around me retreat like the way the water pulls back on the shore before a tsunami.

"Look out!" I roared into the melee, projecting the need to get away into the web of spirit that tied me to the other fighters.

People dove away from Gregor. Not fast enough. It was like what I'd done to clothesline him and his brother, yet where mine had been a cobbled-together attempt, his was clearly a full-on defensive ability.

Force exploded outward from him, hitting me like a swinging boom. Suddenly, I was sailing through the air. I'd barely enough time to register the exquisite bloom of pain in my ribs before I hit the ground, tumbling over the ridge of low-lying grasses into the ditch beside the road.

Stunned, I couldn't make myself move for several heart-beats. I gasped for breath, floundering to stay connected to the others' spirit.

Even with my own spirit recovering quickly, I didn't have enough. And I needed to see if the others had escaped the radius of his wave of force. I scrambled to my feet, my vision swimming.

A scene of total chaos greeted me. Ealasaid lay sprawled twenty metres away, Gregor's knife another five metres beyond her where it was still spinning to a halt on the tarmac. Mòrag must have had some sort of defence against what the siphon had done, because she was still on her feet where I'd been moments before, stumbling and clearly stunned.

Benny still screamed at the hornets; he had dropped all pretence of fighting and was spitting ropes of bloody mucus from swollen lips. Gregor tried to beat the swarming insects away from his brother, to no avail.

With horror, I watched a hornet crawl out of Benny's open mouth, the man's purple tongue engorged from stings.

We needed to end this.

I looked around frantically for some sort of answer— and I found what I needed.

There were pine trees just off the road.

Without further thinking, I lunged for the nearest one, my fingers making contact with rough bark that poured spirit into me. My spirit expanded, and I said a silent thank you to Glòir a' Ghiuthais, the new boon that gave me an hour of a plus-three-hundred capacity.

Tairm waned; I felt as the hornets began to flee.

Some of the fighters had seen where I was, and confusion gave way to understanding that whispered through the web of spirit like a wave.

It seemed as if the remaining warriors acted with one mind: half of them screamed out a battle cry and flew at the MacGregors with renewed vigour, and the other half bolted for the nearest trees.

I cast Tursa, pulling Connection through it as the battlefield lit up before my eyes. Threads of spirit connected everyone on my side, and those threads glowed brightly with the golden light of will.

Through that gold, though, there was also the flaming red of pathos.

Eilidh's stun cascaded through that web, catching both the siphons in its radius. It barely staggered Gregor, but just as he lunged for her, Mòrag and Rhona hit him at the same time from each flank. Mòrag's club took him in the patella, and Rhona's daggers flashed with silver fire as she delivered a litany of laser-precise slashes up the length of his right shoulder.

Rhona's shriek pierced the air once more, louder than before. My arm hair buzzed with it; I half expected to hear the crunch of the thick lenses of Ealasaid's spectacles.

This time, Benny's resistance faltered.

Stumbling to the side, he swayed on his feet.

I formed Spèird into a bludgeon and brought it down on his skull.

Boils burst in a spray of lymph and oozing pus where the hornets had stung all over his scalp. Eilidh seized the opportunity I'd given her.

Her claymore came down on the crown of Benny's head. The blade sliced through his skull, and a roar went up behind me as the tide of the fight finally turned in our favour.

It was as if Benny's death released any and all compunction in the rest of our fighters. They fell upon Gregor even before I could reach him.

I ran for the fray. Yells and screams and curses lit the air on fire. Even as overwhelmed as he was, Gregor fought on, his Constitution and Strength keeping him alive, and his Mind bolstering each of his arcane attacks. I saw his blood-covered hands grasp first a young woman from our ranks, then a man, draining them both the way I'd seen him do early in the battle until they collapsed, greyed husks.

We all watched in impotent horror as he harvested the corpses before they hit the ground.

His power exploded outwards, a torrent of spirit-honed blades of air that cut through the nearest attackers in a spray of blood like a detonation.

I wanted to kick myself for forgetting about my newer spell, Sgàthan, the mirror that would turn an enemy attack back upon the caster. But I also remembered the warning too well—with so many people around Gregor, Sgàthan was too dangerous.

Pouring nearly half of my total spirit into Spèird, I centred my attack on Gregor himself and let it loose.

My goal had been to get people back from him as gently as I could whilst immobilising the siphon himself, and it worked. Injured survivors lurched backwards, stumbling. A few collapsed to the bloodied tarmac. Dazed, they reeled where they sat amid corpses I was afraid to count. Not now. Not yet.

I closed the distance to Gregor, the force of Spèird pinning him to the ground.

"He's the one who rounded us up for Sackington!"

Someone's voice pierced the air, full of anger and the rage of revenge.

"I thought as much." My own voice came out hoarse and ragged. I cleared my throat, moving to stand at Gregor's side where he could see me clearly. "He will soon pay that price in full."

The siphon sneered at me, flexing his spirit so hard, I almost lost my hold on him. I poured another ten percent of my spirit into keeping him immobile. Even then, he was able to reach a hand into his pocket, pulling out a glowing stone.

No, not a stone.

A simulacrum.

About the size of a large scallop, it somehow did not pick up the blood from his hand.

Dread pooled in my gut.

"Kill me," Gregor rasped, a wild and cold-eyed grin spreading across his face. "I dare you. If you don't, I am going to kill every last person here so thoroughly, it'll make Benny's death look merciful."

I had only about fifteen percent of my spirit left, but I had to know.

Keen Eye.

As the text filled my vision, that dread turned to gel, solidifying into a bleak brick of grim determination.

Whispering to Brac-Meanmna in my mind to tell it what I wanted from it, I gritted my teeth. "Everyone get back. Now."

I didn't wait to see if they obeyed.

Bracing myself against the cost took all of my resolve.

My staff came down, a blade of spirit and Purifire taking Gregor MacGregor in the chest. It pierced his sternum, crushing his heart.

CHAPTER
THIRTY-SIX

I thought I could scrub my brain for a thousand years and not be able to burn away the words Keen Eye had shown me.

Wearily, I leaned my back against the pine where I'd settled myself. My back ached from the clean-up. My soul ached from triaging survivors. My heart ached from harvesting our dead—those the siphons hadn't managed to harvest first, anyway.

But even that was nothing compared to the horror that had taken root in my brain, just as Gregor had intended.

Spirit Node Simulacrum

Unlike the larger specimens of a simulacrum, a spirit node is not mobile on its own. It must be transported and kept within the aura of the user to have an effect.

Within the Ascended Alliance, spirit node simulacra are used by beings who travel into danger. Their purpose is to remain with a person in peril, and every spirit node is linked to a nexus simulacrum. In the event of death—of causes natural, violent, or arcane—instead of dissipating or being available to harvest, the essence and resources of the deceased are absorbed into the nexus simulacrum.

This not only informs the holder of the nexus of the fate of the traveller, but it also provides the boon of closure. The nexus holder then receives the spirit resources belonging to the deceased. In the context of conflict—war exists even within the realms of the Ascended Alliance, though it is rare and most frequently caused by attacks from outwith the alliance itself— this ensures that soldiers' deaths do not strengthen their enemies.

In the case of this spirit node, that purpose has been bastardised.

Lord Edwin Thomas Sackington has given this spirit node to his most trusted henchpeople, that in the event of their deaths, he will profit from their power.

I forced myself to read it again.

And again.

The words still sickened me.

Though it had been the right choice to kill Gregor—we had no way to hold him indefinitely, and he would have healed and recovered quickly. As outnumbered as he was, his regeneration could have stymied us. And his skills from his Stalker affinity? He could have hunted down each and every survivor at his leisure.

No, we had made the right choice—but that meant the considerable spirit, pathos, and will gained from this battle was lost. A level-fifteen and a level-sixteen siphon. I shuddered at the thought of how much that would strengthen Bawbag.

We had only barely eked out a win.

Someone had had the presence of mind to harvest Bonnie and the fallen flunky I'd almost forgotten, the mid-twenties lad who died early in the fight.

Rhona, I suspected, since she'd vanished from my awareness for part of the fray.

As much as I wanted to relax, I couldn't.

I needed to work through my notifications even though it filled me with dread.

Eilidh had yet to stop moving that I could see. She'd moved like fury, the wound in her side healed. It was her doing that we'd managed to get word to Nan and the others to find a route around the battlefield that would keep it out of sight of the weans. Time was ticking down towards sunset, and none of us wanted to make camp here. Not now.

Trying to settle my mind, I watched Meeksy help Eala-said in the direction of the rest of the camp. She seemed unharmed, likely healed, but she held tightly to the big old bear of a man's arm anyway. A beatific grin lit her face as she spoke to him animatedly.

I didn't think she was being flippant about what we'd just been through. Far from it. I thought she was trying to cheer him up.

Iain had been one of the first taken back to the others. Despite immediate healing, he'd been in a bad way, his leg almost torn clean off. Even the ascension's wonders took some time to heal such a thing.

Since Rhona was nowhere to be seen, I was alone.

With a sigh, I opened up my notifications.

You have reached Level 12! You have two attribute points and three skill points to distribute.

You have reached Level 13! You have four attribute points and six skill points to distribute.

You have increased your affinities: Nature (Level 10), Synthesis (Level 5)

You have increased your specialised affinity: Coimhearsnachd (Level 3), Wild (Level 5)

Through physical exertion, you have gained a permanent +2 to Strength, +2 to Agility, +3 to Dexterity, and +7 to Stamina. Please note that such increases have diminishing returns as your base statistics grow.

Through arcane exertion, you have gained a permanent +3 to Spirit and +1 to Will. Please note that such increases have diminishing returns as your base statistics grow.

Through diligent use, you have increased the level of your skill: Connection (Level 10), Tàth (Level 4), Purifire (Level 10), Cumhachd (Level 3), Spèird (Level 4), Tairm (Level 3), Tursa (Level 3)

The level up for Purifire also alerted me to an additional line of text in the spell's description, though I had to groan at their choice of pun. Apparently, my—shall we say—heartfelt final attack against Gregor MacGregor had triggered an upgrade.

You have utilised Purifire in myriad ways with efficiency and cunning. In combat, you have often used it in combination with Spèird to great efficacy. As such, you have gained the upgrade Fist of Flame, which you can use to pack an even greater punch.

You have killed a Level-15 and a Level-16 human.

Their essence has been transferred to a nexus simulacrum and cannot be harvested.

You have received experience.

You have killed a Level-7 human.

You have received experience.

You have received 114 Spirit, 57 Pathos, and 21 Will.

You have killed a Level-11 human.

You have received experience.

You have received 243 Spirit, 171 Pathos, and 52 Will.

The implications of that were . . . sobering. I had to guess that the experience gain and Manipulation resources gain from the two human kills were split amongst whomever had damaged them. Before, when we'd fought people, it had been a lot, but I hadn't really thought about that split because there had only been four of us present. Previous fights, we hadn't even harvested our fallen enemies.

But with a wider playing field, this gave a sickening picture of just how much the MacGregors' deaths would have given Bawbag.

If I had to guess, I would say that a level-fifteen and level-sixteen human would have upped his Spirit, Pathos, and Will by a permanent twenty to fifty each. And that was being conservative.

Even if he were burning through low-levelled people and harvesting them, that was potentially a meteoric rise to power. Especially if he did it in quick succession—a killing spree of anything but the anomalies would provide a temporary boost to Manipulation resources. Anytime those temporary boosts ticked over a hundred, it added a permanent point to the stat.

It was only with the knowledge of what our community had managed together that I stayed on the calm side of panic.

There were more notifications to go through, but my heart wasn't in it. I decided, for once, to simply dump all my new attribute points into Mind. Anything to increase my spirit capacity. Anything that could aid us when we had to face down Bawbag and his pet beithir.

To that end, I remembered the book I'd gotten as a reward and hadn't yet read. *The Power of Community in an Ascended World.*

With a thought, I absorbed the book's knowledge.

Images poured into my mind of galaxies far, far away. Alien beings I couldn't have imagined appeared, as real and lifelike as if they were standing right in front of me.

There was a species very like us, a carbon-based mammalian biped that had evolved on a planet like our solar system's Mars, if Mars still had oceans. They were taller and thinner than us, willowy where we seemed almost stocky. Their skin ranged as dark and as pale as humans', but something about their eyes were different to ours—where our pigmentation was merely based on the presence of melanin or not, the latter creating blue eyes, their melanin seemed to work differently in their irises. Fascinated, I fixated on this detail, in eyes that spanned the spectrum from almost silver to the deepest cornflower blue to midnight indigo.

Those eyes allowed in much more light than ours, their pupils expanding to the point that they could see nebulae without benefit of telescope, a painted starscape of colour above their heads under the canopy of night.

I saw them en masse in the bowl of an extinct volcano's caldera that had been flash-heated by some fluke to create a perfect amphitheatre of obsidian. The people gathered there, with a gravitas that belied a special occasion. A cele-bration, a holy day.

As I watched this memory unfold, they raised their voices in song. Gooseflesh poured across my skin as their harmonies filled the caldera, echoing off of the glass-like obsidian like a glass harp. It created an eerie resonance akin to a theremin but with such exquisite precision that where a theremin conjured a sense unreality, this *transcended* reality.

The resonance seeped into spirit, strung through each and every soul connected in the caldera, and from that resonance, light spilled out. It turned the obsidian into a prismatic rainbow of colour, bathing every person present in an ethereal light.

I knew without knowing *how* I knew that any ailments suffered, any pains left to fester, any unhealed wounds would fall away in that effulgent song.

Part of me wanted to remain there forever—but that was not what the book was for.

It was as if the book had led me first to people like me, that I might have some feeling of kinship. How well must this Ascended Alliance know humans if that were the case?

No sooner had the thought crossed my mind than I was shunted onward, this time to a species entirely other.

A fully aquatic world spilled forth before my eyes, their water highly sulphuric on a planet whose seismic activity had never truly ceased.

But oh, what life existed there.

I'd been to Iceland right before I met Susanna, seen the Blue Lagoon where a simple accident had tapped into a font of volcanic-heated water full of silica. The water's silica content had settled onto the black basaltic rock of the lava field, turning the pool white and leaving brilliant blue water visible to the naked eye.

This entire planet's water was like that.

Their people were like our jellyfish, our octopods too, translucent and iridescent in the light of their sun or colour-changing along with the myriad other life forms that inhabited their world.

Instinctually, I sensed that the sun was much younger

than our own on Earth; its light was far more white than gold, and its rays kept the shallow waters of the planet warm year round.

They had no cities as we would conceive them, but they built their civilisation around extensive reef systems, vibrant and alive. Spirit flowed through them with the currents of the waters, a heavy tidal pull from their moon exerting its force upon the world.

These people had built . . . the internet.

It was the only way I could really conceptualise something that was otherwise so literally alien to me; they had created a planet-spanning network of coral and kelp, facilitated by microorganisms not unlike the mycelium that connected root systems underground on Earth. Through this, they shared information, wisdom—even memes. Though I could not understand their humour or the context of what whirled around me in this underwater world, what came across was community. Wealth. Abundance.

Joy.

Where there was danger, their connection allowed them to reach out from across the world to help. Curiosity won out over malice time and time again. In one way, it was utterly antithetical to Earth's internet: it ran on spirit, not electricity, and as such, their interdependence was coded into their communities.

It was, after all, hard to harm someone when you felt the pain you inflicted.

Unlike the book on staff technique that had seemed to flash through me in an instant, this one took me on a universal tour. They showed me life forms made of starlight as minuscule as a human skin cell. They showed me beings as big as nebulae who made their homes *around* entire civilisations. They showed me towers of crystal and mountaintops of the purest diamond, murky swamps full of philosophy so profound, people travelled from the universe's greatest cities to wade through the mud and seek it out.

By the time it let me go, the day had darkened, and clouds obscured the stars.

Irrationally, I resented those clouds. I knew I could not actually *see* the worlds the book had shown me—and cynically, I had to admit that it was possibly a pretty lie—but I wanted that proof all the same.

Starlight from other worlds and the hope that maybe, just maybe, someday we could meet such people ourselves.

THIRTY-SEVEN

By the time I made it to the camp, it was fully dark, the sunset's remnants no more than a smear on the western horizon with the cloud cover.

There was one person I needed to see more than anything, but I didn't get far.

The moment I came into people's line of sight, they mobbed me.

When I was younger, I don't think I quite grokked the meaning of the term "emotional labour," but that night? I understood it down to my toenails.

It took a whole different kind of muscle to withstand the onslaught of other people's trauma.

Everyone who crossed my path had a tearful story, thanks to give, advice to ask for, a trinket, a tale, a task. I lost track of the faces and names of the people who came to me, but one through-line pulled taut through the mire of that madness: they remembered the MacGregors, and those men were second only to Bawbag in the trauma they had inflicted. Maybe not even second; Bawbag had the MacGregors do the bulk of his dirty work.

As anyone who has had someone hurt them just because they were told to or dared to can attest, "just following orders" doesn't float any more than a boat made of Swiss cheese. In some ways, it's almost worse than someone hurting you of their own accord. Vicious in its banal cruelty.

The siphons were the very definition of banal cruelty to the survivors.

Most had not been on the front lines of that fight but back protecting the weans.

It was Eilidh who finally rescued me.

She carried a strange contraption that, at first glance, I thought was a sceptre. I wasn't far off. Someone had crafted a branch to hold a rock. Not a special rock, mind, but your average, well-worn river rock. What made it special was that some intrepid fledgling mage had figured out how to make it glow.

In the gold-white light of that ascension-crafted torch, her face crinkled with exasperation as she pushed through the crowd towards me.

"A chàirdean," she began, then jumped as if she'd heard her greeting and realised she'd meant to use a different language altogether. "Friends, give Calum some space. He's about to keel over."

At that, folk nearly tripped over their own feet to back up, some scuttling away with muttered apologies and others simply looking at their feet, abashed.

"It's okay," I said, raising my voice enough that I hoped they could hear me despite its hoarseness. "I just need some water and a wee sit-down."

"Aye, water and a wee sit-down," Eilidh agreed. "Without interruption."

Her tone brooked no disapproval, and she beckoned at me to follow, which I gladly did.

Everyone had settled in a field this time, just back from the road, and someone had cleared the bracken away to make a path, lining it with rocks. At the edge of the field was a small stand of birches, which is where we seemed to be headed.

Eilidh led me a short distance away where another ascension oddity awaited: a brazier crackling with normal-looking flames and no apparent fuel. The light flickered, turning the silver bark of the birches to gold.

The person I'd been hoping to find sat beside this other-worldly sight, moodily staring into the fire.

I was too exhausted to ask about the brazier and instead plunked my arse down in the moss next to Rhona.

"Hey, kid," I said to her.

She just looked at me, big brown eyes reflecting the flames.

When she didn't curse at me for calling her a kid, I let out a heaving sigh and threw my arm around her, pulling her into a side hug.

To my surprise, she burst into tears, collapsing in on herself as she folded into a ball with her arms around her knees.

"It's—it's my fault," she said through her sobs.

All I could think in that moment was *Jesus Christ, this kid has been through too much already.*

"It's not your fault," I told her fiercely, hugging her even tighter. "I saw you in that clearing when you stood up to them. You did exactly the right thing, made all the right choices. Hell, when we finish off Bawbag, I'm going to raid some jewellery shops, melt down a muckle pile of gold, and make you an Oscar for that acting. You faced down people that could have *crushed* you, and you did it without flinching. Jesus, Rhona. You're a bloody gaisgeach."

"I don't know what that means!"

"It means a hero," Eilidh said quietly from where she sat with one leg stretched out in front of her.

An unintelligible sentence fell into further obscurity with Rhona's mouth being buried in her knees—and the huge sniff in the middle didn't help.

Honestly, kind of a mood. It had been that kind of day.

"Couldn't make that out, love," I said, giving her a brotherly squeeze.

Rhona lifted her face, which was wet and blotchy. "I said it was my fault he caught me at all. I was being stupid, trying to finish my part of the quest, the alchemical hingmy."

That was about as clear as my current view of the stars, which was to say completely blanketed by clouds.

The teenager dropped her head back into her knees again as if she couldn't bear to look at either me or Eilidh for this confession.

"I found a fly agaric, and I got so excited that I didn't notice the siphon sneaking up on me," she said finally, her words slow and deliberate.

"The . . . poisonous mushroom?" I frowned. "Isn't it a bit early?"

"Yes! That's why I got distracted. My book says they're a symbol of luck alchemically, and I wanted to gather them to help us." Rhona lifted her chin only enough to rest it in the crook between her knees. "That—*arsehole* grabbed me right as I was dropping it in my inventory. So aye, it's my fault yous had to come rescue me, my fault we had to fight them, and my fault all those people are—are dead."

"Wheesht," Eilidh said sharply to shush her. "You're not

the only one who's gotten captured here. In fact, you're so *un*-unique that literally everyone else here has also been captured by the enemy. By that particular enemy, no less."

"Eilidh's right." I pulled my arm from around Rhona's shoulders so I could turn and face her. "You were smart enough to lie and buy yourself time. You gave us enough of that to form a plan, and the plan *worked*. If they'd found us unawares, can you imagine what a disaster that would have been? How many more people would be dead?"

"But maybe they wouldn't have found us at all!"

"Maybe," Eilidh said with a shrug. "Then they would have gone on to Oban. And they would have killed folk there."

Rhona was silent at that.

"We're in a shite spot," I said truthfully. "We've got something coming up from the south that's worse than Nigel Farage—"

Rhona let out a snort at that, then scrubbed at her nose with the back of her hand.

"—and we've got a beithir and a ballsack who fancies himself Genghis fucking Khan to the . . . northwestish. To say our situation is less than ideal is an understatement."

"But we're not fucked." Eilidh's eyes were on me when I glanced up at the sound of her voice.

"We're not fucked," I agreed. Then I nudged Rhona's shoulder with my elbow. "And mate, you got the mushroom. If my memory serves from the last notification-palooza, you finish that task and we finish that quest. Dry yer eyes, lass, and make some mushroom magic."

"I guess if all else fails, we can eat it and die tripping balls," Rhona muttered, and when both Eilidh and I zeroed in on her like she'd announced she was going to lick her own toe jam from her feet, she returned our stares blandly.

"I'm nineteen, not a fucking nun. I was joking anyway. Fly agaric won't necessarily make you trip balls. It could, but it'll probably just make you shit yourself and boak tae fuck in the process, speaking of not ideal."

With that delightful imagery, our wayward wraith was off.

· (⚜) ·

Quest complete: The Hills Have Eyes: Part III

Oban is on the brink of war.

In freeing Edwin Sackington's captives—and sparking a mutiny within his household staff—you have gathered a formidable force to come to Oban's aid.

You have also discovered that Sackington is employing the use of spirit node and nexus simulacra to bolster his power; do not underestimate the danger of a foe so emboldened and thus strengthened.

Your quest [Defend Oban] has also been updated accordingly.

Continue on your path of ascension. Do not grow complacent. More than lives depends on your actions.

Objectives:

-Complete your personal quest (Calum Green) (Complete)

-Complete your personal quest (Eilidh MacIntosh) (Complete)

-Complete your personal quest (Rhona Smith) (Complete)

-Work together to craft infused armour (6 sets) (Calum Green, Eilidh MacIntosh) (Complete)

-Create alchemical solutions to aid your party (6 sets) (Rhona Smith) (Complete)

Optional: Take items of value from Sackington's manor. Nothing within its walls belongs to him any longer (Complete)

Reward:
-1 skill point
-5 attribute points
-Blueprint: Communication Crystal
-All cooldowns reset

I wanted to crow with delight at that—the crystal alone sounded like it would be absolutely invaluable if it did what I presumed it did from what was written on the tin.

Not daring to revel in optimism yet, I opened up the next quest notification.

Quest updated: Defend Oban
Make a plan.
Make haste.
Make no mistake: Oban depends on you.
Objectives:
-Reach Oban (Previous Instance) (Complete)
-Seek out the following inhabitants who are most likely to believe your story:
-Catrìona and Iain Whyte and Farid "Meeksy" Meeks (Complete)
-Ross and Jo MacIntosh (Complete)
-Ruaraidh and Ciorstaidh Smith (Complete)
-Jack Miller (Complete)
-Tina Dunlop
-Convince at least twenty fighters of level five or above of the threat (2,415/20)
-Formulate a plan to aid Oban's defence
-Reach Oban with the survivors of Sackington's magic and liaise with the town's defenders

-Survivor population: 297/312

-Optional: Reach Oban with all ultimate survivors having gained at least one level (Survivors having gained at least one level: 312/312) (Complete)

Rewards:

-Experience (commensurate with current level progression)

-1 item (ascension dependent)

-1 skill point

-5 attribute points

-???

-???

The survivor population line hit me like a sack of bricks to the gut.

We'd lost fifteen people. Fifteen.

I didn't even know their names.

My stomach churning, I vowed to find out. Every single one of those people had gone into battle against people who hugely out-levelled them in both strength and brutality. They'd still done it, despite their fear, their doubts—hell, whether or not they thought I'd doomed them personally to die.

My six skill points remained, plus another one from completing the Hills Have Eyes quest. Plus the five I'd not allotted earlier. And another five attribute points.

Twelve skill points.

At this stage in my personal commitment to forgetting important shit, I really needed to start doing press-ups or something, because I was heading into himbo territory. I could probably live with that. I was always the guy who got near-perfect marks in school, but basic life shit? Yeah, I'd been known to walk into glass doors. *Jazz hands.*

I could always aspire to be the Scottish version of Brendan Fraser in *George of the Jungle*. That didn't sound half bad.

But the self-deprecation was just stalling.

It was a bit overwhelming to think about where to put all those points, and as I was still trying to learn to use my existing active spells and skills efficiently, I wasn't about to go unlocking another seven new spells.

I *could* put them into existing spells, active and passive alike—and passive spells could trigger evolution as they grew in level.

I decided my best course of action would be to look at passives. If there were passive skills I could unlock that would boost me in the fight that lay ahead of us, bring them the fuck on.

For a few moments, I sat in my meditative state, simply breathing and allowing my spirit to ebb and flow through and around me. Part of me hoped—in vain—that it would give me some clue as to which skill tree to start with. No answer emerged from the murmur of the camp.

With a small sigh, I opened my Draoidh tree. It was where I wanted to concentrate the most anyway, and so far I'd not seen a skill I didn't want.

What met me gave me a shock.

Normally, when I concentrated on a particular spell tree, the tree itself would appear in my vision with whatever was already unlocked glowing like a star, unavailable spells greyed out, and anything I could unlock lit up.

This time, I only saw a single message that sprawled across the obscured tree.

Darach evolution available.

Warning: Skill evolutions take several minutes to complete, and during that time, you will be left vulnerable. Do not trigger a skill evolution if you are in hostile territory or if there are any hazards that could harm you in the surrounding natural world.

Would you like to trigger this evolution now?

Damn.

I shook myself out of my screen, looking around for Eilidh. She was sat much where she had been, though Mòrag was at her side. Eilidh's seanmhair didn't look like she'd been in battle only a couple hours before. To the contrary, she calmly sipped tea from her birchwood quaich.

"I've got a skill I can evolve," I said quietly. "I'll be out of commission for a few minutes, so please don't slap me this time."

"It was a *pat*," Eilidh protested. "And you just spasmed and passed out!"

Mòrag glanced back and forth between us, the skin at the corner of her eyes crinkling despite her gallant effort to keep the smile off her lips.

They twitched anyway.

"No slapping," I repeated, and against my better judgement, I winked and added, "unless we've established informed consent."

To escape my bad life choice, I hurriedly reopened the Draoidh tree and told the system to evolve Darach.

But not before I saw Eilidh's cheeks turn bright red as her lips parted ever so slightly in a look I had not expected to see on her face.

I didn't have time to consider whether or not that look meant my ill-timed flirt had landed.

My head bounced off the moss as I hit the field.

CHAPTER
THIRTY-EIGHT

D*arach (Passive) (Evolved)—Some believe that the word for druid, and thus all magic, originated from the word for oak. This word in the old language was* dair, *and whether or not the etymology proves true, it is undeniable that the oak is a symbol of magic and protective power even now.*

As a Draoidh, you will slowly begin to demonstrate a Draoidh's connection to the power of trees. The first of these is always the oak, for it is within the stalwart oak your power finds its roots.

Darach allows the Draoidh to draw consciously from this power, which grows stronger when using staves of oak or when in contact with living oak.

Your skill has evolved due to the connection you have forged not only with living oak trees, but also with your living oaken weapon and the spontaneous cultivation of a live oak.

You have gained an increased efficacy with all woodcraft made in communion with oak. Items you create will now be 20% more likely to bestow an additional blessing upon the user, and crafting with oak will no longer draw as heavily upon your spirit well, allowing you to create more complex items and also to upgrade existing items in both quality and arcane properties.

This skill may evolve once more.

Evolution of Darach (II): unlikely

For perhaps the first time ever, I woke with a migraine pressing at the borders of my skull.

My vision swam with the words, and I read them without really seeing them at first. It mostly resembled alphabet soup, like those colourful magnets on the fridge-freezer we'd had when I was a bairn.

When my mind cleared enough to actually make sense of them, excitement attempted to slap fight the burgeoning pain.

"You look awful," Eilidh's voice said. "That was way longer than a couple minutes, too."

I opened my mouth to ask how long, and a wave of nausea threatened to make me boak in lieu of speaking.

Eilidh seemed to interpret my goldfish-mouth gag clearly enough. "About half an hour. Everyone's getting ready to leave."

Nodding was about all I could manage. I rolled over on my side—away from the woman I fancied so if I did boak, the vomit would not be in her direction—and pressed my cheek against the cool moss.

I lifted my right hand in a feeble thumbs up, and I heard a chuckle.

"Might want to . . . check your face," Eilidh said. Amusement crept into her tone now that I was back in the land of the living.

Oh, no.

That was incentive enough to risk puking. I scrambled to a sitting position, pulling my quaich and my jug of water from my inventory. It wasn't like I kept a compact on me to powder my nose, but I hoped the water would at least give me an idea of the damage.

Had I stabbed myself in the face with a pointy stick or something?

Pouring the water into the quaich, I angled it so the still-burning fire illuminated the surface.

And immediately groaned.

"Rhona!" I bellowed to a burst of youthful tittering from the camp.

Apparently, she'd found some peers her age.

"Yes?" Rhona's voice called back.

I pinpointed the source of her voice in the crowd. "I will get you for this, mark my words."

The eruption of laughter that followed did not increase my confidence.

Worse, I heard the belly laugh of a certain Scottish-Iranian bear and the unmistakable snort of his wayward partner in the mix.

The giggles seemed to be contagious. I even saw Diana from Kilchurn doing her best to disguise a grin, and even the storm cloud that was her grandson Andy seemed to be losing the battle against amusement.

Groaning, I scrubbed at my forehead with my fingers and some water to no avail.

"I'm going to yeet her into the Minch using the Sound of Mull as a bloody *cannon*," I muttered. Where the fuck had she even scrounged up a permanent marker pen?

By the time I'd manage to scour the ink free of my forehead with Purifire, the laughter had died down, my skin

was bright pink—and not from the scrubbing—and throbbing, and my pride was a bit rumpled.

Rumpled pride was, however, a small price to pay to
hear laughter after that battle.

I could deal with that.

Besides, I'd been successful at removing Rhona's
artistry, a true comfort and relief.

No way in hell was I going to face Bawbag with a
muckle cock on my forehead.

"Call me Dickhead, and I will end you," I said to Iain as I fell
in beside him not long after.

"I wouldnae dream of it, mate," he said, far too inno-
cently for that to be the truth.

My head still throbbed, which was unfortunate for
myriad reasons, not the least of which the migraine itself,
but it also added the further indignity of my brain helpfully
combining the word "throbbing" with "member." Great
job, Rhona. A few strokes of a pen, and she'd made me the
poster boy for bad puns about 80s kilt flippers and bodice
rippers.

At least I wasn't in danger of taking myself too seriously. Ronald, who walked a short distance away from me
and Iain, looked like he was more offended than I was at
Rhona's prank.

It was past midnight, and we were almost in sight of
Oban. The plan was to stop at Luachrach Loch to regroup
and try to liaise with anyone in Oban who could get the
kids to a safe place. The one thing I was waiting for hadn't
happened yet—the wren was napping, which was fair play,

and once he was awake, he would hopefully give me an idea of the safest approach into the town.

Until then, we'd sit tight with as strong a perimeter as we could manage and figure out a more specific plan.

Ealasaid made her way through the crowd, almost as if I had summoned her.

The woman moved with even more fluidity and grace than she had a day or so ago despite getting thrown across the road by the siphon.

She gave me a sweet smile and handed me the notebook where we'd been keeping track of people's progression. Sure, it wasn't a high-tech solution, but we were living in a no-tech world, and no one had worked out how to reinvent the internet. Something told me the coral reef model from across the universe would not work for landlubbers.

I paged through the notebook, trying to disguise the grin that wanted to creep across my face. "Folk have not been slacking."

"An fhìrinn a th' agad!" Ealasaid confirmed my words as truth. She glanced at Ronald, who had given her an irritated look, then she sighed and changed to English. "We've now got a handful of people at level eight, a much larger handful at levels six and seven, and the bulk of folks are around level five now. No one is below level three, and the one person who's not hit level four yet is having an existential crisis."

"An existential crisis?" I asked, morbidly curious. "Who *isn't* having an existential crisis this year? Or hell, for the past six or seven years?"

"Perhaps I misspoke, m' eudail," Ealasaid said. "'Crisis of faith' might be the more appropriate term."

"Ah," I said. "Jesus faith or otherwise?"

"He's a Free Church minister from Lewis," Ealasaid said. "Very devout. Bless him."

"Well, he can debate teleological conundrums after we solve our Bawbag—erm, Sackington problem." My face still hadn't quite calmed down from the abuse.

Ealasaid snorted. "I may be old, but you've not managed to shock me yet."

"Good to know." I gave her a fond smile. "Is Rhona back?"

She'd gone back to scouting ahead, this time with a solemn vow not to get side-tracked by local flora, and it was a tossup whether she or the wren would be our best source of intel.

"Not yet," Ronald said shortly, before Ealasaid could answer. Then, almost under his breath, he muttered, "I hate waiting."

"You and me both, pal," Iain said. "But after the excitement of earlier and nearly having my best kicking leg torn out at the joint, I'm no in a hurry to get past the boring bit."

Ronald seemed to sober momentarily at that, but he still looked as if something was bothering him.

Not without reason—we all had plenty of bothersome things going on, to put it mildly.

"I just hope we can get in touch with someone in Oban to coordinate. There are too many moving pieces here for my liking." I blew out a breath. "With a little luck, Bawbag bought our ridiculous ploy and the flunkies who fled told him we'd taken out some of his people. His spirit nodes will tell him the rest, hopefully with little more information than that we killed the MacGregors."

While it seemed like we'd been moving slowly, we'd actually been making good time, all things considered. What I couldn't figure out was why Bawbag wasn't yet making his move. My Draoidh tree passives as well as my Nature tree passives would sense if something was amiss, and the world was quiet.

Too quiet.

One of my mother's favourite stories about me as a bairn was the time she and Iain's mum Catrìona had been having tea at ours, and Iain and I'd buggered off. We were only about two, an age where noise is the norm, and after a time, they'd realised things were awfully quiet.

They'd immediately put down the teacups and made for the upstairs, where they found the two of us completely starkers, dipping my plushies in the loo and wringing them over each other's heads.

Bawbag was nothing if not an absolute toddler, and if I could guarantee a single thing about his silence, it was that it'd spell bad news.

And be a lot worse to clean up than a pile of plushies and a pair of weans who'd given each other a sponge bath in—thankfully clean!—toilet water.

While Iain and Ronald bickered about strategies, I mulled over my skill points, which I still hadn't allotted due to the unexpected evolution of Darach.

Before I opened myself up to temptation, I wanted to prioritise. Knowing me, the second I saw a flash new spell, I'd be ready to grab it, but I wanted to hone my existing skills more than create a scattershot approach.

The spells I used most were obviously Connection, Spèird, Purifire, Cumhachd, Tàth, and Tairm but Tursa and Mac-Talla had come in clutch more than once as well. Whilst walking, I managed to flip through my spell trees to see where most of them lay.

Even though I was aware of it, the enormous bulk of my active spells fell under the Arcane tree, and all of those played off of my Nature, Synthesis, and Staves affinities. If I were to just go on that alone, it would be a clear sign to put more points in Arcane skills.

Only thing was that it didn't show the whole picture. By numbers alone, Nature and Wild were my weakest trees, with one active spell in each. But Nature held a whopping *four* passives, each with subtle-but-potent benefits to my understanding this brave new world. Both Tàthadh and Slàinte—animal bonds and healing, respectively—had two active spells.

My level-nine class was draoidh, and that tree had only one hybrid passive-active spell, Tursa, and Darach, which had just evolved.

As much as it *seemed* logical to go with the Arcane tree, something stopped me. Without a doubt, I'd gotten a lot of mileage out of Purifire and Keen Eye, and Spèird had obviously saved our arses when I used it to pin down Gregor MacGregor.

It took me fifteen minutes listening to the dull buzz of Iain and Ronald's back-and-forth volleys to put my finger on why, exactly, it didn't sit well with me to simply go for the easy choice.

Our recommendation is to use [your points] not according to the life you have led thus far but according to the life you wish to lead.

That was what the ascension text had said in the first moments.

I'd opted for the draoidh class despite my Pathos being my slowest-rising stat. And while I'd hit the bare minimum, that was a far cry from exceptional.

I felt a bit like Dorothy in *The Wizard of Oz* realising I'd had the answer all along, and I could jet on back to Kansas with a click of a pair of fabulous ruby heels.

Perhaps I'd been resisting adding points to Arcane because I already knew I wanted to focus on the Wild and Draoidh trees.

With a ghost of a smile pulling at my lips, I opened up Wild.

I was not disappointed.

CHAPTER
THIRTY-NINE

The first thing I saw in the Wild tree was a passive. After Tairm, I'd not looked farther in the tree because I'd been distracted by, well, everything. Shiny new class took precedent over shiny new affinity when I had six active skill trees.

Seven, if I were to count Coimhearsnachd, which I absolutely should.

Mentally, I allotted myself four skill points out of my existing twelve to use for passives—or to increase existing skill levels, in a pinch—in Draoidh and Wild. The other three I would save for Coimhearsnachd.

I had to smile wryly when I saw they'd gone for a Gaelic alliteration and followed up Tairm with Tuairmse. That'd likely be confusing for folks who had no Gaelic due to their similar spellings, but I had plenty of Gaelic, and the only thing funny about it was that it meant, quite literally, *guess*.

Tuairmse (Passive)—Whilst most flounder with patterns in the wilds of nature, you thrive riding the waves of weather and landscape alike. Tuairmse is like a volcano; it may lie subtly dormant for a time, but when it wakes, the results can be course altering.

Tuairmse works best in tandem with the Nature tree's root-level passives: Gu h-Ìosal, Gu h-Àrd, Taobh a-Muigh, and Taobh a-Staigh. It is recommended to learn those skills prior to learning Tuairmse.

Once all of these are unlocked, however, your innate under-standing of nature increases tenfold. You will not only be able to sense the turning of the seasons like the woodchuck who builds a thicker-walled den before an intense winter, but you will also judge the tides, the whip-quick shifts in weather, and most importantly, how to use those things to your advantage.

I confirmed that skill immediately.

With the tumultuous properties of the gales that blew in from the Minch despite Oban's naturally shielded harbour, rain could—and did—pelt you sideways. If we were heading into a prolonged battle and had the abilities to use mist, storms, and wind to disguise our movements and unsettle Bawbag? Aye, we'd take any advantage we could possibly use.

The activation of a new passive didn't always happen palpably, but this one did. My skin rippled into gooseflesh from head to toe, like the world's most effective ASMR. I gave a wee shudder and saw through the overlay on my vision that Iain had noticed and was looking at me ques-tioningly.

Trying to reassure him, I waved a hand dismissively, which seemed to work.

Next up in the Wild tree was an active, and though I itched to look at it more closely, I instead concentrated on bringing up the Draoidh tree. A surge of excitement followed the goosebumps. Just knowing I had hit the minimum Pathos threshold to be able to use more Draoidh abilities made me way too giddy.

Even the snide, cynical part of me shut up, though I was all too aware that the coming battle could truncate my chance to actually use all this new magic.

I was already fairly sure I wanted to add a point to Tursa, which I hoped would increase the efficacy of the spell to the point of allowing us more avenues of escape if things went to shit in Oban. We needed contingencies upon contingencies. I could only hope there was only one Bawbag making waves in Scotland, though that may have been an exercise in futility.

With a grimace, I braced myself for an active I'd have to talk myself out of.

It gave me a wee start for being the first of this tree to not be in Gaelic.

Liminality (Passive)

The Gaels and the Celts both venerated liminal spaces—the place where land meets water, dusk and dawn, and the traditional markings of the year for equinoxes as much as solstices. There is power to the between-places, where the world becomes veiled. Neither shore nor sea, yet both at once.

Liminality increases all Nature and Wild affinity abilities based on the following temporal-spatial locations: dawn, dusk, Imbolc, Samhain, Beltane, Lughnasadh, equinoxes, being within nine metres of a body of water, and being in places that house the dead.

Your magic shall respond with alacrity in these times and spaces, and you gain a 10% chance to bend others' magic to your own will to disarm it if it seeks to harm.

Any permanently bonded animal companions immediately unlock this passive skill.

As the bridge between the physical and the spiritual world, the Draoidh draws power from both.

This spell cannot be increased with skill points after unlocking, but mastery of its ways may trigger evolution.

That was an immediate unlock as well.

As with Tuairmse, I felt the reaction of my body like a ghost passed through my flesh, sinew, and skeleton.

If I couldn't add an extra skill point to Liminality, so be it—I went back to the Wild tree and placed a second point in Tuairmse, immediately getting a new type of notification.

Through use of a skill point, you have increased the level of your skill: Tuairmse (Level 2).

Which left one more in my passives budget, leaving me nine total. I was tempted to put one into Tairm, yet I kept that idea in my back pocket, instead flipping over to the Coimhearsnachd tree for the first time.

The word meant *community*, and it always triggered in me a particular type of fondness. I had a vague memory of my mum—a massive etymology nerd—telling me that the literal definition was *shared doorpost.*

I'd not asked if others had unlocked the tree, so when it unfolded before my eyes, I actually did miss a step to the point that Iain grabbed me by the upper arm.

"Watch where yer walkin', mate," he said, slapping me on the back when he let go.

"Have you seen the Coimhearsnachd tree?" I blurted out.

"Aye," he said as if it was no big deal.

I made a strangled noise, and Iain shrugged, turning back to his conversation with Ronald. How they'd not throttled each other yet was a mystery for another time.

The thing that had so wildly caught me off guard was that until that moment, I had not realised there could be such a thing as a *shared* skill tree.

If I hadn't been musing internally about the etymology of the word coimhearsnachd, I might have missed the pun. Shared doorpost, indeed.

As it was, the tree—shaped like an enormous maple—was lit up like Father Christmas's elves had had a rager and barfed fairy lights all over its base.

A lump formed in my throat at the sight of all the root-level abilities shining bright.

There were six of them illuminated, leaving the first ability on the trunk tantalisingly within reach. A quick glance told me that not only had people been unlocking new ones—each seemed to take nine skill points rather than just one—but adding to existing skills to increase their potency.

The names of the skills were those of hearth and home, of breaking bread and loving thy neighbour.

Just looking at it brought to mind Hogmanay nights, clasped arms and flushed faces as folk belted out "Auld Lang Syne" in its original Scots.

I paged through the root-level skills, seeing them pretty well sorted.

The first trunk-level skill threatened to have me greetin' even more than the general emotion of the tree's existence.

Aw. I'd lost track of my new emotional range, but I was officially experiencing more than the singular.

Eilidh was gonnae be so proud.

It required a whopping twenty-seven communal skill points to unlock the first spell on the Coimhearsnachd tree's trunk. Quick maths showed that it would take a total of eighty-one to get that far in the first place. I didn't doubt the skills higher on the tree would take more and more points to unlock—but their bounty would have to be extraordinary.

Clach-Cheangail (Active -> Passive)

If a community reaches this skill in the Coimhearsnachd tree, they will have already demonstrated a commitment to ensuring that all within their circles can benefit from the boons of the ascension.

Clach-Cheangail allows for the creation of a keystone which, when placed in an existing community, will provide said community with a limited area invulnerable to attack. This can be used to protect the most vulnerable among you as well as serving the purpose of a repository of communal knowledge.

This skill can only be activated once to create the keystone and requires a community working in tandem, connected by shared spirit, pathos, and will. It cannot be activated in disputed territory, nor can it be used to secure disputed territory. The placement of Clach-Cheangail requires existing connection to the land it will serve, and it cannot be taken by force.

Further skills in the Coimhearsnachd tree cannot be unlocked until Clach-Cheangail is triggered. Additional points in Clach-Cheangail prior to activation will count towards the next skill once the keystone has been created and placed.

Points to unlock: 21/27

There was no question in my mind as I practically slammed six of my nine remaining points into Clach-

Cheangail. The star on the trunk blazed to life as a bell-like tone resounded through my mind.

This time, I wasn't the only one who missed a step. A ripple went through the entire crowd as a notification flashed up.

Community Announcement:
Clach-Cheangail is now available.
Status: No keystone crafting available
Requirement needed: Undisputed placement locale

As I looked around, blinking back the sudden stinging in my eyes, cries of excitement rose up among the survivors —my community.

The reasoning that I'd felt on an instinctual level materialised in my mind. We were going off to fight, yes, because our community here *and* our wider community in Oban were under threat.

But unlocking that skill for the benefit of all served yet another purpose. It didn't just solidify our existing ties; it gave us hope.

Hope that on the other side of the fear and violence, there was something more.

From bonuses to crafting to shared knowledge, the Coimhearsnachd tree had nowt to do with war.

It had everything to do with people—and making sure everyone had the best chance at life.

And *that*, more than revenge or rage or mere need to stop Bawbag, *that* was worth fighting for.

Naturally, after that triumph came catastrophe.

Or, more precisely, cat-ass-trophy.

I hadn't forgotten about Sailean, per se, because I could

always feel her presence, but when someone yelled "Oh god, get the cat!" and it was accompanied by a sudden sense of kitten panic, I went on high alert.

A wave went through the people walking in front of me, heads bobbing as folks hurriedly got out of the way. A wean's squeak or two punctuated the scene, as presumably the adult giving them a cokie-back jostled the kids suddenly to avoid the horror of a trod-upon kitten.

Though I'd never tried to do such a thing before, I concentrated on the bond I shared with Sailean and, for lack of a better description, gave it a tug.

Immediately, her frantic flight shifted direction. From one heartbeat to the next, a ball of blurred fur pelted out of the crowd and flew through the air. Sailean landed, claws out, on my leg and began to climb.

Grimacing with each puncture wound, I endured her ascent. The tiny wildcat finally settled on my shoulder with a loud and disgruntled *mewp* that brought with it a whiff of kitten breath . . . and something else.

"Ugh, Calum—" Someone began to address me and cut themself off.

I looked over to see a harried-looking middle-aged woman pushing her way through the crowd. Tina, I thought. Or Christina? Maybe Kirsty.

She stopped in front of me apprehensively, eyeballing the kitten. Sailean hissed.

"Erm, care to explain why you were chasing Sailean?" What was that *smell*? "I've never heard her hiss before, so I hope there's a reason."

"There's a reason," Tina-Christina-Kirsty said flatly, wincing. She floundered as if trying to say something delicately.

"Just spit it out." The smell was growing stronger, and

while Sailean started to purr, which was cute, I had a sneaking suspicion fermenting.

"I was trying to catch her," Tina-Christina-Kirsty said, voice prim, "because she has a dingleberry."

Turning my head like I was a character in *The Exorcist*, I attempted to look at the kitten. Sailean, for her part, seemed unperturbed by the accusation that she'd been running through a crowd of giants—to her—with a turd hanging from her furry wee arse.

All empirical evidence seemed to support that claim.

I very carefully reached up and plucked the wildcat kitten from my shoulder, where she dangled, squirming indignantly.

The smell grew noxiously potent.

"Does anyone have any toilet roll? Or a large leaf, by any chance?" I managed to ask, trying not to breathe.

Three handkerchiefs, a maple leaf, and a ragged tea towel appeared in hands, paired with wrinkled noses on the faces of those offering.

I took the maple leaf.

Sailean squawked when I removed the . . . encumbrance . . . from her bum, and with a burst of Spèird, I launched the biological weapon in a high arc above the crowd much like Eilidh and Rhona and I had once done with bricked grenades.

A quick flash of Purifire over both the kitten and my hand—leaf or no leaf, that wasn't sanitary—and I replaced Sailean on my shoulder. Thankfully, the smell was gone, replaced only by her usual warm-fur scent with a hint of pine and grass.

Not wanting to embarrass myself, I cast Keen Eye on Tina-Christina-Kirsty to find her name was exactly zero of those options and that she was a level-seven hedge witch with a Contact Sports specialised affinity, of all things.

"Amanda, thank you for your service," I said, about to shake her hand but thinking better of it despite my fool-proof cleaning method. "I'll keep Sailean."

"Grand," she replied, relief escaping her words with a wee sigh. "Cute little bugger, but if you turned the arse end of her on Bawbag, she might just solve all our problems for us."

A ripple of uneasy laughter followed as Amanda turned and left with a half-hearted wave.

Not long after the dingleberry incident, we reached Luachrach Loch.

Sailean clung to my shoulder like a pirate's parrot, purring contentedly as she swayed with the movement of my gait. I could feel her happiness through our bond; she was delighted to be reunited, which filled me with a surge of warmth.

It was that, along with the knowledge of what awaited us in the coming days, that made me sure the time was right.

"A Shailein, a ghràidh," I said to her softly. "An dèan sinn Caidreabhas?"

I'd never been particularly afraid of rejection before, but for whatever reason, reaching out with a soft question of spirit to a wild animal hit me with the jitters.

I'd known, deep down, that she was who I was meant to bond with Caidreabhas. I also knew damn well it was her choice every bit as much as mine, and she was, as the children say, smol.

Who knew whether she'd understand what she was getting into?

Her wee kitten mind was a jumble of images, patterns,

the elation at evading Amanda, joy at being with me again. I also saw Eilidh's face in the mix, which gave me a further pang. I was turning into a right softy.

But soon, Sailean's own spirit caught hold of my own, and her purr grew louder as she stood on teetering paws and nudged her forehead against the side of my neck.

"Ceart, ma-tà," I said. "Rachamaid."

Let's go.

FORTY

W e stopped just short of the loch where the police college had a well-tended lawn—or had, until the ascension made it overgrown. The grass was still plush and far more even than trying to pull up in the middle of a bog or on the slope of a hillside covered in gorse.

The sky turned murky behind us with the oncoming dawn. My wren friend would be stirring soon.

Even as I thought it, he woke, and I got the impression of a wee birdie yawn so wide, his little beak felt danger-ously close to coming unhinged. I sent what I hoped was a thread of affection through our connection. He and the other birds had done more than their share in our battle with the siphons, and things had been so frantic and jumbled since then that I'd not really had the chance to thank him.

His feathers puffed up at my gesture, and he did a delighted wee shimmy on his branch before launching into the air to hunt for a breakfast of bugs.

The human camp was nowhere near breakfast time, but that didn't stop anyone's stomach from growling.

Nan set to barking orders, as usual, and her minions scurried to follow them. With all the unknowns, any opportunity to get a solid meal in was well seized.

I moved to the fringes of the group, also as usual. There was no way to really know what to expect from Caidreabhas when I cast it; I'd just have to do it and hope it didn't knock me on my arse like the evolution of Darach had. I didn't *think* it would.

People seemed to have learnt that when I wasn't up for conversation, I'd keep to the edges, and no one came over to speak to me. My own habitual pulses of Connection told me that the others who had been honing their use of the skill were taking up their posts around our perimeter. The amount of pressure that took off my shoulders was not negligible.

To calm my nerves, I pulled up the spell information about Caidreabhas, since it had been so long since I'd unlocked it.

Caidreabhas—This skill is a foundational one in the Tàthadh tree, but it is not one to be used lightly. Caidreabhas, like Tàth, forms a consensual bond with an animal companion, but unlike Tàth, this bond is permanent and will persist until your death or that of your companion.

Many animals in an ascended world stretch past their previous limits, often ranging from sentience to outright sapience, in time. Caidreabhas encourages such growth in your companion, bolstering the animal's natural strength and adaptability as well as their intelligence.

Unlike most active skills, Caidreabhas will not level, as for it to do so would cause first bonds to eventually lose their appeal with the ability to form more complex bonds. Instead, Caidreabhas evolves—with each animal you bond, your rela-

tionship with your companion will shift depending entirely upon what you invest in it.

Your current abilities allow you: 1 companion

For safety's sake, I settled myself in an even patch of grass, leaning back against a wooden fencepost. I placed Sailean in my lap, and she perched with her paws precariously on my knee, her tiny tail whacking at my arm.

I gave her cheeks a scratch, chuckling as she leaned into my fingers so hard she almost fell over.

"Here we go, m' eudail," I said to her under my breath. "Deiseil is deònach?"

Ascension or not, Sailean still couldn't answer me with words, but she head butted my hand. The gesture came with a surge of affection through our existing bond.

I took that as all the confirmation I needed.

Placing my hand at the scruff of her neck, I cast Caidreabhas.

Unlike the other spells I was used to, Caidreabhas didn't respond immediately. Instead, it initiated a swirl of spirit. The minuscule vortex hovered in the air between my heart space and the kitten, visible to my Connection-enhanced eyes. I watched as it slowly grew in intensity.

At first, I expected it to be like a cyclone, spinning itself out of the air and whatever particles made up the meat of magic. But as it grew, it also shifted. Threads came together and dove apart, acting in circles almost like a spiral but branching off like the fractals of a snowflake.

That strange pattern widened and expanded outward, rising until it hovered above my own head.

Sailean's wee ears had pricked up when I'd begun, and she scrambled around to sit on my crossed ankles, whiskers puffed forwards and her pupils fully dilated.

She could see the weave as well—she tracked it as it moved.

Like a perfectly symmetrical pour at the absolute zenith of a sphere, the bonding spell slowly began to expand back downwards, widening to encompass the both of us. From there, it curved back inwards. As it passed beneath my knees, I got the utterly bizarre sensation of a layer of spirit somehow weaving between me and the grass upon which I was sat.

I knew the exact moment it converged beneath us once more, because a pinprick of silver flashed in Sailean's eyes.

And an altogether new awareness blossomed in my mind.

Sailean's soul.

I had thought that bonding Sailean would help me feel less worried about her with the impending showdown.

Aye, I was a numpty.

The moment her furry wee presence became irrevocably intertwined with mine, I knew I would become mayhem incarnate to keep her safe.

Her gratitude almost overwhelmed me. It was the gratitude of a baby for whom the world was still enormous and new and full of wonder and fear—but it was also the gratitude of a traumatised orphan.

My mum had done wildlife rehabilitation her entire life; she was a veterinarian and a tireless advocate for Scotland's indigenous creatures. I grew up seeing first hand that animals could—and did—express emotions.

As Sailean's soul wove itself around mine like the cat she was rubbing against my ankles, I remembered Mum reading me a book about Koko the gorilla and her fellow gorilla Michael.

Michael had watched poachers kill his family, and as he slowly learned to sign, he told the scientists how he felt. Anger. Sadness.

Sailean had no need for British Sign Language or any other human language—her grief and terror and panic deposited themselves directly into my psyche.

I felt the way her tiny body had sprung into the air when the shot rang out, before she knew her mother was dead. And I felt the scrabble of her claws in the underbrush and the way she ran to her mam's prone form where it lay cooling on a bed of moss.

The man-thing who laughed and caught her with rough hands.

The smell of her mother's blood.

Then more humans, more strange smells, more fear.

Her memories poured into me, Bawbag's crow of triumph when the hamper opened, exposing her nest of comforting dark blankets to the harsh fluorescent light of the hunting shed. She had been barely a week old when that happened, and then the ascension had hit.

The first memory even of Rhona dripped anxiety and fear. Along with Sailean, I relived the hissing, the bottle-brush tail, the clumsy swipes of paws.

Fear coated that house, seeped between the floorboards.

Ultimately, it was that shared fear that sparked Sailean's trust for Rhona.

The young woman was no wildcat, but she was as afraid of the man-things as the kitten was. Sailean herself didn't understand this, but adult Calum did.

Sailean purred for the first time since her mother's

death in Rhona's arms, on a trundle bed in the servants' quarters where Rhona cried herself to sleep at the thought that she might never see her parents again.

The ascension changed *everything*—when the starling I'd sent to spy on Bawbag flitted to the balcony of the manor, Sailean had felt another presence.

And then I saw myself through her eyes.

My own face, full of the fear the kitten knew all too well. Sailean sensed the protective determination I held both for her and for the girl who had shown the kitten such love.

And Eilidh, as we travelled, a heart as broken as her own. Complex emotions for an infant creature, but we had taught her, even without realising we were doing such a thing, that fear was not the end.

No wonder Sailean had tried to find us.

We had left her in Oban for her own safety, but she didn't know that. She only knew that we were her family.

When I opened my eyes, Sailean mewed, a mournful sound that I felt through to my core. I picked her up and cradled her against my chest.

"I've got you, a ghràidh," I murmured to her. "You're home."

FORTY-ONE

There was still no word from Rhona.

The sun crept towards the horizon, and my anxiety climbed ever higher right along with it. For every moment that passed, I wanted to go running after her. We'd let her go off alone once more—Rhona had *needed* to go off alone again—to let her prove to herself she could conquer it.

Now, regret threatened to keep me from eating the hearty serving of porridge and nuts Nan had ladled into my quaich. Sailean lay asleep in the grass, a wee ball of exhaustion, and I didn't want to wake her. The use of Caidreabhas had taken a lot out of both of us.

A smile ghosted across my face as I thought of the notification that had popped up once the bonding process completed.

You have permanently bonded Sailean.

Many animals in an ascended world stretch past their previous limits, often ranging from sentience to outright sapience, in time. Caidreabhas encourages such growth in your companion. This will bolster Sailean's natural strength and adaptability as well as her intelligence.

Caidreabhas evolves—with each additional animal you bond, your relationship with your companions will shift depending entirely upon what you invest in it.

As Sailean is your first companion, she receives a permanent bonus of +5 to Mind, +3 to Strength and Stamina, and +10 to Constitution.

Sailean has unlocked the ability: Camouflage

Her current abilities are: Pounce, Camouflage

Your current abilities allow you: 1 companion (Sailean)

Of the pair of us, I thought it was the wee kitten who had taken the brunt of the shifts. I could feel her even now, her kitten mind full of busy images as she dreamed. Only snippets made it into my own consciousness, but what did made me smile; she was dreaming about pouncing the willow switch that had given her her name.

If the wren hadn't been winging ahead to seek out Bawbag, I would have asked him to find Rhona. As it was, the wren was off to the north, which could also explain why we'd not seen any further evidence of Bawbag's main force, just not why said force was taking the long way around. Maybe our ploy *had* worked, and he'd turned north once he got wind of us coming. There was no way of knowing until we could ask him face to face, assuming he had a face left when we were done with him.

Part of me had held on to my three remaining skill points just in case punting them into one of my existing skills could turn the tide of battle, but with Mòrag and Ronald on the other side of the garden working on the communication crystal blueprints and fussing over what they needed to craft it, I had nothing better to do.

It was anybody's guess whether we'd see more of the

anomalies any time soon. Until they made themselves known, I had more pressing issues.

Taking a breath to steady myself, I consciously relaxed into Connection. Muscles around my eyes softened. Shoulders pried away from my ears. Frown lines on my forehead smoothed out. Spirit and breath in for four heartbeats, spirit and breath out for four heartbeats.

I couldn't find Rhona right this second, and I couldn't teleport to Bawbag and give him the hefty kick to the cojones he so deserved. All I could do was what was within my power.

Passives still felt important, but Bawbag's erratic decision making wore on my mind, gnawing like a dog with its teeth in the marrow of a particularly juicy cow bone. I wasn't sure if my Pathos stat governed intuition or if I was just restless, but I figured it was worth a look at the next things in my Draoidh and Wild trees either way.

I started with the Draoidh tree this time. A stroke of luck—the next spell I'd not even briefly glanced at before was actually relevant, this one enigmatically labelled "seen and unseen." It fitted perfectly with Liminality.

Faicte 's Neo-Fhaicte (Sustained)—The Gaels have long known that there are more worlds beyond the physical, worlds into which people sometimes slipped, unseen or unheard or both. On occasion, they reemerged with tales of delight or horror or a mingling of the two.

Food so delicate and sweet all else would taste forever of ash. Beauty so rare and tantalising one could weep—but denying it would bring swift and brutal death.

The fuath, the glaistig, the beithir—all of these are creatures of your world and always have been. Now, though, they slink through the veil. Now, all worlds are one.

Faicte 's Neo-Fhaicte is a sustained state, first activated and then reserving a portion of your spirit the longer you maintain its flow of perception. It alerts you to the presence of the other-worlds' beings and may, for the canny, provide insight into its inner workings and motivations.

I would have left it alone but for one tantalising lure.

It mentioned the beithir.

The skill swallowed one of my three remaining points.

I activated it immediately.

Again, the spell's incorporation into my repertoire came with a shiver and an ethereal perception of expansion.

I had the strangest sense of existing in more than one moment at once, as if I could run my fingers both ways in time's river rather than simply forwards as we were so often constrained. The more I concentrated on it, the more I could almost feel it.

That was too much for me to take in at the moment. Miles to go before I had time to sit round and play with magic.

Deactivating the spell again, I waited for my spirit to regenerate, but it hadn't taken much at all. Moreover, it seemed that even inactive, it functioned in a subtle way like a passive ability. Or perhaps that was simply the shift in my awareness—up till now, I'd not actually considered the confirmation of the worlds beyond or that they could merge with our own.

There was cultural belief and what we called seanchas or dualchas, our lore and heritage and traditions, and there was kissing the hand of a glaistig and feeling the petal smoothness of her skin and knowing without a doubt she was real. There was the beithir's stinger crushing a warrior's skull. There was the fuath dragging Rhona to the bottom of Loch Awe.

My worldview adjusting further still, I looked at the next skill in the Draoidh tree.

This one was a passive, and it was one that immediately tugged at me, so strongly I knew even without reading it that it was necessary.

Bas-Ogham (Passive)

Ogham is a form of writing that, much like the runes of the Nordic peoples, was also used for divination. Its letters correspond to the trees of the Gaelic alphabet. Bas-Ogham is the art of divining with small rods of wood into which the letters of the ogham are carved.

The writing can be found carved into stone, though wood carvings would have also proliferated at the time of its peak usage. Those have largely been lost to time.

Regain the knowledge of those who came before. In an ascended world, your connection to your ancestors is as real as that to those who walk and breathe beside you on your path.

The uses of ogham are limited only by your imagination— and your will. They can be formed into sacred trees, etched into weapons, tattooed into skin. Be mindful of what you create. Allow Bas-Ogham to guide you.

Bas-Ogham as a skill will improve with each tree attunement you cultivate.

Your current attunements:
Darach

Despite the piddly list feeling utterly lacking, I confirmed the skill point.

It was as if I'd been gifted a book.

The new knowledge ran through me like a harp string, and upon it, Bas-Ogham gave me every letter I needed to write destiny onto that string. It whispered the importance of the ite, the feather that formed beginning and ending of the intended message.

That left me with one skill point remaining, and almost shaking, I looked to the next in the Draoidh tree. It was seventh of the nine root-level spells. My first glance made me do a double take because I forgot *dubh* meant other things besides just *black*. It could also be the pupil of the eye —or it could mean ink.

The moment I remembered that, the more excited I got.

Dubh

The Draoidh knows there is nowt to fear in darkness.

To the contrary, darkness is the source of all things, including light. It is from darkness the universe was born, and in that darkness is the potential of all creation.

Dubh allows you to tap into the creative power. Coupled with Bas-Ogham, it can be used to write ogham into your skin. In the heat of battle, the Draoidh can use Dubh to obscure an enemy's sight. While it will only work upon a foe who lacks the Draoidh's understanding of the true nature of darkness, on a fearful opponent who relies fully upon sight and light, it is a powerful weapon.

The skill taps into our most ancient connections to a time before time itself, before light, when all was one in the womb of the endless void. Dubh does not ascribe fear to this void; for the Draoidh, it is a source of comfort and solace. In returning to Dubh, the Draoidh finds the will to write reality into existence.

I needed no further convincing.

While the note about battle would certainly help, I'd no doubt, it was far from the first thing on my mind.

My brain whirled through something practical—something magical—I could do while we sat on our arses and waited.

Already, I could see script unspooling along that harp string at my core.

I could see how to use it.

Like a thoughtful mad scientist handed a primordial power from the dawn of existence, I prudently decided to start my experiments on myself.

Bas-Ogham had instilled in me the knowledge that ogham was most often read from bottom to top, though long inscriptions could also be read left to right.

It felt fitting that my first mark should be for my first attunement: darach, the oak. In the ogham alphabet, it was called dair.

Moving yet further away from the busy camp of people, I pulled my staff from my back. I carefully stripped off my armour and my undershirt, juggling my equipment for a moment before I spotted an ideal place. There was a large pine on the eastern edge of the grass. I made my way to it and stepped behind its trunk, under the shadow of its branches.

My staff, I leaned against the trunk of the tree, nestling its globe of wood in a deep crack in the bark.

The slowly lightening morning illuminated my pasty white skin to the point that I wryly thought I had better make sure I was dressed again before the sun came up so I'd not warn Bawbag and his Band of Bams by turning myself into a beacon of blinding light.

I'd not had much occasion to see myself naked lately, and because of that, I'd missed the effects of hard travel and physical exertion on my body—along with the ascension's spirit influence.

Eilidh had changed dramatically. *That,* I'd noticed. Her beauty had shifted from soft to fierce. She'd never been a shrinking violet or a shrinking anything, but now she was a warrior.

For whatever daft reason, I'd not considered that I had changed just as much. Even the few points I'd haphazardly gained in Strength had filled out my chest and shoulders. Where before, I'd been a rangy wee cunt, now I was . . . well, still rangy, but definitely no longer wee. The cunt bit was debatable—I'd choose to think of it as the Scottish affectionate epithet, though I was sure others' mileage would vary.

My abdominal muscles were visible and pronounced, Adonis lines giving me a slight internal crisis.

"Christ," I muttered under my breath.

I'd never had trouble finding a date—or a casual shag—but if my clothes needed washing, I'd the board for it attached to my bloody torso now.

That humbling imagery was enough to shake me out of my literal navel gazing.

Sober now, I sat down with my back to the pine. It gave me a wee start as my spirit capacity expanded with the boon, Glòir a' Ghiuthais.

It felt a bit awkward to be enjoying the benefits of the auld Scots pine's parting gift whilst about to tattoo another tree's name over my heart.

The tree at my back must have felt my sudden shift in demeanour, because without me trying to establish a connection to it, it gave me the ascended-tree version of a pat on the head as if to say, *Aw, human. You are very young and cute.*

Fair enough.

Reaching over to where I'd leaned my staff against the

pine, I moved it into my lap. I held it in both hands, allowing Brac-Meanmna to sense my intent—though more and more, I didn't think I had to worry about the living weapon catching my meaning. While it was still early, I was beginning to get a sense that the staff had glimmers of a personality emerging.

With a little—or a lot of—luck, we'd both live long enough to see what shape it ultimately took.

In confirmation, I felt a flare of spirit from the staff, almost fondness.

Both for myself and for the first tree I'd communed with, it felt extra right to create the symbol.

The ogham for dair, when horizontal, was one horizontal line—an ite at each end—with two short marks pointing upward, perpendicular to the first line.

>‖<

Raising my staff to chest level, still holding it in both hands, I imagined the strength of the oak.

My skill Darach rose up to meet me.

Oak was protective, ancient. Its roots dug deep into the earth, and its branches reached high into the sky. They could spread out to cover enormous ground when left to grow. Unbidden, my mind retrieved an image of a burr oak in Kelvingrove Park in Glasgow.

The tree had to be at least two hundred years old, and it stood at the junction of two paths that were always busy. People rolled out picnic blankets in the oak's shade, skateboarded by it. Its many mahoosive burls covered its trunk with easy hand and footholds, and they were shiny with the oils of human fingers that had found purchase upon them over the centuries.

Its canopy covered easily fifty-metres in diameter, and despite humans using it as a climbing gym for likely all of its long life, it seemed to thrive. Its boughs were wide and welcoming—more than once when I was studying at Glasgow Uni, I'd personally scrambled up there with a textbook.

Oak held the passage of time within its branches. It would watch short human lives come and go with gentleness, never bending until its own time came.

Be like me, oak seemed to whisper.

With more peace than I had felt in weeks, I acquiesced.

I had no need of casting when it came to Dubh—all that mattered was my agreement with Brac-Meanmna and oak that straightened my spine from within even as the pine braced me from without.

As Dubh took root upon my skin, the spirit of Darach seeped into me with it, further and further with each beat of my heart.

When it was done, I sat taller. The sun had peeked above the horizon, a single sliver of gold turning the edge of the pine's needles to sparks with the night's dew.

Across my chest, the letter dair in ogham stretched directly over my sternum. It thrummed with my pulse, steadying me.

It was time to share this gift.

FORTY-TWO

The sun slowly climbed in the sky as I worked with Bas-Ogham and Dubh as people saw fit. Most asked for inscriptions on their weapons—and, increasingly, armour as people crafted it—but several hours in, I finished up with the last of a whole queue of people only to find found Eilidh sitting beside me, her legs crossed.

Surprised, I turned to face her.

She dangled a bit of heather rope over one knee with her long-fingered hand, which Sailean was busy pouncing ferociously.

That alone would have been funny enough, but Sailean also had a couple abilities of her own. And she was using them.

Pounce—A fundamental attack for an ambush predator. Currently most effective against slow-moving flora.

This ability can evolve.

Camouflage—Another staple in an ambush predator's arsenal, Camouflage allows Sailean to blend in with her surroundings.

Currently limited by the kitten-level understanding of object permanence best summarised with the phrase "If I can't see you, you can't see me."

This ability can evolve.

Both Eilidh and I were distracted by the subtle—and sometimes not-so-subtle—differences between pre-ascension kitten behaviour and post-ascension kitten behaviour. Aye, she did the butt wiggle, the tail lash, the whisker puffs. But on top of that, not only would I sense the flows of spirit as Sailean used Pounce or Camouflage, but we could see plain as day the contrast between her fumbling baby pounces and the ability Pounce. With the former, she'd often tumble arse over teakettle—or just tip over. Adorable, but not particularly predatory. When she triggered Pounce, though?

Sailean's trajectory was precise, and though she still tumbled in the aftermath, her strikes hit the end of that heather rope unerringly.

Camouflage, well. Let's just say that a black-and-brown wildcat in green grass suddenly stood out a lot less whenever she used it. More than once, I blinked and she was barely a blur. Not gone, but depending on how this skill of hers evolved, I wouldn't want to be the one Sailean was hunting.

You know, once she was bigger than a shoe.

As it was, while Eilidh had simply come to sit by me with the kitten, I got the feeling that wasn't the only reason for her sudden proximity. I'd not seen much of her as we made the trek to Luachrach Loch, but that didn't mean this was purely a social call.

I wasn't about to flatter myself.

It took about fifteen minutes, but Sailean eventually petered out again. Catrìona, Iain's mum, had luckily had Sailean's food and bottles in her inventory, so at least we'd been able to feed her. When the wee wildcat picked her way between Eilidh's knees and mine and collapsed asleep, that left the two of us sitting in sudden silence.

"Did you want something?" I asked her carefully, doing my best to make my tone warm enough that it wouldn't come across as *go away*.

Eilidh hesitated, but after a moment, her chin dipped in confirmation. "I was wondering if you would engrave my sword."

"Of course," I said immediately. "Give it here."

She'd laid it in the grass beside her in its scabbard, and she unsheathed it for me, balancing it on her outstretched palms so I could take it by the hilt.

"Did you have something specific in mind?"

It felt strange to hold her sword. Had it really only been a couple weeks ago that I'd seen her with it for the first time? The claymore felt like it was part of her now.

I placed the sword across my knees, careful of the keen edge of the blade.

"Whatever you think is best," she said softly. Then her lips curled into a rueful grin. "You're not Rhona, so I think I can trust you not to engrave it with a giant dick."

"Oh, god, I wouldn't dare." I groaned at the memory.

Goddamn kid—where was she? If she didn't make it back to us, I was going to kill her myself. Very rational feeling. Not at all symptomatic of growing familial fondness and affection.

I swallowed, deciding to continue to trust that Rhona was okay.

Clearing my throat, I went on. "But seriously, Eilidh,

that's a big thing to trust me with. I'll honour that—I promise. Thank you."

"You've earned it." Her words were not particularly soft, nor were they especially shy. She said them in a simple declarative sentence with no hint of defensiveness lurking between vowels and no sign of doubt in her blue eyes.

This time, when I swallowed, it wasn't fear. I wasn't sure what it was, but it very much wasn't fear.

Not trusting myself to say anything else, I turned to the task at hand.

Bas-Ogham spoke to me of the trees, of their own affinities and strengths. With my hands against the steel of Eilidh's sword, each time I cast Connection, I delved deeper into the essence that her own spirit imparted into the metal.

She treated it with principle, energy. Eilidh embodied nobility and strength, but she also encompassed purification and will, the initiative to do what was right and necessary and the conviction to carry through what she had begun.

The whisper of Bas-Ogham accepted all of that, and images took shape before me. Silvery birch with its elegantly draping branches and delicate bark. The steadfast bounty of oak, too, and the essence and energy of one who stood by her ideals. For the last of those, it was holly, brilliant and green with blood-red berries.

As my thoughts coalesced into something more substantial, I directed my spirit into the blade.

On impulse, I activated Faicte 's Neo-Fhaicte, further expanding my awareness into the unseen realms.

The effect was instantaneous. Eilidh's claymore was fully Earthbound, but under my directed spirit, I wove together strands of will like I was making a heather rope of shining gold. It sank into the steel with a resonance like a singing bowl.

The threads tightened, their twists and turns drawn together until I only knew it had not begun as one piece because I was the one who had created it. That golden, glowing rope stretched along the blade. It formed the canvas for the message.

The itean I placed at either end, complementing the shape of the weapon. Oak, dair, belonged closest to the guard where the sword's wielder could exert the most pressure, utilise the strongest leverage. It was there the sword most needed to be unyielding, rooted in the warrior's strength.

In the middle, I placed holly, tinne. That would guard the bulk of the blade, honing its cutting edges upon the whetstone of courage and principles.

The tip of the sword was the weakest part. Most would assume that because it was the bit that did the stabbing, it was the most dangerous. But anyone with any experience in the art knew: if your weak is against their strong, they don't need to stab.

They can turn your pointy end away from themselves and make you into a target for the edge of their blade in one skilled move.

No, the tip of the sword was where flexibility was needed. It was the purification of intent to know when to disengage, when to regain the advantage of your strong against an enemy's weak.

When I was done, I opened my eyes.

I hadn't realised I'd closed them. Dubh hovered in the background of my mind, a reminder that I did not need to see to create.

Eilidh's sword had been . . . transformed.

She stared at it, wide eyed.

The claymore had previously been the medium grey of commercial steel. Now it gleamed like white gold, but it carried within it the comparative strength of a centuries-old oak trunk. Instinctually, I knew that barring a meteor smashing into it, this sword would not break.

The crossguard and the hilt had been similar, the hilt wrapped in leather of unknown origin. That had fallen away, landing beside my right knee in a nest of pitiful scrap. In its place was what looked like bark.

When I reached out my hand to touch it, it felt like it, too. But where bark was brittle and crumbled and cracked with ease, this would not. Dark brown swirled with silvery white in an intricate pattern that formed the grip.

Before I could satiate my curiosity and cast Keen Eye, someone broke through my spellbound haze with a loud cry.

"Rhona's coming!"

The urgency of the call was, as it turned out, premature.

Our eager community crier shuffled his feet, abashed, as the brown skin of his cheeks turned ruddy. I thought his name was Alejandro, but after Tina-Christina-Kirsty had turned out to be Amanda, I didn't exactly trust my memory.

Rhona *was* coming; those at our perimeter who had been casting about with Connection to get forewarning of any threats had also been looking for her return.

Relief unspooled in my core. Rhona was okay. She was okay, and she was heading our way.

Eilidh seemed to be experiencing the same release of tension. Our eyes met over the sword, my hands still on the blade. At some point, she had also put her hands against the metal, close enough that her pinkies brushed the knuckles of my thumb.

Sparks seemed to jump from her skin to mine, and from the way she startled, I suddenly wasn't sure it was only on my side. Eilidh broke eye contact, carefully taking the blade back.

The spell of the moment broken too, Eilidh hastily sheathed the sword with a murmured "Ceud taing an da-rìreadh" of earnest thanks and got to her feet. I followed, shaky on my own legs as I noticed that my spirit had taken a steep dip.

And because after waiting for half a day for any news it *had* to all arrive at once, I felt a sharp tug against the thread of spirit that connected me to the wren. It felt different this time, insistent.

"You go," I said to Eilidh. "I'll be right behind you—the wren has news."

She gave me a strange look, but she nodded. I couldn't help but notice that she held her scabbard to her chest as she walked away.

I scooped up Sailean, who protested with a surprised "Prrow?" Nestling her into the crook of my arm and tucking her heather rope through one of the straps on my chest-plate, I also balled up the remnants of leather from Eilidh's sword. Waste not, et cetera. It may have been bedraggled, but it didn't have to be chucked into the bin.

The wren had eyes on Bawbag himself—and the beithir.

That filled me with elated glee for a whole two seconds before the wren turned ever so slightly midair and I got a glimpse of the scenery.

Of the *familiar* scenery.

My stomach practically dropped out through my colon at the sight of Beinn Mheadhonach on the far side of Loch Etive, Beinn Bhreac visible through the haze to the northwest.

He was between Taynuilt and Connel.

Bawbag really was coming at Oban from the north. I couldn't fathom why he would do such a thing.

But Faicte 's Neo-Fhaicte was still active, and spirit hummed through me, connecting me with the unseen as well as the empirical.

That view was familiar to me anyway, but now, it was even more so. It was familiar now because we'd fought the beithir in Connel with nearly that exact backdrop, and everything in my new senses screamed that this was not a simple coincidence.

"He's following the beithir," I murmured to myself, certainty making its home in my chest. "He's following the *fucking beithir*."

Sailean mewed in my arms, so I gave her a boost up to my shoulder, where her claws dug into my armour.

A couple people nearby looked at me sharply, one of them so hard that it gave new life to the old saw "glaring daggers." I registered a moment later that there was a small gaggle of weans clustered around the man, who had a small basket of foraged fibres half completed in his hand.

One of them was wee Rachel, oor buggy lass herself, and she crowed, "Calum said a bad word!"

Oi.

"Very sorry," I said, "truly. Beg your pardon."

With that, I promptly buggered off, making a beeline for the clump of people who would not announce to the entire camp if I dropped an F-bomb.

Iain and Meeksy may not have fought the beithir themselves, but they'd sure heard about it. I quickly told them my suspicion, Mòrag and Catrìona listening intently to every word as well. They weren't the only ones—the grassy garden we'd occupied was far from large, and I'd no desire to hide this from people.

Those closest to us made no effort to disguise their eavesdropping, and silence spread as I talked, the buzz of conversation dying off like sea foam pulling back into the ocean after the crash of a breaking wave.

"I don't reckon wee Rhona's findings will dispute what you've essentially seen with your own eyes," Mòrag said slowly, "but we will need to consider everything she says before we are able to make a plan."

"Aye," I agreed. "Bawbag's being reckless. Oban's had time to prepare now. *We've* had time to prepare. Either the man's so bloody stubborn that he's unaware of the word 'retreat' or he's got some sort of deadline."

They all knew my hunch about the beithir, and again, I couldn't quite help but feel sorry for the beast. It hadn't asked for any of this, and more and more, it looked as if Bawbag was puppeting it as a battering ram and little else.

When we killed it—and we would—he would simply find some other poor soul to consume.

CHAPTER
FORTY-THREE

When Rhona finally appeared around a curve in the road, the entire camp had gotten to their feet to see her.

And she wasn't alone.

Not only that, but I recognised the man with her.

Angus. I could have hugged him.

He was the bloke who, along with his wife Eliza, had taken us in when we'd first made it to Oban a lifetime ago. A lifetime—or what, four days? Five? I honestly didn't know at this point.

I'd remarked on the changes to my own body and Eilidh's, but seeing them in his brought the point home even further. He was in his sixties, and when I'd first met him, he'd moved like it. Now, though, he walked beside the nineteen-year-old wraith with the easy, flowing gait of a fighter.

Rhona had a triumphant—almost cocky, to be quite honest—grin on her face as she approached. She turned to look up at Angus and said something I was too far away to hear, but he laughed, and the burst of noise reached my ears a split second later.

Their mood filtered through the waiting crowd, turning anxiety to eagerness.

"Hello, the hoose!" Rhona called when she was about fifty metres away.

"Did something steal yer eyeballs?" Iain hollered back. "There's no hoose in sight!"

It seemed the excitement was contagious. Though I saw a few wary glances, ripples of chatter spread throughout the gathered cloud. Diana of Kilchurn caught my eye, a wry smile on her face. Beside her, Andy still looked haunted. His hair was lank and greasy despite people having figured out how to clean themselves with Purifire and the abundance of water to wash in.

That poor lad—I resolved where I stood to do something for him. I kept thinking I needed to and then getting distracted with other things. Meanwhile, the lad was sliding deeper and deeper into this funk every day. What would be useful to him, I couldn't say. I needed to figure it out. Anything that could encourage him, anything that could give him some sort of lifeline into the future of this new world.

Rhona's face, by contrast, was bright and shining. Her brown hair had some flyaways from exertion and drying sweat, but her brown eyes were clear. She reached the drive that led back to the police college with Angus and gave me a beaming wave.

I waved back at her, and Sailean made a squeaky wee mew as if trying to say hi.

If Rhona was this excited, *something* good must have happened.

No offence intended to Angus, but he wasn't exactly an

archangel descending from the heavens to lend us his flaming sword of justice. He was, as I was myself, pretty much just some guy.

Rhona waited for the buzz to die down a little bit. The sun broke through the swiftly passing clouds, lighting the green of the field with gold that haloed both the teenager and Angus as if to somehow prove me wrong.

"Two things," Rhona said, eyes still gleaming. "One, Oban now has over three and a half thousand fighters ready to defend the town."

That was enough to get the chatter buzzing again, but a sharp whistle from Eilidh quickly silenced it, though Rhona waited long enough to speak that I started to think she was taking the piss.

"The second thing is that Bawbag is retreating."

What? My breath caught in my throat. I stared at Rhona, though she was looking at someone else and didn't notice. There was no way—no way in hell—that was correct.

I clearly wasn't the only one who felt that way.

This time, it was a ripple of unease that went through the crowd like a shiver. It mixed with a few excited noises, quickly hushed as the people who made them realised they were in the minority.

Jeezo. I hadn't expected the wren's tidings to travel quite *that* fast.

There was no need for Eilidh to whistle again; it was quiet enough that I heard someone's stomach growl from ten feet away.

It was clearly not the reaction Rhona had expected. Consternation drew her brows together.

Angus was the one to speak. "I assure you, one of our

best scouts himself brought the news. The man's on the run."

That absolutely did not fit.

"What exactly did this scout say *made* Bawbag retreat?" I didn't need Òran na Cloiche to project my voice—the silence after Angus's pronouncement had only deepened. "He's been moving towards Oban for days, so what made him turn tail and head home?"

The people here had lived through the fight with two of Bawbag's *flunkies*. Fifteen of them had not lived through that battle. Even if I had kept the wren's report a secret, this would have rung false.

"Freddy said his team harried Sackington's flanks for two days and that his own people started to desert when they realised Oban was so strong," Angus said slowly.

"Did anyone verify this?" Eilidh asked, her voice sharp.

Another ripple went through the crowd, unease turning to distress.

"Freddy's reports have been spot on this whole time," Angus said. Defensiveness crept into his tone, intensified by the way he took half a step back and crossed his arms in front of his chest. "We have no reason to doubt him."

Rhona, on the other hand, did not echo his posture. The excitement drained from her face visibly, wariness taking its place. She looked to me as if begging me to reassure her, but I could do no such thing. I simply mouthed the word "Beithir" to her. She paled.

"What about the beithir?" she asked.

Angus stopped with his mouth half open as if he'd been about to go on defending Freddy and Rhona had chucked a live fly into his mouth. "Pardon?"

"The beithir," Rhona repeated. "The one we fought in Connel."

"It's not been seen since you lot drove it off." Angus's shoulders had stiffened, but even I could see the cognitive dissonance.

He was starting to realise something was very wrong.

"Is Oban ready for battle?" I asked softly.

Angus didn't have to answer, but when he spoke and it wasn't an answer at all, dread coated the inside of my stomach like crude oil. "We've watches set and our highest-level fighters are on rotation at all times."

"Just how high a level are we talking?" Iain asked bluntly. "Fifteen? Sixteen? Seventeen, maybe?"

"Twelve," Angus answered promptly, though he side-eyed Iain as if Iain had said something ridiculous. "Freddy's the highest in town at thirteen."

Fuck nuggets.

"Angus," I said, "I need you to listen to me very, very carefully and then do exactly as I say. Everyone's life depends on this—yours, Eliza's, all of Oban's and maybe all of Argyll's."

The older man simply stared at me.

"Bawbag is coming at Oban through Connel. He's taken control of the beithir the same way he's puppeted those stags, do you hear me?" At his jerky nod, I went on. "On top of that, just last night, we fought a level-fifteen and level-sixteen siphon, along with a level-eleven nature's blade and a poor sod of a bloke at level eight. We had almost sixty fighters. We lost fifteen of them, and we barely eked out a win."

Angus's face had started to turn red with his irritation at the peak of his defensiveness, but now it drained of colour, leaving it splotchy from the edge of his leather armour to his receding hairline.

"This next bit is maybe the most important of all of

this." I went on, trying to stop my own panic from rising. "Bawbag is using something called spirit node simulacra and nexus nodes. We told you about the simulacra when we were in Oban, yeah? Well, these are different. The highest-levelled blokes we fought had spirit nodes on them. Those are connected with spirit to nexus nodes controlled by Bawbag himself."

"What do they do?" Angus asked, confusion fighting a war with every other emotion flashing across his face.

"When the person holding them dies, the spirit node funnels all of the deceased's Manipulation resources into the nexus node. Into Bawbag. When that happens, it's as if he's harvested the dead himself." I did my best to let my breath out in as controlled a manner as possible, watching Rhona's face turning bleaker and bleaker with every passing second. "I need you to tell our fastest and highest-stealth runners where to go to warn the town—in a way that will *not* reach Freddy—and I need you to direct the parents here where they can take their children. Wherever you've planned as sanctuary for Oban's kids."

That, of course, relied on the assumption that Oban had such a contingency plan to keep the bairns safe. In all the hubbub when we'd first arrived there, it hadn't come up. Gods, I hoped they had thought of that, at least.

I was all too aware that the weans *here* were listening to every word I said, and from the complete and total silence and the bairns' lack of crying, my heart broke a little bit more. There was no hopeful naïveté left within me that they didn't understand what was happening. They'd seen too much in too short a time, and they were merely accepting the inevitability of the coming trauma.

It was up to us to make sure that was *not* an inevitability. We owed that to them. Safety was the first and most important promise adults made to the children they brought into the world, and it wasn't always one that was in parents' power to keep, but these kids were all of our responsibility now. That promise was ours to mend. Ours to protect.

"Mobilise everyone, and I mean *everyone*," I said. "I hope yous have got a contingency plan in place, because we cannot depend on numbers for this."

"We ought to outnumber Sackington's forces by easily four to one at the most conservative estimate," Angus burst out, scrubbing his hand through his grey hair. "It's more likely forty to one!"

"It was thirty to one last night for most of that fight," Eilidh said quietly, but her voice rang out through the crowd. "Thirty to one. We lost fifteen of our people before we managed to take them down. Iain almost lost his leg, and he's almost level ten. Believe me when I say that Calum's right. We cannot depend on numbers. Not with the beithir, and not with Bawbag. If I had to guess, just an estimate, I'd say he's hit level thirty by now."

The crowd collectively flinched at that, myself among them. I hadn't articulated that myself, probably because it was too terrifying a thought to entertain. But Eilidh was very likely right. Even if she was wrong, it was far safer for us to assume he was stronger than he was rather than gamble on him being level fifteen only for him to curb stomp the toon before we could stop him.

"Even considering diminishing returns on experience, he's been slaughtering people, and he's rigged it so that when his own people lose, he grows stronger," I said.

"They're right." Ronald's voice chimed in, the lanky man's head and shoulders visible above the folks of more average height around him. "Those he hasn't killed outright, he's tried to use as puppets like those stags and like the beithir."

Angus swallowed. Finally, after a beat that seemed to last a year, he nodded.

"I can't afford not to believe you," he said. "And in that case, we need to hurry. There's—there's no time to lose."

"You believe us?" Eilidh pressed.

"Aye."

"Why do you suddenly say there's no time to lose?" Rhona asked slowly. "What am I missing?"

"There was such a rush to come back with you that I didn't have a chance to tell you," Angus said bleakly. "Oban's not only not ready—Freddy's convinced them to celebrate Sackington's retreat. Festivities were supposed to start mid-afternoon."

Almost every eye went to the sky, where the sun was well past its zenith, already dipping back towards the western horizon.

I understood why he had hedged early on—denial was a heady force—but this was precisely the thing we needed to hear.

If we couldn't do something to turn this around, the night would be a massacre.

CHAPTER
FORTY-FOUR

We gave everyone fifteen minutes.

Fifteen minutes to gather up everything they could.

Fifteen minutes to figure out who would be the runners to sound the alarm in Oban.

Fifteen minutes to adjust our expectation from "prepare for frontal assault" to "prepare for Bawbag to strike while Oban is celebrating his retreat and folk are pished tae fuck."

Rhona came to me, practically wringing her hands, so I deposited Sailean into them to keep them occupied. She immediately pulled the kitten against her chest. Her brown eyes, though, looked lost.

"You did good," I told Rhona before she could say anything. "Not only did you bring us someone who revealed a full-on betrayal from inside Oban itself, but you gave us the chance to get the jump on Bawbag."

When she blinked at me, I put a hand on her shoulder. I could hear Sailean purring like a rattly motor in Rhona's arms.

"I'm serious. Whether he bought our ploy or not no

longer matters—what matters is taking this ambush and making it into a trap." My heart pounded against my ribcage thinking of the million and one ways this could end in atrocity. I tried to shove each and every one of those eventualities into the recesses of my mind. "We will do everything in our power."

"I like the idea of traps," Rhona muttered, still looking uncertain. "Particularly the idea of a mousetrap, the cartoony ones that snap shut. Particularly one of those on Bawbag's bawbag."

"Reckon just about everyone here would happily help craft you one," I told her dryly. "Now give me your daggers. I'm going to gussy them up for you. They've got a party to go to."

Without hesitating, Rhona shifted Sailean into her left arm and handed over the daggers one by one, though she cocked her head inquisitively at my choice of words.

The vibrations of everyone's hurried movements resonated through the ambient spirit around me, but I tried to tune it out. I sat down in the grass again, placing Rhona's blades in front of me.

Rhona was different to Eilidh, but I thought I knew what to do. This young woman was survival and creativity, fierce protectiveness and courage. She retained a child's wonder and clarity of focus despite mistrust and turmoil around her. Despite coming closer to death than any of the rest of us, she had persevered.

Her hardiness was a Highland hardiness, built of brine and burrs, but she also deserved softness. A kitten's cuddles —a community's love.

Ash and hazel and blackthorn—nuin, coll, straif—these were the trees I called up with Bas-Ogham, instilling Rhona's daggers with their power.

This young woman could pierce like the blackthorn's two-inch-long spikes. She could bend like hazel and withstand ash's challenge.

Wind whispered across the grass as Dubh wrote those roots into her weapons.

When I finished, I picked both daggers up by the hilts and stood to present them to her.

The ogham etching upon the blades was subtler than with Eilidh's sword, but the other changes were no less profound. The steel shone like platinum but with a beaten lustre that seemed to want to fade into mist.

These were the weapons of a wraith.

Rhona moved closer to me to allow Sailean to climb back onto my shoulder. As she took back her daggers, she frowned up at me.

"Calum, how did you get taller?"

FORTY-FIVE

E xistential considerations on height differentials were the last thing on my mind in terms of the day's trials, but even as I continued helping the group prepare to move, I couldn't help but wonder the same thing.

Angus caught my eye around the heads of a couple people I knew had been working on their stealth and speed: the unnervingly good-looking couple who'd gifted me the spork. At Angus's wave, I went over to him. Iain and Meeksy convened at the same time, each giving me a brief nod.

"I'm not sure it'll be enough to just warn people," Angus said. His lips had the too-slack appearance of someone who was in the midst of a significant shock, and his tone when he spoke was distant, as if he were hearing himself from a long ways away. "It's not that I doubt the town will mobilise, but Freddy is one of the best-connected people in our forces. If he's a spy for Sackington . . ."

"He'll notice something's wrong," I finished. "Aye, of course. You sound like you have a suggestion."

"I know where he'll be," Angus said, his voice squeezing around a knot of anger. "He's off shift for the night because of the 'retreat,' but he volunteered to guard the road to Ganavan."

"Ganavan," I said bleakly. "Did he, aye?"

Angus responded only with a terse nod for a moment. "His position is meant to be the Dog Stone, and to get there from Connel, he'd either need to come into Oban proper and then cut north or go overland."

I shook my head, gazing northward as if I could see Ganavan from where I stood. The Dog Stone was an enormous pillar of rock, narrower at the bottom than it was at the top. Legend had it that Fingal the Giant had used the stone to tie up his equally giant dog and the dog's chain had worn away the bottom of the stone.

The tale was a favourite among Oban's many sea life-slash-sightseeing-slash-ferry trips.

In an ascended world, I supposed it was too much to hope Fingal himself might turn up with his enormous hound and give us a hand against the beithir.

It would be less than ideal if he turned up and instead ground our bones to make his bread. I'd stick with the known evils.

I jolted myself back to the task at hand.

"There's a cycle route that cuts through to Ganavan from Connel," I said. "That's their easiest route to avoid the A85."

Iain nodded. "Also takes him past some perfect staging areas if he settles in for a protracted battle. The meadow just south of the castle, for one, not to mention Dunollie Castle itself."

Meeksy's black eyebrows knitted together. "If he were to somehow take the castle, it'd be a bugger to get him out of there."

A moment of grim silence followed.

I knew that cycle route, because I'd used it a hundred times as a kid with Iain when we'd bugger off on long summer nights to swim at Ganavan or—in later years—sneak a wee tryst with Connel-based folks we fancied.

Extending a tendril of thought to the wren, I saw he was still tracking Bawbag, who had now just about reached Connel proper.

That set off all sorts of alarm bells in my head; he wasn't trying to be stealthy.

"You look like you just bit into a cat turd someone told you was almond roca," Iain said, with his characteristic poise and charm.

"Gies a sec," I muttered.

Tàth had levelled up with the near-constant use. This was the longest I'd kept a bond with an animal, and belatedly, I realised that must have been part of how the wren was able to coordinate his aerial attack in the battle with the MacGregors. I'd not had the time to really explore the possibilities fully, but now I'd no time *not* to.

Giving myself over to the bond, my friends' faces fell away, and a burst of excitement from the flighty wee birdie told me he had been waiting for this.

Loch Etive spread out before me as the wren skirted the shoreline. The brackish meld of freshwater and salt filled the air, and with the now-setting sun, the rays cast golden fingers to trail in the loch's surface.

I wasn't sure what had happened with Connel's population after the battle with the beithir; they'd evacuated at the time, but we'd been away, so I'd had no idea whether people had gone back to their homes.

Now, though, I got an answer.

Through the wren's eyes, I saw glows in windows,

heard movement of people going about their business. A few weans played outside in a back garden.

The songbird took a turn southward, circling the village to give me the lay of the land . . . and then he aimed us back to the east.

Barely half a mile out of town, I got my first glimpse of the beithir in a while.

Where before, it had been nearly invisible, its camouflage so effective that it appeared to reflect its surroundings back at its beholder, now the beithir looked almost piebald. It was clear they'd been using some sort of arcane fire to control it like a cattle prod. Burn marks stood out across its skin, unhealing. Its scales cracked to reveal suppurating sores, which oozed a virulent green discharge.

Acid swirled in my stomach at the sight.

But that wasn't the worst thing.

No, that honour was reserved for the people.

I'd expected the deer; Bawbag seemed to have hunted down entire herds of them. That he could puppet so many effectively ate away at my guts, reinforcing Eilidh's assertion that his level had to have skyrocketed.

I hadn't expected the people.

Bawbag's flunkies sat atop their puppeted hinds and harts, a macabre cavalry heading towards Connel.

They formed the rear guard of the invading force, and while I was thankful to count only about twenty— including a few familiar faces we'd encountered at the manor what felt like ages before—sandwiched between the brutalised beithir and Bawbag's ruinous knights were humans.

Well over four hundred of them stumbled along, eyes vacant and arms trailing listlessly.

There were familiar faces there, too.

I recognised faces from the battle against the beithir, people from Connel itself who had fought by our side with whatever they could possibly gather. They'd attacked the beithir with rocks.

How exactly he'd managed to puppet so many, I didn't know. I'd not been party to Bawbag's advances around Loch Awe, only knew he had thoroughly depopulated my homeland.

But this had the look of a honed strategy. Bawbag himself sat atop a seven-point stag that moved with the same mindlessness as the other puppeted deer. The same rotting patches scoured the hart's pelt, and his eyes wept rivulets of water, strangely clear and pure.

The wren chirped, his heart fluttering with fear.

He banked away from the grotesque column, and while I wanted to urge him to stay in order to gather more information, it was too much to ask.

His urge to fly south, out over the sea, north towards the mountains, anything—it nearly overwhelmed me.

I knew then, beyond any shadow of a doubt, that the compulsion that had driven all life away from Bawbag's manor was at work here, too.

Through the wren's senses I felt the barren land, the encroaching dread that triggered every animal's instincts to flee.

Ceud mìle taing, a charaid, I thanked the bird.

He trilled a response, his voice the only lonely song on the wind. In it, I felt his desire to be far away. Even now, his wings itched to soar to safety. It had cost him to continue this long in my service.

I couldn't in good conscience keep him when he had already given us so much.

Resolved, I made my decision.

Though it pained me to offer, I gave a gentle touch on the wren's mind to let him know that I would release him from his bond if he wished. He'd flown into danger for me, ignored his instincts for me. And he had shown us much—his intelligence and strength was our best hope.

When he took the chance I offered, I let out a shaky sigh. *Mo shoraidh leat.*

I bid him farewell with a heart that grew heavier by the beat.

As my consciousness flowed back into my body, I met the three pairs of alarmed eyes watching me.

"I know how Bawbag took so many people," I said, "and I think our group of survivors here were a test run to see how many he could control at once."

I told them what I'd seen, watching their faces darken more and more with every passing word as the understanding sank in.

Bawbag had hostages. It had to be his strategy, how he'd cowed people unused to threats of violence. If he'd begun slowly, house by house stealing someone and taking over their mind, well. It would be an effective strategy, and in a rural area, there would be more distance between houses. Fewer chances for the village and hamlet dwellers to raise an alarm.

Fewer opportunities for them to warn each other.

With Bawbag aiming at Connel now, I'd no doubt he would employ a similar strategy. Connel was bigger, and the people there were fighters, but would they fight their own?

I knew the answer to that in my gut.

We would be too late to save Connel.

If we moved now, we might be able to save Oban.

My core group constituted the highest levels in Oban, and we would be the strike team to intercept Bawbag whilst our runners rallied a defence.

As much as I wanted to believe that Oban's highly superior numbers could crush Bawbag's offensive, it would be suicide to make that assumption. Our survival today would depend on coordination—and thankfully, the system had given us a way to do that.

By the time we were ready to set out, Mòrag and Ealasaid had crafted a handful of communication crystals. One by one, Eilidh fused them into armour or existing jewellery. They didn't look much like crystals—they were made of smooth river pebbles—but a touch of spirit made them glow silver, and when Eilidh whispered into hers, I heard her voice from twenty metres away as if she'd come up behind me and whispered in my ear.

The sensation was unnervingly intimate.

Mòrag tasked some of the other mages with creating more of them as soon as they could. She herself was coming with us.

Eilidh's grandmother had hit level ten in our journey, and her class, ealantair, could be read as both artificer and artisan. I'd no doubt we'd have need of her. I watched as she gave Iain's mum Catrìona a tight hug and kissed her on the cheek, murmuring something to her in Gaelic that I couldn't hear clearly but sounded suspiciously like *Bidh mi coimhead às an dèidh*, which meant "I'll look after them."

I looked away, swallowing, when Catrìona threw her arms around Iain, and with a glance at Meeksy's face, which was a war of envy and worry and gratitude all at once, I turned to Nan.

"Nan, you've everything you need?" I asked the chef just as we were about to leave.

"Aye. I'll work with the folk in Oban to see what we can do to keep you supplied." She gave me a strangely motherly look—strange because "motherly" was perhaps the last word I would use to describe Nan Reynolds, and sure enough, it faded almost as soon as it had appeared. "Gie it laldy, lad."

With that rallying sentence, she spun on her heel, setting off to finish getting folk together to head into town. I fought a brief internal war as I handed Sailean to Catrìona, the kitten's plaintive mew almost changing my mind.

"You've got tae go with her, a ghràidh," I said to the wildcat. "A battle is no place for a tiny kitten."

I felt indignation—or the kitten equivalent—bloom in Sailean's wee mind through our bond. It hit me with a pang of guilt as she clambered up to Catrìona's shoulder and swiped at the air with a hiss as if to say *See? I fight!*

"You are very dangerous," I told her seriously. "Which is why we need to keep you in reserve."

Catrìona, for her part, had jumped with the proximity of the kitten's hiss, but now she stared at me, bemused. "Are you having a conversation with the cat?"

"She wants to come with us," I said, tone bland.

Sailean gave me a long stare with a slow blink that told me my words had mollified her, if not fully placated her, and she mewed again. I reached out and gave her a wee scritch behind the ear, leaning in to give Catrìona a peck on the cheek.

"You be safe," she said gruffly. "Your mum'd never forgive me if something happened to you."

I didn't trust myself to reply to that, so I simply nodded, clearing my throat and turning away.

The rest of us were ready to move. Eilidh, Rhona, Meeksy, Iain, and the grans were to be accompanied by Angus, Ronald, and a group of ten of our highest-level mages who could keep up. Each of them carried what, at first glance, looked like a shillelagh, but on closer examination, it became clear it wasn't a tool for bludgeoning. With Brac-Meanmna able to cling easily to my back while I was running—not to mention the staff's sapience allowing it to keep itself from tangling up with my feet and sending me sprawling—I didn't have to worry about portability. The other mages did.

They'd crafted belts with simple loops, through which they could put their sceptre-sized wands. The wands had a solid grip to them and a pommel at the end that would keep them from slipping through the makeshift holsters, but they would serve as well as a staff for their general utility. And in a pinch, they could absolutely bludgeon someone.

The mages' job would be support, staying out of the heat of battle as best they could but hopefully keeping us fighting.

At least until our own cavalry came.

First order of business, though, was Freddy.

"That's us," I said tersely. "Let's go."

We set out at a bracing pace. I was a bit worried that the grans—Ealasaid and Mòrag—would struggle more than Meeksy running, but Ealasaid instead simply looked elated at the sensation of the wind in her hair.

That was almost as concerning, considering what we were heading into, but I wasn't going to begrudge her joy on the way to battle.

A few weeks ago, the thought of running a handful of miles through the up-and-down hillscape of coastal Argyll would have given me the fear. But now, with the ascension-boosted Stamina and even my middling Strength, we covered the two miles into town in less than ten minutes.

Oban was bustling with celebration already. We gave the centre as wide a berth as we could manage, with Rhona running ahead to find us quieter streets away from the boisterous sounds of merrymaking. Last thing we needed was someone to spot us and ask questions. Thankfully, Rhona's stealth and speed got us around without us tripping over anyone who might be alarmed by our sudden appearance.

That was, until we came to the roundabout at Markie Dans just at the edge of the Oban promenade.

We'd been bound to have some sort of bad luck at some point today, but I'd sincerely hoped it wouldn't have happened so soon. On a scale of stubbing a toe to stumbling into the waiting maw of a kraken, it wasn't *that* bad of luck, but part of me thought I might prefer the kraken.

Alison, the smitten primary-school science teacher from Kilninver, was stood at the rail that overlooked the bay.

The jolt that went through me shocked me with the reality that I'd not even thought of Alison since I'd heard Eilidh'd gone off with the rescue squad to Kilninver, nor her tearful collapse in my arms.

And there she was, standing and staring moodily out to sea like she was waiting for her long-lost sailor to return to Oban harbour.

"You've got to be kidding me," I said before I could help myself, and then I winced.

Eilidh's gaze snapped towards the young woman with my words, and though she said nothing, an irritated sigh escaped her, and she pressed her lips together as we ran.

We did not have time for this. With our pace, we were closing on her quickly, and before I could say anything, Ronald called out, "Alison!"

Gods damn it.

"Ronald, we do *not* have time for a reunion or an explanation," I hissed to the beanpole of an ultrarunner.

"But—"

I waved him off, slowing my pace, as it was already too late. Mòrag gave her granddaughter a shrewd look.

Alison's face absolutely lit up at the sight of us, her eyes searching until she found mine. I gave her a tight wave.

"Oh, my god. You're back! When did you get back?" Alison looked as if she were about to run into my arms, but thankfully, there were enough strangers with us that she didn't.

Eilidh standing by my side like a perturbed angel of justice likely contributed to her hesitation as well.

Alison's brown eyes widened as she saw Angus among us, as well as Mòrag and Ealasaid and the mages who'd accompanied us, none of whom were familiar to her, clearly.

"Just," Eilidh said, answering Alison's question before anyone else could. "And Ronald's story is one you should hear eventually—just not now."

I stifled my urge to cringe as mortification spread across Alison's face, making it all too clear she'd been talking about me and not Ronald—who, last she'd heard, was presumed dead.

Ronald seemed to realise the same thing, and his posture grew stiffer. "Indeed. We are in a hurry."

To punctuate his sentence, a ripple in the air betrayed Rhona's presence a split second before she seemed to step out from behind a veil, looking exasperated. "Why did you sto—oh." She eyed me askance. "Calum."

"I know," I said to her. "Alison, I am glad you're safe, but we need to move. You should go into town and find Eliza."

I glanced at Angus with that, and the older man took my cue with a perfunctory nod.

"Aye, lass, do that. Find Eliza and tell her to look out for Nan Reynolds. Middle-aged woman with dark hair with a white streak—she's hard to miss. Tell Eliza I said to listen to anything Nan says and do it." Angus's tone had the quality of someone who would brook no refusal, to the point that I wondered if he himself were a former school-teacher. Or a drill sergeant. "We'll explain later."

He didn't add *If we're alive* to the end of that, for which I was grateful.

I could see Alison was about to protest, and I'd an even stronger sense that she was not susceptible to Teacher Voice, since she was one herself.

"We're depending on you," I said after considering—and rejecting—several blunter options that I deemed more likely to get the opposite result.

"What are you all doing?" Alison asked, her embarrassment fading as she seemed to realise something was very wrong.

"We literally do not have time to explain," Rhona said breezily. "We didn't have time to stop, either, but here we are. If you don't mind . . ."

I guessed Rhona, unlike me, had not tried out any softer options. While the nineteen-year-old wraith didn't look at either me or Eilidh, I had a sneaking suspicion she'd already made up her mind about me and Eilidh—even if Eilidh and I hadn't yet.

Alison bristled at Rhona's brusqueness, but she gave a stiff nod, her eyes lingering on me. I had done nothing to inspire such a sudden crush, I didn't think, but this was growing uncomfortable, and it was a distraction I didn't need.

"Let's go," I said to my group, and a few of the mages murmured in relief, wiping sweat from their foreheads.

"Wait—" Alison started, but I cut her off as gently as I could.

"We can't. Do as Angus said, please."

I didn't give her time to protest further, breaking into a run.

"That was awkward," Eilidh's voice said softly in my ear, making me jump before I remembered the communication crystal.

These things would take some getting used to. Jeezo.

"Aye," I muttered in reply, hoping she could hear me. "For the record, she's a nice woman, but I don't reciprocate her . . . unfortunate infatuation."

"I know."

"You know?"

"I don't want to belittle her. She's allowed to fancy whoever she pleases," Eilidh said, "and so are you. But I know you don't fancy her."

Oh.

This was not the time to talk about this, not even a little bit, but I was dying to ask her how she knew that I didn't fancy Alison. I mean, she was right—very right—but I hoped I'd not been that obviously disinterested. Embarrassing Alison tae fuck was not on my list of action items, today or any other day.

From the way the others all kept on running without reacting to this little side conversation, I guessed they couldn't actually hear us. That was a relief. Even so, I didn't know what else to say.

I gave Eilidh a nod and a tight-lipped smile instead of responding, which she returned, a wistful look in her eyes.

Rhona had trotted on ahead yet again, and now she returned as we approached the Oban war memorial.

"Heads up," she said, motioning at all of us to halt. "Freddy's up ahead with a group of about five others."

Her brow furrowed with a frown.

"What is it?" Ealasaid asked, squinting up the road as if she could see around the road's curve.

She wasn't so much as panting after the exertion. If this is how we'd all be at ninety, that would be a hell of a boon.

"I don't know," Rhona said in answer. "Bad vibes."

The young woman shifted her shoulders like something was crawling between her scapulae.

"Did they see you?" Ronald asked, his voice still a bit sour after the Alison encounter.

"Of course not." Rhona's frown turned into a scowl. "That's part of the problem—they don't look like they're seeing *anything*."

FORTY-SIX

As awful as Freddy's betrayal of Oban would have been, it's almost worse to see the reality.

None of us quite knew what to make with Rhona's pronouncement, but as we moved through Dunollie Forest to get a look at Freddy himself, my stomach sank immediately when I laid eyes on him. The forest came to an abrupt end at the edge of a large meadow, but at the Dog Stone itself, the meadow was a narrow strip of grass, cut off from the main road on the other side with a waist-height stone wall. And with the sun on its way down, the shadows from the trees grew even darker despite the rays filtering between the trunks where we stood. A walking path ran along the fence a few metres in front of us, deserted.

Rhona had been right—Freddy and the mixed group of other scouts and fighters clustered around the Dog Stone with vacant expressions I knew all too well.

"Fuck, he's managed to make puppeted people *talk*?" I said aloud before I could stop myself.

All eyes turned towards me.

"You think he used Freddy to tell Oban they were safe while puppeting him?" Eilidh asked.

Ronald's face was a mask of horror. He had to be thinking of his own experience cut off from controlling his own body.

"Yes," I said, grasping at straws in my mind. "But I don't think he can do it convincingly for long."

When my companions met that with confused looks, I shook my head.

"He's got hundreds of people shambling after him in Connel." The thought of it made me sick—even now, Bawbag was likely invading the village. "He's got the beithir. He's got the puppeted stags. He's got the simulacra. It's one thing to hold things in a kind of stasis, but getting them to convincingly act human? Look at them."

Much like our band of survivors had in the corral, Freddy and his team stood listlessly, vacant-eyed expressions staring at grass. Though I couldn't smell them from where I was, I was willing to bet they'd also lost control of their bowels.

"I think he can either control them completely or not at all," I said. I thought back to what I'd observed through the wren's eyes. "Maybe the mounted cavalry at the back wasn't there as a rear guard—maybe they'd been put there to make the humans march."

"How does he control the stags, then?" Rhona pointed out. "Or how does anyone?"

"We can ask him when we get to him," Eilidh said grimly. "Pointedly, and I mean that in a literal fashion."

"Amen," muttered one of the mages in the back.

Iain and Meeksy had been silent all this time, and now they seemed to hold an unspoken conversation.

At my questioning look, Meeksy gave a hesitant nod.

"They're pretty much in the same state as those in the corral, judging by how they feel to my diagnostic skills. I think you'd guessed that Ronald's compatriots—for lack of a better term—were a trial run of sorts, but what if they were more like overflow?"

That got my attention. "What do you mean?"

"Auld Bawbag bit off more than he could chew," Iain said succinctly. "Reckon he's still pushing at his limits, like you speculated about the beithir."

"Right," I said, mind spinning through the possibilities. "The beithir they're having to control with pain in addition to whatever mind link he's using to take over its will."

"Poor bastard," Iain muttered.

"I wouldn't say that 'til you've seen it." Rhona kicked at a clump of bracken, then muttered, "Poor bastard, he says about the bloody beithir."

Ignoring that, I cleared my throat. "I don't want to hurt them. They seem placid enough—reckon we can restrain them somehow?"

"Why?" Ronald asked, irritation creeping into his voice. "They're clearly not a danger like that."

"Young man, I don't think we want to risk Lord Bawbag influencing them again, do we? Or let them roam free for him to do just that?" Ealasaid cut in, and I held back a snigger at her use of Bawbag's nickname. At Ronald's silence, she sniffed. "That's what I thought. We don't know what will happen if he tries and this lot is all tied up, but that alternative is preferable to turning them loose on the toon."

Nods bobbed around the group.

"Then let's do that—and then we need to get eyes on Bawbag himself." With a grim smile, I reached out for the nearest tree, which happened to be an oak. "Our friends here will make sure they don't do any more damage than they already have."

We worked quickly with the help of the trees, whose branches became bonds with the encouragement of our mages. Two of the ten who'd come with us exclaimed as they apparently got a level-up notification.

"Take care of that as soon as we've got Freddy and the others tied up," I said shortly. "We'll not get another chance."

It didn't take long.

Angus knew the others with Freddy, and he worked with a gentle efficiency to guide the puppeted humans to the fence, where Eilidh and I helped lift them over it. It was awkward work. The people were virtually deadweight, and they didn't squirm, so physically picking them up was a bit like trying to pick up a five- or six-foot-long sack of potatoes.

As much as it would have been fitting to tie up Bawbag's hounds to the Dog Stone in tribute to Fingal the Giant, we wanted them at least nominally out of sight just in case someone ventured by and found them before Oban mobilised.

We worked as quickly as we could for the sake of Ronald and the mages, if nothing else. Their revulsion and pity struck me; they'd been like this only a few days before, soiling themselves and shuffling about a literal paddock.

When we finished, I cast Purifire over everyone, including the puppeted detainees. Cleaning them up so they weren't lingering in their own filth seemed like the bare minimum of kindness to share with them.

"Use your points to your existing strengths as best you can," I said shortly.

Exchanging a glance with Eilidh, I decided to follow my own advice to look at my notifications, since I'd a persistent pulse of gold.

Quest updated: Defend Oban

Make a plan.

Make haste.

Make no mistake: Oban depends on you.

Objectives:

-Reach Oban (Previous Instance) (Complete)

-Seek out the following inhabitants who are most likely to believe your story:

-Catrìona and Iain Whyte and Farid "Meeksy" Meeks (Complete)

-Ross and Jo MacIntosh (Complete)

-Ruaraidh and Ciorstaidh Smith (Complete)

-Jack Miller (Complete)

-Tina Dunlop (Complete)

-Convince at least twenty fighters of level five or above of the threat (3,702/20)

-Formulate a plan to aid Oban's defence (Complete)

-Reach Oban with the survivors of Sackington's magic and liaise with the town's defenders (Complete)

-Survivor population: 297/312

-Thwart Sackington's plans:

-Alert Oban's forces to the ruse

-Use Saorsa to free the puppeted deer from Sackington's influence (Calum)

-Slay the beithir

-Deliver justice to Sackington and his compatriots

-Optional: Reach Oban with all ultimate survivors having

gained at least one level (Survivors having gained at least one level: 312/312) (Complete)

Rewards:

-Experience (commensurate with current level progression)

-1 item (ascension dependent)

-1 skill point

-5 attribute points

-???

-???

-???

I didn't love the new objectives. The "alert Oban's forces to the ruse" one in particular got my hackles up, because it wasn't yet marked as complete. The others were more obvious—of course we were going to do everything we could to kill the beithir and Bawbag. I hadn't forgotten about Saorsa, either. Knowing I could free the stags was a relief, but the warning also rang in my mind. They could turn on *us* if we weren't careful.

Shaking myself free from worrying about something we'd set into motion and could no longer affect, I had to focus on what *was* within my power.

Rifling through the rest of my notifications, I was slightly disappointed to find only a few wee points additions. Two to Stamina, three to Mind—welcome, but not earth-shattering. That I'd gained another level in Tàth was bittersweet. I knew I'd made the right choice with the wren, but that didn't mean it didn't sting.

We could really have used his eyes.

That thought brought me jarringly back to the present as I realised what was missing around us: birds.

A pulse of Connection confirmed it, but the silence told that story without need of magic. Oban was built on a bay —seabirds were omnipresent. Gulls, cormorants, sandpipers, plovers, terns, ducks, little grebes, gannets, even the occasional eagle or puffin, though the latter were far more likely to be found farther out in the islands.

If hills were alive with the sound of music, Oban was almost always alive with the sound of squawking. Gulls kicked up a racket, clustering near the pier where the seafood stand churned out mussels gu leòr and tourists were likely to drop chips on the pavement.

The silence was almost worse here than it had been inland.

When I closed out of the notifications, Eilidh was looking at me, a bleak expression on her face.

"You saw the update?" I asked, already knowing the answer.

"Aye," she said.

"We've got a quest?" One of the mages—I really needed to learn their names—blurted out the question before giving me an embarrassed look.

"Guess that means you're in it with us," I said. "Look at it if you want, but we need to move. I was hoping for a clue that our runners have already let people know, but it looks like something's held them up."

Silence greeted my words.

"Oban's not a big city, but it's also bigger than a single room," Mòrag said pointedly. "Especially because you told them to be unobtrusive about it."

"Aye," I agreed. "Just could have done with the reassurance is all."

I didn't have to voice what. The faces in front of me all understood the stakes here—and exactly what they'd volunteered to run into ahead of everyone else.

"We're a community, right?" I said, almost more to myself than the others, but there was a chorus of ayes in response. "We'll have to trust that our people will do as they set out to do and trust that Oban will too."

"And that they'll set up a better plan for verifying integral intelligence in future," Ealasaid said, eyeballing Angus.

"Yes, Mrs. Masson," he replied automatically.

"Good lad."

I blinked at their exchange—our ninety-year-old retired primary school teacher had taught *Angus*?

Ealasaid winked at me. "You too, Calum. Let's jump out of this frying pan and into the fire now, shall we?"

Uneasy laughter followed in the wake of her words.

We gave the puppeted humans one more good looking over—Meeksy did, anyhow, muttering into his communication crystal to Catrìona that they were here and we were moving onto the next stage of the plan.

He waited for a moment after he finished speaking.

"Anything?" Iain asked, frowning.

"No." Meeksy glanced at me. "Maybe it didn't work?"

"Try again as we move," I told him, gesturing at the path down to the road.

Without another word, we were on our way, again surrounded by the eerie silence both natural and magical alike.

FORTY-SEVEN

N one of us were used to moving quite so quickly yet. By the time we reached Ganavan Sands, Connection still told me that there was nothing and no one around us, but that would not remain true for long.

The silence from our people in Oban continued, much to our dismay. Even if we did everything in our power, we'd barely be a delaying tactic without reinforcement from the Òbanaich.

Light faded. Clouds had rolled in from the Minch, obscuring the view of Mull and the Ardnamurchan Peninsula, which also blanketed the sunset and the day's remaining brightness into a shrouded and too-still early gloaming.

Ganavan on a good day was braw, white sands and sparkling teal water didn't quite hold a candle to the jaw-dropping pristine beaches of the Isle of Iona off the south-western corner of Mull, but the beach was a stunner anyway. Today, though, it felt as empty as the skies without their birds.

The cycle path branched right off the carpark at the

edge of the beach, and around us, empty homes told a doubly depressing tale of a Highland housing crisis that preceded the ascension—holiday homes owned by distant investors, homes that stayed shuttered ten months out of the year while locals were increasingly priced out of the area much as I'd been myself. There were plenty of reasons Iain and I'd stayed in Glasgow after uni.

Now we were fighting for the chance to live at all, and I'd have been lying if I'd said my long-squashed homesickness didn't play a role in my desire to beat Bawbag down permanently. He was an extreme example of the commodification of the Highlands, without a doubt, but like the shells of white houses that surrounded Oban's loveliest beach, Bawbag's ugliness and bullshit had preceded the ascension.

"Too quiet," Eilidh murmured.

"Still nothing on the home front?" I asked Meeksy, hoping for a refutation of my expectation.

A minute shake of his head made me press my lips together.

Rhona hovered at the edge of the carpark, staring down the cycle path. "You all wait here."

"Be *careful*," I said at the same time Eilidh said, "Don't get too close if you see him!" to which Rhona just rolled her eyes as if she were trying to be as teenager-y as humanly possible.

"Yes, Mum and Da," she said, and then the little twit blew us a kiss and vanished.

"Nobody say a thing." Eilidh's voice was sharper than the edge of her sword, and considering she kept that thing honed to the point of being able to split a single strand of hair down the middle, that was saying something.

More silence as we waited, the slight boost of levity dispelled with the cold wind that whipped in from the sea.

Minutes stretched out, and I coped with my now-customary mechanism: Connection meditation.

Meeksy and Iain began talking in low voices about strategy, and not far away, I could hear the mages murmuring about something else I couldn't hear.

Rhona was back so quickly that her sudden reappearance was more unnerving than a prolonged absence would have been.

"Get ready," she said. "He's on the move. I found him just outside Dunbeg, which is probably pants for Dunbeg as well as Connel. You were right—he's oan the cycle path and looks like he's a king taking a tour of his lands."

Rhona's face darkened on the last bit, and I didn't blame her. Connel was her hometown, and if Bawbag had somehow neutralised Connel and Dunbeg both this quickly, that was not a good sign.

"There's something off with him," she added after a beat.

"Something's *not*?" Iain said under his breath.

"Something worse than his usual level of gobshite nonsense," Rhona replied immediately. Despite her usual quick retorts, though, she looked worried.

"Your family stayed in Oban after the beithir, right?" I asked her.

"That's what they said they were doing." Rhona didn't look entirely convinced.

"They did." Angus piped up to reassure her. "Your parents especially didn't feel safe in Connel anymore."

Rhona blanched but tried not to show it, looking down at her feet.

Her parents had been among the beithir's victims

in the first major battle with the beast—Eilidh and I had saved their lives by practically chucking them into the burn that ran alongside the road where we'd fought. I couldn't exactly blame them for wanting to avoid the place a giant scorpion-snake-thing had plunged a venomous stinger into them and almost killed them.

My next use of Connection stretched out as far as I could manage, and sure enough, just at the edges of my range I could feel Bawbag's presence.

Not *his*, specifically, but my spirit recognised the hart he rode.

"We've got maybe five minutes," I said shortly.

"You're sure you want to go behind enemy lines?" Eilidh asked me, her expression far too neutral to actually *be* neutral.

"Nope. But our best bet is chaos that benefits us more than him, and if we wait until our reinforcements arrive for me to use Saorsa, there's too much chance of causing more collateral damage."

I didn't mention the fact that there would almost certainly still be collateral damage—Bawbag's puppeted human hostages would be in danger.

"*Yes!*" Meeksy burst out, drawing all our attention. At our movement, his face broke into a grin just as a pulse of gold surrounded my vision. "Finally! That was Catrìona. Oban's mobilising."

I felt as much as heard the collective sigh of relief that swept through our small group. There was no such thing as out of the woods yet, but at least we had a shot of being more than merely a speed hump in Bawbag's path.

Maybe a speed hump laced with pressure-triggered spikes.

The momentary relief proved short lived, because naturally, I was up next.

"You're sure you don't want me to go with you?" Rhona asked me. "I'm sneakier than you."

"I've got Connection," I told her. "I'm the best suited. Besides, you've got your own job to do."

"Kick Bawbag in his own bawbag, got it."

"Rhona."

"I know, I know." She stuck her tongue out at me. "But if I get the chance—"

"If we get the chance, I will personally hold him for you whilst you kick him in the baws," Eilidh told the younger woman dryly. Then she looked at me, blue eyes dark in the gathering twilight. "You be careful."

I held her gaze perhaps a moment or two longer than necessary. "You too."

A bracing slap between my shoulder blades made me jump, and since Brac-Meanmna was clinging there, the staff retaliated with an audible *bzzt*, which made the culprit —Iain—jump as if he'd stuck his tongue in a power socket.

"Feck, sorry," he exclaimed, and I didn't think he was apologising to me. Iain cleared his throat. "What Eilidh said, mate. Thoir an aire ort fhèin."

"'S e a nì mi," I said, glancing at Meeksy, who, being the bear he was, wrapped me in an unabashed hug. "You lot too —look after yourselves, and I'll be back as soon as I can."

"Do not get dead," Rhona said, "or I'll kick you in the baws too."

"What, and add insult to injury?" I grinned at her. "Actually, naw, fair play. If I die, kick away."

It was stupid, but I'd almost rather this be the last

memory of me if I did kick the proverbial bucket. With an acknowledging nod and a few inane words to those I didn't know as well, I took off.

Whether or not it was the right choice was moot; we had few advantages, and Saorsa was one of them.

It wasn't just that Bawbag was almost upon my friends; the sun hadn't actually set quite yet. With the combined power of my many passives—Tursa and Liminality and the quartet of complementary skills in the Nature tree—I could tell time by the mere feel of the day. Saorsa would reset with the sun, and I had about ten minutes of a window to use it.

Part of me hoped it would also free the people caught within the radius, or even the beithir, but I didn't think the glaistig had concerned herself overmuch with humanity or monsters. Her focus was singular; it was my freeing of the first puppeted hart that had earned her respect, and the humans at Bawbag's manor had simply been a bonus when we righted the damage their presence had caused to the land.

It didn't take me long to find the putrid procession myself.

Rhona's assessment had been all too correct. Bawbag rode at the front of the column astride his seven-point stag, which stared vacantly even though its hooves clopped along the cycle path so smartly, it was practically a dressage horse.

On the hart's back, Bawbag sat ramrod straight, his perfectly chiselled face every inch aristocratic masculinity. Broad shoulders encased in armour that somehow resembled early nineteenth-century fashion if someone had redesigned it out of leather and what looked like glass plates. I recognised that strange magic; it was the same image that I'd seen before as he shot Eilidh's chest full of glass needles.

Bawbag looked like he belonged on an advert for haute couture apocalypse attire that would cost the equivalent of the UK's median annual salary for one outfit. His skin was flawless, clean shaven, and his eyes looked straight ahead, somehow managing to smirk.

But that wasn't the most disturbing bit. The entire panorama was obviously disturbing as fuck, but just the sight of Bawbag struck ice into my spine.

Even though I knew it was a risk, I had to know, because if we were totally buggered, at least Eilidh could warn the Òbanaich who were moving to join us.

I cast Keen Eye on Bawbag.

My spirit dipped seventy-five percent.

I almost staggered where I stood, and it wasn't the massive outrushing of spirit.

Eilidh's guess that he'd hit level thirty was correct; it was just conservative.

Edwin Thomas Sackington

Level 37 ???

Affinities: Simulacra, Mind, Arcane

Specialised Affinities: Proxies, ???, ???

This man is wanted for crimes against the Ascended Alliance. In full knowledge of his abuse of ascension tenets, he wilfully refuses to comply with demands that he cease his attempts to subvert the free will of Earth's inhabitants. He bears no title. He has been stripped of his class and all requisite boons. All possessions are hereby forfeit.

Anyone to dispense justice on behalf of the Ascended Alliance shall receive:

-Experience equivalent to 1 level

-Book: Ascended Alliance: A Legal History

-1 boon
-Mark of Esteem: Mark of Justice
-Access to the Ascension Champion skill tree (3 skills)
-Blueprint: Scrying Pool

Before I could recover from that, more text popped up on my screen.

You have discovered a quest: The Hills Have Eyes: Part IV
*   Ensure Sackington's horror ends today.*
*   Reward:*
*   Bounty rewards only.*

Fucking hell.

Leaving aside the revelation that the Ascended Alliance had just confirmed that they were both aware of what was happening and also either could not or would not intervene directly, I had to wonder if no one else had gotten this quest yet. Perhaps it took casting Keen Eye on the man, and maybe no one else had gotten close enough to do that.

I was eminently grateful that I'd unlocked that skill after the last time I'd seen him.

The quest and his level—*thirty-fucking-seven*—had stalled me. Gulping a breath to calm myself, I also cast Fuaran to help along my spirit regeneration, imagining a shield around myself as I did as if it could protect me from anyone in his macabre entourage catching wind of my presence.

If Bawbag wasn't oblivious, he *was* arrogant, and spirit eddied around him without direction; he was simply out for a jaunt, expecting no resistance. Truth be told, I wasn't sure even Fingal the Giant would qualify as "resistance" at this point.

I'd not seen the beithir yet, and under the darkening skies, I was almost afraid I'd trip over the damn monster before I laid eyes on it. At least that particular worry seemed unfounded—no sooner had Bawbag moved past me than the beithir made itself known.

Even knowing how Bawbag had mistreated the creature couldn't quite prepare me for the reality.

The beithir slithered in the midst of the puppeted humans, who themselves half stumbled and half shuffled, spread out onto the field on either side of the cycle path haphazardly. How none of them fell over was beyond me, but part of me was glad they couldn't see the monster in the middle of their hodgepodge assembly.

The massive snake monster was a mess.

Even in the failing daylight, I could see burn marks all over the length of its hide. Hell, I could *smell* charred flesh and pus from where I was, a healthy twenty metres into the field.

Iain'd had the right of it. Poor bastard. I couldn't help but feel sorry for it, even though the first time I'd encountered it, it had just murdered a pair of off-season tourists. That had been in the first twenty-four hours of the ascension; it had likely barely even burst into being.

What would have happened if Bawbag *hadn't* taken hold of it? His influence was what had sicced it on Connel in the first place. Now it was a husk of a beast—albeit a brutally dangerous husk.

The beithir wasn't what I was here for.

I waited until the puppeted people passed by completely, simmering in my own rage. The people were normal Argyll folk, a full range of ages just like in the corral, from a tottering old bodach with a hump on his back from long decades of hunching over to weans. A mishmash of genders, skin colours, hell, clothing styles. There was a middle-aged white woman in what had once been a pristine Harris Tweed suit and a brown-skinned gent in a suit himself that probably cost more than my previous monthly wages. Footy blokes in trackie bottoms like Iain's usual wardrobe. And there were pot-bellied empty nesters in dressing gowns and teens in jeans and T-shirts. It was a cross section of modern Scotland, turned into zombies.

Who knew whether the Ascended Alliance was actually a model utopia of their ideals? Maybe we'd find out one day, but until then, all I knew was that in this particular case, I was one hundred percent on their side of the line. Bawbag could not be allowed to run free.

As the first of the puppeted harts came into view, that fury solidified even farther into my soul.

Unlike Bawbag's own mount, these ones had none of the strange grace. They moved jerkily under the weight of their burdens, and though I didn't dare cast Keen Eye again this soon, I held my breath as I watched Bawbag's finest lackeys on parade.

My senses told me none of them were under level fourteen. I'd celebrate my increasing sense of spirit deductions at a later date if I lived to cross it off in my diary, but for now, it just made my stomach slosh.

I counted them as they went by.

Twenty-seven.

There were twenty-seven of these bastards.

They ranged somewhat in age and gender, though they were overwhelmingly male—about twenty men to seven women, and I was vaguely surprised he'd accept women outwith his kitchen and his bedroom.

Thinking of Nan, the late chef of Bawbag's kitchen, made that somehow worse.

A few more puppeted stags picked their way along in the crowd, riderless. I wondered why they were riderless and if that meant someone had relieved them of their riders or if Bawbag simply planned to put more butts on them.

"Eilidh," I murmured into the communication crystal. "Yous got eyes on them yet?"

"Not quite," she replied, and again, the sound of her speaking right into my ear almost made me shiver with the imagined sensation of her breath tickling me.

"Let me know when you see them."

"I will."

Slinking along beside the monstrous column, I followed at what I hoped was a safe distance. Saorsa was effective to a hundred-metre radius from me, and while the column wasn't so stretched out as to put that to the test, I didn't want to risk disaster.

Connection was my touchstone as I moved step by painstaking step in time with the procession. As much as I hated the waiting, my spirit recovered more and more with every passing minute.

The procession seemed to have slowed. The sun inched closer to the horizon. I didn't want it to become a race against sunset; I wanted Saorsa in my back pocket just in case.

And then, just as I was about to curse for losing the chance to take advantage of the cosmic cooldown reset, Eilidh's breathless voice bloomed in my ear.

"They're here. Do it."

CHAPTER
FORTY-EIGHT

I wasted no time.

As part of the glaistig's boon, Saorsa wasn't one of my learned skills, and I'd not yet had occasion to use it. Its name meant *freedom*, and while the glaistig was too new to this world to get that this was a very droll reference to a certain dubiously historical film about good-auld Willy Wallace, the irony was not lost on me.

Saorsa was meant for one thing and one thing alone: protecting those the glaistig had deemed her own.

The deer.

Even as I triggered the spell, spirit converging upon me like I was a magnet, I recalled what the system had said about it.

Saorsa bloomed outwards from me with a scent like fresh, rain-washed moss.

As a skill tied directly to a boon, Saorsa is part of no skill tree. It may be used twice per day and resets with the rising or setting of the sun. Saorsa affects all creatures within a hundred-metre radius of the caster and creates a web of Purifire and spirit that severs puppeted creatures from their bondage.

Be wary; whilst in the aftermath of Saorsa, all living beings may become violent or unpredictable, depending on the complexity of their minds, how sapient they are, and how long they have been in captivity.

For those who turn violent, they may attack anyone who threatens them, including their rescuers. In very rare cases, the trauma of their former puppet strings may cause irreparable damage.

I was very, very glad I'd stayed off to the side even a little.

For a moment, it was as if nothing had happened except a sudden gust of forest-tinged odour riding in on a rogue breeze off the loch.

Every single puppeted deer, hart and hind alike, reared up, panicked screams coming from their throats.

More than half of their riders crashed to the floor then and there, unprepared for the sudden bucking of their placid mounts.

It didn't stop there.

The stags began to bellow, hooves coming crashing down with the unmistakable crunch of breaking bones. The ascension had grown these deer to a size they *could* be ridden, adding easily a hundred stone to their weight. All of that weight now pummelled Bawbag's flunkies.

A surge of spirit exploded outwards from the freed deer, and yells cut off abruptly, though the sounds of trampling continued like a percussion of terror.

Looking once at the maelstrom of rampaging harts and hinds told me enough—something with Saorsa had stunned the riders for now.

The glaistig would be getting a fucking fruit basket from me if I lived through this.

I couldn't afford to hang about to see the aftermath of

what I had wrought. There was no time for me to waste. Whatever happened was a gamble—normally, I'd hope the deer would take out a few of Bawbag's henchies, but considering every single one of them likely had a spirit node simulacrum, I didn't dare wish for that eventuality.

Light exploded in the sky ahead of me.

My legs pumped as I covered the distance back to Ganavan, not daring to distract Eilidh now that the battle was officially on.

The beithir had been well within the radius of Saorsa—though it seemed Bawbag's mount had not—but as I'd expected, the spell hadn't touched anything that was neither hart nor hind.

Which made the beithir my next priority.

Purifire was by far the most effective weapon I had against the monster, and now, with my new upgrade, I knew exactly how best to use it.

With my spirit nearly recovered, I poured my energy into the spell, gathering it like an adder preparing to strike. The beithir wouldn't appreciate such a simile, but I could live with that.

Though I had not intended, miles back in the moors, to strike the enormous anomalous bunny in its sphincter, that unfortunate mishap did give me an idea. Not the exact same one, but a thought I hoped would pay dividends.

As the beithir surged forwards in the centre of the crowd of humans, I watched the rhythm of its tail.

Like the adder that had brought forth the beast in the first place, the beithir moved like a snake—for the most part.

Unlike an adder, the beithir had a scorpion's stinger-tipped tail. That surged forwards and back with the undulating movement of the monster. Like the harts had been, the beithir moved without the unpredictability of animals in control of their own action. Its slithering body instead kept a strange, unnatural tempo.

That it didn't deviate from that pace worked in my favour.

The next time it dipped, I loosed Fist of Flame.

Purifire exploded from the scorpion tail of the beithir in a splash of sizzling venom.

The venom? Flammable.

It showered down upon puppeted humans in an erratic cascade of blue-green sparks that might have been beautiful if the circumstances had been literally anything else. As it was, I watched in horror as the beithir simply kept moving, not reacting to the destruction of its stinger.

Ahead of the crowd, Bawbag let loose a torrent of silver-white glass.

Concussive force roiled backwards from the point of impact in a wave that shook the ground beneath my feet.

"Tell me you're okay," I said into the communication crystal embedded in my armour.

"Shield" was the one-word answer I got in reply, and it was the single most beautiful word I'd ever heard.

I refreshed Fuaran on myself, continuing my rolling use of Connection to keep an eye over my shoulder at the mayhem I'd left behind. None of Bawbag's people seemed to be up yet, or at least they were still regrouping.

And from the south, I heard another beautiful sound, one that I'd never heard in the context of war.

Bagpipes.

My body lit up with the melody that rose on the wind, the melody that could mean only one thing.

The Òbanaich were here to join the battle.

Before I could move to rejoin my companions, the earth erupted beneath my feet.

My head rang like someone had smashed a pair of enormous cymbals around my skull. Abused eardrums shuddered with the din.

I lay sprawled in the field, a clump of heather digging into my side. Groaning, I pushed myself up only to see a booted foot coming at my face.

On instinct, I cast Spèird on the foot from the side, and there came a near-simultaneous cartilaginous *pop* and the thud of the attacker hitting the floor bedside me.

No way was I waiting for them to get up. I scrambled to my feet and snatched Brac-Meanmna from my back, thankful yet again for my many passives that helped me orient myself in the midst of pure chaos.

"Calum!" It sounded like Eilidh was yelling right beside my throbbing head, but it was the sweetest pain I could have imagined.

"Coming your way!" I took off running, trusting my feet to go the right direction.

I'd no real avenue to know what had happened, but my stomach turned with the smell of blood, guts, and loosed bowels across the battlefield. The beithir was nowhere in sight, but the puppeted humans milled about aimlessly, tripping over corpses of their fellows. Several had collapsed across dead bodies.

My stomach wanted to retch. Casting Connection told the story too clearly—most of the harts had fled, but a few were down.

I needed to find Bawbag and the beithir.

Whatever had thrown me had dropped me in a clearing, blocked from view of Ganavan by a single line of trees.

Running straight for the trees, I threw out a hand to touch the first pine I encountered. Spirit rushed through me as my capacity expanded, and I renewed Fuaran on the spot.

I also activated Faicte's Neo-Fhaicte; I needed to make sense of the calamity.

The strange sense of duality opened my consciousness again, lighting the world with spirit that transcended layers of time and space.

The beithir.

Though I couldn't see it from where I ran, it had carved a path through the underbrush opposite me, on the other side of the cycle path. Screams and roars sounded from the direction of the beach.

In the midst of the cacophony, the bagpipes played on.

Without breaking stride, I shifted to follow the beithir's tracks.

Connection warned me someone pursued me, and I flung Spèird back behind me. I didn't look to see if it had hit. As I crested a small ridge, the battle splayed out before me.

Oban had come in force.

The beithir lashed its damaged tail, under siege from at least a hundred attackers—attackers who had learnt the hard way last time not to hit it with lightning.

Instead, Purifire rained down upon the thrashing beast, and though it tried to stab its many foes, it was limited to blunt-force action. No more stinger.

And I noticed something else.

Lines of spirit ran from the beithir to its right. I followed them even my feet continued to churn forwards.

The spirit led straight to Bawbag.

I almost lost my breath at the sight of the carnage around him. The concussion that had thrown me had clearly done far worse to those in the direct radius of its blast.

Even more terrible was the sight of more puppeted humans. They stumbled around Bawbag where he still sat atop his seven-point stag. Some still bore weapons, half unsheathed or trailing behind them. These people Bawbag had clearly drawn from the ranks of Oban's fighters in the midst of battle.

Slowing my stride, I kept to the edge of the trees where they jutted out to meet the cycle path.

I couldn't see Eilidh or the rest of my core group in the pure pandemonium of battle. The Òbanaich surged around Bawbag, mostly attacking him at range. From the moat of corpses around him, that seemed wise.

My pursuer must have been routed, because nothing else came at me from behind.

Seconds slipped away as I formed several plans of action and discarded them just as quickly. While I thought I could manage to cut Bawbag's tethers to the beithir as I had learnt to do with the simulacra, that would be disastrous.

Whether it would demolish Bawbag or us or both—that I could not predict.

I didn't dare cast Keen Eye on Bawbag again, but with his attention on the army facing him down, this was an opportunity I might not have again.

If I could find the nexus node he held, maybe I could destroy it.

And if I couldn't, maybe I could catch him off guard with something else.

Creeping closer, I saw the muscles in his mount's legs quiver. The majestic beast did not deserve to be treated like this.

At twenty metres, Faicte 's Neo-Fhaicte grew . . . strange. Stranger than usual. The hart seemed infused with something otherworldly, an energy not its own for sure, but it also didn't feel like Bawbag's.

In fact, he wasn't using the hart to charge into the battle, where an enemy of his level, mounted, could have caused even more casualties.

Suspicion dawned with increasing horror.

I cast Connection, listening with spirit.

My own spirit remembered the signature of the spirit node simulacrum from when I'd identified it, and while this wasn't the same, it was similar.

The nexus node.

Bawbag had somehow installed it *inside* his mount.

"Eilidh," I said softly into the communication crystal, "Where are you?"

"Fighting the beithir, but Bawbag's going to try something—each time he's stayed back instead of attacking with his magic, he's unleashed a fucking nuke. Where are you?"

"Right behind him," I answered. "I'm going to try something before he gets a chance."

Just then, a yell sounded from behind me, and I hurriedly cast Connection again as I closed the distance to Bawbag. The din of battle covered the sound of my footsteps and the ones gaining on me from behind.

The riders from the puppeted stags.

Whatever had stunned them with my use of Saorsa had run its course.

But the sun had dipped below the horizon, and they were too late.

I could use Saorsa again on the one target I'd missed the first time.

No hesitation.

No announcing my presence.

I gathered my spirit and cast Saorsa on Bawbag's puppeted seven-point stag at point-blank range.

CHAPTER
FORTY-NINE

This time, the effect was almost instantaneous.

Bawbag's hart bellowed, the trumpet-like sound rising above the screams and crackling magic. I hurriedly backed up, just in time. The stag reared up on his hind legs, bugling again with a sound like tearing vocal cords.

How that fucking barnacle managed to keep his seat was beyond me.

But the stag had been freed—and he was ragin'.

Unable to remove his scrotal burden with his first attempt, the hart began to buck and kick. I leaped further backwards to avoid the moose-sized deer's hooves. Each of them would hit with the concussive force of a sledge-hammer propelled by hydraulics, and I did not want to catch the business end of those pistons.

Knowing I had only moments before Bawbag realised something had gone seriously wrong—or worse, managed to recapture the stag—I cast Keen Eye on the frantic animal.

Liberated Monarch of Glen Etive
With the use of the glaistig's boon, you have granted

freedom to this noble creature, who has been twisted into an abomination by the one who rides him.

Though he has regained his free will, he retains an object that is not supposed to be housed in flesh.

The only way to free him fully and to destroy this object is with his death.

Something in me crunched at that last line.

I think I had suspected as much—a living being wasn't a piece of armour one could simply implant a communication crystal into—but suspecting and having to do it myself were two different things.

So I did something stupider.

Gathering my spirit, I reached out to the frenzied animal with Tàth. Not to offer a bond, but to show him my intent.

At first, he didn't even notice me, and with the fighting raging before his eyes, it was no wonder.

But after a moment, I felt his mind brush against my spirit.

The touch of his rage was like expecting a cool sip of water and instead pouring lava into my mouth. My whole body seemed to rise to a simmer all at once, and I forgot the danger of Bawbag, forgot the beithir, forgot the other opponents who even now were going to close with me and probably kill me.

All I could think about was the stain upon my back, the horrid usurping of my autonomy, the fury of seeing my own kind made into mindless shells.

Oh, I could relate.

Everything I'd seen since we'd reached the corral at Bawbag's manor bubbled to the surface, and my rage further fanned the hart's into an inferno.

It took me over, remade me from the inside out.

The hart seized my offered bond and took it willingly, wanting only my vow to destroy the man-thing on his back in return.

Before, my bonds with the starling and the gelding and the wren—they had all been gentle things.

This was different.

All at once, I felt the weight of Bawbag on my back, his knees digging into my sides, and though I knew it wasn't actually me, my vision went crimson with incandescent fury.

Pain lit into my shoulders as I saw with my human eyes: Bawbag's gauntleted fists, spikes slamming into the hart's neck.

I felt their impact, the punctures in my hide.

Dual roars rose, from the stag and from my own throat, torn free by agony and a need for vengeance.

It was that, finally, that made Bawbag spin and notice me.

I had succeeded at one thing; I'd caught him off guard.

Bawbag's magazine-perfect face contorted with rage, lips wet with uncontained spittle, and in that moment of his distraction, I felt as the stag's powerful muscles bunched. The hart reared again, balancing precariously on his hind hooves, and Bawbag slipped off.

Whether it was my impulse or the hart's, I'd never know. All I know is that as the stag regained his freedom from Bawbag's weight, he rocked forwards onto his front legs.

Those sledgehammer hooves caught Edwin Thomas Sackington in the chest.

Level thirty-seven or not, that force was incredible. The hooves hit with a crunch that punched straight through Bawbag's glass-magic-plated leathers and sent him flying backwards—directly into the chest of an onrushing lackey.

I leapt for the stag.

With Tàth in place, he was ready for me as I vaulted onto his back. It was not graceful; I was no classically trained rider, and this was no horse. Even so, I managed to scramble up and throw a leg over even as the hart pranced, wheeling to face Bawbag, who lay in a heap with two of his flunkies.

Forming Fist of Flame with Purifire, I let it loose from my staff, aiming it straight at the existing wounds in Bawbag's chest.

It struck with a wet *thunk* that immediately began to sizzle. Bawbag's body jerked with the impact, blood exploding from his mouth.

The hart's fierce joy at that sight echoed through me. Time. I needed time.

I cast Tursa.

The pandemonium around me slowed, stretching out like black treacle dripping from a spoon.

Behind Bawbag were the rest of his flunkies, barely moving to my eyes as they raced towards the battle.

The beithir still struggled with its attackers. It was as if Bawbag's puppeting had somehow weakened it. I didn't even know if it could paralyse someone without its stinger; its teeth were a danger, of course, but though it lashed and snapped, it lacked the drive and the animosity we'd seen when we fought it in Connel.

The Òbanaich would overpower it eventually—as strong as it was, they were whittling away at it more with every passing moment.

I tried not to look at the scores of dead, instead seeking out the faces I needed to see more than anything.

Eilidh. Her auburn hair looked black in the twilight, but it lit up with flashes of Purifire and other magic as she charged towards the downed Bawbag. Iain and Meeksy were nowhere to be seen, but Ealasaid spun great wheels of Purifire, which she launched into the advance of Bawbag's henchies.

The vantage point atop the hart was valuable—and it couldn't last.

In the momentary stillness as Tursa ticked onward, giving me the time I needed to plan my next move, I felt the majestic stag's resignation.

Now that the forced bond with Bawbag was gone, the putrid weight gone from his back, he could feel the nexus node inside of him. He knew. He knew what had to happen next.

He offered me a gift.

His spirit whispered to mine, guiding me to where the nexus node sat against his heart. Every time his pulse thumped in his chest, its expansion touched the nexus node. An invader, implanted with vile magic, meant to pervert what the ascension had tried to impart.

The heart itself, I could sense with Connection.

Tursa ran its course.

I moved before I could second guess myself or the stag.

Throwing my leg over to his far side, I called upon Brac-Meanmna to guide my strike. The hart eagerly seized upon the living weapon's own spirit, and as my feet hit the ground, I spun.

The stag reared once more, this time to expose his belly to me.

His heart sat in his chest cavity, just behind his front legs. I spun Brac-Meanmna in a downward motion, and an arcane blade erupted from the globe at the staff's head.

Built of pure force and fire with the cutting edge of wind, it cleaved through flesh and bone alike.

I felt the exact instant it struck the stag's heart, and a split second later, it hit the nexus node.

A gurgling scream rose from Bawbag where he still lay prone. The entire shift had taken maybe five seconds.

The nexus node plopped onto the blood-wet grass and bounced.

As the stag breathed his last, I accepted his gift.

His spirit poured into me, as did his pathos and will. My vision flooded with white, white, white.

When it faded, the hart was gone. No trace of him remained except for the bloodied, fist-sized simulacrum.

"Eilidh!" I yelled, feeling her presence ever nearer. "The nexus node!"

I kindled Purifire, slamming it down atop the nexus node even as Eilidh halted her charge. Breathing heavy, she raised her claymore above her head, point down.

Bawbag's mouth moved, but no sound came out. He would be healing—I felt the urgency pressing down upon me that we needed to hit him *now*, while he was still injured—but the nexus node was the most important thing.

Warriors from Oban streamed past us, falling upon the flunkies as they reached Bawbag.

Eilidh's sword came down.

With the other simulacra, there had been no noise, just an anticlimactic deflating jellyfish thing like a sad balloon.

When the point of Eilidh's ogham-engraved claymore hit the nexus node, it detonated with a blast of golden will.

For the second time in only a few minutes, I flew backwards from the explosion and knew nothing.

The only positive thing about getting knocked unconscious twice in a quarter of an hour—however briefly—was that this time, I had heaps of company.

Not only myself and Eilidh, but *everyone* who'd been in even moderate proximity to the nexus node when Eilidh'd destroyed it.

Even as I came to, Eilidh's hand appeared above me, and I grabbed it without thinking. She pulled me to my feet, somehow already alert.

"I know how I'm up already, but how are *you* up?" Her blunt question lacked bite. "Your Constitution can't be more than what, twenty?"

"Nineteen," I muttered. "Your guess is as good as mine."

It had to have something to do with the hart's gift, whatever he had bestowed upon me when he offered himself up to die and be harvested, but that would have to wait.

There had to have been a couple hundred people caught in the blast, and few were stirring.

Bawbag was among them.

"Shit," I said. "He's healing."

The massive chest wound was still there, but he was no longer frothing bloody foam at the mouth, which meant his lungs had healed. I'd thought we'd have more time. None of us knew yet how to quantify level differentials at such an extreme as this, and any guesses were probably wrong.

We didn't get a chance to so much as move.

Bawbag let out a rumbling roar, his teeth still stained with blood. Behind us, the beithir bellowed.

Startled yells and grunts followed, and I spun to see the massive snake-scorpion beast convulsing as if it were waging an altogether different war. Its tail strained towards us, whipping away and then jerking back, but its head lunged towards the Òbanaich who were hacking away at its front half with everything they had. Blades and magic scored and scorched its scales, but Bawbag roared again, and the beithir screeched. Its enormous bulk writhed, bunched, and then bowled through an entire line of twenty fighters.

"You will pay for what you have done," Bawbag rasped, speaking for the first time.

"Probably," I replied without thinking, "but we'll make you earn every penny."

This was the wrong thing to say.

I'd expected Bawbag to use magic like he had once when I'd encircled him with Ring of Fire, but in one impossible moment, he threw himself to his feet and launched at me.

This time, he'd caught me off guard. He wielded no weapon except those gauntleted fists, and I found out why the second they gained purchase on my upper arms.

Muscle crunched under their grip. I had only fractions of a second before my bones would snap.

Luckily, Eilidh didn't hate me. She did hate Bawbag.

I felt the swooping motion of her spirit as she planted her claymore point down in the spongey ground. Her stun, Tuairneal, had been impressive before—but it wouldn't have touched a level-thirty-seven opponent.

Now, with the force of the ogham I'd engraved into the blade, it hit with a beam of light that was palpable. Even without being the target of it, I felt as it rammed into Bawbag with the force of her enormous will.

It still didn't budge his feet . . . but it had hit him in the side.

The power of the spell wrenched Bawbag's hands from my arms, and I swung Brac-Meanmna, channelling a third of my spirit into Spèird to hit him while he was off balance.

It wouldn't have been enough, if it weren't for Rhona.

Even as he staggered—I could hardly call it reeling—Rhona materialised at his shoulder. Both of her daggers came down in the overgrown trapezius muscles at the sides of his neck at the same time that oor teenage banshee turned her ear-shredding shriek up to eleven.

Bawbag made the mistake of taking one stumbling step to the left, which put his legs a too-convenient distance apart.

Rhona was an absolute brat, but she was *our* brat, and right then, she did the brattiest thing she could possibly have conceived.

She brought her leg up in a powerful kick—right between his legs.

Being on the back side of him, she did not get to witness the look on his face. I'll admit, my own nuts cringed at the force of her kick, but despite his overwhelming levels, Bawbag's bawbag was still, at the end of the day, a fragile sack of tender testicles.

His rage-reddened face went white as he buckled over.

Rhona danced backwards, narrowly avoiding his grasping gauntlet.

She flashed me a single triumphant grin just before the beithir's tail caught her in the gut in a splash of gore and venom.

CHAPTER
FIFTY

I would have gladly taken that blow for the kid—she'd done what several thousand people wanted to and had done it with aplomb.

Instead, after Bawbag's beckoning, the giant snake monster threw itself into our midst, its massive body hurling itself to the ground and cutting off our route to reach Rhona.

In the distance, I saw Ealasaid facing down one of Bawbag's henchies, magic swirling around the old woman like she was the Cailleach of old, the mother of Scotland who crafted the land with the work of her hands. The henchman's blade flashed out through that magical maelstrom, and all I saw was a flash of red before the battle swallowed them. *Ealasaid.*

People were dying.

A flash of Connection told me Rhona was as unharmed as she could be, already in stealth and scurrying out of the beithir's path.

I wasn't going to overestimate Bawbag's recovery time again.

Eilidh seemed to have the thought at the exact moment I did, and we both sprang into motion. I refreshed Fuaran myself and Eilidh alike. Moving as one, we closed on our enemy.

She was the front-line fighter, not me, but I could set the stage for her.

The hart's memory was still fresh in my mind. So was the ancient pine, the corral, Sailean. Sailean's mother's pelt with a bullet hole in her head—had that fucking poacher waited one day more, maybe Sailean's mum would have lived when the ascension ruined guns. My memory held the silence of the land without animals, the hush of stillness both unnatural and wrong.

And if that weren't enough, all I had to do was look around.

Bodies of Òbanaich littered the darkened field around us. There were undoubtedly familiar faces among them, and I couldn't bring myself to search for Iain and Meeksy with Connection—or Ealasaid or Mòrag or Ronald or any of the others who had come with us to this fight.

All I could do was funnel all of that grief and rage and needless, pointless pain into my spirit and present it to the land as an offering of our need.

I cast Tairm.

The roar of battle around me rose and rose and rose.

Eilidh's sword shone, the blade giving off its own ethereal light as it arced towards Bawbag's head.

He caught it with one gauntleted fist, stopping the downstroke of that massive blade as if she'd hit him with a piece of straw.

Bawbag's other hand flashed out towards Eilidh's throat.

All I could feel was the strength in his hands on my

upper arms and the knowledge that he could have broken both of my humerus bones with one squeeze.

I heard, as if it were already happening in front of me, the snap of her neck.

Fury rose within me, and because I doubted my ability to move Bawbag, I caught Eilidh instead.

With a rope of Spèird, I yanked her out of the reach of Bawbag's gauntlet, and not a moment too soon.

Eilidh reacted immediately dropping her centre of gravity as Bawbag overshot her previous position, and she brought her claymore up in a diagonal strike at his now-unprotected side.

The blade connected with a flash of light and sparks as the magically altered steel met his bizarre protective glass.

I didn't even realise her move was a feint until she danced backwards. In one fluid motion, she used the claymore's heft and momentum to turn her retreat into an overhand slash.

Had it connected, her blade would have severed his carotid artery.

But Bawbag was level thirty-seven.

He dodged it as smoothly as she'd executed the strike, and a basket-hilted broadsword of pure glass materialised in his hand.

Edwin Thomas Sackington brandished it as if he'd trained his entire life for this moment—and that likely wasn't far from the truth.

Behind him, the beithir screamed.

I'd cast Tairm and nothing had seemed to happen; I should have known better than to assume that meant nothing would.

Even though we stood on a bare expanse of grass, the earth still lay beneath our feet.

Until it didn't.

With a rumble I felt through the soles of my boots came a tearing sound that prickled the back of my brain. It sounded like a glacier calving.

Bawbag made sense of it before I did. He leaped backwards just as the ground split in front of his feet.

He still wasn't fast enough.

Layers of grass and root and sod and peat and soil appeared immediately beneath him; one more heartbeat, and he'd have plunged downwards into the belly of the earth's crust.

Maybe farther than that.

As Eilidh and I scrambled backwards from the edge of the new-made abyss, a blast of heat struck me in the face.

The erstwhile lord drove himself back from the edge even as it crumbled beneath his feet.

Smoke filtered through the air.

Belatedly, I realised the blast of heat hadn't come from within the fissure; Bawbag's Scrotal Squadron was trying to herd the beithir towards me and Eilidh.

Though I'd suspected it from using Mac-Talla to catch the echoes of what had transpired in the clearing days before, seeing it with my own eyes still sickened me.

Five of Bawbag's thugs wielded staves that blazed orange, far too saturated and intense to be anything resembling normal flames. They beat at the beithir's sides with them, the arcane fire roasting the beast alive wherever it struck.

"Beithir," I said to Eilidh, pitching my voice low enough that I hoped she'd be the only one to hear me.

She glanced at me, sweat dripping down her temples. Her eyes held as much disgust as I felt as she gave me a single decisive nod.

With Faicte 's Neo-Fhaicte still active, the radioactive orange fire's damage shimmered like an oil slick in my vision where it licked up above the ridge line of the beithir's back. The beithir, caught between Bawbag's previous call and the constant pain raining down upon its scales, made a sound like tearing sheet metal.

It was weakened and in agony.

With a touch, I spoke into my communication crystal, this time tugging with spirit to make sure it hit everyone wearing one. "All hands to the beithir—we end this thing now!"

Wordlessly, Eilidh launched herself at the monster.

At the same time, I poured half my spirit into Ring of Fire.

I'd done it once before to protect us from the beithir, with the beast on the outside. This time, I caught the snake in its circumference. As Eilidh passed through the blazing wall of blue-green flame, her sword lit up like blue topaz in sunlight.

On the far side of the Ring of Fire, I saw henchies go up in flame, screaming as they got a taste of their own burning medicine. The Òbanaich, responding to my call, fell on them en masse.

Compared to Bawbag, the lackeys were easy targets.

I wasted no time casting Fuaran again, and as the battle around me shifted, I drew deep on my breath. Trying to ignore the stench of death, I took spirit into me, moving through a staff form even as I cast attack after attack, chan-nelling my spirit into a flow state.

Everything I had done on our arduous trek to the manor and back had brought me to this moment. With every wave of Connection, I drew more spirit back to myself. While I recognised the spells that flew from Brac-Meanmna—

Cumhachd and Spèird and Purifire and even Slànaich cast upon a wounded comrade—it was as if my staff took over the direction. It calculated the trajectory of every screaming lackey that came barrelling towards me, and whoever wasn't stopped or diverted with one of my spells took Brac-Meanmna to the face or arm. Anything that came in contact with the centre of the shaft came away with torn gouges from the goshawk claws which, disturbingly, grabbed hold of tender flesh and tore.

There was no way of knowing which way the tide of battle flowed; my entire aim was to guard Eilidh's back as the beithir screamed.

So caught up was I in the river of spirit I wielded that I almost missed the beithir's death blow.

It was Bawbag's roar of rage that drew my attention to it—no fewer than a hundred Òbanaich pelted him in waves with magic and projectiles, and even that barely kept him at bay.

I looked up to see Eilidh balanced on the beithir's back as she ran along it with her flaming sword from tail to the base of the monster's skull.

Bawbag had been shoved back ten, then twenty metres from the beithir, and when he saw her plunge her sword *through* the crown of the massive snake's head, he howled like a spoilt toddler who's had a toy taken away because they wouldn't stop bashing people in the face with it.

The first time he'd triggered his ability, I'd been too far away to see it. This time, I had a front-row seat.

Even where I stood, closer to the beithir's now-cloven tail, I barely escaped the blast.

Most of the Òbanaich had wisely kept their distance, but a score of them hadn't been quite as prudent.

As the shockwave boomed out from the epicentre that

was Edwin Thomas Sackington, anyone within ten metres of him got instantly vaporised.

The next circle of them flew backwards as I had the first time, the sound of breaking bones a massive crunch that cut through the crackling atmosphere.

Eilidh leapt from the writhing back of the beast—which hadn't quite realised it was dead—and rolled on the blood-wet ground.

Bawbag moved so quickly, he was a blur.

He leapt the chasm Tairm had opened in the field in a single bound, firing off explosions of his glass needles in every direction. I aimed a blast of Spèird directly at the incensed arsehole, and while it smashed the needles into glittering dust, Bawbag didn't so much as grunt.

His aim was perfect, and when he'd started, he'd had the room to get around the beithir's head.

But the beithir did not know it was dead.

Like a chicken after the chopping block, the snake monster flailed and writhed, and the moment Bawbag reached what he thought was his opening, the beithir's final death throes lifted the bulk of its girth from the ground and crashed back down metres from where it had been—directly onto Bawbag's head.

For a moment, everyone stopped.

The image was so surreal, so cartoonish, that I half expected the entire battle to burst out laughing, but no one did.

That impulse vanished in the next second, as a thousand shards of icicle-like spikes of glass made mincemeat out of the chunk of beithir that had dared land on Bawbag.

He *dripped* beithir guts and blood and a viscous slime that reeked worse than all of the faeces and death that smeared this once-pristine field.

I cast Connection.

The tie to the beast was no more; all lines had been cut.

And that wasn't all.

Before, I'd had a sense of all the strings that led from Bawbag to the puppets, to his servants—the nexus node had severed the spirit ties, but the death of the beithir seemed to have left Bawbag marooned.

I saw the precise moment he realised it, that he had no more flunkies, no more unwilling beasts to flog.

Oh, his henchies were still alive; there had been twenty-seven of them at the beginning, and I could still see at least half that many. But they seemed to shake themselves out of some kind of fog, and in a jerky, stumbling motion, they turned and scattered.

A fireball soared over our heads towards Bawbag from a mage far on the other side of the battlefield, practically in the Ganavan carpark.

My head swivelled to see where it'd come from, and I almost didn't believe my eyes: Andy.

This time, his act of destruction was bang on.

Bawbag didn't dodge. He must have been so used to simply swatting attacks away like annoying gnats; he stood there as the fireball careened towards him.

It hit him square in the chest. None of us were prepared to see him keel over with a startled grunt as the arcane attack knocked him clear off his feet. He sailed through the air, sticky threads of beithir slime trailing behind him like a St Bernard's strings of drool.

I was moving before I could stop myself. My feet launched me over the crevasse in the grass, and I hit the ground on the far side with the sound of others' pounding feet building into a rumble people came running.

Lucky me—I reached him first.

His chiselled face was a mess of bodily fluids, and his armour was a charred ruin.

There was something I'd been dying to get out of my inventory for ages after a few close calls. With a burst of Spèird, I loosed an entire mahoosive goshawk worth of feathery down from my storage and aimed it at the turd who'd made my people's misery his mission.

Pristine white floof coated him like an egg-washed fish fillet dipped in flour.

Eilidh landed beside me a split second later. Within another three heartbeats, Bawbag was surrounded, spitting feathers and wheezing. There was no sign of his flunkies anywhere; it was as if they'd given up or buggered off when they saw their master yeeted through the air. Whatever magic had shielded him, it seemed the beithir had indeed been the key.

"We should do this together," I said softly.

Bawbag stared up at me with hate-filled eyes, but he could barely draw breath.

Eilidh gave me a questioning look. "We?"

"All of us."

At that, Bawbag somehow managed to look even more outraged, like it mortally offended him that I wouldn't deign to end him myself. He gasped a breath, but though his lips moved, he couldn't speak without choking on goshawk down.

Thank all the gods—we wouldn't have to hear him fucking monologue.

"'S e seo ar coimhearsnachd," I said loudly, knowing damn well Bawbag didn't have a word of Gaelic. This was *our* community, one he'd tried for years to undermine.

At some point in the battle, the pipes had gone silent, but now someone picked them up again. The drone of the chanter filled the air as the piper adjusted them, and I saw Bawbag's lip curl with disdain as "Flower of Scotland" filled the air.

"Plenty of Scots don't care for the pipes, it's true," I told him conversationally, "but I'm sure everyone here'll love them right this moment just to spite you for all that you've done."

With that, I opened myself to spirit, feeling Eilidh's blend with mine, then more from surrounding people. Rhona's, to my extreme relief, and Iain's and Meeksy's, though Meeksy's was tenuous, grasping onto a thread of life.

Ealasaid stumbled forwards to stand beside me, and without thinking, I held out my arm to her. She'd a makeshift bandage around her throat that was far too red, but she was alive. I looked around for Eilidh's seanmhair, for Mòrag, but the beithir's body obscured half of the field.

Ronald appeared next, his beanpole frame appearing above the heads of bloodied fighters near the corpse of the beithir, and when the fighters moved slightly, they revealed Meeksy with Ronald's arm wrapped tight around the big bear's waist, Iain supporting his partner's other side. Meeksy's head lolled, and I cast Beannachd Shlàinte, hearing his gasp even at this distance.

Bawbag was still choking on his own spit and goshawk floof, but healing my friend was more important in that moment than killing my enemy.

Bawbag wasn't going anywhere. Not now.

I'd thought I would savour this moment, seeing him broken and pitiful before a vengeful crowd of people he'd tried to destroy. Instead, though, I just felt disgust.

The pure hatred in his eyes was tangible—or maybe

that was just that every one of my senses had experienced the rot he brought to the world.

Spirit grew and melded with the survivors as one by one, we reached out to one another with the ascension's magic.

"Calum," came Iain's voice in a near croak.

"Aye?"

"Tarring and feathering's an appropriate end for this sort, aye. And the Lios Mòr's a wee jaunt from here, but what d' you reckon, we find an appropriate urinal here in Oban to memorialise him once he's gone?"

An evil grin spread across my face, but when I glanced to my right and saw Rhona limping towards me, *hers* was positively vicious.

"If anyone deserves it, it's Bawbag," she said.

If I'd thought the man himself couldn't look any more outraged, getting taunted by the teenage girl who'd once served him made him literally spitting mad. His lips moved, dripping bloody drool that made mud with the clouds of down stuck to every inch of him.

"I dinnae ken what's got you so cheesed off, mate," I said to him. "You're the one who ruins everything you touch. You could have just *not* been a fucking cunt, and you'd have lived to a ripe old age. Now, you just got chucked across a field by a boy whose family you destroyed. That wee kitten whose mam you poached? She's part of our family now, and even she hates you. Your staff, your home, all of it—they all chose to bugger off and leave you, and you've no one to blame but yourself."

Bawbag actually managed to make a squeak at that, but the sound of it must have enraged him even further to sound so pitiful.

"Oh, I almost forgot," I said, moving slightly to the side from Eilidh to give myself space. "This yours, king?"

With that, I pulled a massive mahogany door out of my inventory. Even if it hadn't been emblazoned with his family crest in ivory relief, he'd have recognised it, but as it was, his eyes bulged nearly out of his face.

I put it back with a thought, ignoring Rhona's exasperated head shake that I could see out of the corner of my eye.

"That was actually my parting gift to you." I leaned over to look Bawbag in the face, feeling the thrum of hundreds of people's spirit flowing with mine. "You've been tarred and feathered by your own hand. Enjoy the logical progression."

His last words were lost in a grating wheeze and an ignominious puff of feathers and spit.

Where his corpse would have lain rotting, instead of harvesting him, we poured his spirit back into the earth. The roots whispered to me, explored the seeds lying dormant among them, and from those seeds, they selected one.

Edwin Thomas Sackington's body returned to the earth and brought forth new life.

We watched as a green shoot unfurled in the centre of his chest, and roots dug down through his flesh. The fungi and insects burrowed into him, doing their work on a sped-up timescale as spirit fuelled them. The shoot gave way to a sapling; the sapling grew into a tree. Red-brown bark shone in the light of magic glow stones, and branches sprang off of it, unfurling flat needles.

When it was done, a single yew stood in the centre of the meadow.

I felt a strange weight on my head, ponderous when I shifted my neck. Spirit seemed to surge within me, extending like antlers. Gasps rippled around me, along with a muttered "Bloody hell."

Eilidh turned to me, her face curious and somehow hungry, and she reached out one hand to touch something.

"He blessed you" was all she said.

Before I could ask what that meant, from the south, the ghostly white shape of a hart appeared out of the corner of my eye. I turned to greet him, the stag's presence as heavy upon my spirit as the sudden appearance of antlers upon my head. I felt him recognise the gift the Monarch of Glen Etive had bestowed upon me.

I bowed to the white stag, my hands crossed over my heart. With that motion, the weight atop my skull slipped away with the vestiges of spirit from our combined act. What it meant, I didn't dare guess. Not now. Not today.

The hart dipped his snout towards the yew, and like before, he turned and walked away.

A symbol of death begetting new life.

It would be our memorial, now and forevermore.

FIFTY-ONE

I t's been said that only a battle lost can compare to the melancholy of a battle won, and every last one of us felt the truth of that down to our smallest cells by the time dawn lit the sky.

The sunrise ascended over the last remnants of clouds drifting off to the east, leaving behind a morning soaked in gold and the luminous blue of a cloudless day.

Ganavan Sands were postcard worthy, white and brilliant, the teal water clear and calm.

A hundred metres beyond, though—that was a different story.

We had triumphed, without a doubt, but we had paid a steep and painful price.

As the sun climbed in the sky, I walked the field of the dead. It was almost eerier without corpses, but the memory of them had burned itself into the synapses of my mind even after harvesting them.

We had all seen and dismissed another world first message; reaping rewards from the night's trauma felt too fresh. Healers came from Oban with the news of our victory, and even now, they gathered in the carpark tending to the wounded. The ascension's healing was fast for the body; the soul was something else altogether.

Where I had used Saorsa on the puppeted deer, many of them had not escaped. There had been perhaps forty, and among the slain were at least five. None of Bawbag's flunkies had died there, which I counted as a stroke of luck. Some had died later, after I destroyed the nexus node.

The mighty stag, which Keen Eye had labelled the Monarch of Glen Etive, had given me more of a boon than I'd expected. In my inventory—which had expanded to fifteen slots—was the pair of his antlers.

I left them there to ponder later, wondering if they were truly separate from me at all.

The night had been gruelling enough.

We had harvested our own dead one by one, waiting for each body to be identified before offering their spirit to their next of kin.

It shook me to see a new funerary rite established in front of my eyes, and this was far more raw than the keening at the pine. Keening would come later. We would honour our friends and comrades.

My core group had survived intact. Except one.

As I ended my circuit of the battlefield, my eyes sought out the shape I knew hadn't moved since I'd walked away.

Eilidh still knelt over the body of her seanmhair, unmoving, without weeping.

People were beginning to move back towards Oban with the shellshocked gait of those unsure whether an ordeal had been real. I saw Rhona hovering at the edge of the battlefield and caught her eye.

Go, I mouthed to her. *I'll stay.*

After a moment of hesitation, Rhona gave me an uncertain nod and turned towards Iain and Meeksy. Meeksy had spent the night healing everyone but himself, and from the slump of his broad shoulders, it had nearly broken him. Iain held his hand tightly, speaking to him with a tender expression on his face as they waited for Rhona.

When she reached them, my best mate turned to look at me and Eilidh, a questioning look on his face. Rhona said something to him, and I could almost see Iain's internal battle not to yell out something daft, like "Oi, we'll leave the light oan fer ye!" I almost wished he would.

I reached Eilidh's side and sank to my knees next to her in the dew-damp grass.

She didn't look at me, and I didn't look at her. I just sat beside her as my knees grew soggy and the sun rose higher and higher, burning off the dew.

Mòrag did not look peaceful. Her kindly face was bruised, the Highland steel in her spine replaced with rigour mortis.

Some time later, an hour or an eternity, cold fingers found mine. I took hold of Eilidh's hand to warm it with my own. That, more than almost anything else, nearly broke me.

For all our half-serious jokes about me having exactly one emotion, here I was, near to greetin' for the fact that after hours on our knees in a sunlit vigil, Eilidh had finally decided to let me comfort her in some small way.

Sometimes even the strongest people just need someone to sit beside them in the dark, no matter how bright the day.

Our fingers interlaced, her right hand and my left, Eilidh reached out her free hand and placed it over Mòrag's heart.

Her grandmother's body dissolved into motes.

"Siubhail i thuige," she said hoarsely.

She went to be with him.

When I met Eilidh's eyes, they shone with unshed tears. Without another moment's thought, I pulled her to me and held her while she cried.

I thought of how I had found her, fighting for her life at Mòrag's side, how I'd now watched two members of this family harvest those who preceded them into death.

The thought came to me unbidden.

Whatever happened next, whatever threat was rising in the south, I would make sure this woman was not alone. I would stay by her side as long as she'd let me. Through everything she'd lost, she'd held herself together—I'd never for one second let her regret breaking down in front of me.

I'd said it once before for myself, and I thought it again then.

If we can't admit we're sad at the end of the world, when the fuck can we?

I wrapped my arms around her just a little tighter and held on.

World first!

In Oban in Western Scotland, there has been a second community ascension. One community has performed a legendary feat by being the first on Earth to eliminate a threat designated by the Ascended Alliance.

The people of Argyll have again demonstrated their under-standing of one of the ascension's most basic cornerstones: a community is stronger than the sum of its parts. Furthermore, they have fought back against one who sought to steal power at the expense of anyone who stood in his way—and they have won.

Edwin Thomas Sackington was wanted for crimes against the Ascended Alliance and against his home planet and all who dwell therein. In full knowledge of his abuse of ascension tenets, he wilfully refused to comply with demands that he cease his attempts to subvert the free will of Earth's inhabitants. He has been stripped of his title, his class, and all requisite boons. All possessions are hereby forfeit.

For dispensing justice on behalf of the Ascended Alliance, all veterans of Blàr Ghaineamhain shall receive:

-Experience equivalent to 1 level

-Book: Ascended Alliance: A Legal History

-1 boon

-Mark of Esteem: Mark of Justice

-Access to the Ascension Champion skill tree (3 legendary skills)

-Blueprint: Scrying Pool

Bonus:

For bringing Sackington to justice communally and for using his spirit to create life rather than harvesting it, all veterans are also awarded the following.

-Blueprint: The Resplendent Throne

-Blueprint: Spirit Well

-Blueprint: Communication Beacon

These blueprints can be shared with other communities for the betterment of your ascended world.

Quest updated: Defend Oban

You have eliminated the threat and saved your community.

Objectives:

-Reach Oban (Previous Instance) (Complete)

-Seek out the following inhabitants who are most likely to believe your story:

-Catrìona and Iain Whyte and Farid "Meeksy" Meeks (Complete)

-Ross and Jo MacIntosh (Complete)

-Ruaraidh and Ciorstaidh Smith (Complete)

-Jack Miller (Complete)

-Tina Dunlop (Complete)

-Convince at least twenty fighters of level five or above of the threat (3,702/20)

-Formulate a plan to aid Oban's defence (Complete)

-Reach Oban with the survivors of Sackington's magic and liaise with the town's defenders (Complete)

-Survivor population: 273/312

-Thwart Sackington's plans:

-Alert Oban's forces to the ruse (Complete)

-Use Saorsa to free the puppeted deer from Sackington's influence (Calum) (Complete)

-Slay the beithir (Complete)

-Deliver justice to Sackington and his compatriots (Complete)

-Optional: Reach Oban with all ultimate survivors having gained at least one level (Survivors having gained at least one level: 312/312) (Complete)

Rewards:

-Experience (commensurate with current level progression)

-Blueprint: Storable Armour

-1 skill point

-5 attribute points

-Book: Ascension and the Truth of Universal Bounty

-Book: Preparation and Ascension: Prerequisites and Understanding

-Book: Intergalactic Treatise on Wartime Law

. . .

I stretched out on the twin bed I'd commandeered in Iain's mum's house, feeling my feet dangle off the end. That was new. I really had gotten taller. I might have been chuffed a couple months ago, but now my ascension—ha—to the over-six-feet-two club was the last thing on my priority list.

Sailean snoozed by my side, her tiny whiskers twitching in her sleep. I deeply envied her that peace.

My mind was not ready to process all of the quest info, and I blinked at the three books that, for all intents and purposes, looked about as exciting as reading a government white paper.

At least they'd be dumped into my brain.

These were paired with the not-so-subtle hint that we were expected to share knowledge.

Some might have been ruffled by the thought of sharing their rewards with people who hadn't bled on the battle-field, but I could not be less bothered. No one I knew who'd faced down the beithir would want the burden of being the only special snowflake with the power to stop a threat. It took a village to raise a child? Aye, well, it'd take a bloody planet to survive this ascension if there were more Bawbags out there.

We'd get nowhere without empowering everyone around us who gave a shit. I'd take all the bloody help I could get, for fuck's sake.

I tried to calm myself by reading through the more mundane of my notifications, but even that was wild—the combination of the battle and completing the Ascended Alliance's bounty on Bawbag had earnt me three levels' experience. We may not have harvested the bastard, but we still got extra credit for making him deid.

. . .

You have reached Level 14! You have seven attribute points and four skill points to distribute.

You have reached Level 15! You have nine attribute points and seven skill points to distribute.

You have reached Level 16! You have eleven attribute points and ten skill points to distribute.

You have received a boon!

Boon: Blàr Ghaineamhain

As a veteran of the Battle of Ganavan, you have proven your mettle and that of your newly combined community. Once you have placed your Clach-Cheangail as a community, your people shall all receive a 50% bonus to spirit regeneration whilst within the radius of its influence. Because you have paid the price for your community's homeland in blood, the keystone will prevent further bloodshed within its area of influence. You have already unlocked the community skill Clach-Cheangail as part of the Coimhearsnachd (Community) skill tree.

Congratulations! Your community is providing an example to your planet.

... Thanks?

I understood that they didn't expect us to survive an' aw, but did they have to be so patronising?

. . .

You have been honoured with a Mark of Esteem.

For being the part of the first community on Earth to perform a legendary feat and dispense justice on behalf of the Ascended Alliance, you now bear the Mark of Justice.

This will be visible to all who have access to your information, whether by ability or your choice to share. A Mark of Esteem distinguishes you among your people as one who has taken vital steps on the path to ascension.

Should you survive, your name will be recorded in the Halls of the Ascended Alliance for all time.

The Mark of Justice also grants you the following bonuses, which you must accept to receive:

- Access to the Ascension Champion skill tree (3 legendary skills)

- An increase in an existing affinity of your choice

-Specialised Affinity: Justice

Do you accept this Mark of Justice and its requisite rewards along with the ramifications of renown that accompany such esteem?

Hell. I told it to hit me. It was interesting that each of my three Marks of Esteem had wildly different rewards, but to tell the truth, I was relieved to not have more of a pile-on of points. My brain was officially ready to retire into pathetic himbo hamster mode, at least for a little while.

The boon was a simple one called Soul Shield, and it was one I wish we hadn't had to prove we needed to unlock. It provided a fifty percent resistance to mind-control effects and made me wonder just how sadistic this Ascended Alliance was. If they had the power to give us such things, why the hell wouldn't they lead with that?

Then again, we were the plebes who weren't even

supposed to ascend, so maybe it didn't matter to them if we slap-fought each other to extinction.

With the knowledge I had three legendary skills waiting, I opened up the Ascension Champion tree to get a peek at what they considered to be "legendary."

If I'd not been lying down already, I'd have fallen over.

Ionad-Siubhail

Your human concept of borders died with the ascension.

Ascension Champions are able to collaborate in order to designate a specific location as an Ionad-Siubhail. Once at least three Ionadan-Siubhail have been established at points at least three kilometres apart, the network may be activated.

An activated network allows instantaneous travel to any connected Ionad-Siubhail.

Points to Unlock: 3

Tosgaire na Coimhearsnachd

As an Ascension Champion, you have demonstrated your commitment to the ascension directive and have worked tirelessly on behalf of your community. This skill marks you as an ambassador.

As Earth's communities around the planet ascend, it will become beneficial to share progress, information, and wisdom with people outwith your existing locale.

Similar to Ionad-Siubhail, ambassadors can establish a line of communication at any scrying pool in order to convene with anyone globally who has this skill.

Points to Unlock: 3

. . .

Clach-Cànain

Language is one of the most personal aspects of a culture, a community, and a shared bond. This skill allows you to contribute your native language into a spirit-infused stone, which can then be accessed by anyone in the community.

In the earliest ascensions, it became clear that the betterment of all does not include the eradication of differences. The biggest benefit to the Clach-Cànain is that it allows for the preservation and spread of endangered languages, particularly minoritised and indigenous languages that may have few living speakers.

Points to Unlock: 3

That was it for me. I didn't even have to think about it. Nine of my available skill points went into unlocking every single one of those skills.

I had used magic for weeks, felt it pouring through me. We had made miracles happen amid the fear and the grief.

Deep down, I'd felt the terror of wondering if we would be cut off from each other. In a world so used to mobile phones, the internet, planes, trains, everything—I could barely believe my eyes.

Instantaneous travel.

Global communication would be restored.

Even with those two enormous gifts, it was the last one that broke me.

My language.

Mo chainnt.

I couldn't help but mourn for Mòrag all over again. She had taught Eilidh, of course, from childhood.

Mòrag's native Gaelic was different to ours. Ours inched closer and closer to English all the time. Our phrasings, our colours, our numbers, our idiosyncrasies—when learners found them too complex, *we* gave way and not the other way round. We were somehow politely consigning ourselves to the death of our language with an apology and a bow.

But no more.

Seeming to sense my inner turmoil, Sailean stretched and opened sleepy eyes, crawling up onto my chest to nuzzle into the crook of my neck.

Even as I'd held Eilidh while she cried, I'd not shed a tear myself. That was her grief, her time.

I wept now, Sailean purring against my chest.

A seed sprouted in my soul. This ascension had changed everything for us—everything.

It had ended our world.

But now?

We had a hope of making the new world better.

All of us could not just survive—we could thrive.

FIFTY-TWO

"Calum!"

Iain's voice woke me from my exhausted nap. My eyes were scratchy—gods, I hated crying and almost never did it—and my neck ached from lying on it funny. It was also sweaty where the wee fur ball had made her nest.

Gently extracting the kitten, I managed to lever myself onto my feet. "What?"

"You need to come to the harbour. There's—fuck, just hurry!"

I placed Sailean on the bed, where she promptly went back to sleep.

With that eloquent endorsement Iain, I grabbed the nearest jumper and threw it on over the trackie bottoms I'd nicked from Iain's room earlier. They were high waters on me, so my ankles got a chill breeze as I followed my mate out of the house.

He was off like I'd hit *him* in the arse with Purifire, and I had to jog to catch up with him. The streets of Oban were crowding already as people poured out of their homes, everyone headed to the pier.

The reason why appeared moments later, between the isles of Lismore and Kerrera.

Boats.

Fuck if I wasn't about to start greetin' again.

Sailboats, rowboats, anything that could float and move in a forwardly direction without benefit of motor, there had to be at least fifteen of them.

People wept openly as the boats sailed in from the Sound of Mull, through the natural gateway that sheltered Oban's harbour from the winds and weather of the Hebrides.

And from high in the air above them, I felt a familiar— and unexpected—peck on my spirit.

The wren.

The bloody *wren*.

I wove my way through the crowd, hearing Iain's squawk behind me as he saw me leaving him, but I didn't care. The boats were too small to berth at the CalMac terminal, so I headed towards the old quay that now mostly housed birdwatching tours and Oban's English-phonics-spelled, Gaelic-named seafood restaurant Ee-usk.

Sure enough, just as I reached the edge of the quay, a tiny shape fluttered in the air above my head, singing out a jaunty tune and sounding *terribly* pleased with himself.

"Dè fon ghrèin a rinn thu, a charaid?" I asked the bird, bemused. What the hell. First he rallied a dozen avian species to battle the siphons, and now he led an entire fleet —albeit a motley one—in from the isles?

In response, he simply landed on the rail a short distance from me and gave me the closest thing to a shit-eating grin a songbird could muster with a beak.

He puffed up his feathers and trilled.

The first of the boats reached us a few minutes later, the

creak of the sails coupling with the splash of waves against the bow.

"Hello, Oban!" called a sailor at the helm. "Wee birdie told us yous needed some help, so we've come from Mull!"

"You wee shit," I said to the wren. "You went to the *wren island* and brought the Muilich."

The bird preened.

Catrìona's voice made me jump—Iain's mum had snuck up on me with her son, and she was stood with her thumbs through the belt loops on her trousers and a smile on her face. "You're a touch late, Mull, but I've never in my life been so happy to see a bunch of washtubs in this harbour! Fàilte chridheil oirbh uile!"

A burst of laughter came from both quay and boats.

"Instantaneous transport be damned," I said, more to myself than anything. "Should have known we'd manage."

"Dè air a bheil thu mach?" Iain turned to me with a grin as wide as his mum's. "Instantaneous travel what?"

"I swear, mate, you need to read your notifications." I shook my head at him, and then, surprising us both, I grabbed him in a bear hug. "We'll be all right."

"Aye, reckon we will." He pulled away, giving me a slap on the shoulder and a sidelong glance. "You been greetin', pal?"

When I didn't answer, he slapped me on the shoulder again. "It's good for you, you emotionally constipated jobby."

"Thanks awfully."

"Yer welcome."

"Don't just stand there, you two," Catrìona said, pointing down the quay. "Help them!"

"Aye-aye, cap'n," Iain said, then scooted down the ramp as his mum swatted him on the bum.

·ᛙ ᚲᚻᛦᛒᚢ ᛢ·

The night flew by in a whirlwind of hugs, tears, and the biggest cèilidh Oban'd probably ever seen.

Sailean, contrary to most people's conception of cat socialisation, took to the crowd with alacrity once we retrieved her from her nap. She was busy making friends far and wide, the warmth of her presence within my mind a glow of satisfaction and excitement to be part of something.

Aye, I was done for. Cover me in tweed and call me a cat person. Sailean was stuck with me.

The "Muilich" weren't *just* from Mull—they'd gathered folk at Lismore on their way, and they'd all come as armed as possible to help us against Bawbag.

It was a sombre affair relating the battle to them, and I had some severe regrets that I let Iain tell the tale, because despite the grim litany of our losses, he wisnae about to downplay the drama.

There was no disrespect in his recounting—to the contrary, we've a long tradition of storytelling to honour the dead *and* the living—but more than once, every eye turned towards me and Eilidh. And when he got to the bit about the goshawk down, we all let him get away with the fib that it was he who'd added the feathers to Bawbag's tar.

I found myself at Eilidh's side partway through the evening and never found reason to leave it again. Sailean, worn out from her stint as a social butterfly, parted the crowd like the Red Sea, trotting up to us with her tail held high. The wildcat kitten wiggled her bum and leaped at Eilidh's leg, clambering onto the redhead's lap.

Eilidh sat close without touching me, stroking Sailean until the kitten fell asleep. We'd emptied all the local restaurants of chairs, and with the lack of light pollution, the clear sky above darkened to show a breath-taking display of stars. The Milky Way cut a paler swathe across that celestial expanse. I wondered who out there was watching us. Wondered if anyone was hoping against hope that we'd find our way through the shitstorm that had landed on our heids.

A few times, I caught sight of Alison in the crowd. I was glad to see she seemed to have heeded our warning and stayed away from Ganavan but relieved she didn't venture closer.

The Muilich told us that they'd a bàrd—a proper bàrd, in the Gaelic tradition, the keeper of songs and stories and poetry—who'd the ability to communicate with the wrens of the island.

The old name for Mull was An Dreòluinn.

That was, coincidentally, the word for wren. Whether that was the reason for the name or merely happenstance, it seemed oor feathered pal had decided it was his island anyway.

Said wren friend had gone to him—that was why he'd broken the bond with me.

The wren himself stayed close all night, flitting about like the belle of the ball, as was right and proper. He may have been late, but he'd brought us ragtag naval support.

Ealasaid came over to us as evening stretched into night. Someone had gotten out the box and was giving it a good wheeze—accordions were a lot like bagpipes in that way, needed some warming-up squeaks before the magic happened—and fiddles had poofed into existence as well, which meant the night was just beginning.

The old woman's fond gaze lingered on two bickering bodaich who had clearly spent the last fifty years arguing over which set of tunes to start with and didn't care to cease their tradition now.

"Am faca tu Clach-Cànain?" Ealasaid's voice was a harsh croak.

Though her throat showed pink scar tissue that was already fading, I winced at the sight of just how close the old cailleach had come to death.

"Chunna," I answered in the affirmative. I absolutely had seen that skill, and it didn't surprise me one bit that Ealasaid's curiosity had led her there as quickly as my own.

"Well, I don't think I'll be able to sing you a puirt tonight, a ghràidh," she rasped after a moment, and Eilidh reached out and took her hands to give them a squeeze, which the old woman returned with an affectionate pat. "An gabh thusa òran, ma-tà?"

Since I'd not expected to be asked to sing in the slightest, I choked on my own spit. "Erm—"

"Gabhaidh," Eilidh said brightly, making me rethink my decision to sit by her.

Sort of.

Naturally, Iain chose that moment to arrive with Meeksy and Rhona, and that was it for me. Done for. Kaput. I knew it even before Iain opened his gob.

"Calum's gonnae sing us a tune," he said to Rhona, elbowing her in the shoulder.

"Oh my god. *Yes.*"

I groaned.

"Siuthad, m' eudail," Ealasaid said to me encouragingly, making a shooing motion with her hand.

"One song," I muttered.

Part of me wanted to pick the shortest one I could think of out of pure belligerence, but the shortest Gaelic song I could think of where I knew all the words was, in fact, the exact right choice.

Ealasaid pressed something into the palm of my hand, and I knew what it was without looking. Clach-Cànain.

She'd made one and already used it. The stone swirled with spirit, potent and triumphant. I felt Ealasaid's Argyll Gaelic in the stone like my mother's embrace.

Fuck. It was like she'd handed me a bowl of chopped onion. My eyes prickled yet again.

Before I could completely chicken out, I cleared my throat and started to sing.

"Fhir a' chinn duibh, thug mi gaol dhut
 Fhir a' chinn duibh, thug mi gràdh dhut
 Thug mi gaol is thug mi gràdh dhut
 Thug mi gaol nach tug mi càch dhut
 Fhir a' chinn duibh, thug mi gràdh dhut"

The moment I began the lament, my voice rang through Oban harbour like a bell.

Hamster himbo that I am, I'd forgotten Òran na Cloiche yet again.

Everyone—including the two bickering bodaich—fell silent.

The song had been written by a seventeenth-century bàrd called Pàdraig Mòr MacCrimmon in the Isle of Skye after seven of his eight children died of a smallpox outbreak.

It was a short lament, one my mother used to sing sometimes on days she lost an animal she was rehabilitating or thinking on friends and family who, as we say in Gaelic, nach maireann. Those who do not remain.

When I began it for the second time, I was surprised to hear Eilidh's voice joining mine. And then Catrìona's—and then Iain's, followed by Meeksy's bass rumble.

Rhona stood for a moment looking unmoored, and I continued to sing and stood up, taking the stone Ealasaid had pressed into my hand and placing it in Rhona's palm. I closed her fingers around it, waking the stone instinctively with a thread of spirit.

The young woman closed her eyes, eyelids flickering like she was in the middle of a dream.

Tears squeezed out through her lashes and trickled down her cheek. She clung to the stone like it was life itself, and maybe it was.

When she opened her eyes, they were shining.

And when we began the song for the third time, Rhona's voice joined ours with perfect Gaelic.

I didn't think I was imagining the shining brightness in Eilidh's own eyes at that sound.

Bawbag was gone.

He was gone, and we were home.

Our friends had joined us from the isles, and tomorrow, we would begin to build a new world.

For tonight, that was more than enough.

EPILOGUE

R onald may have been an ultra-runner, but by the time he found me on the Oban promenade, a week after Blàr Ghaineamhain, he was dripping sweat and looked like he'd just *sprinted* a fifty-kilometre race.

Sailean, from her perch on my shoulder, mewed.

"Hold out your hand" was all he said to me, though he reached out and gave her a scratch with his free hand.

I obeyed, naturally. When a human string bean brining in their own perspiration tells you to do something, you do it first and ask questions later. And probably wash.

The things he dropped into my waiting palm looked like little balls of clay, but they hit my skin like they were made of solid uranium.

"Fuck," I said.

Sailean hissed at them.

"Aye." Ronald took a deep breath through his mouth, his eyebrows doing a strange dance that may have been agreeing with Sailean or possibly trying to get her to pounce them.

"How far away were they?" While I asked the question, I dreaded the answer.

"Kilmelford."

For a week, I'd nursed a vain hope that the anomalies had ended with the great big killer rabbit and its bouncing bundles of woe.

I peered at the petrified hearts in my hand. "Birds?"

Ronald nodded, leaning forward on the rail of the sea wall to stretch his calves. We weren't the best of mates, and I didn't know whether we ever would be, but after the battle with Bawbag, well. *Family* was likely the best term for it.

"Magpies. Only reason none got past us is because Alison's worked out some kind of Purifire mesh. She threw it straight up in the air and they hit it and exploded. Only reason that wasn't the most feathers I've ever seen in one go is that you set that record when you dropped a tonne of them on Sacking—Bawbag's soon-to-be corpse."

"Hey, and just think! Couple months ago, you'd never get to say a sentence like that." I gave him a wide grin to let him know that yes, I was joking. To my surprise, he actually returned it. "Alison still out there, then?"

"Why do you ask?" Just like that, Ronald was ramrod straight again.

I sighed. "I wasn't trying to disappoint her."

Just in time, I stopped myself from using the *In other circumstances* excuse, but I had to be honest with myself, if nothing else. I wasn't interested in the science teacher. If I were truly honest with myself, Eilidh'd caught hold of me even when I thought she hated me. Call me a masochist—it seemed to be working out okay.

"I'm not judging." Ronald cracked his neck, making me wince.

"You are definitely judging."

"Okay, I'm judging a wee bit. Just a hair." The smile was back, but too tight at the edges, giving away that it was forced.

"People are not my strong point," I said with an awkward shuffle of my feet that tipped Sailean off balance. She scrambled to right herself. I was still wearing my armour as a safety precaution against kitten claws. "I usually figure out what they expect from me too late."

Ronald snorted and wiped away some sweat from his brow. "I'm really not judging. This"—he gestured vaguely at the air—"has put everyone in a state. Everyone's looking for a lifebuoy. And you didn't lead Alison on or anything. To the contrary, to my eyes, you were sending big 'I'm spoken for' messages."

That startled me. "Was I?"

He rolled his eyes, then waved at the petrified hearts. I guessed the awkward bit of the conversation was over.

"We're going to need to figure out what to do about that mess," Ronald said after a beat. "Sooner rather than later. I ran back to make sure we get the word out to everyone else since I didn't have a communication crystal on me."

"Aye, well, you should grab one, even if you're only going as far as Kilmelford. At least then you wouldn't need to show off by setting new land-speed records." When I paused, Ronald's face took a sheepish turn. "I think the crafters have been working double time making more crystals. Plus, the scrying pool is just about ready, the communication crystals we do have are good up to ten kilometres now, and we've got about half of what we need for the first Ionad-Siubhail."

At his blank look, I took the chance to roll my eyes right back at him.

"The teleportation hingmy."

"Ah." Ronald did not look nearly excited enough for real, live teleportation.

"Well, good talk," I said, moving to hand him the petrified hearts back.

He waved me off, still looking distracted.

"Was there something else?" The petrified hearts wouldn't fit in my inventory, because it was full of random shite I kept meaning to drop off somewhere or another. I shoved them in a pocket instead, where they clattered against one another.

"I was thinking of trying to capture one of the anomalies," Ronald said slowly.

"Capture one? You don't need my permission." It took all my self-control not to eye him askance. "I mean, obviously, don't try to capture an anomalous heery coo the size of an elephant, but if the opportunity arises, it could be useful."

God, I hoped I never had to fight an anomalous Highland cow. I'd hate every second of it. I loved those things and their fuzzy ginger faces.

"You don't think it would be dangerous?"

Now I really did look at him sideways. "It's beyond dangerous, but if we want to know how to stop them, knowing more about them sounds wise. Just . . . no torture."

"I was thinking more 'see if we can heal them' than 'make them suffer,' but thanks for the line in the sand."

"Why exactly *are* you asking me about this?" Now that he seemed friendly—or friendli*er*, anyway—I was genuinely curious.

The skinny bloke shrugged. "Believe it or not, I respect you, and especially respect the fact that you're not trying to be the next Bawbag."

"Speaking of lines in the sand." I snorted. "Thanks, pal. You don't have to worry about me trying to kickstart feudalism for the twenty-first century."

"I think the ascension might have actually pulled the plug on that, way things were headed with our corporate overlords."

"Touché."

I reached up to give Sailean a wee scratch. Her rattly purr started up straight away. Something intruded into my mind, so I pulled up the anomaly quest to double check. Sure enough, there was the line. *To the south, Will Grayson and Ezekiel Bosworth III have also encountered and identified this anomaly, which has since claimed the latter with its corruption.*

That confirmed—or seemed to—the gnawing thought at the back of my brain. "Going back to the anomalies, it would be good to see if we can heal them. The quest we got says that the corruption 'claimed' someone, which implies that it's contagious. If that's true, we should find out how it spreads and how to fix it."

Another pandemic, ascension style, was the last thing anyone needed after the past few years on Earth.

I'd finally put a spark in Ronald's eye. Fully recovered already, he bounced on his toes. Man's Stamina stat had to be off the charts.

But then I saw the pulse of gold in the corner of my vision and that the sudden spark had turned in to the vacant gaze of someone having screen time.

I glanced at mine only long enough to see two dreaded words on the anomaly quest.

Quest updated . . .

Bugger.

Guess it was time to go see a lass about shoring up our armour.

As if to confirm it, Sailean pounced a curl hanging down over my now-pointed ear.

"Aye, aye, you wee beastie. Next time we won't leave you behind."

Her answering purr was far too satisfied.

A Note from Mati

Thank you so much for reading *The Ascendent Sky*!

If you're new to LitRPG, there are some great places for you to get your fix! Try the LitRPG Books group on Facebook to chat with fellow readers and authors!

I've had an absolute blast writing in this world, and I really wanted to bring LitRPG to my homeland. Figured it'd be good craic, and I think that proves true. Calum isn't so much a pathetic hamster now, I reckon—I'm stoked to see where he goes from here.

If you've not yet read it, I wrote a wee book for the Inkfort Press Publishing Derby this year that was a concurrent prequel to *The Transcendent Green*. That book is called *Terra Incognita*, and you can find it right here.

I'm hard at work on getting new books out to you. If you want to get first crack at them, find me over on Patreon! You can follow me there for general news updates or pledge at a couple different tiers if you want to really gie it laldy!

One last thing: if the Gaelic has you floundering at all or you're just burning with curiosity about how things sound, check out LearnGaelic. Their dictionary has over seventy thousand sound files, and whilst you may not find everything due to me taking a fluent speaker's licence to play with things for alliterative purposes (or, in Brac-Meanmna's case, to make up a word), you'll find most of it.

If you fancy going all out and *learning* our language, some fantastic folk (including an Oban lad!) worked their tails off to get it on Duolingo, where you can learn exciting and useful phrases like "Tha mo thòn dìreach àlainn" (my arse is just gorgeous) and "Tha Irn Bru sgoinneil" (Irn Bru is brilliant) and "Obh obh, thusa a-rithist!" (Oh, no, you again —AKA what people say when I walk into the room).

Great craic. And contrary to popular paranoia when people see our spellings, Gaelic is worlds more regular than English once you learn the rules. I believe in you! Gur math a thèid leat!

CALUM'S STATS AND SPELLS

Name: Calum Green
Age: 36
Level: 16
Class: Draoidh (Further class specialisation at: Level 27)
Affinities: Nature (Level 10), Healing (Level 4), Synthesis (Level 5), Staves (Level 5)
Specialised Affinities: Wild (Level 6), Coimhearsnachd (Level 3), Justice
Marks of Esteem: Life, Connection, Justice

Alteration:
Strength: 20
Dexterity: 28
Agility: 34
Mind: 75

Regeneration:
Constitution: 23
Stamina: 52

Manipulation:
Spirit: 60
Pathos: 36
Will: 38

Boons:
Blessings
Làmh na Glaistige
Glòir a' Ghiuthais
Blàr Ghaineamhain
Boon: Blessings
Adds a permanent +5 to Will.
Boon: Làmh na Glaistige
By fulfilling your word to the Glaistig of Earra-Ghàidheal, you have received a token of her favour. As she is guardian of the hind and hart, you receive a

bonus to freeing the minds of those she protects. This can be used once between sunup and sundown and again between sundown and sunup.

Boon Skill: Saorsa

As a skill tied directly to a boon, Saorsa is part of no skill tree. It may be used twice per day and resets with the rising or setting of the sun. Saorsa affects all creatures within a hundred-metre radius of the caster and creates a web of Purifire and spirit that severs puppeted creatures from their bondage.

Be wary; whilst in the aftermath of Saorsa, all living beings may become violent or unpredictable, depending on the complexity of their minds, how sapient they are, and how long they have been in captivity.

For those who turn violent, they may attack anyone who threatens them, including their rescuers. In very rare cases, the trauma of their former puppet strings may cause irreparable damage.

Boon: Glòir a' Ghiuthais

With the creation of the birlinn and by virtue of its recognition as a mythic feat, you have been favoured by the forest.

When under tree cover, your spirit regeneration increases, the rate itself increasing the longer you linger.

Touching a pine tree will temporarily increase your total spirit capacity by 300 for one hour. This effect does not stack.

Boon: Blàr Ghaineamhain

As a veteran of the Battle of Ganavan, you have proven your mettle and that of your newly combined community. Once you have placed your Clach-Cheangail as a community, your people shall all receive a 50% bonus to spirit regeneration whilst within the radius of its influence. Because you have paid the price for your community's homeland in blood, the keystone will prevent further bloodshed within its area of influence. You have already unlocked the community skill Clach-Cheangail as part of the Coimhearsnachd (Community) skill tree.

Congratulations! Your community is providing an example to your planet.

Bas-Ogham (Passive)

Ogham is a form of writing that, much like the runes of the Nordic peoples, was also used for divination. Its letters correspond to the trees of the Gaelic alphabet. Bas-Ogham is the art of divining with small rods of wood into which the letters of the ogham are carved.

The writing can be found carved into stone, though wood carvings would have also proliferated at the time of its peak usage. Those have largely been lost to time.

Regain the knowledge of those who came before. In an ascended world, your connection to your ancestors is as real as that to those who walk and breathe beside you on your path.

The uses of ogham are limited only by your imagination—and your will. They can be formed into sacred trees, etched into weapons, tattooed into skin. Be mindful of what you create. Allow Bas-Ogham to guide you.

Bas-Ogham as a skill will improve with each tree attunement you cultivate.

Your current attunements:

Darach

Beannachd Shlàinte (Level 3)—This skill can be used once per day to heal a severe injury of tissue trauma and infection. You gain an increased affinity for Healing, allowing you to intuit what is necessary to save lives of humans and animals alike.

Increased use of this skill allows for more complex healing, including but not limited to: internal haemorrhaging, progressive disease, antivenin formulation, purging toxins, and limb regrowth. Additionally, greater knowledge of the body's anatomy and physiology makes you more effective in combat.

Through your growing Synthesis affinity, you have combined this spell with others to great effect, and your increasing understanding has cut the cooldown time by 50%.

Affinity: Healing

Skill Tree: Slàinte

Caidreabhas—This skill is a foundational one in the Tàthadh tree, but it is not one to be used lightly. Caidreabhas, like Tàth, forms a consensual bond with an animal companion, but unlike Tàth, this bond is permanent and will persist until your death or that of your companion.

Many animals in an ascended world stretch past their previous limits, often ranging from sentience to outright sapience, in time. Caidreabhas encourages such growth in your companion, bolstering the animal's natural strength and adaptability as well as their intelligence.

Unlike most active skills, Caidreabhas will not level, as for it to do so would cause first bonds to eventually lose their appeal with the ability to form more complex bonds. Instead, Caidreabhas evolves—with each animal you bond, your relationship with your companion will shift depending entirely upon what you invest in it.

Your current abilities allow you: 1 companion

Affinity: Nature

Skill Tree: Tàthadh

CALUM'S STATS AND SPELLS

Connection *(Level 5)—You gain a deeper affinity to the earth and its needs, and it whispers to you. With this skill, you are able to see how things around you interact, be it the tracks of a deer hunted by paw prints of a stalking cat or the passing of a band of hunters.*

Increased use of this skill enables you to take in an entire scene at a glance and appropriately assess its secrets. Additionally, the skill will allow you to ascertain the needs of the natural world, giving you the power to aid creatures and plants that may one day return the favour.

Your use has granted you a bonus to clarity. Your ability to see and identify patterns has increased, and you are now 12% more likely to spot items of import, foes in stealth, and escape routes.

Affinity: Nature

Skill Tree: Nature

Cumhachd *(Level 3)—This spell is one of the most versatile in the hedge witch's arsenal. By tapping into the ambient spirit that surrounds you to augment your own, you are able to form missiles based upon your environment. Not only does this spell shift dramatically from mage to mage, but it also enhances your acquisition of points in Spirit. This ability is bolstered by and best used within your existing affinities, but it also rewards creativity.*

Continued use may unlock additional benefits and upgrades. As with all things in an ascended world, the limits are your own imagination. (ch23)

Affinity: Synthesis, Nature

Skill Tree: Arcane

Darach *(Passive)—Some believe that the word for druid, and thus all magic, originated from the word for oak. This word in the old language was* dair, *and whether or not the etymology proves true, it is undeniable that the oak is a symbol of magic and protective power even now.*

As a Draoidh, you will slowly begin to demonstrate a Draoidh's connection to the power of trees. The first of these is always the oak, for it is within the stalwart oak your power finds its roots.

Darach allows the Draoidh to draw consciously from this power, which grows stronger when using staves of oak or when in contact with living oak.

While Darach will not increase in levels as active spells will, your understanding of magic will, on occasion, trigger evolution.

You have already demonstrated your connection to the oak, both in your creation of the living weapon Brac-Meanmna and with your spontaneous cultivation of an oak tree in Kilninver. Evolution of Darach: Imminent.

Dubh

The Draoidh knows there is nowt to fear in darkness.

To the contrary, darkness is the source of all things, including light. It is from darkness the universe was born, and in that darkness is the potential of all creation.

Dubh allows you to tap into the creative power. Coupled with Bas-Ogham, it can be used to write ogham into your skin. In the heat of battle, the Draoidh can use Dubh to obscure an enemy's sight. While it will only work upon a foe who lacks the Draoidh's understanding of the true nature of darkness, on a fearful opponent who relies fully upon sight and light, it is a powerful weapon.

The skill taps into our most ancient connections to a time before time itself, before light, when all was one in the womb of the endless void. Dubh does not ascribe fear to this void; for the Draoidh, it is a source of comfort and solace. In returning to Dubh, the Draoidh finds the will to write reality into existence.

Affinity: Draoidh, Wild
Skill Tree: Draoidh

Faicte 's Neo-Fhaicte *(Passive)*

The Gaels have long known that there are more worlds beyond the physical, worlds into which people sometimes slipped, unseen or unheard or both. On occasion, they reemerged with tales of delight or horror or a mingling of the two.

Food so delicate and sweet all else would taste forever of ash. Beauty so rare and tantalising one could weep—but denying it would bring swift and brutal death.

The fuath, the glaistig, the beithir—all of these are creatures of your world and always have been. Now, though, they slink through the veil.

Faicte 's Neo-Fhaicte alerts you to the presence of the otherworlds and may, for the canny, provide insight into its inner workings and motivations.

Affinity: Draoidh, Nature, Wild
Skill Tree: Draoidh

Fuaran—*Like its name, Fuaran is a skill that brings with it a wellspring of refreshment. This skill increases your spirit regeneration by a base of 20% for 3 minutes, and if comrades are within 10 meters of you, it will also do the same for them.*

Increased use of this skill will increase its efficacy and area of effect and may also bestow other boons that can benefit you and your party. (ch23)

Affinity: Arcane
Skill Tree: Arcane

Gu h-Àrd (Passive)—You gain an understanding of all things above the earth: the currents of the air, the patterns of the clouds, and those that make their home therein. You receive an immediate +2 to Mind and a bonus to calling upon the powers of weather, wind, and creatures of the heavens. With experience, you may also summon the storm.

While Gu h-Àrd will not increase in levels as active spells will, your understanding of magic will, on occasion, trigger evolution.

Affinity: Nature, Synthesis

Skill Tree: Nature

Gu h-Ìosal (Passive)—You gain an understanding of all things below the earth: the waters that flow, the roots that grow, and those that make their home therein. You receive an immediate +2 to Mind and a bonus to calling on the powers of flora and earth-bound fauna. With experience, you may also free the forest to do your bidding.

While Gu h-Ìosal will not increase in levels as active spells will, your understanding of magic will, on occasion, trigger evolution.

Affinity: Nature, Synthesis

Skill Tree: Nature

Keen Eye (Level 3)—This ability allows you to examine an item, foe, or location, and in conjunction with Connection, it can reveal secrets or vital clues that will push you towards helpful information. Keen Eye comes with a one-time bonus to Mind of +1.

Continued usage will improve the complexity and usefulness of the information Keen Eye provides. As your knowledge of its uses has grown, you have discovered the boons to this subtle skill. As with many worthwhile things, you get out of it what you put into it.

Affinity: Synthesis

Skill Tree: Arcane

Liminality (Passive)—The Gaels and the Celts both venerated liminal spaces —the place where land meets water, dusk and dawn, and the traditional markings of the year for equinoxes as much as solstices. There is power to the between-places, where the world becomes veiled. Neither shore nor sea, yet both at once.

Liminality increases all Nature and Wild affinity abilities based on the following temporal-spatial locations: dawn, dusk, Imbolc, Samhain, Beltane, Lughnasadh, equinoxes, being within nine metres of a body of water, and being in places that house the dead.

Your magic shall respond with alacrity in these times and spaces, and you gain a

10% chance to bend others' magic to your own will to disarm it if it seeks to harm.

Any permanently bonded animal companions immediately unlock this passive skill.

As the bridge between the physical and the spiritual world, the Draoidh draws power from both.

This spell cannot be increased with skill points after unlocking, but mastery of its ways may trigger evolution.

Affinities: Synthesis, Wild

Skill Tree: Draoidh

Mac-Talla—*Like Tursa allows you to connect with the turning of the earth and the constancy of the stars above in the present, Mac-Talla opens you to echoes of the past.*

When you use Mac-Talla, you gain insight into what has come before to better prepare you for what is ahead. Your Earth philosopher George Santayana once said that "those who cannot remember the past are condemned to repeat it"—the Draoidhean live by this understanding. It is also said that a smart person learns from their own mistakes, but a wise person learns from the mistakes of others. Listen to the echoes. Learn from them. Use them to chart a stronger future.

Affinities: Wild, Arcane

Skill Tree: Draoidh

Òran na Cloiche—*When the Draoidhean speak, the people listen. And when the Draoidhean sing, the people weep. With this passive skill close to your heart, your words will reach receptive ears. Once per week, you may also find inspiration to weave words into song, and those songs will ring out through your lands to touch all those who hear them. Friend or foe, the listener will not remain unmoved—for better or for worse.*

Affinities: Wild, Synthesis

Skill Tree: Draoidh

Purifire (Level 6)—*This skill is most used in combat, instilling basic fire with the power of the arcane, making it burn hotter and brighter than typical flame—and all within the mage's control. This fire is not friendly fire in more than one way. Magic is will and intent, and it will strike only your foes. While a staff is needed for advanced use, this skill can be wielded without need for a weapon.*

Increased use of Purifire allows for more complex use. Many mages utilise it with metal weapons to great effect, adding burning damage and spirit damage to physical. Others prefer a staff's elegance and the advanced precision a mage finds therein. At its heart, this skill moulds itself to its wielder, and only the mage can decide its limits.

You have discovered the utility of this offensive skill in using it not only against your opponents but also to control your environment. As such, you have gained the upgrade Ring of Fire, which you can use to encircle your foes.

You have utilised Purifire in myriad ways with efficiency and cunning. In combat, you have often used it in combination with Spèird to great efficacy. As such, you have gained the upgrade Fist of Flame, which you can use to pack an even greater punch.

Increased use of Purifire allows for more complex use. Your use of it has been diverse, from illumination to cleansing to combat, and you are only scratching the surface of its potential. At its heart, this skill moulds itself to its wielder, and only the mage can decide its limits.

(upgrades: Ring of Fire, Fist of Flame)

Affinity: Nature, Staves

Skill Tree: Arcane

Slànaich (Level 2)—A basic healing spell, Slànaich provides a general increase to inherent healing in both speed and duration. While it will not stave off death in the event of a mortal wound, it will both refresh tired muscles and soothe smaller injuries, which may make the difference between life and death even if it feels less dramatic.

Affinity: Healing

Skill Tree: Slàinte

Spèird—Often the first spell a mage learns, Spèird is a blast of force that can be used to fling projectiles and foes alike to buy the wielder precious time or space to manoeuvre.

Increased use of this skill allows for more targeted applications and, with the power of a true proficient, can be as lethal as a martial arts' master's fists.

Affinity: Staves

Skill Tree: Arcane

Tairm—This spell calls upon the land around you to respond, which it will, based on your affinities and your own intent. As this is wild magic, the results are difficult to anticipate for the caster, though if that is true, it is all the more confounding for the targets.

Be clear in your need, and nature will respond to your call.

Affinity: Wild (Special)

Skill Tree: Wild

CALUM'S STATS AND SPELLS

Taobh a-Staigh *(Passive)—You gain an understanding of the intrinsic qualities of all life and its relationship to spirit. Rooted in Connection, this skill grants a permanent +1 to Mind and +1 to Pathos, and you receive a bonus to all spells and skills that deal with things internal: healing, buffs, and your understanding of your own spirit.*

While Taobh a-Staigh will not increase in levels as active spells will, your understanding of magic will, on occasion, trigger evolution.

Affinity: Nature, Synthesis

Skill Tree: Nature

Taobh a-Muigh *(Passive)—You gain an understanding of the relational qualities of all life and ecosystems as well as their place in the web of spirit. Rooted in Connection, this skill grants a permanent +1 to Mind and +1 to Will, and you receive a bonus to all spells and skills that deal with things external: bonds, brawls, and anything that acts upon the outside world.*

While Taobh a-Muigh will not increase in levels as active spells will, your understanding of magic will, on occasion, trigger evolution.

Affinity: Nature, Synthesis

Skill Tree: Nature

Tàth *(Level 2)—This ability allows you to form a consensual bond with an animal, giving you the power to see through the animal's eyes and guide the creature's movements where necessary. These bonds, once created, will bring a consistent drain on spirit until released, but the benefits far outweigh the sacrifice. Tàth comes with a one-time bonus of +1 to Pathos.*

Continued usage will improve the usefulness of these bonds, providing a symbiotic balance for both you and your companion. You gain eyes and ears and mobility—they gain intelligence, protection, and, in rare cases, special abilities. (Ch 18)

Affinity: Nature, Synthesis

Skill Tree: Tàthadh

Tuairmse *(Passive)—Whilst most flounder with patterns in the wilds of nature, you thrive riding the waves of weather and landscape alike. Tuairmse is like a volcano; it may lie subtly dormant for a time, but when it wakes, the results can be course altering.*

Tuairmse works best in tandem with the Nature tree's root-level passives: Gu h-Ìosal, Gu h-Àrd, Taobh a-Muigh, and Taobh a-Staigh. It is recommended to learn those skills prior to learning Tuairmse.

Once all of these are unlocked, however, your innate understanding of nature increases tenfold. You will not only be able to sense the turning of the seasons like the woodchuck who builds a thicker-walled den before an intense winter, but you will also judge the tides, the whip-quick shifts in weather, and most importantly, how to use those things to your advantage.

Tursa—The ancients moved twenty-tonne slabs of rock hundreds of miles to build their monoliths. From this we have gleaned not only their technological capabilities but also their astronomical understanding. Many of these ancient monoliths were built with an intimate knowledge of the stars in the sky and the movements of the sun's path.

This skill is the bedrock upon which the Draoidh builds their power. In unlocking it, you will gain an instinctual knowledge of astronomy and its relationship to you. While this may not seem like much, it will root you in time, in the seasons, and upon the surface of the earth itself. For what is more constant than the stars for navigation? To get anywhere, you need to know where you are.

Both a passive and an active skill, Tursa will allow you to carry an instinct of time and the turning of the wheel, but upon casting, it will give you an innate understanding of your environment, a precious glimpse that can allow you to strategise in the heat of battle or work your way out of natural obstacles when you can see no escape.

Affinity: Nature, Synthesis

Skill Tree: Draoidh

LOVE LITRPG?

To learn more about LitRPG, talk to authors including myself, and just have an awesome time, please join the LitRPG Group!

About the Author

Mati Ocha is a Scottish author of LitRPG and progression fantasy. He likes scrambling up mountains, jumping in cold lochs, and generally making mayhem in Gaelic and English. When he's not being chaotic in the wilds, he can usually be found ruining his characters' days or grinding yet another seasonal character in Diablo III.

His social media game is less than ideal, but you can follow him if you really want to on Twitter, Reddit, or Patreon, and if you want to support his Patreon, you can get first crack at new stories!

MORE FROM ROBOT DINOSAUR

R.J. Theodore's Peridot Shift:

(Swashbuckling Science Fantasy)

Flotsam

Salvage

Cast-Off

· ⟨ ⟨⟨ ⟩⟩ ⟩ ·

The Worlds of Novae Caelum:

Magnificent (A Superhero Novella)

The Throne of Eleven (Epic Fantasy)

The Truthspoken Heir (Epic Space Fantasy)

· ⟨ ⟨⟨ ⟩⟩ ⟩ ·

The Many Marvels of Merc Fenn Wolfmoor:

Wolf Among the Wild Hunt

Friends for Robots

These Imperfect Reflections

Monster Girls Don't Cry

· ⟨ ⟨⟨ ⟩⟩ ⟩ ·

Robot Dinosaur Press

robotdinosaurpress.com